Amie Whithouse is a weirdo reader who lives in a small mountain town in sunny South Africa, with too much time on her hands and several casts of characters demanding their stories be told. She spends most of her days daydreaming at a café, or with her nose tucked in probably another disappointing BookTok recommendation, but she'll finish anyway out of principal, or she's staring at people's faces so she can use them as references.

To Inger: my bestie, my Ingie, my Thingy, my CEO of sound effects. I couldn't have done this without you. Now finish *insert work-in-progress name here*, you have a civic duty to bless my screen and you're taking too long to do it! Love ya…

Amie Whithouse

MISSGUIDED

AUSTIN MACAULEY PUBLISHERS™

LONDON ★ CAMBRIDGE ★ NEW YORK ★ SHARJAH

Ordering Information
Quantity sales: Special discounts are available on quantity purchases by corporations, associations, and others. For details, contact the publisher at the address below.

Publisher's Cataloging-in-Publication data
Whithouse, Amie
MissGuided

ISBN 9798889108979 (Paperback)
ISBN 9798889108986 (ePub e-book)

Library of Congress Control Number: 2023924480

www.austinmacauley.com/us

First Published 2024
Austin Macauley Publishers LLC
40 Wall Street, 33rd Floor, Suite 3302
New York, NY 10005
USA

mail-usa@austinmacauley.com
+1 (646) 5125767

To be honest, I never even thought this story would see the light of day, yet here we are. I don't have anything fancy to say yet, so I'll just stick with the most important ones. First of all, thank you to my best friend, Inger, who this book is dedicated to, for being there with me through it all. I couldn't have done this without you. Though not by blood, thank you to the best and only brother I've ever known, Grayson. Thank you for pushing me to get my shit together and finish the story all while annoying you in the process. Solid advice. Skip over the sex parts, please. To Jessica Bosak. I screamed when you sent me that first email. Cops were called. It was fantastic. To the wonderful production team, that you all for your hard work in making *MissGuided* a reality. And a very, very special thank you to my senior year English teacher, Ms. Mariët Jordaan. You've started it all and you don't even know it.

Table of Contents

Chapter 1
Emryne
Welcome to My Kingdom

Do me a favor, will you? Next time you blow out your birthday candles, don't wish to be a princess. Sure, the pretty dresses and fancy balls look fun, but trust me, it's not all its chalked-up to be. Tiaras are uncomfortable, corsets do in fact squeeze the life out of you and despite what you may believe, after several hours baking in the sun at an afternoon tea when, like the goddamned idiot you are, you forgot your sunscreen, silk? Chafes.

If you do like wearing said uncomfortable tiaras while simultaneously focusing on *not* letting the thing fall to the ground and shatter your precious family jewels when bowing your head, princessing is for you. If you like sucking up to Parliament members and visiting royals, sitting through never-ending parliamentary assemblies, never having time for yourself, your friends or anything other than your duties and being an overall pain in the ass, princessing is definitely for you. But if you're like me and you can't stand the idea of any of that, well then… do I have a secret for you.

Parliament has officially entered its third hour of argument regarding recent events surrounding Alorewyn's most famous vigilante. Should King Loryne Gennady order more knights to patrol city streets after dark? Should a special unit be dispatched to hunt this person down? The justice system exists for a reason, there are no shortcuts. This vigilante is insulting His Majesty. Blah, blah, blah.

What they should ask themselves is why this vigilante decided to take the law in their own hands in the first place.

But I'm getting ahead of myself. My name is Emryne Charlotte Gwendolyn Gennady. A mouthful, I know, Emryne is just fine, and I am the crowned princess and future queen of Alorewyn. Well, I will be, if my sister doesn't get married before I do.

You will be pleased to know that we don't live in the Middle Ages, and it is in fact 2021. Yes, we have Wi-Fi, cellphones, working cars, and toilets that flush. And yes, we still live a humble lifestyle, only with a staff of two hundred and sixty-five, and entire battalions of highly trained and skilled knights valiantly guarding Alorewyn day and night, yet to find the identity of the hooded watchdog who delivers criminals to Guard Dispatch's doorstep.

Yes, we have common criminals living among decent people. It would be incredibly naïve to think a kingdom of Alorewyn's size wouldn't house a sinister underground. You see, while said citizens are safely snoozing in their homes, I'm in the streets keeping the unholy scum from stealing, dealing, and shooting my kingdom to shit.

Am I a vigilante? Yes. Do I have a name? Also yes. They call me the Dark Warrior. Probably because of the signature suit of pitch-black armor, a gift from my older sister Ophelia (which, to this day, she has no idea about).

"Princess Addylin," Prime Minister Fredrich Hastings starts, dragging his burly fingers through this short, salt-and-pepper beard, "in your opinion, should Parliament be more concerned with the recent developments regarding this vigilante? Do we have enough resources devoted to our criminal justice divisions?"

Despite his kind tone, my twin sister's face falls. Opening and closing her rosy lips while scrambling for an answer, "I… think we do. I think there are plenty of viable threats we are aware of and are working tirelessly to defend our great kingdom."

Addylin Rose is my twin sister. We're fraternal, thank God. The only thing we actually have in common is our parents. And I have no problem with that.

The Gennedy family was blessed with five children. Two of which hold Ph.Ds, the other a queen in another thriving kingdom. Which left Addylin and me, fighting tooth and nail for our mother's crown. Three guesses as to which of us Mother dear is rooting for.

Addylin is the quintessential princess. Beautiful, delicately featured, with our mother's stunning, deep brown eyes, and an award-winning smile to dazzle the citizens with the flash of her perfectly white teeth. Addylin's only problem, despite her lovely smile, the people don't trust her. She overcompensates, stutters, and ends up shoving people away instead of assuring them she is trustworthy. I, on the other hand, have no problem with people.

What can I say? I know how to schmooze, always have. I get it from my father. Alongside his inherited thick, dark coppery brown hair and deep blue eyes. I wouldn't say my features are robust, but given my vigorous workout regimen, my mother often refers to me as the rhino in the family, mostly because of how defined my muscles are. After all, it's not normal for a princess of twenty-one years to have a six-pack and live a non-vegetarian, full lactose lifestyle while running for queen. Addy and I might not always see eye to eye, but I hate seeing her struggle, so I straighten my shoulders, ready to step in.

"What my sister is trying to say, Prime Minister, is that every citizen of Alorewyn should be taken under consideration. From what I'm reading, the general consensus among them is shows whoever this vigilante is, they have been making a great leeway for their peace of mind."

There is an art to answering diplomatic questions confidently. Keep eye contact, breathe deeply, stay calm and stick to the rehearsed lines you practiced with your father the evening before seared in the crevasses of your brain.

"Alorewyn has a legion of Knights Guard for exactly that purpose. Statistically—" Minister DuMarc, Alorewyn's minister of defense, starts.

"And where have they been?" I interrupt, raising the page again. If he wants to talk statistics, so be it. "So far, petty crimes have increased by three percent since last quarter. Several of those cases remain open today. And why? Does your statistics mention that?" I place my hands in my lap after setting the page down, "Four-hundred-and-ninety-four million people call Alorewyn their home. *Statistically*, there is no way to guarantee every crime, however small, will be attended to, regardless of how many knights are stationed around the city. Alorewyn is simply too large."

Which is only the first half of the answer, now comes the old razzle dazzle. "That being said, should these crimes escalate, I agree it would be wise to appoint a specialized unit, several, as a matter of fact, while we're on the topic. If not to capture this vigilante, then at the very least to increase pressure on prosecution as well as assure the safety of our citizens remains our highest priority." All this is a test. Or should I say, another one.

Since becoming eligible on our twenty-first birthday, Addylin and I have been requisitioned to attend more assemblies for the sole purpose of testing and our competency in solving both minor and major issues pertaining to the kingdom. Should I be nervous of them discovering my identity? Sure, and while I do realize the irony of setting myself up for a capture that'll never happen, these old greasebags grumbling and battling among themselves, fighting for the king's attention is wonderfully amusing to watch. It's like I said, the Knights Guard have better things to attend to than small crimes.

That is, until a new threat befalls Alorewyn streets.

Father's beard is neatly trimmed today. Defining his square jaw and accentuating his nobility in earnest. His blue eyes bright and alert as he beams, giving my hand a squeeze. Mother gives her signature single nod of approval. Whether or not she in fact did approve I'll find out once we've adjourned. And so begins the final stage of our grooming. A new generation of queen to rule the kingdom until new leaders follow in their parents' footsteps. All of which I am fully prepared for.

What I'm not prepared for is the news my mother delivers, once we step into the throne room.

Chapter 2
Emryne
Not Welcome to My Kingdom

Two years ago, my eldest sister Asaria was assaulted in the streets of our own home, in broad daylight. Five men held her at gunpoint and escaped with about half a million dollars' worth of goods. Most of which I recovered. My grandmother's pearl ring and emerald necklace were already sold on the black market when I caught up to them.

And her guards? Nowhere to be found. Now, I am my father's daughter, and we Gennady's have illustrious tempers, but I do not have a single word in my vocabulary to describe the fury that sprinted through my veins the day I heard about the robbery. My father completely lost his shit when he heard of the attack. Lost it all over again when he was informed of her missing guards. Did the knights in question lose their heads that day, very, very publicly? Yes. Yes, they did.

Did I go on a city-wide manhunt to find the scumbags who dared touch my sister? You bet your sweet, buttered buns I did.

It took a while, but I tracked them down one by one. Until I found the mastermind, a common street rat named Charles 'Cheech' Morris, feigning his ignorance on who I was or what I wanted, and dragged him to Guard Dispatch, hogtied and bloody with a makeshift sign tied around his neck that read: *I Robbed Princess Asaria Gennady. Punish Me.*

Or when I happened to stumble upon one George Pauley, a registered sex-offender prowling the women's locker rooms at Ember City Country Club, but somehow outran the knights every time someone caught him. His sign: *I Like to Watch Girls Through Bathroom Windows. Find My Stash.* Which was conveniently stapled to his forehead.

I know what you're thinking… a princess in line for her throne shouldn't call underprivileged citizens 'common street rats', but being trapped in a car with the barrel of a pistol pointed at your head changes you. Trust me, I've been in the situation enough times to know.

It changed my sister. Changed my family. And it definitely changed me.

And so began my days as the Dark Warrior.

It was the least I could do given the only way to act otherwise would be to join the Alorewyn's Knights Guard, and I had no interest in spending my days surrounded by horny, smelly men when I outrank them by… a lot given my extensive knowledge of martial arts, weapons, and close-quarters-combat. All of which I've learned under my father's watchful eye.

Every day, we'd spend at least a few hours training so I'd be prepared if any idiot, outside and inside palace walls, tried his luck with me. None of which my mother or my siblings were aware of, and I savored our time together.

I may hate traditional princessing, but I'll do it if it makes my father happy. Because I love him more than anything. Respect him. King Loryne Gennady is perhaps the greatest ruler in Alorewyn history, and I will do everything in my power to uphold his kingdom's legacy, and if it meant wearing tiaras, corsets and attending assemblies, so be it.

It wasn't all bad. Prime Minister Fredrich was a scream when he wanted to be. He might look like a grizzly bear, but he's harmless for the most part. Mother's burgundy gown, a favorite in her wardrobe, quietly swishes along the marble floor as she paces the Emerald Library outside Farrow Hall where assembly is held.

The dress is stunning. The thick material hugs her curves perfectly, the delicate jewels and golden embroidery along the Bardot neckline accentuates the brown in her eyes something fierce. A dress fit for a queen.

Addylin and I are dressed more subtly. Like Mother's, her porcelain skin is clad in an arctic blue high-neck gown with a silver, jeweled belt around her tiny waist. Father asked me to wear something complementary to the peach tie he wore with his slate gray suit, so I went with the semi-sweetheart tulle cantaloupe gown Beth, Tory and I bought on one of our bi-weekly shopping sprees. I fell in love with the feminine sequin flowers embroidered on the bodice and along the skirt the second I saw it on the model. Father approved.

Mother… Her arms are folded at her waist, brow pensive as her mind runs through our performances.

"You might want to remember to speak the next time the Prime Minister asks you a question, Addylin Rose. At least your sister had answers when addressed."

"Thank you, Mother."

"That wasn't a compliment, Emryne," she bites. Of course, it wasn't. "That was a travesty. What was the point of the hours of preparation if you fail at replying to the simplest of questions?"

Addylin crosses her arms over her tiny chest and puffs her cheeks like a disgruntled bunny rabbit. If the daggers she shoots at me is meant to intimidate, it wasn't working. I'd pinch her cheeks if she didn't say, "I would've been fine if she hadn't interrupted me."

My eyebrows shoot skyward. "Really? That's what you choose to say to me after I just saved your ass in there?"

"Oh, get off your high horse, Emryne," she spit my name like a cheap slice of cake. A full fat, non-vegan, all sugar cake.

I bit back, "Speak for yourself, Addylin."

"Enough. Everyone," Father scolds. "We don't have time for this now. Comment on their ineptitude later, the princes are arriving soon."

Addy and I exchange confused glances. "Princes?" she asks.

Mother rolls her shoulders, flicking an invisibly piece of lint from her dress. "Without a king, a princess of Alorewyn cannot be queen. Since you are both are officially eligible, it's time we consider our options."

This is the part I almost run from the room terrified. I would have, were it not for my father's steady hand in mine. I squeeze to the point of cutting off both my and his blood supply.

I swallow. "They're here already?"

Father knows I'm not comfortable with this arrangement, but what choice do I have?

Fine, I'm not entirely against the idea of being with one person for the rest of your life. If you find your soulmate, or whatever, you should be together. What I don't get is why marriage is a prerequisite for a crown. My great-grandmother ruled Alorewyn alone for many years before my father became eligible. I guess it makes sense that having both a king and a queen ruling would present a more united front, put the people's worry at ease, still—the whole thing just freaks me out.

Cameron, my brother, and Asaria never had to go through this. Then again, both of them fled the kingdom as soon as they graduated. He had no interest in following in Father's footsteps and chose study medicine instead. To this day, he is the youngest MD ever to graduate from Johns Hopkins University and pass the medical board exam.

He's already cured one form of cancer and is busy curing another. Don't ask me how or which ones it is, but apparently it has to do with growing a pancreas on a bird, or in a bird. That's it. That's all I know.

Asaria followed closely behind. After she was attacked, she had no interest in becoming queen. With a Ph.D. in ancient languages and a master's degree in archaeology, she abdicated her eligibility and she's been traveling the world ever since.

I should've gone when I had the chance. Addylin and I became eligible on our twenty-first birthday back in March. My mother has been preparing us since we were eighteen, and now she's invited the eldest princes from the eligible kingdoms to stay with us for the year, in hopes to win one of our hearts and serve alongside us as king.

"They should be arriving any minute," Mother says, for once with something resembling a smile, while Addy calmly fixes her hair.

Not a second after Mother finished did the heavy oak doors swing open as my cheeks redden and my heart beats a million miles a minute, and the first of them crosses the threshold.

All these pretty-boy princes do absolutely nothing for my libido. Not that that's all I think about, you understand, but sometimes a little something, or someone, is nice to look at.

All except one.

The prince I've been in love with since my junior year of high school. The prince who took my virginity and shattered my heart in doing so.

Skylan Dormer.

Chapter 3
Skylan
The Pleasure is Mine, Princess

When my father first told me of Emryne's eligibility, the conversation went a little something like this.

I woke up to a request for a video call. Contented, yet surprised to see the picture of Dad's dark brown eyes, slowly greying hair, and strong jaw pop up above the answer button, a cheery expression on his face. I was in Naples for two weeks helping a friend out with a video for her film study the day before and only walked through the doors of the penthouse apartment I rented at three that morning, hence my lying in bed at eleven a.m.

I lifted my laptop on the bed in front of me and hit answer. "It's five a.m.," Dad's never awake before eight-thirty at least. "What are you doing up?"

"It's been two weeks since you called. What? I can't check up on my favorite son?"

"I'm your only son," I chuckle. At least he looks rested, as opposed to the call we had a few weeks ago.

"For now," he shrugged.

My spine straightened. "You're seeing someone?"

"Not officially, no. But your old man's young. I still got it, ya know?"

I shook my head, grinning. No arguing with that. "So, what's up? I know you're not awake on accident."

"You're right," he raised his shoulder and leaned back in his office chair. "I just thought you might like to know."

"Is everything okay?" My body tensed as I grabbed at the first question begging for attention. "Is it Greenland?"

"Yes, and no. Would you calm down?" Dad rolled his eyes. "Hell, you're worse than Maverick. Everything's fine."

I sighed my relief. "Okay, so?"

"Emryne turned twenty-one," he scratched his chin.

"Yes. I know," I swallowed hard. I saw the posts, news stories, excitement. It took everything I had not to pick up the phone and call her, explain, but it wasn't exactly a conversation I wanted to have over the phone.

Dad leaned forward again and grabbed some fancy envelope from his right. "Got this yesterday."

"Another legendary party?" I chuckled. If there's one thing the Gennady's knew it was how to throw a party.

He put the fancy white envelope back down. "She's officially eligible for queen."

After those words left his lips, I stopped listening and flew to my suitcase.

Throwing in every item of clothing I could carry at once and not bothering to fold it like I always did. Got on a plane, and flew home.

And here we are.

Situated on the East Coast, the kingdom of Alorewyn proudly thrives as governing party of the Consolidated States of Emarica. I'd say I missed this place, but I didn't. Okay, maybe a small part of me did. But that's mostly because of her. The driver enters the wrought iron gates and slows down to turn off to the monolithic sandstone palace inching closer, the forty-six great spires, each representing a ruling king and queen, kissing the cloudless summer sky, windows gleaming in the sunshine. And, should this year prove successful, a forty-seventh to be added shortly, I have no doubt.

My father, King Harryson Dormer, and I are the first of the royal families to arrive apparently. Princess Emryne's and my father have been best friends since childhood, and served together as Grand Commanders in King Adelio's, Emryne's great-grandfather, Knights Guard during the Second Great War in 1965. Inside, the air is cool, a welcome relief from the basking heat outside.

The grand foyer hadn't changed at all either—still adorned with the expensive red Persian rugs, portraits of the Gennady predecessors, decorated with antique furniture. The only new items around the room are the fresh flowers, all still in the heirloom vases.

"It's wonderful to see you again, Prince Skylan." She says, bowing her head.

"Likewise."

But I'm not paying attention to her. Not with the diamond of Alorewyn, the ethereal beauty that is Emryne Gennady standing next to her father.

My mind switches to autopilot as I bow to her mother, Queen Lilliette. Barely registering the hand King Ryne held out to me after shaking my father's, but I shook it, nonetheless. My eyes never left Emryne. Neither did hers mine. Both of us frozen in time. The time we lost. The time we had. And her face remains unreadable.

Her dress hugs her body stunningly. Her eyes are already impossibly blue, but the way they capture the afternoon sun makes them almost violet. And her lips… God, her lips are still perfect. I've spent so many days thinking about kissing her again. Being with her again, if only for a second. I don't know how, but she's even more beautiful now than she was that night, and she already looked like a goddess bathed in neon lights when we…

My heart is beating outside of my chest. I bow deep, gently take her hand, soft as the finest silk. Her palm is warm against mine; just as delicate as the first time I touched her. "It's wonderful to see you, Princess Emryne."

A callous smile tugs at her lips, and I already know what's coming.

This should be good.

"Prince Skylan," she says sweetly. Much, much too sweetly. And she has that warrior-huntress look in her eye. Never a good combination, either of those. She takes her hand back and steps closer. My body stiffens, her intense gaze studying every inch of me as her eyes sweep from head to toe.

I won't lie, the fist that flies into my face a second later catches me completely off-guard.

My head whips to the right and I stumble backward, trying my best to compose myself as a startled gasp escapes Queen Lilliette's and her hands fly to… and she's at my side in a flash, "Oh, dear God."

My eyes flick to Emryne, a funny combination of pride, amusement, and horror on her face when she sees the blood running from the cut where I bit my lip. I'd say the same for the shock on my face but given the circumstances, I fight to keep my laughter at bay. This is going to be an entertaining year.

I'm watching her every move. God, I missed her. She was feisty then, and she's feisty now. I feel the desire in my body ignite as my eyes sweep over the gentle curve of her breasts. Ached to play with those delicious nipples again.

I know her body better than anyone, it's obvious my teasing eyes are getting to her, and when she wrings her hands and shifts on her feet the way she is now, she's just as turned on as I am.

A lusty grin spreads over my lips, and she flies up the staircase and out the foyer.

I'll make you pay for this later, my Princess.

"I apologize profusely, Prince Skylan," the queen consoles, running her hand along my back. "I have absolutely no idea what came over her." Unfortunately, I do. And I don't blame her.

"You okay there, Ace?" her father asks, gripping my shoulder, and I grin at my old nickname, despite my spinning head. Never thought I'd miss hearing that.

"I'm fine," I wipe the blood from my mouth and turn to her father. "That right hook of hers is no joke. You have trained her well, Your Majesty."

Because only King Loryne would teach a woman to fight like a man.

Better, in fact. It's his nature.

"Yes, I know. Excuse me," he follows her up the staircase.

I feel her hand tighten on my forearm. "Please, allow me to escort you to our medical rooms, Your Highness."

"Thanks Lil, but that won't be necessary," Dad says and slaps my shoulder. "I think my son and I have a few things to discuss."

Chapter 4
Emryne
He Deserved it

Why? Why, of all the eligible princes in the goddamned world, did she have to invite the one I want nothing more than to shove through a woodchipper. Every memory I had locked away came swarming back when he flashed those mischievous chestnut brown eyes at me.

But you missed those eyes…

No, I did not, brain.

I fly through the door of my father's study and beeline for the antique, gold-accented side table with the cutglass decanter filled with my father's favorite whiskey. The Single Malt Macallan was a gift from me on his fifty-first birthday; he first shared it with me on my twenty-first birthday.

My knuckles throb from the unexpected violence as I pour myself a double to ease at least some of the nerves, and gulp it down like a lifeline on a talk-show.

My body warms as the smooth, amber liquid glides down my throat, welcoming its elegant flavors and calming my rapid heartbeat.

Father's study smells like him. The expensive, oaky musk he wears lingers even after he leaves. It complements the rustic leather couches and rich oakwood bookshelves and trophy cases perfectly. And the art on the walls, every picture imaginable he's taken of his children, candid or otherwise.

He knocks before peaking in. Not that he had to, it is his office after all, but out of respect. It's the one place in the palace other than the training room I feel completely safe. Especially if he's with me. He makes me feel safe, as a father should.

Funny, it used to be the same with Skylan. Then he vanished without a word, and left me heartbroken and alone with no way to get home.

I drown the memory in whiskey too.

Father shuts the door and joins me where I'm leaning against the desk, brows furrowing at the crystal cutglass in my hand, half of it already in my stomach, but he's grinning. Such a daddy's girl am I. "Is that my expensive whiskey?"

"Just a little bit," I shrug, smiling.

He smirks, "And how would you describe it?"

"Award-winning," and it was. A perfect balance between citrus and smokey. No wonder people became alcoholics.

Father chuckles, and kisses my forehead as I hand him the glass. He takes a long drink before handing it back. "Are you alright?"

I worry at his gentle voice. "Is it bad?"

Father shrugs. "He's right about that hook of yours. He'll have one hell of a shiner tomorrow, that is for sure. Who taught you to punch like that?"

"Some guy," I nudge his shoulder. Though the situation didn't make me feel any less like an idiot. "I'm sorry, that was stupid. I shouldn't have done that."

"Do I want to know what happened between the two of you to make you lash out at him?"

I finish the remaining whiskey and set the glass down behind me. "I don't think so."

"Well, whatever it is, I trust he deserved it." Father takes my hand, and settles his gaze on mine, shifting into what I like to call 'King Mode'.

"I understand you are upset with this agreement. It's strange, and terribly awkward to think you'll be marrying one of these boys in a year." He squeezes my hand. "You assured me before we announced your eligibility that you were all in. But, I'm giving you one last chance to back out."

I'm at a loss for words. My mouth opens, closes, and nothing comes out but a strained, "Father?"

His gaze turns concerned. "I hate seeing you so uncomfortable. If this isn't what you want, then you are free to abdicate."

Tears threaten to escape my eyes. No other king would give their child a chance at freedom like King Ryne did his. It was considered an embarrassment, and there was talk believe you me, but my father couldn't care less. The wellbeing of his children is his first—only priority. Over his dead body would he let any of us suffer.

Before I could answer, the door bursts open and Mother barges through. "Emryne Charlotte Gwendolyn Gennady, have you lost your damn mind!" Funny, I could ask her the same thing. I should ask her the same thing.

"Why did you invite him?" I glare at her.

"Every prince of the eligible kingdoms was invited, Emryne. Are you telling me you have a problem with *all* of them? Should I expect more bloody lips and bruised eyes this week?"

I scoff, crossing my arms. Brooding. Like a two-year-old. That's what I was doing. "Maybe."

Mother's brows draw together and her voice is tight as she closes the distance between us. "Is there something I should know?"

Father's words echo in my head. *I'm giving you one last chance to back out. If this isn't what you want, then you are free to abdicate.*

I can't do this to him. Not now. He was so excited to announce our eligibility on our birthday. I'd be the worst daughter in existence if I left now. Father deserves reassurance that his kingdom will be taken care of. Deserves rest even more. The man hasn't had a vacation since my senior year of high school.

So, I stand tall, and smooth out my dress before turning to my father. *Time to put on your big girl panties, Emryne. You made a promise to your father. And you never break a promise.*

"No. I'm not going anywhere," then to Mother, "I let my emotions get the better of me. I'll apologize to him."

Because he'd just love that.

#

If I'm going to endure Skylan's stupid face for the year, I'll need to up my workout regimen, find a way to tame the beast so the urge to disfigure him every time we run into each other doesn't cloud my better judgement. Which I'm sure will be often.

Up at the butt-crack of dawn, dressed and headed for the training room, I gulp down a peanut butter protein shake. No one other than the knights are around, none of which pay attention to me other than a curt nod. The ideal time to work up a sweat. As expected, my knuckles are ugly and red. So, I wrap them carefully before my workout.

Two and a half hours of switching between weights, heavy bag and cardio, and my body is drenched.

It's eight-thirty by the time I emerge from my bedroom, freshly showered, with my earbuds in and the music blasting on my way to the kitchens for breakfast.

Monique, one of my lady's maids, is waiting at the end of the massive turquoise granite island, matching the intricate features of the cupboards and light fixtures. The palace has three kitchens—the first used for grand events like balls or birthdays, the second is the main kitchen where Sir Stéphane, the French chef trained among the greatest in the world, and all but jumped at the chance to cook for King Ryne, prepares his seven-star meals, and the third smaller one a level down for staff use. The Monique holds out a jar of freshly made raspberry yogurt as I turn and pause my music. "Good morning, Your Highness," she beams.

"Morning, Moni."

When I was younger, pronouncing her name was a struggle. It took me a while to master the 'K' sound 'Q' has, so Monique became Moni. And she wouldn't have it any other way. She's a tiny, well-rounded woman, with golden skin and deep, playful brown eyes with little lines of crow's feet in the corners, who came from well-rounded women who've served the king and queen since before my siblings were born, all of which were retired now. Her gray hair is immaculately plaited on her head, no doubt Des's doing, and her simple beige linen uniform is perfectly ironed as always.

My mouth waters in anticipation as I lift the spoon to my lips, savoring the sweet tartness. In case you're wondering, I am a total raspberry whore. If I could bathe in it, I would, but eating it is so much better.

Hollerback Girl is next on the playlist and my lips turn up. Something about the lyrics sits right with me, and I'm knocked back to my cheerleading days. Alongside my good friends Annebeth and Victory, or just Beth and Tory, believe it or not our squad was nationally ranked. We never made it to championships mostly because of a technical error, and by that time I'd lost interest anyway.

Royal duties were impatiently waiting.

Finally, the song hits B-A-N-A-N-A-S, and I yank Moni closer and stick an earbud in her ear. She sings with me, as she always does, and we share a good laugh. Both of us without a care in the world, as if we didn't have work to do.

Without her Monique and Desirée, my other lady's maid, my life would be chaos.

The song comes to an end, and Moni is back to business, smoothing out her apron and tucking her baby hairs behind her ears. "How was your workout, Highness?" she asks with a motherly smile.

"Vigorous," I reply and take another bite of yogurt. "I needed it." Despite my hand throbbing every time, I jabbed the heavy bag. I fought through the pain and imagined it was Skylan's face. Worked wonders.

"I've always admired your morning savvy," she says, leaning her elbows on the island. Were Mother here, she'd surely have a fit. It's all business all the time with her lady's maids. Des and Moni were different. They basically raised me and my sister. Worked wonders. Sometimes they felt like more of a mother than my own did.

"My great-grandpa always said, 'Early to bed, early to rise, makes a young woman smart, pretty, and wise.' I've stood by those words my entire life." I smile at her. Moni always spoke so fondly of her grandfather. It made me miss my own.

King Adelio died when I was seven. Though he wasn't formally king after my father was crowned, he still held the title. As most royals do.

"He was the wisest of kings," she smiles solemnly. "When you've finished with breakfast, Queen Lilliette is waiting in the grand foyer with Prince Zimo."

I sigh and roll my eyes. "Oh, goody. The whoring begins already."

Moni knows of all my hardships, including my aversion to marriage. Her tiny hands fly to her lips to keep herself from laughing out loud. "Princess!" She playfully slaps my wrist. "You mustn't speak in such a way. It is most unladylike."

I stifle a shrug. "It's the truth."

She shuffles closer and bends down, her voice low, "Might I ask a question, Your Highness? If it's not too forward?"

I spoon some yogurt and take a bite. "Only if it doesn't have to do with my hand." But I already know that's exactly what she'll ask about.

"Prince Skylan is very handsome," she starts after clearing my empty jar and handing me a bowl of fresh raspberries. Did I mention I'm a raspberry whore?

My eyes find hers and I bite down on my lip. She tries to hide her curiosity, bless her, but Moni's face is quite expressive, and she does a poor job hiding her emotions. "The other maids heard about… something that happened yesterday," Here it comes. "Did you really punch Prince Skylan, Highness?"

I laugh. "You girls never miss anything, do you?" Not exactly an answer, but an answer enough.

"Did he act inappropriately?"

"No. He was the perfect gentleman." Damn him.

"Then… why?" she asks confused.

Why is a long-ass story. One I have no interest in telling, no matter how deeply I care about Moni.

Luckily, the storming footsteps echoing down the passage toward the kitchen belong to Addylin and cut the conversation short.

She breathes a sigh of relief. "There you are. What are you doing? We're going to be late!" she urges, sweeping a disapproving gaze over the oversized t-shirt and white knee socks I'm wearing. I didn't bother with clothes since 'spending time' with anyone is not particularly high on my to-do list. Especially *him*. "That's what you're wearing? Mother's going to have a cow!"

Next to her perfectly ironed, soft pink, off-the-shoulder gown, ever the apt representation of overall put-togetherness, I prevail as the epitome of disappointment. Exactly what I'm going for.

Never in her life would Mother let me anywhere *near* her guests dressed like this. Also exactly what I'm going for.

I pop my earbuds back in, and follow Addy out of the kitchen to the foyer at a lackadaisical pace, casting Moni a wink as I grab my bowl of berries, music blasting in my ears. Mother's arms are at her waist, fuming with the swan-like grace she's mastered over the years. Beside her with his hands behind his back, all the way from the Fán Róng Kingdom in the Grand Asai Empire on the other side of the world, stands a very earnest Prince Zimo. Handsome in that classic prince way; his deep, soulful, almond-shaped brown eyes shine in the morning light, hair of raven black, and arguably the sweetest smile seen on a prince.

Mother says something and gestures to him, he smiles and nods my way, bowing after his reply, but his words are lost on me given the music in my ears being too loud to hear my own thoughts, exactly the way I like it. He sweeps his eyes to mine, flashing a crooked smile and waves.

Is this rude? Definitely. But I don't have it in me to keep up appearances today. Not with Skylan lurking somewhere in my home with God only knows what intentions.

My phone vibrates in my pocket with a lifesaving text from Tory, I could kiss her for. I should kiss her for.

TORY: *Pls, pls tell me ur free?*

I smile at her begging. She'll think up any excuse to get out of her weekly visits with her grandparents.

My fingers fly over the keyboard as I happily type my reply.

ME: *As a matter of fact, I am. Burberry & Burratas?*

TORY: *Read my mind babe. Bethie's meeting us there.*

Beside me, Addy curtsies deeply and speaks. He must've replied with something charming since her cheeks redden and her gaze drops to the ground.

Perfect opportunity to make my escape. I throw a peace sign Zimo's way and dance off toward the staircase that leads to my bedroom, less than uninterested in swooning and smiling at a prince I don't know.

I have no interest in any of them for that matter. Especially not *him*.

Like Skylan, a few princes have seen Alorewyn, but this is the first time for many, Prince Lando of Parson and twin princes Obren and Herwin of Jaunor for example, and it falls to my sister and I to show them around. A task I'd happily take on, *after* seeing the girls. Probably. And well after throwing back a shot or two, or six, of Beth's favorite, ridiculously expensive vodka.

Desirée is waiting when I enter my room. She's much younger than Monique and has only been here for about two years. Her skin is a shade darker than Moni's and her eyes are the brightest sky blue. Des is trained in cosmetology. Her make-up is subtle and perfect as always and her blonde hair, expertly plaited just like Moni's, is my favorite part about her.

Both her and Moni grew up in a small county outside of the kingdom and is well taken care of, granted they might not earn a fortune but it's more than enough to live. And for Des, any extra money she saves she uses to buy more quality products; the ones I haven't already given her.

She finishes my make-up and ties my hair in an intricate knot at the nape of my neck. I spend a good few moments admiring her expert handiwork with a beam before entering the massive walk-in closet to get ready. I go with a deep purple crop-top and black, high-waisted jeans with a pair of strappy stilettos and a simple black wrap to cover my shoulders.

Satisfied with ensemble, I grab one of my Hermès purses, the limited addition scarlet red snakeskin, before heading out the door and back downstairs where the knights are waiting with the Rolls Royce. I could've driven myself or taken any car in our fleet given all of them are armored, but since our eligibility, it wasn't beneath any disgruntled citizen to act as callous as they did with Asa, we couldn't be too careful, so Father insisted.

I send Beth a quick text telling her I'm on my way and throw my phone along with my favorite grapefruit lip balm and sunglasses I grabbed from Des's hand on my way out in my bag. An effort rendered moot since I round the corner and crash into a solid chest, the contents spilling out anyway.

"Jesus."

To be fair, the chatting voices should've told me someone was in the vicinity so I could look up and actually pay attention to what I was doing.

A smooth voice caresses my senses and warms my body. It would've made my day had it not come from him.

"Afraid not, darling," Skylan smirks. Far too impeccably dressed in his navy Oxford shirt and simple beige slacks with brown loafers. "A couple more seats down to earth. But I am eligible for king, so I guess I'm halfway there."

I roll my eyes and look over his shoulder for his accomplice. I could've sworn I heard two voices. "Who are you talking to?"

His eyes glitter with mischief as he leans forward. "Why, are you jealous?"

"No," I deadpan.

"Then why do you want to know?"

"Because it's my palace, dickhead."

His head falls back with laughter. He lifts his phone, showing a familiar face on screen. Maverick Dormer, Skylan's cousin, waves at me.

A few years older and a softer jaw, but a spitting image of his cousin, the signature Dormer charm alight in his brown eyes, Maverick says, "Hey you. Don't mind this dumbass. As always, he has his foot in his mouth."

Or in yesterday's case, my fist in his face. I laugh. "Trust me, I know."

"How are you? Hey, is it true Alorewyn has a vigilante running around? Man, all the good stuff happens when Sky's there." I'm not sure where exactly in the palace in Callior he is, I don't remember much about Sky's home, but when he leans his broad body back, it has to be somewhere more formal with the rows of bookcases behind him.

Much as I'd love to chat, "I'm sorry. I want to catch up Mav, but I'm so late."

He chuckles. His wild curls shaking with his head. "I expect a story about why you socked him!"

He swings the phone back to him. "I told you already, jealousy."

Ass. I roll my eyes. "Get out of my way, Skylan."

"Or what? Are you going to hit me again?" his smooth voice challenges.

"Seriously considering it," I seethe. In no mood to continue this… whatever this is, I step to my left to get around him, only for him to do the same.

"Skylan, I am late. Please move."

His grin never falters as he drops his gaze down to my feet. "Aren't you forgetting something?"

I follow his eyes and remember my purse, huffing my irritation, and bend down to gather the scattered contents. Sky holds out a hand for me to take, but I slap it away and he simply chuckles.

I straighten and smooth out my wrap. "If you'll excuse me," and I step to my left once again. And Skylan follows me. Again.

Oh, for God's sake, what now?

His hands cross behind his back and he leans toward me. "I'm still waiting for my apology."

"You'll be waiting until your death. Actually, please do, you'll be doing me a massive favor. Now if you don't mind," this time, I'm held in place by his enigmatic gaze. The same gaze he had the first time we kissed…

"What are you staring at?"

His lips turn up in a devilish grin. "How many times have I asked you not to wear purple when we're in public, Em-Em? You know it turns me on."

God, I hate that nickname. I hate him too.

"Ever think that maybe that's my plan? Distract you so I get close enough?" *Then kick you in your teeth.*

Those twinkling eyes send slivers of fury through my body. "I knew you wanted me."

"Goodbye, Skylan," I ground out, stepping around him. By small mercy, he lets me.

But just as I reach the doorway leading to the foyer, I'm stopped in my tracks once again.

"*You never close your eyes anymore when I kiss your lips,*" his voice echoes the hallway. My heartbeat speeds up and I swallow hard.

Of course, he'd sing that now.

"*And there's no tenderness like before in your fingertips.*"

Skylan's voice has always been my kryptonite and he's perfectly aware of it. It was already as smooth as Tennessee whiskey when we were teenagers, but now? Now that his voice has broken, that he's not a boy anymore and all man… it's even better.

"*You're trying hard not to show it. But baby, baby I know it…*"

I can't help smiling as I turn and face him. "Stop."

"Why? You love Top Gun," he teases.

"No, I love my father. My feelings for Top Gun run much deeper." For very specific reasons.

I've loved this song since the first time I heard it, but the movie because of Kelly McGillis's character Charlie Blackwood. Lady pilot at the top of her field training know-it-all boys with chips on their shoulders? Yes please. And don't think none of us missed the irony of Sky's cousin is also being named Maverick. We teased him about it almost daily.

"*You've lost that lovin' feeling,* back me up, Mav," he says to his cousin and saunters closer, taking my hands and lifting them onto his shoulders, like he's done countless times before. Two voices sing the rest, "*Whoa, that lovin' feeling. You've lost that lovin' feeling now it's gone… gone… gone… whoa-oh.*"

I feel my cheeks warm as laughter bubbles in my stomach, along with several other feelings I'd rather not say out loud.

The first time he sang to me, the second time he kissed me, I ultimately fell in love with the movie.

It didn't hurt that Sky, only nineteen at the time and the youngest pilot to graduate from Callior's Air Force Academy, got his license that year either.

I remember it like it was yesterday. We were the only ones on a lovers' seat in the palace movie theater and it happened almost exactly as it did now. Skylan singing, smiling, pulling me up to dance with him. I knew he could see my bright red cheeks, even in the darkness, which only made his smile wider. He's always had this way of charming me into doing whatever he wanted.

Nothing too heinous, he was still the crowned prince after all, not to mention his father would kill him if he acted poorly, but small things like dancing, or helping with prepared speeches when he made me practice in a mirror over and over again while he watches, making small corrections as I speak, or when I cried after a fight with my mother. Skylan was there in a heartbeat, pulling me into his arms, letting me cry against his chest until I felt better.

Maybe, that's why I fell so hard for him.

We'd watched it so many times we knew every word. And that night, after Carole said her famous line, "*Goose, ya big stud! Take me to bed or lose me forever!*" I did the same, as I always did. Skylan laughed. I laughed. And them something between us changed.

His arms came around me, he lowered his head and to my ear, and he whispered, "Show me the way home."

I close my eyes and chase the memories back to where they came from. That won't be happening again ever. Skylan Dormer, the boy with the smoldering eyes and the dashing smile, took more than just my virginity that night.

He took my heart. And he never gave it back.

"Are we ever going to talk about what happened?" My voice barely breaks the sound barrier, but I have to keep it low. Walls have ears. And in my case, as I've seen so many times, eyes too. The night I'm referring to had nothing to do with Top Gun, but he knew.

Skylan's smile fades, and he shrugs. "Nothing to talk about. If you ask me, actions speak louder than words anyway. Put your hands against the wall and bend over. I'll prove it to you."

"I'm serious, Skylan. That can never happen again."

"Never say never, darling," he whispers in my ear.

"I will if it means you'll stay away from me."

"Oh, come on. You loved it."

"I did not. That was hormones, adrenaline, and a bottle of Don Julio you stole from Asaria's bedroom." A four-hundred-dollar bottle of tequila was the least of my worries then given that my mind was blinded by lust, my body ached for his and my mouth was around his cock. Lapping up every drop of the expensive liquor he poured down his body.

Sometimes I miss it, sometimes I don't. Especially not when I'm in bed with another man who'd try so hard to please me, yet he just can't, and I'd blame Skylan. Every time. I haven't been able to get off since then.

Did Sky ruin me for other men? Yes. Damn him. Yes, he did. And I'll be kicking his ass for it, come hell or high water.

Chapter 5
Skylan
The Art of Making Amends,
Or at Least Trying to If I Don't Keep
Getting Interrupted

"You slept with her," my father scolds after I filled him in on our lovely welcoming debacle. "Of all the stupid things you've done, you thought sleeping with her would be a good idea? My best friend's daughter, and a princess no less! What in blue blazes were you thinking?"

"Dad, I—"

"No, I'll tell you what you were thinking. You weren't thinking at *all*, that's what you were thinking!"

"I know, okay! I know."

"This could spell out a heap of trouble for Callior, Skylan. Trouble we can don't need."

"It just happened, alright?" I really had other no point to argue. Because he's right. "I thought she would've let it go by now."

Dad throws his hands in the air. "Have you met the girl's mother? The Gennady's aren't exactly level-headed people."

"Yes. I know that now," I bite.

His finger pinched the bridge of his nose and he squeezed his eyes shut, "If you're serious about this, about her, then you need to fix it, Skylan. I'm serious, fix it now." Then left without another word.

That was how the conversation with Dad went before calling my cousin and filling him in about the recent events surrounding my busted lip and black eye, and I'm relieved to see his cheery face today.

Maverick, heavy with laughter, the asshat, falls off his bed when he sees the state of me. "You really do have a death wish, don't you?"

"I'm here for a reason, Mav," I remind him.

"Then make sure she knows what it is."

Oh, I plan to. I need to. "I can't believe after all this time she still holds a grudge."

Mav raises a mocking eyebrow. "Really? I thought that's the way it works when women get their hearts broken?"

"I was a kid, Maverick. What did I know?" He's well aware of this. I don't know why I need to keep reminding him about it.

"It doesn't matter. You still left without so much as a goodbye," he sets down his phone and gathers his things before heading to class. "You're bound to mess this up without my brotherly advice but just remember I'm here for you."

We talk for about another ten minutes about this and that. The guy is wicked smart and sharp as a tack. Maverick is a Tri-Nations Scholar currently completing his Ph.D. in political science at Acadan's most prestigious college, Harvada University.

Growing up in Callior whenever we weren't spending time here, Maverick and I were inseparable. My mother died from Amyotrophic Lateral Sclerosis in the same year Mav lost his parents in a bandit attack traveling from a vacation in Alaska while we were in Alorewyn. Since he had no immediate family, Father insisted he stay with us in Callior. It was his brother's son after all, and he'd sooner shoot himself than let Mav go into foster care. Poor kid was destroyed after losing his parents. I didn't leave his side for weeks after he moved to the palace, pushing him to attend balls, parties, and holiday celebrations to keep him from disappearing into that wallowing shell he kept himself in sometimes.

Naturally, since he was adopted and was officially crowned Prince Maverick Dormer and became eligible for king alongside me. Which lifted an immense pressure off my shoulders thanks to princely duties being divvied up between two of us instead of falling squarely on me. I'm an only child, and the thought of taking on such a ridiculous amount of responsibility clawed at my sanity on more than I cared to admit at the time.

The resemblance between us is uncanny. His dark brown eyes and defined chin matched mine almost exactly, the only difference being his dimpled cheeks. When I say women fell at his feet when he hit puberty, you better believe it. He's six years older than I am and three inches shorter, which I pester him about constantly, and an internationally ranked polo player.

Give me anything from football to lacrosse, hell even tennis, I can play it. Give me a jet, I'll fly it. But horse riding? Not even when my mother stuck me on the tiniest pony at a traveling fair. I hated it.

My grandfather believed that a horse is a creature of admiration, worshipped for their otherworldly grace, not ridden and whipped for the pleasure of man. I guess I shared that sentiment.

But when Mav and I would play Which Animal Would You Rather he'd usually pick some dinosaur, I'd pick a horse. Not necessarily for the height, I tower over my father with at least two inches at six-two, but definitely for the genital girth.

Mav lets me know he's late for class and clicks off. And not a minute too soon. We've been through this conversation too many times.

If it weren't for the icepacks I held against my eyes, it'd be swollen shut by dinner. A wonderfully dull throb remains, which I'm sure will accompany me for days, that I could see out of it was nothing short of a miracle. Perhaps a sign that Emryne wasn't as pissed as I expected her to be. But the cut on my lip suggested otherwise. And something about the way she glared at me this afternoon tells me it's only the beginning.

I change into Callior's dress uniform, pin the respective medals under our nation's emblem, and fasten the coat buttons. The red coat is heavily embroidered, and the lapels reach mid-calf with an accompanying sash displaying Callior's red and white colors.

Different uniforms have different medals, and for tonight's occasion, it's mostly decorative: the Medal for Crowned Prince, the Honor of Eligibility, Medal for Accepting Eligibility and the United Nations Services Award, an honor most royals don't bother with, but I wear proudly. Mav and I both received the award when I was still in high school. Callior welcomed citizens from Alaska when temperatures plummeted to an all-time low and the country's electrical grid was all but destroyed.

I fasten the golden aiguillettes under my shoulder and head out the door.

I'd say Queen Lilliette outdid herself for tonight's formal, welcoming the eligible princes from their respective kingdoms around the globe, but then again, she does every time. She may be the angriest woman you'll ever meet, but she throws a hell of a party.

The Grand Banquet Hall is decorated for a feast of two hundred instead of the ninety people standing around. Trays of fancy pastries, savory snacks, and towers of sparkling wine line the famous Alorewyn turquoise marble tables. A string quartet plays in the southeast corner and dancing couples enjoy the melodies.

I scan the crowd, spotting Addylin with her positively anxious mother, deep in conversation about something or other, and King Ryne laughing with my father and Kings Lodran and Gavriel of Eugavis.

Addylin meets my eye and bows her head. I bow mine in return. She looks very princess-like in her sky-blue silk gown with its delicate flower embroidery on the waist, but Addylin isn't the crowned beauty I'm trying to find.

She's nice enough, I've always liked Addy and we get along just fine, but it's the flame in her sister's heart that I've always been addicted to.

Queen Lilliette follows her gaze and before I knew it, she's at my side.

"Oh, wonderful," she starts. "Would you mind, Prince Skylan, lending Addylin your voice? I'm afraid the soloist I'd hired for tonight has fallen ill and couldn't attend." I guess that's what they were talking about.

Had anyone else asked, I'd have said no, but I need to stay in this woman's good graces if I have any hopes of winning Emryne back.

"I would be honored, Your Majesty."

I give the crowd another sweep, finally spotting who I'm looking for. As if she couldn't get any more stunning, her lilac evening gown made her dazzlingly spectacular.

I take a step toward her but stop short when the queen announces Addylin's performance, and before I knew it, I'm beckoned onto the stage and a black microphone stand is settled at my feet.

"Thank you for doing this," she whispers over the applause. "I know it was totally last-minute."

"It's my pleasure. Wouldn't want your voice missing from tonight's occasion," I wink and Addylin laughs. Not a lie. She has a phenomenal voice, befitting the gentle princess she is. Polar opposite to her firecracker of a twin.

The crowd hushes and settles in their seats for the performance. As the small choir joins us on stage, a wave of panic at the lack of preparation hits me.

"Uhm, Adds, mind filling me in on what we're supposed to be singing?"

She smiles. "Maybe I'm Amazed, Paul McCartney. You know the song, right?"

"Of course." Thank God.

"Feel free to add your own spin to it. Let's make it a night to remember," she smiles, bumping my shoulder.

The pianist begins, and the lyrics form with ease. In the ocean of endeared faces, all I see is Emryne. In all my years pleasing women, no one quite excited me like she did. Challenged me like she did. And God knows none of them gave me such ridiculous hard-ons like she did. Ever.

How am I supposed to concentrate on singing when all I can think about is tying her up, spreading her legs and filling up every inch of her?

The choir begins their bridge, and Addylin and I adjust. Might not have been what Paul necessarily intended, but she did say make it my own. So, I glide into the most comfortable *G#4* I've sung in my life, all while my eyes are on Emryne. I'm sure she tries to fight it, but I see the adoration in her eyes; the way she used to look at me all the time when I'd sing for her.

That's right, sweetheart. This is all for you.

The music finishes, crowd on their feet once more, and to my surprise, Emryne included. Though that could be for her sister, but I take the opportunity and smile at her anyway. To my further surprise, she's beaming at me.

I take Addylin's hand and we step around the microphones. I bow my head, she curtsies, and we turn to the musicians and choir for their well-deserved applause. She takes my arm I hold out to her, and we climb off the stage.

She leans her head toward me so I can hear her over the new music, "I can't believe I forgot what an incredible voice you have."

I do the same. "Well, we haven't seen each other since your graduation." Since I'm an eligible prince, I'm technically supposed to be spending time with both princesses, so a small part of me feels bad for releasing myself from her hand, "Would you excuse me?" but I need to see Emryne. I'll find some way to make it up to her.

Her sister seems to want the same thing. We meet each other's smiles and make our way toward one another. Only to be stopped halfway to the massive dance floor once again by another unwanted presence.

Even I can't deny Prince Caneic Loundry of Eikenish is handsome. His smooth features give him a clean-cut look with hair styled to perfection. And, of course, there is the English accent women all but come over.

My annoyance hits ceiling-level and I stifle a growl as Cane holds his arm out to her, and she gives me an apologetic smile as they exit through the white French doors to the gardens outside.

I knew what I was signing up for when my father announced our invitation to Alorewyn to court the princesses, but I'd be lying if I said this didn't drive me to insanity.

In no mood to endure the festivities any longer, I walk to my father, still in conversation with King Ryne, and bid him and the king a good night. I did the same with Queen Lilliette and an obviously disappointed Addylin, and head back to my room. I admit I slammed the varnished oakwood a little hard, but I'm too pissed to care.

I can't stand seeing her with another man. Emryne was the first and only woman who gave her virginity to me. It meant something that her trust was absolute, and I cherished that to this day. A feeling I have no doubt she'd never share with suave-e-o Caneic, no matter how great his accent is. A woman's virginity is a gift, something not everyone deserves. *She* is a gift he definitely doesn't deserve.

I rip off my uniform until only my pants hug my hips, enjoying the freedom my bare chest brings. Don't get me wrong, I'm not in any way ashamed or embarrassed to wear Callior's colors, but with the hours I'd already spent smiling, greeting, and singing in it, not to mention my frustration, the material begins to annoy.

I get why Emryne's pissed, I would be too, I acted like a coward. But that's exactly why I'm here. To explain myself. To prove why I'm worthy of her.

And if there is one thing I detest more than sharing, it's sharing a woman.

I'm surprised I don't burrow a trench in the carpet from my unsteady pacing. What are they doing in those gardens? Is he holding her hand? Is he touching her the way I used to touch her? Is she smiling at him the way she once did with me? Kissing him the way she used to kiss me? Coming apart on his fingers the way she used to do mine?

Over, and over, and over again?

I feel myself stiffen at the memory. I wish I could describe the way she moaned when my tongue licked hat sensitive spot in her neck, her body inching closer to mine, just as starved for touch as mine was. And when my greedy hands adored every inch of her, she all but begged me inside her. No longer able to control myself, I unzip my pants and pull my boxers down and I wrap my fist around my cock, working my fingers around my shaft, squeezing harder, pumping faster, as I imagine my princess.

Down on her knees.

Looking up at me with those gorgeous eyes, just like she used to.

Emryne.

That incredible body. Wearing the lacy lingerie I love so much.

Emryne.

Those full, luscious lips around my cock, sucking softly, then taking my hard length into her delicious mouth. Bringing me closer and closer to the edge with those impossibly blue eyes of hers, sparkling as she keeps my gaze.

My Emryne.

No longer a girl. All woman.

Her soft, wet pussy wrapped around my cock. Her deep moans filling the air.

Taking her against the wall, against the desk. The floor. The shower. Every-fucking-where.

Mine.

My orgasm hits me with the force of a cargo ship, and I sink into the black silk sheets on the massive four-poster bed behind me, willing my heavy breaths to even enough to form any coherent thoughts other than wrenching the door open and barreling dick first into Emryne.

It's been a while since she possessed my thoughts as she did once. But seeing her now, how much she's matured into Alorewyn's future queen?

It made my goal crystal clear.

I *have* to have her.

Chapter 6
Emryne
The Lavender Complication

Am I disappointed that I didn't get to talk to Skylan? Honestly, I am a little. And he surprised me.

Addy was perfect as always, but I wasn't expecting to see him singing at all, let alone how beautifully he did. I did my best, but there's no denying the rush I felt when he did.

My plan was to congratulate him, he seemed giddy to talk too, but Cane appeared at my side at the speed of light and pulled me away before I could blink.

I know that I'm supposed to make time for all the princes—yes, I'll make it up to Zimo somehow—so I accept his request for a walk in the gardens.

"This is your third time back in Alorewyn, right?" I ask as we near the wild orchid garden, Ophelia's favorite flowers. My father insisted a garden be planted for her at once, and it's grown into quite the exquisite display. Father did things like that for all his children. Cameron loved cars and wanted to race, so my father had the racetrack built around the palace.

Asaria wanted Arabian horses, so my father flew her to the United Arab Emirates, and they came home with two champion stallions and three prized mares. Ophelia wanted flowers, and I wanted to fight. Addylin… sticks to my mother's side like Velcro; barely speaks to Father unless she absolutely has to.

The Gennady children are quite the enigmatic bunch.

"It is. Happy to be back," his smooth accent caresses my senses. Prince Caneic Loundry has quite striking features. His round chin and forest green eyes are typical Loundry characteristics and resembles his mother's, Queen Carmen, the closest.

He looks much sweeter than Skylan. *He is much sweeter than Skylan.*

"I must admit, I was surprised to receive your invitation. I'm honored." Technically my mother's invitation, but he doesn't need to know that.

I feign modesty as best as I can. "You were?"

"I was. We haven't spoken much other than balls or diplomatic visits to one another's kingdoms. This is the most time we've spent together. I'm quite enjoying myself," he says, warm eyes settling on mine. He's right. Whenever Father would visit Eikenish I rarely went along. Addylin would, she loved everything about Adlengn, but again—she was glued to Mother's side.

"I'm glad you are," I say with a smile. "I realize the situation is a little awkward, but I'm looking forward to getting to know everyone."

He leads me down the path to the rose fields. A gentle breeze infuses the air with their gentle scent, and I take a deep breath in. I'm not a huge rose fan, I love the pop of color daffodils add to summer, but Alorewyn roses are among the most famous flowers in the world, and one of our kingdom's leading commodities. The coral petals produce an oil so rich it's used in everything from perfumes to antibiotic powders. But it's most famous for its stress-relieving and sleep-restorative properties. Cameron's discovery, believe it or not.

"How are you coping so far?" Cane asks.

"It's too early to say," I answer politely. "You've barely been here a week and I haven't been able to really spend time with everyone yet."

He nods, smiling. "Well, if you ever find yourself bored and in need of company, my door is always open."

I squeeze his arm and smile thoughtfully, "I appreciate that." Spending time with Cane, all the princes, would keep me as far away from Skylan as possible. I can't avoid him forever, I know, but if he could make me wait three years for an explanation, if I ever get one, then he can be damn sure I'll make him wait too.

We continue our stroll until we reach the cobblestone path to the diamond rotunda, one of my favorite places to relax in the palace. The hibiscus canopy provides the perfect shade in summer, so I arranged a sitting area with snow white couches, an antique coffee table, had speakers mounted and a fire pit for Alorewyn's colder months. Just a few things to make the space a little homier.

"And if there is anything in particular about Alorewyn you would like to see, feel free to let me know," I tell him.

He inclines his head politely. "I appreciate that. There is something quite interesting I heard about Alorewyn in the few days before my arrival."

Color me curious. "Do tell."

"Well, word on the street in Adlengn is that a vigilante is loose."

I stifle a sigh. Is that all people can talk about? "It seems to be circulating in a few news outlets, yes."

And that's all I'm saying on the matter. I straighten my shoulders and change the subject. "So, tell me a little more about yourself?"

He takes the bait and nods. "What would you like to know?"

Everything. What are your intentions with my kingdom? What are your intentions with me? "Did you leave behind a string of broken hearts when you accepted the invitation?"

His lips turn up and he laughs. "Oh, yes. None of which I knew personally. Mostly fans and admirers of the kingdom." Fair. He is Adlengn's most eligible bachelor. "How about you?"

"Same thing. Some posts about who the Parliament will side with, me or Addylin. A few videos have circulated expressing their excitement for a new king and queen. That kind of stuff."

"No broken hearts?"

I shrug. "Nope." The only broken heart in this frickin' soap opera is mine, but he doesn't need to know that.

A look of satisfaction fill his eyes. "So, I don't have to worry about a disgruntled ex-lover poisoning my wine?"

I shake my head with a laugh, "No, you're fine."

"Good," he says. The relief in his voice is as obvious as moonlight.

"Funny, I always thought—"

The heel of my sandal slips against the cobblestones, "Oh!" probably because the stones are wet from the earlier sprinkler systems, more so because I'm a real klutz sometimes. Cane's hands steady me at once, his grip is warm and firm. He takes my hands after sweeping his eyes over my body, checking for other injuries.

"Careful, Princess." His eyes are bright under the garden floodlights. I haven't missed how close he's now gotten, and I'd be insane not to get lost in the intensity of forest green. Something about Cane excites me. I know nothing about him, and the prospect of something new is quite appealing and there really was no telling where this could go. He is attractive, maybe not Skylan attractive. But, if I am to find a companion, I need to focus on more than just pretty.

Whoever the future king is, should at least have some interest in Alorewyn. And in me. Both of which I know Skylan has given that he spent most of his childhood with me, but he's not the only prince here. And I owe it Father to at the very least get to know all of them and see who would make an agreeable husband.

Hey, maybe even fall in love with. Wouldn't that be a dream?

"Thank you," I say and his hands release me, and a curious wave of regret passed over my body. Another new feeling. I like it.

Sky can sing all he wants; these panties are staying right where they are, thank you very much.

I may have a moderate to severe shopping addiction.

Seven hours, thirty-four bags and nine iced toffee-nut mocha latte's later, with aching feet and bellies overflowing with laughter, the girls and I walk through the palace doors at exactly three fifty-five that afternoon. Moni and Des are waiting to take our bags and summon a few knights to help bring the rest to my bedroom.

It's been three months since the princes' arrival and three of them have already gone home. Herwin and Obren kept good conversation, but none of us had anything in common. Neither were bothered; it was obvious they weren't into it.

It's Prince Zimo I'm most worried about. Moni woke me up in the middle of the night three weeks ago saying my presence was needed in Father's study. Everyone was waiting when I'd arrived, including the remaining princes, all equally concerned, and Addy gripping Zimo's hand tightly. Father announced that King Xiang-Lin had fallen gravely ill. Rebel uprisings from the Pirate Islands southeast of the continent were at an all-time high. The monarchy suspected the king was poisoned by a knight or servant, possibly even a cook posing as a staff member. Zimo's return to the Grand Empire was imperative in case of his father's death and he needed to be crowned king. Zimo was a sweet guy, and I regretted not being able to spend more time with him, but I promised him a visit after the unrest calmed again.

When the study emptied, I asked Father if I could speak with Parliament to arrange for a battalion of Alorewynian knights to prepare themselves should the kingdom need assistance. Father's eyes beamed with pride as he fought back his tears. He nodded and promised we'd meet with them first thing in the morning. We did. Grand Empire was grateful, and Parliament was thoroughly impressed.

Score one for Princess Emryne.

"What time should we leave tonight?" Beth asks as we climb the staircase on our way outside. With summer in full swing, days are much too beautiful to spend indoors.

"Ten-ish? You know how crowded it gets if we don't get there before eleven," Tory replies. She declared tonight Girls' Night and demanded we head to Alorewyn's most famous VIP club, The Lavender Forum, to celebrate my running for crown. The three of us hadn't seen each other much after graduation since they're busy with work and I've been training to run a country. This is the first time since Beth's birthday in November last year we've really been able to catch up besides quick lunches here and there.

"I'm not going anywhere until we've eaten something," I state, ice coffee was all we had while emptying out the shelves of Louis Vuitton, Off-White, and Manolo Blahnik.

Yes, I'm spoiled. No, I regret nothing.

Since the club didn't have a kitchen, and I have no doubt Tory planned for us to leave with an unacceptable blood-alcohol level, food is an excellent idea. My stomach rumbles in agreement so I call for Monique and she promptly meets us at the white floor-to-ceiling French doors leading to the South Gardens.

"Yes, Your Highness?" She says friendly.

"The girls and I are going to have lunch in the rotunda. Please have the chef prepare three bowls of fried rice and chocolate-pistachio crepes for dessert?"

She bows her head. "Of course, Your Highness. Raspberry tea?"

I smile. She knows me so well. "Please."

"Oh, can I have an ice coffee with the butterscotch syrup you added last time?" Beth asks.

Moni bows politely and heads downstairs to the kitchens.

"More coffee?" I raise a brow.

The knights guarding the doors open them for us to exit, and a symphony of summer aromas fills the air. I love spending time in the gardens. Every flower is in bloom, the lawn is perfectly manicured and most important, there is not a fleck of snow in sight. Winter fashion may be gorgeous, but winter weather is enemy number one in my book. I might even declare it illegal if I'm elected queen.

Arm in arm, we make our way down the sandstone steps toward the rotunda.

"Have I ever told you how jealous I am that you have people who do everything for you?" Tory sighs when we reach the shaded couches.

"Every time you're here," I laugh. "But I know. I wouldn't be anything without her. Either of them, really."

"So, what's the newest with Sky?" Tory flops down and props her feet up on the armrest like she always does. Her unruly blonde curls fanning out on the couch behind her.

I lift her legs and sit down under her, laying them over my lap like I always do. "I don't know. Other than the day he cornered me in the hallway I haven't talked to him much since—"

"You socked him in the keister?" Beth finishes with a giggle, sitting down on the loveseat opposite us and tucking her legs under her.

"He deserved it," I sit up and Tory drops her feet as Moni and Des set out our lunch. Sir Stéphane has outdone himself once again. I cannot begin to describe the mouth-watering aromas floating from the steaming bowls. Not to mention the chocolate crepes with the generous drizzle of pistachio, cooked to perfection. As if a Five-Star Michelin chef would cook them any differently.

"God, I wish you guys could've heard him the night of the welcome dinner."

"You mean the dinner we weren't invited to?" Tory asks with a teasing tone.

"That was for state and diplomatic officials and you know it. Not like I didn't want you there."

"Still hurts," she mumbles, rolling her eyes.

"And? Is she still as drool worthy as we remember?" Beth asks with a mouthful of rice.

"And then some. He hit this high note and I swear I almost came right there." Moni staggers and nearly drops the teacup and saucer. My lips turn up and I help steady her as I take the fine China and set it down. She smiles gratefully and pours us a cup of tea. Not that she hasn't heard me mouthing off before, but being nearly seventy and a widow with no children, it shocked her almost every time. Beth reaches for her bowl. "I'm not surprised. You've always had a hard-on for Sky's voice."

And Sky's always had a hard-on for me.

"Have you heard him? He sounds like a god."

"What about the others?" Tory asks. "What're they like? Any potential?"

I take a bite of my fried rice and consider her question. "I've seen the most of Cane." I say between chews. "Lando is nice and Allister's hilarious."

"But no spark yet?"

"Nope. And I'm kind of starting to get a little discouraged."

"Don't," Tory consoles, gripping my knee. "It's only been three months. You can't expect sparks to fly if you don't know a thing about these guys." She's right, of course. Honestly, this whole thing is like our own twisted version of The Bachelorette, minus the cameras and scripted responses, which made it even more difficult. At least with a script they had some sense of what to say to one another while I didn't have the faintest idea.

The remaining princes were more charismatic, but keeping conversation with Herwin and Obren was a more obtuse venture than training a goat to pilot an airplane.

All Obren kept talking about was water. Walking in water, swimming in water, bacterial growth in water, spring water versus reverse osmosis water… after twenty minutes of talking, I would've flooded my home if I didn't flee to a bathroom. Herwin mostly stared at his phone and replied with cryptic half-answers when I asked him something.

"Seriously, E," Tory snaps me back. "I don't know how you do it. I don't think I could go through something like this."

How do you imagine I feel? "Be thankful it's not you."

Beth takes a sip of her coffee then sets her cup down. "I don't know if this question is allowed, but how's Addylin doing with all of this?"

"I have no idea. She's barely said a word to me since Asa's accident." Which made my heart ache. The four of us were inseparable in school. And then she disappeared. Wrote us off in the middle of the night without so much as a goodbye or explanation. It's the strangest thing.

A thought crosses my mind. "Maybe we should invite her tonight? I'm sure she could use a little fun just as much as I do."

The girls smile. "That'd be great. It would give us a chance to—"

"Fuck. Me."

Both Beth and I grimace at each other. "Why on earth would we… Oh. Yes please." We follow her line of sight, and I press my lips together to keep from laughing out loud.

Bare-chests, big arms, and metal clashing against metal in a stunning display of power. Seems like as good a day as any for Skylan and the others to take their workout outside, I wouldn't waste it indoors either. Although I find their choice in that particular spot by the giant checkers board, when they could've picked anywhere on palace grounds, very interesting. Or maybe they've been there all along and we hadn't noticed.

Their bodies are glistening, they're laughing as they spar, and it blows my mind thinking my king may be among them as we speak.

"Geez, is that Prince Allister? The hot get hotter." Tory smirks before she gets up. Beth and I follow her, leaning against her and admiring the show. "I didn't know you invited him?"

"My mother did. And I literally told you the second the invitations were sent out?" I say, her bewildered gaze intently focused on them. "You might want to wipe your mouth." I joke. "You've got some drool hanging in the corner."

"God, I wanna ride his dick like Luke Collins rode that bull," she bounces.

I burst out laughing. "You are unbelievable!"

Every one of the them are built like boulders, yet I can only focus on one— perfectly styled hair despite the heat, sun-kissed skin despite his fair-skinned parents; the one whose eyes are trained on me even from the short distance.

He bears his teeth and hops off stool he's resting in, and he and Lando begin their round. Somehow an even more powerful one. Though I don't know why I'm surprised, Skylan has been training with his father for longer than I've been training with mine. And on a battlefield, I haven't seen it myself but I heard it's brutal, King Harryson Alexandrius Dormer III was a force to be reckoned with.

Skylan flashes a devilish grin before leaning closer to Lando, mumbling something he obviously takes personally given the force his sword comes down at Sky's head not a second later, jumping him and firing a string of Italian words I don't want to know the meaning of.

Boys.

"No wonder you're having a tough time. Infinite potential at your fingertips, babe." Beth says over her shoulder, brown eyes sparking with anticipation.

I feel my laughter disappear. "I can't sleep with anyone. You know that." Not because I'm a virgin, but because of how much trouble we could get into since we're supposed to keep this clean. Which I get on one hand, but on the other? Emotional compatibility is important sure, but so is sexual compatibility. How are you supposed to know if you are without getting naked? It's why I don't believe in high school sweethearts. Sure, they're all you want then, but as soon as you leave the confines of the familiar and feel the rush of the exotic… familiar? Just can't compare. And a good orgasm says a lot about a person. Giving and receiving.

That hasn't happened since Sky. All these goody-two-shoes princes don't exactly excite me either.

Even with the piercing. Guys either go way too fast, or they run with their tails between their legs. What can I say? It's intimidating. But I've gotten used to people's misperceptions of me. Sometimes faking it is easier; most don't swallow the truth the same otherwise.

"Sky seems like the perfect candidate to get you back on the horse girl," Tory remarks. "And the way he's been looking at you tells me he'd be happy to oblige." She smirks.

"No, he's not. He's the devil," I deadpan, throwing her a scowl.

"If you mean devilishly fuckable, then yes," Beth chimes.

I frown at her. "You two are out of your minds."

"Are you kidding? He looks like the type of man who'd handcuff you to his bed and torture you one, sweet, slow, *hard* orgasm at a time. Exactly what I like in a man."

"Even if I was to consider it, which I'm not, to go through the same thing I did after graduation? Yeah, no thanks. Besides, the guy has slept with half the women in Alorewyn."

Beth turns to me. "Have you still not talked about what happened?"

"I've tried," I shrug. "But he always changes the subject."

I'm not sure when, but the boys' sparring halted and now all four were staring at us, ending in chuckles after Skylan whispers something in Allister's ear. I roll my eyes.

"I think trying new a prince is a great idea. Especially if he looks anything like the one coming over now."

I turn and spot Cane jogging up. "Good afternoon, Princess." He really is something to look at, especially with his bare chest and solid arms. He smiles and falls into step beside me. "Sweltering afternoon, isn't it?"

"Tell me about it. Would you like some water?" I offer and bounce up the steps.

"That would be lovely," he follows me to the water bottles. "Afternoon, ladies." He nods to Beth and Tory. "I don't believe I've had the pleasure?"

"These are my best friends Annebeth and Victory."

He smiles and bows deeply, "Prince Caneic Loundry of Eikenish, at your service. Please, excuse my improper attire."

"Hey."

"Please don't," they answer in unison, somewhat dumbfounded.

His kind eyes settle on mine and he clasps his hands behind his back, squaring his shoulders.

"I apologize for the interruption, Your Highness, but I was wondering if you had plans tonight? I have tickets to the Ember City Philharmonic, and I was hoping you would accompany me? There's a fantastic restaurant nearby. Perhaps we can have dinner after?"

Right, because I absolutely listen to classical music.

Behind him, Beth and Tory lean their elbows on the back of the couch with their chins on their fists, flashing puppy-dog eyes and mocking pouts. I avert my gaze before I break out in laughter, smiling sincerely, "I'm so sorry, but the girls and I have plans."

Cane gives a nod. I can tell in his eyes he's pretending not to be offended, but he accepts the answer. "Another time perhaps. Anything fun?"

"Actually, we're heading downtown to The Lavender Forum. It's DJ Velocity's last night in Alorewyn before she heads to Belgium for Tomorrowland," Tory says, turning her smile to me, and I already know what she's thinking. I shake my head as subtly as I can, but of course, she ignores me. Her effervescent smile never faltering. "Why don't you come with? It'll be fun."

"Do we get an invite?" Behind Cane, Sky and the others saunter closer, his sword resting on his shoulder, and stop just short of the canopy.

I glare at him. "No, you don't."

Obviously amused, he inclines his head and grins. "Why?"

Because I have no self-control when it comes to you and I don't want to be stuck in a confined space for longer than absolutely necessary.

None of which I say, so I groan and agree. There really is no use resisting when I know he'd keep pestering and I'd eventually end up giving in anyway. And eyeing my best friends, I know they'd bring them along regardless of my vehement protests.

I cross my arms over my chest. "Fine. But none of you are coming anywhere near me until you take a shower." Lando and Allister exchange high-fives and head off in the palace direction with Cane behind.

Except Skylan, who's still grinning at me. "Care to join, Princess?"

Cocky bastard. I roll my eyes and hold up my palm dismissing him. "Just be ready by ten, moron."

He laughs. And I can't stop my smile as I turn away.

#

The conversation on our drive downtown flows easily. We left just in time too since traffic near the club is already piling up.

My excitement doubled when Addy agreed to join, and she hasn't left Cane's side since we got in the car.

Next to Allister, Tory's giggle draws my attention. She decided tonight would be a black off-the-shoulder top kind of night, with faded blue jeans and black pumps. Her thick blonde hair is tied in a ponytail on her head, "just in case I happen to get lucky tonight."

Leave it to her to be prepared. Beth's in an all-white jumpsuit, and next to her, Addylin chose a simple pink blouse, blue jeans and white pumps, her shy smile turned to Cane who seems to be enjoying her company. Good.

And Skylan? He's next to me with his arm draped behind my headrest, brow furrowed as he observes the world passing by us. I'm trying not to focus on his warm next to mine, or the fact that our knees have been touching since we got in the car and focus on, knowing exactly how they can be, setting some ground rules for my friends instead.

"For the sake of the princes, can the two of you at least try to behave yourselves tonight?"

"I will do no such thing," Tory protests. Beth answers with a stomach-full of laughter.

Can't bring these two anywhere.

I feel Sky's shoulders shake beside me, but he keeps his eyes outside. He's been doing that all night. "Are you including yourself in that ultimatum, Em-Em?" He asks.

I ignore his question, yanking my vibrating phone from my pocket instead.

"Please stop calling me that," I mumble as the screen lights up and my pulse quickens. *Perfect, just what I need.*

Given the lack of privacy, I angle my phone away from Skylan to read.

UNKNOWN*: Heads up: new drug's hit the streets. It's brutal, YH.*

YH being short for Your Highness. And they're not kidding. The string of images flooding my phone nearly has me losing my lunch all over myself. The crime scene photos have obviously been taken from the Knights Guard database, and display the bodies of recent OD victims, laying in pools of weird brown vomit, and foaming at the mouth.

Jesus, what'd they put in there, cyanide? I try not to focus on the gut-wrenching images too long and scroll away before texting back. No one deserves to die like this.

ME*: Details?*

UNKNOWN*: Some punk's selling in Midtown. If ur headed to Forum, keep ur eye out for baby-blue pills. Name's Purple Sprinkle.*

Another image comes through, a mugshot of a local drug dealer. I've seen his face before, but as with most of them in Alorewyn, he's never really been on my radar. There's simply no way to wrangle up every dealer when another one comes crawling through their devious cracks not a second later.

UNKNOWN*: Don't know much yet. I haven't been able to get my hands on it 'cause it sells out crazy fast. Dealer's Markus Millman, goes by Rolo. Likes to keep his stash in leather jacket & wears black ripped jeans. He'll probably show up.*

ME*: Thanks, Cas.*

UNKNOWN*: Anytime, YH.*

It's been a couple weeks since a report's been slipped to me from my informant, Castor. It took me a while to get into a good groove when the Dark Warrior first took to the streets, but you'd be amazed at the allies I've already made and tonight, I feel like I need a little action to take the edge off. In the meantime, I stash my phone away and survey the car. No one seems to notice.

Except Skylan. Who's eyeing me in the strangest way. I know he couldn't have seen; I've practiced discretion more than once. So, I roll my eyes and turn back to the girls. "I'm serious, you two."

"Oh no, girlfriend. We're letting loose tonight. At the end of the year you'll be married, and we'll never get to do this again because you'll be too busy being the badass queen we deserve."

I exchange awkward glances with the princes. None of us really wanted this but hanging out and getting to know each other this way is better than arranged marriages. So, I'd endure awkward for now. Not much I can do to change reality.

Or maybe I could with the amount of cocktails Tory orders when we're settled our suite. The club is completely packed, strobe lights lining the stage flashing blue and silver to the beat of the music, and I'm relieved for calling ahead and reserving a private suite.

"See, I told you!" I tell Beth over the blasting music as we walk through the VIP entrance, another perk of royalty.

Beth mocked me as we were getting ready, but something told me since it's Velocity's last night getting a private suite wouldn't be easy especially with the fifteen-minute photo-op outside the club, and there's no way any of us could mingle with citizens without being mauled, hence the bouncers escorting us and their photography prohibition of any kind inside.

"Yeah, okay, Princess Prepared. Your psychic abilities never cease to amaze." She hooks her arm around my neck and pecks my temple as the hostess calls for the private bartender, waiting for the MC to announce the main event. I do my best to keep my eyes on my surroundings. The club is lit enough to see each other's faces clearly, hearing is another thing though.

Sky's sitting all the way at the opposite end of the sequined golden couches, and I can't keep myself from wondering why. It's not like I haven't tried having a real conversation with him after the welcome dinner, but he's been avoiding me and it's enough to annoy. So, I leave my seat and move over to his brooding figure, crossing my leg on my knee as I do so, and I lean into him. "Hey."

He keeps his eyes on the dance floor below. "Talking to me now?"

"I want to know why you're avoiding me."

His lips thin and he shrugs. "I haven't been avoiding you."

I scoff. "Yes, you have. So, tell me why."

"I thought you hated me," he rolls his eyes and finally turns to me.

"Well, if I can get some answers maybe I won't have to."

"We both know it's not that simple."

My chest tightens, and I grip his forearm, feeling his muscles harden under my touch. The sleeves of his white button down tighten around his biceps as he battles whatever emotions my question awoke, and I fight the urge to run my finger to his clenched fist and over the corded veins. "It can be if you would just talk to me."

"It wouldn't make a difference," his voice is strained as he pulls his arms away.

Even knowing he probably won't answer, I ask anyway, "Sky, please just tell me where you disappeared to? Where have you been all this time?"

"Just let it go, Emryne," he barks and moves to the other side of the suite, grabbing another beer as he does so. Even in the darkness I can see the turmoil in Sky's eyes. I don't want to hate him. He was my best friend, our parents stuck us in the same bathtub for Christ's sake.

Though I gave him my heart the last night we had sex, and it broke me in more ways than I could explain, we've always had an unbreakable bond between us.

Skylan understands me in a way no one has before. I never wanted to lose him. I'm not saying it would go back to exactly the way it was before, we've both grown up too much since then, I just want this figured out so we can move on. If not as friends, then at least we can be free of one another and live our lives.

I swallow the ache in my chest and chose to focus on the tasks at hand. Have fun with my girls before they head back to work and keep an eye out for this so-called 'Purple Sprinkle'. Should it make an appearance, the Dark Warrior is going hunting tonight.

I leave Skylan to his drinking and head to the private bar where Tory and Allister are perched on barstools laughing, completely wrapped up in one another. Good, at least someone is getting some action.

Their conversation halts as I step between them and pull a bottle of Vodka from behind the counter, unscrew the lid and gulp down a generous swig, welcoming the stinging in my throat. I've had enough of Skylan's moods. I've had enough of Skylan, period.

Beth's right, we are here to have a good time before I get married and become queen. Maybe even without a king if I can get my say in.

"That's the spirit, E!" Tory exclaims happily and claps her hands.

Allister leans in over the music, concern shining in his eyes. "Are you alright, Princess?"

I gulp down another shot, answering with tight lips, "Fine. Just fucking fine."

The private suites have plenty of space for dancing, but nothing quite beats the thrill of having your senses engulfed in the full force of beats blasting from the speakers around you.

Beth rushes through the glitter strings and beckons us to the main dance floor below. "Girls! What're you doing? Velocity's starting, let's go!" I unzip my bomber jacket and my blood-red strappy sequins top glitters in the house lights. It cuts off mid-stomach and complements the black leather jeans and my favorite pair of Christian Louboutin's perfectly.

I take Tory's hand and we make our way to the stairs. But not before we turn back to Addylin, "Aren't you coming?"

She shakes her head and smiles, lifting her drink and sinking further into the couch next to Cane. Alright then.

The energy is electric when we make it down the illuminated stairwell to Beth on the massive main dance floor. Beth's nearly all the way in the front, her eyes glued to Velocity, fingers expertly work the turntable below her. Tory is as lost as Beth is, but I stay focused. I committed Castor's texts to memory, even the OD victims, and scan my eyes over the crowd. Some bewildered smiles along with waves flash my way. All of which would've ended in autographs and pictures for their Instagram accounts were their blood-alcohol levels not way beyond legal limit. Not to mention God knows what pumping through their veins.

Forum has produced some of the greatest names in electronic music's history. Every DJ who's made a name for themselves have presented here, and Velocity is next to head to the big leagues. And since it's her last performance, there's bound to be someone selling to the elated masses.

Though I might be mistaken. No one in their right mind would wear a leather jacket inside this place tonight. Even with the air-conditioning blasting, the strobe lights and grinding bodies still drives the temperature to ridiculous heights.

There's no way I can resist losing myself as the beat drops, especially not next to Tory, or Beth for that matter. I grab my friends' hands and hold on tight as we sway to our favorite song and just for a few moments, the world around me melts away and I feel a sense of relief for the first time in weeks, months actually. We've shared so much heartache between us, so much history, being here with my girls now, it's never been easier to forget everything around me.

That is until my eye catches someone, and I'm ricocheted back to reality.

As the crowd closes around us, I use the opportunity to my advantage and slip through the sea of young adult angst, hormones, and gyration until I'm on the other side of the dance floor while my friends remain oblivious to anything other than the bass.

The bartender throws her head back in laughter as he reaches out his hand and slaps his palm.

Bingo. *Castor, your information is thoroughly appreciated.* Tall, dark, and handsome is indeed sporting the same jacket as Millman.

Even with the main bar directly in view of our suite, Sky and the others are the least of my worries now.

She hops up on the bar and kisses his cheek, waving as he strides away. I turn my head away and duck behind a pillar before they spot me, and make sure to follow him as he exits the main floor.

The overhead LED lights from the bar allows me to see just enough to know he handed her something, and the flash of blue confirms my suspicions.

Not in my kingdom, you don't.

Checking and double-checking that I'm not seen, I follow him almost all the way out of the club. But when I round the corner, no one was there.

"Looking for me, Princess?"

My head whips at the direction the voice comes from. And there he is. In all his leathery glory.

This isn't my first rendezvous with a dealer, so I turn on the charm. "Do you have eyes on the back of your head?"

"In my line of work? Occupational hazard, I'm afraid."

"Well, thank God I found you," I say as sweetly as I can without breaking his jaw, and saunter closer. "I was hoping you would have something to… take the edge off."

He smiles. Did I mention tall, dark, and handsome? "And you chose me?" His hand touches his chest. "I'm honored, Your Highness. Anything in particular you're in the mood for?"

Oh, we'll get to that in a minute. "What's your name?"

He considers me for a beat. Then smiles wider. "Name's Rolo."

"Okay Rolo, I'm feeling in a dangerous mood."

"Can't be too dangerous given those goody-two-shoes princes you're here with."

Of course, he'd notice. The snapping phones and gleeful smiles outside the club before we came in was indication enough as well.

"That's exactly why I need you. Think you can help a distressing damsel out?" I flash my sweetest smile, gluing my eyes to his dark gaze as I lean into him and reach for his zipper, playfully running it up and down the teeth. If this doesn't work, nothing will.

A dark chuckle escapes his throat, and he takes my hand, opening his jacket and flashing his product, and it's enough to make me throw up. I recognize a few of them, mostly because I—I mean, the Dark Warrior—threw the dealing jackasses to Knights Guard to deal with.

Everything from Molly to an ecstasy derivative called Sleeper, several of what I assume is cocaine and god knows what other pills and powders. "Pick your poison."

I scan the rows of contraband lining his jacket. But I don't see the pills.

"Actually, I was hoping for something a little stronger? Or maybe something new?"

He nods, eyes flashing with excitement. "New seems to be the flavor of the evening. I got you," he reaches behind him and he pulls out the baggie of baby-blue pills. "Allow me to introduce you to Purple Sprinkle. Hit the streets a couple days ago."

"What is it?" I ask, taking the baggie from him.

He pauses, then a slow smile spreads. "Trust me, Princess, it's better if you don't know. It's safe enough that you won't OD, but you're in for a wild night." Please, as if I'm putting this junk in my body.

Ready for this exchange to be over, I slip the pills in my bra. "How much?"

"Three thousand," Dollars, of course. Ask me how I knew I needed to come prepared.

For five hundred dollars a pill, whatever this is must be premium stuff if it carries such a hefty price tag. With his type of clientele, money is the finest object.

I reach in my back pocket and pull out a flattened wad of bills, making sure to toss in a few extras.

To my surprise he holds up his hand. "That's not necessary, Your Highness. You're not the first royal I've sold to, and you definitely won't be the last. I'm no snitch. And I have a business to run."

"Keep it anyway. For your troubles," I wink, flashing a flirty grin. He hesitates at first, but nods and stashes the money in his jacket. No one in their right mind would refuse free money. Especially not from a member of the royal family.

"Pleasure doing business with you," he bows and exits the club but not before turning back, "Word of advice, don't take more than two at a time. Shit gets a little... weird... after that. Enjoy your evening, Princess." And he disappears behind the closing door.

Won't be enjoyable for you, Mr. Millman.

All I need is my equipment, and he's mine.

Chapter 7
Skylan
Old Habits Die... Never

Don't think I wasn't aware of exactly what game she's playing. Same old Emryne. Only much, much finer. I don't know how, but she's even curvier than I remember. And I remember pretty damn well. I think about that night more often than I care to admit.

Was our little workout this afternoon strategic? Maybe, but it was only the first step in my plan to get Emryne back. And she took the bait exactly like I hoped.

Of course, I saw the Instagram post she shared about her favorite DJ's last headliner at The Lavender Forum tonight, so getting them up and moving was the natural thing to do, a preview of the festivities. And inviting us along? Icing on the damn cake. Or at least it was until Emryne walked downstairs in those jeans and that damn red strappy thing.

My heart rattled against my chest when she smiled at me. It took a ridiculous amount of will power not to pay attention to the blood rushing to every nerve in my dick, shove her against the wall and tell everyone else to fuck off while driving into her, making her scream my name.

I should've known Emryne wouldn't be shy by any means, about her body, or her sexuality. Not after the way our first kiss happened.

Sixteen-year-old Emryne, sitting next to me on a rainy Tuesday afternoon in one of the lounges only the princesses ever used. Being best friends growing up, whatever her parents couldn't fill about relationships, which was nothing at all, she'd ask me.

She was reading some fantasy novel about a boy who finds out he's an angel, and I was going over notes for my flight exam later that week...

"Can I ask you something?" her innocent eyes turned to me.

"Given your age and lack of general knowledge, I encourage you to ask as many questions as possible, Em-Em," Innocent joke, but I meant it. She once held an iron out to me and asked what it did. Though no one could blame her. Royal lives are sheltered; there wasn't much that the staff didn't do.

Mom was old-school. She taught me how to do pretty much everything from ironing my own shirts to changing a tire.

Emryne sucked on her teeth and slapped my stomach playfully. "You're like two years older than me."

"Exactly, and don't you forget it," I teased, earning me an eyeroll. "What would you like to learn about today, Princess?"

She didn't reply immediately, so I closed the handbook and angled my body towards her. Her cheeks turned a rosy-red as she kept her eyes downward. "Have you ever… kissed anyone?"

I pressed my lips together in a poor attempt to keep from laughing. "Yes, of course."

"What's it like?"

Her question caught me a little off-guard, but I couldn't stop smiling at her genuine curiosity. I had to think about it for a second since I've never had to describe kissing before, so I answered as best as I could, "Well, it can be a lot of fun if the person you're kissing knows what they're doing."

"How can you tell if they're any good?" she asked and cocked her head to the right like she always did when she was curious about something. It was one of my favorite things about her.

I'd be lying if I said I'd didn't cross my mind who she planned on making out with. Her father would have a cow if he knew she was dating.

Her mother? Would have the whole barn.

But it had to be why she asked.

I gave a shrug, "I mean, the only way to really figure it out is to kiss them. Why? Who do you want—"

I barely had the sentence out when she grabbed my face and closed her lips over mine.

Her silky lips moved over mine, opening ever so slightly and all my thoughts disappeared, my senses possessed by Emryne, and my body lit up like fireworks on the Fourth of July.

I let her control the kiss at first, not wanting to scare her away and gently ran my tongue over her bottom lip, testing, teasing her and when hers parted against mine, I knew she was comfortable enough for me to take over.

What I didn't tell her, couldn't because I have no idea how to put it in real words, is that a single kiss with the right person could change your entire life. The way you look them, how they feel in your hands, their smiles when they walk past you and you remember exactly how their lips danced over yours. A good kiss with the right person becomes a separate language entirely, and I wanted nothing more than to speak in tongues. Over every inch of her body.

My hands snaked around her waist and pulled her into my lap so my fingers could reach her neck, guiding her, holding her even closer and the kiss went from sweet to desperate.

Then the sweetest moan escaped her, I knew I had to break the kiss before I did something I knew she wasn't ready for.

Both of us were breathless when we came up for air and I can, without hesitation, say I've never entirely lost myself in a kiss before.

"Like that?" she whispered. My response was a single nod, and I went right back to pressing my lips against hers, hungry for more.

And it was secret meetings and stolen kisses ever since.

Until we were sparring in the palace's private training room one night after watching Top Gun for the thousandth time, and something just… changed. She was a year older, had a few boyfriends here and there but nothing serious, and I was averted to serious girlfriends. It was kind of perfect. And so, so wrong.

I have no words to describe how or what changed, but something did. Maybe it was her natural talent for fighting, although it never really surprised me when she was her father's daughter, or maybe it was that she wasn't an innocent little girl anymore.

And it would start the same way as it did then.

We'd spar, she'd counter, and every time we'd end up inches from each other. She tried to disarm me, only for me to counter her advance and pin her to the wall with her back against me…

I let her go just enough to move her loose hair off her neck, and gently pressed my lips against the soft skin on her shoulder.

I took a leap of faith when she didn't free herself as she always would and felt her relax into my body. So, I tested the waters, and brought my hand around her hips and down to stroke her precious center. With no objection, I continued to kiss, rubbing until her sword slipped from her fingers and clattered against the floor, and her head fell to my chest.

Emryne reached backward and pulled me even closer as my lips moved to her neck. She eventually let go and put both hands against the wall to support herself, and pushed her butt into me, I growled my approval and ran both hands down her body again. She moaned in response, no doubt feeling my erection jump at the sound.

I swept her hair over her shoulder and began to unzip the black training suit she wore, but then her hand came around mine and stopped me.

"No," she breathed. "Sky, not here. Someone could walk in." I grinned at her aversion. I'm no stranger to exhibitionism. In fact, the prospect of getting caught only doubled my excitement. "Let them."

"No, Skylan. I'm not the one who'll get in trouble, you will," she finally spun around to face me, cupped my cheeks as she whispered, "I want you, but not here."

As much as I hated moving, I understood where she was coming from. Wars were started over less than sex, but our kingdoms' allegiance hung in the balance.

So, I let her take my hand and guide me through the infamous corridors hidden behind the inner walls, until we're inside her room. She locked her bedroom door and slowly kicked her trainers off as she made her way back to me. She had her lip between her teeth, her eyes devouring me as she stopped at my feet and rose on her tiptoes. My arms closed around her body as hers slid over my chest and around my shoulders. She whispered again, "I want you," her voice desperate, body craving release.

I knew she was a virgin, knew I should've stopped her, that we shouldn't be doing this, but I was too far gone to care. I needed to be inside her, and the way her body responded to mine told me she wanted exactly the same.

"Are you sure?" I searched her for the slightest sign of hesitation, anything at all and I would've ended it, but her impossible blues sparkled as she nodded and pulled my lips to hers, lighting my body on fire once again.

"I trust you, Skylan."

When my fingers slid the zipper down, she let the suit fall, and stepped out of it. For a second, I could do nothing but stare at her; nothing more than a flimsy lace bra and matching black panties on her body, and my mouth watered in anticipation.

My hands cupped her butt, and I lifted her onto my hips and carried her to her massive four-poster bed. A bed fit for the queen she'd one day be.

I lay her on her back, and guided her backward until she hit the mountain of pillows against the velvet headboard. Her eyes blazed with desire as my fingers undid her bra's clasp and slid the delicate fabric off her skin, freeing her gorgeous breasts. No longer able to resist, I lowered my tongue and took her pert nipple in my mouth, teasing her and earning another throaty moan.

Emryne's fingers gripped my shirt and lifted it over my head, then slid her fingers down and firmly gripped my erection, and hissed my approval. I bit the inside of my mouth to keep from coming apart before I tasted her, so I let her go and flipped her on top instead.

She was so innocent. So beautiful. A part of me thought I was sleeping, about to wake up at any minute and she'd be part of some fever dream, an unlikely reality. Then she took my hands and cupped her breasts as she ground into me, gave me all the encouragement I needed, and kept going.

I moved her panties to the side and played with her while she got comfortable. Her delicious wetness coated my fingers. Her head fell back as her hips moved again, riding my fingers. "Feel good?"

That beautiful smile; ocean irises focused on nothing but me as nodded. "Yes."

I hadn't anticipated exactly how wet she was, but it played in favor of my manhood in the very best of ways. Better yet, for her.

"So wet," I breathed.

She stopped moving then. "Is… is that bad?" she asked shyly.

"God no. It's perfect," she was perfect. And the need to feel her around me became unbearable, so I took her hands and flipped us back before I got up and stripped down.

She propped herself on her elbow. "Have you done this before?"

"Had sex? Of course, Em-Em. Plenty of times," I teased, hoping to relieve some tension. She tried to hide her disappointment, but I knew her well enough to know something bothered her. "Oh." I lifted her chin and gave her a reassuring smile.

"Hey, look at me," And when she did, my heart broke at the tears forming in her eyes. "What is it?"

"What if..." she started as her eyes searched mine.

"If?"

"What if I suck at this?" My brows furrowed, and I waited for her to continue. "You've done this before and... and it's my first time and what... what if..."

"Breathe, darling. It's okay to be nervous," I say and place a tender kiss on her soft lips. "I've got you. I promise. Okay?"

She found her smile again as she released a shaky breath, and her arms closed around my neck.

"Okay."

"Okay."

"Do you..." she swallows. "Do you, uhm, have a condom?"

Shit.

I sat up, silently cursing myself for not coming prepared. Then again, I had no idea today was going to turn into this.

"Bedside table," she motioned with her eyes. Suspicion creeped into my narrowed eyes as I waited for an explanation, and she grinned. "Asaria brings them when she's home. I usually throw them out but kept some just in case."

Relieved, I chuckled as I opened the drawer and reached in. I tore open the wrapper before I stripping down, then rolled the condom on, hooked her leg over my butt, giving me the perfect access to her.

"Ready?" She nodded one final time and moved her leg higher, and earned a smile from me.

"Tell me if it hurts too much and I'll stop, okay?" I needed reassurance, that she really wanted this and I wasn't letting my hopes run away with me. "I need to hear you say it."

"I'll tell you." Her hands cup my cheeks. "I trust you, Sky."

Suffice it to say, some people's addiction were drugs, others alcohol. After that first kiss, after the first time we had sex, Emryne Gennady became mine. So much that my feelings for her began to scare me.

I left that afternoon with nothing more than, "So, I'll see you tomorrow?"

And her look of confusion, "Uhm, yeah."

But tomorrow came and neither of us mentioned a thing. In fact, we avoided each other like the plague; barely spoke a word until her graduation. And even then, the conversation dragged.

What could I do? Our relationship dynamic changed and I had no idea what to do with that.

I was a coward. I wanted to see the world, taste the freedom travel brought, that's why I was opposed to relationships.

I gave her the time she needed. Let sweet old Cane think he has a shot with her, but I have news for him: Emryne's mine. And I have no intention of sharing her ever again.

If I didn't keep my eyes on the floor, or out of the window every damn time she shifted in her seat or her perfume intoxicated me, I would've jumped her right there, her friends be damned. I tried making jokes, but it only made it worse. No, what made it worse was when she lifted her hips to reach for her phone I almost leaped from the car. If I'm going to make this work, I'd have to get ahold of myself. There would be no touching Emryne until she said so.

Instead, I let my thoughts guide me to something other than a naked, breathless Emryne, though after the text she received, her behavior in the car was weird. Like she grew more distant.

Mav requested an update earlier today, but I changed the subject almost immediately. I care about my cousin, but sometimes he's a pain in my ass.

I spent the better half of my two months since I arrived looking into this Dark Warrior though. Maverick seems to think it's the best thing to happen to world since sliced bread. He even went as far as to text me a link to a fan-filmed video of them fighting.

RICK-O: *Dude, this chick is unstoppable! Check this out!*
Chick?
ME: *U think it's a woman?*
RICK-O: *No doubt, look at the way she fights!*

And the more I replayed the video, the more I saw what Mav did. Don't ask me how, but I swear I've seen that fighting style before.

And I have my suspicions about who exactly this Dark Warrior is.

Her sister gets assaulted and all of a sudden, a justice-seeking vigilante pops up out of nowhere and begins cleaning up Alorewyn's streets? Doesn't take a rocket scientist to do that math.

I keep an eye on her regardless, and when she disappears, I'd be lying if I said it didn't make my pulse race. It's not like her to leave Annebeth and Victory. Those two were dancing the night away, not a care in the world, and Emryne was… there? Making her way back to the suite.

I'd recognize her red sequins anywhere, she wore it the last night we had sex, but it baffles me how she just appeared out of nowhere when I could've sworn she was gone.

She winds her way through the crowd and back up the stairs to our suite and headed straight for her purse, hastily shoving something inside and shutting the clip. I leave the railing and sneak up behind her, leaning down. "Marco."

She yelps and shoots upright, clutching her chest. "Oh, hi."

"You were supposed to say Polo," I say, crossing my hands behind my back. "Where did you disappear to?"

She scoffs and crosses her arms. "Oh, so now you're talking to me? First, I find you lurking around every corner of my home, then tonight you can't stand the sight of me. You are so confusing, Skylan."

"Speak for yourself, Princess. You're the one who punched me in the face, remember?"

"You deserved it, and you know it," she argues, stepping right in my face.

"Yeah, I guess I did," I chuckle softly, rubbing at dull ache in my cheek. "So, where did you go?"

"Stop answering questions with other questions!" She pushes at my chest but stops short. "Are you wearing cologne?"

I lick my lips and flash my teeth. "Saint Devious, Complex Blend Number Seven," her favorite, just by the way. "Want a taste?" I tease, extending my back to her.

"No," her back straightens. She can pretend to hate this all she wants, but I'm nothing if not persistent.

"Why? You know it's your favorite."

She chokes on a laugh. "I'm fine, but thanks for the offer."

"Suit yourself. It's only a matter of time," I wink at her. "So, are you going to tell me where you went now, Princess, or am I fucking it out of you like old times?"

Her brows draw together, and her head cocks to the side, voice sweet as sugar. "Why is it so important for you to know, Prince Skylan?"

"Because you won't be any good to Alorewyn dead," *And I think you're the Dark Warrior.* "Just looking out for the future queen."

She shrugs and flashes an innocent smile. "Nowhere. This is so much fun! Are you having fun?"

I've known Emryne my whole life, and I know exactly when she's hiding something. Naturally, I turn on the charm and close the distance between us, backing her up until her back hits the wall.

I eye her suspiciously, but my lips are turned up. "I saw you leave, Emryne?"

She turns away, and flips her hair over her shoulder. Typical Emryne, now I *know* she's hiding something. "Bathroom," she proclaims.

In the opposite direction? Trust me, I've been dragged to the bathrooms enough times it's seared in my mind.

I take another step toward her, caging her between by arms and sealing my gaze in hers, lean down, and whisper, "Liar," reveling in the heat of her body against mine, her beautifully feminine scent ensnaring my senses.

She rolls her eyes and makes a failed attempt at pushing me back. "You are the one who's lying. Just tell me why you keep avoiding me."

"You want to know why I keep avoiding you?"

"Yes, please."

I grab her wrists, pinning them above her head and lowering my voice. "Because I can't keep my fucking eyes off you, Emryne. And you know I have no control when it comes to you."

Her body stills, eyes flicking between mine and my lips, and our breaths tangle. "Why did you come back? Isn't there anyone in Callior good enough to make your queen?"

No, Emryne. There isn't.

"No."

"Why? Why are you here, Skylan?"

Because they're not you, I'm here… "For you," God, she's so close. If I leaned down another inch, our lips would be touching. I want to. I want to feel her soft lips move against mine. Taste her, tease her until she begs me for more. But pushing her too far is not what tonight is about. I need her to know, "I came back for you."

Having her this close, her luxurious—because she wouldn't settle for less—perfume draws me closer to her. Gentle notes of gardenias and roses—a new one for her since she hates roses—and something else I can't quite place. Sandalwood maybe?

I breathe slow, deep, couldn't stop my fingers from trailing her neck even if I wanted to. She's never looked this good, never smelled this incredible before. Don't think I don't notice the mischievous twinkle in Emryne's eyes, her breathtakingly beautiful eyes, beckoning me closer. And her skin, God, her skin is flawless. There's no stopping myself from admiring the determined rise and fall of her puffed chest, the curve of her round breasts peeking out of her top. Begging for my touch.

I drag my eyes to her plump red lips, her chest raising and falling in gentle rhythms.

The need to taste her burns through my body like wildfire, searing my skin and fueling a primal desire I haven't felt in years.

Her breathing deepens, eyes settling on my lips, and a gentle gasp escapes her when my forefinger sweeps her exposed collarbone, over her gorgeous breasts, down her stomach until I curve my hand around her hip down to her perfect ass. "Well, what are you going to do now?" Her eyes never left my lips as she did so and tilts her pelvis into me.

"Something incredibly stupid," as the words leave my mouth, my lips slam onto hers.

My body rings with ecstasy as she opens her mouth, her tongue massaging mine. I give her supple ass another squeeze, earning a breathy moan, "Sky…" she murmurs, willing me to go further.

My body protests profusely, but I release her mouth. Not yet. Not here. "I won't touch you until you ask, but I want you to do something for me."

"What?" she whispers, eyes fluttering closed.

"Go home, and touch yourself tonight," I rasp, twirling a lock of her hair in my fingers. "Tell me what you felt when next we meet."

Chapter 8
Emryne
The Dark Warrior

Stupid Skylan.

Stupid feelings. Stupid hormones.

Stupid need to listen to every word he says and tell him exactly how hard he made me come which I didn't because I won't be doing anything until the asshole apologizes for—

He moves from the shadows and finally crosses the street. I've been tailing Markus Millman for the past three hours, and I still can't get a handle on this guy. He's never in one place long enough for me to tag him, hence the Midtown runaround at two… thirty-three in the morning, according to my watch. And every stop he's made so far included Purple Sprinkle.

I went by the P.O. Box Castor and I use to drop off forensic evidence, flash drives, or in tonight's case, illegal substances that need testing.

When I caught up to Castor, huddled in the abandon smelting factory in Lower Industria, he begged me not to drag him to Guard Dispatch.

Parliament was notified about a string of knights' uniforms selling on the black market. The custom-made armor is fashioned out of the finest titanium Alorewyn dollars could buy. Every set of chainmail is hand-butted for each knight assigned to the Guard; the precious metal sold for a fortune. Our justice system does *not* take kindly to thieves, especially when it involved our nation's protectors. You can imagine what happened when my father discovered it was a retired knight who supplied the uniforms after being dishonorably discharged for running illegal weapons through our major coastal shipping yards to Greenland separatist clans. Depending on your feelings about gruesome public mutilation… actually no.

I'll spare you those details. Needless to say, when the Dark Warrior found him in the holding cells before his execution, we struck up a deal. There was no way this guy was working alone, but no names were given other than Castor's, and as much as I wanted to turn him in, he's proven his worth time and time again, including creating my armor and the programmed voice scrambler built into the mask hiding my face. We've been partners ever since.

Castor's been my inside person, computer extraordinaire, and overall eye in the sky for about a year now, and I couldn't be more thankful. Especially when my phone lights up with Markus's address.

I abandon the useless pursuit and make a beeline down Barker Avenue, heading straight for his building.

Markus lives on the third floor of a newly renovated building a few miles from South Piedmont Gardens, Alorewyn's largest public parks, and of the most expensive neighborhoods on the East Coast. The winding ivy, the massive windows, and neat gardens is… ritzy, for a drug dealing pest.

Scaling the fire escape behind the building is child's play. As is finding his bedroom window open when I climb through and dash across the floor and into the living room, grabbing an iron figuring from the TV stand and heading to hide at his front door. The apartment looks like a typical bachelor's pad: minimal decoration, and no color to speak of, with basic furniture and a single light gray carpet in the center of the living room.

It's three forty-three by the time the lock turns and he walks in, gripping his phone to his ear.

"Yeah, I just sold out. What did I tell you, man, this shit's gonna make us a fortune." He kicks off his black boots and heads to the kitchen, still not bothering to switch a light on. Why would he when there's never been a justice-seeking vigilante hiding in his apartment?

"Yeah, totally," he gabs on as I step up behind him, "Nah, three grand like I told you. I'm not giving that asshole a penny more. Besides, a little commission never hurt—" and swing the statue at the back of his head at the perfect angle to knock him unconscious.

Time is of the essence. I need to get him awake, talking and have enough time to get him to Guard Dispatch before the sunrays arrive in an hour. I pull a chair closer, perch his unconscious figure and tie him down, checking that he's still breathing as I do so. A pound too much force, and he would've been dead. But again, not my first time doing this.

I grab a porcelain planter bowl from the kitchen table and dump the dead houseplant in the sink, then fill it with water. Satisfied with the ties around his hands and ankles, I slip on the brass knuckles Father gave me for my nineteenth birthday—no school like the old-school, amirite?—just in case, angle the bowl at his face, drenching him in water.

Markus startles awake and yanks his bonds upward as he fights to free himself. "What the *fuck*?"

Only when I speak did his head whips up. "Markus Millman. Nice place you've got here," the color drains from his tanned face. It's times like this when I thank Castor for his excellent work. I may not understand the technology that went into this thing, but it works every time. The deep register can be quite threatening if I lowered my own voice while speaking.

His throat bobs as he swallows anxiously and shakes his head, "I didn't do it! I swear!"

"Do what, Markus?"

"Whatever it is you think I did, I didn't do it! It wasn't me!" he pleads.

"Oh, okay. So, you're not selling the drugs that could lead Alorewyn into a narcotic epidemic?" Him and whoever the hell his buddy on the phone was.

"Oh, come on," he rolls his eyes and laughs. "That's what this is about? It's just some pills, man. No harm done."

"Just some pills, huh?" I reach into my back pocket for the pictures I'd printed out earlier. Among them a kid no older than fifteen. It made me sick just thinking about it, how his poor family has to survive without their son for the rest of their lives. That could easily have been me, or any of my siblings for that matter. "Call that 'just some pills'? You're selling this shit on my streets, Millman. And it stops tonight."

Markus isn't phased in the slightest, he barely blinks at the gruesome images. "That's not my problem. I warn them every time not to take more than two."

"These people were addicts, you stupid moron. What makes you think they'd listen?" Not to mention most of them probably couldn't stand up straight. I flick the photos at his face; the good ole Gennady temper rising from its peaceful slumber.

Nights like these either go one of two ways, first being where they deny all involvement and plead innocence which ends with me returning home with bloody knuckles, second being they sing like canaries and pour their hearts out to me, pleading they had no other choice.

I can't see Markus fitting the latter's description at all. "Who's your supplier?"

Markus rolls his eyes and shrugs, unfazed. "I don't know."

The former it is then.

Fantastic. I see it's going to be that kind of evening. "Uh-uh, we're not playing that game tonight."

He barks out a laugh. "And what exactly are you planning to do? Last time I checked, the Dark Warrior isn't exactly violent."

"Then you clearly don't know me very well."

The brass clobbers his cheek. He lets out a painful yelp as his face wrenches to the side. I grip his cheeks between my fingers and force his eyes to mine. "One more time, who is your supplier?"

He spits out a mouthful of blood at my chest. "Fuck you!"

The knuckles crack his cheek again and he releases another howl. I grab a handful of his greased-up hair… seriously what man uses this much product? And jerk his head upward.

"I've got all night with nowhere to be. Either you tell me who your supplier is, and I arrange a deal with Guard that you were very cooperative which only gives you a few months in jail, or you stay quiet and spend the rest of your natural life in jail. Your choice."

"How about a deal that doesn't end up in me going to jail at all?" He whines, barely able to keep his head up.

"Someone has to go to jail, Markus."

"I don't know," he says through bloody teeth.

I suck on my own, "Wrong answer," and strike him a third time. "Who is your supplier?"

"I don't know!"

Ready to deliver a fourth punch, his hastened shouts stop me as I raise my fist. "No, no! Wait! Wait! Wait! I'm serious, I don't know who the supplier is! I don't deal with them directly!"

I eye him curiously, brows drawing together. "Meaning what?"

"Our product is delivered through the postal service," he answers through bloody teeth. "None of us deal with them unless we need more pills. There's an email address in my laptop I contact when my supply is running low. That's it, that's as far as communication goes."

I pause, studying him closely through squinted eyes. I'm good at reading people, but pain makes you do strange things. There's always a chance the asshat could be lying to save his ass. "You better be telling me the truth."

"I am! I am, I swear! Take my laptop, you'll see. It's all there," he says, frantic.

"You aren't very bright, are you Markus?" I shake my head, striding to his kitchen, grabbing the duct tape I found after digging through his drawers in case he had more pills.

"What?"

"A part of you, no matter how small, must've known I'd catch up to you eventually. Most people would've bargained for their lives by now, you know, negotiate for some kind of plea deal. You haven't said a word," and you know what they say... snitches get stitches. Although, in Ember City State Penitentiary, where most of these dealers end up, snitches mostly get dead.

"I told you everything I know. Please, I don't want to go to jail," he tries again.

"You should've thought about that before selling that shit to innocent kids," I deadpan.

I tear off a strip of tape and lean forward to stick it over his mouth, but he wrenches his head away and shouts, "They'll come for you!"

I drop my hand and straighten. This I've got to hear. "They who?"

"The suppliers, they'll come for you."

I scoff. "Is that supposed to be a threat? I've taken out punks bigger than you."

"It's not about me, but they know who I am, who all of us are. If any of us are off the streets, if their product isn't moved and they figure out you interfered, they'll come for you."

I can't stop the laughter escaping my mouth. "Oh, I'm counting on it."

Sweet really, thinking that'll scare me. But I meant what I said, I look forward to catching these bastards if it's the last damn thing I do.

Finally, I stick the tape on and pull a pillowcase over his face.

Thirty minutes later, and I park the rental Chevvy Cruze Castor arranged for tonight a few blocks from Midtown Guard Dispatch and yank him out of the backseat, along with the hood covering his head.

"What the fuck, man! You said I wouldn't go to jail!" Markus protests, yanking at his restraints.

"No, I said if you cooperate, I'd strike a deal. I told you, Millman, someone has to go to jail. I am keeping your laptop, though. You did kind of give it to me," I say, then shove him toward the doors. Castor would handle the decryption, and hopefully track the emails. Let's see how truthful he was.

"When you get to City Pen, tell Tiny I sent you. He'll keep you protected."

Markus stops and scoffs. "Am I supposed to thank you for that?"

"Given your considered prime white ass in a place like that, you should be on your knees kissing my feet, my guy. Off you go." I wave my hand for him to keep walking.

And I laugh as I weave my way through the streets and back to the palace, thinking about Markus's statement upon walking into Guard Dispatch:

I sell Purple Sprinkle to innocent children. What Am I Made Of?

#

I climb through the throng of webbed green ivy concealing the gate of several hidden tunnels below the palace, pull the hood off my head and roll my shoulders, relieving tonight's pent-up tension as I sink to the ground with a heavy sigh.

In a time of bi-monthly jousting matches, overflowing Meade barrels and court jesters, the tunnels served as a quick escape route for the royal family in case of attack, before close-quarters combat was an option.

I insisted on taking the one bedroom still connected to them since most were sealed off after the Second Great War when weapons and training became more sophisticated and they were no longer of use. Sky, when he wasn't in Callior, and I explored every nook and cranny when the opportunity presented itself.

And now, they're my secret weapon to securing victory and bringing my kingdom closer to safety. Even if I only scratched the surface, I'd file tonight's mission under success. With at least one of the known Purple Sprinkle dealers off the streets, Castor can decrypt the emails on Markus's laptop along with his phone I stowed in our P.O. Box, and texted he's looking through before I dropped off the rental. Hopefully leading us to the rest, and, with any luck, the suppliers.

Midtown is about forty minutes outside of the palace gates. I've traversed those streets enough times to know exactly where I'm going. But every time I do, it hits me exactly how much work is cut out for me. The alleyways were filthy, mostly abandoned and littered with trash but easy enough to maneuver without causing too much noise or attention. Whatever squatters called it home were usually asleep or too drunk to care.

Sure, I wouldn't be able to change it overnight, but I could at least pay some attention to improving these people's lifestyles. Something Mother should've done ages ago, but again, she's been too busy selling her children out to anyone who'd take us.

Fine, I'm being harsh. But wouldn't you feel the same way if all your mother cared about was getting you married and getting rid of you and of her title? And they may say otherwise had I bothered to ask, but some of the princes want the same thing. All except one it seemed, his words echoing in my mind as I catch my breath in the peaceful darkness.

I came back for you.

I want to believe him. Trust me I want that more than anything. Those were the first honest words he's said in the past two months if he's telling the truth, and the way he kept looking at me proved that, but I wouldn't fall for it so easily.

Other than a single night after Ophelia and her husband King Kaleo's, then Prince Kaleo, wedding announcement, we kept hanging out like nothing happened. Frankly, it shouldn't have. Both of us knew it perfectly well, we were best friends, and you aren't supposed to have any kind of feelings about your friends, but there was no stopping us. It only lasted so long until we both gave in after avoiding each other for three months.

Exactly three months, and we once again tore into each other like rabid animals at Maverick's twenty-seventh birthday and the emotions just came flooding back, all the while he often teased me about it, saying things like, "Hey, you remember when I fucked you against the wall that one night? We should do that again." Or, "Forget the fighting, why don't we fuck instead?" or, "Hi, darling. Fancy a fuck tonight?" all to which my answer was a right hook to the jaw.

I went with a date I knew from high school. Keith was decent and fun to be around, until Prince Skylan intercepted and promptly shooed him away, and of course, no one in their right mind would dare defy the crowned prince of Acadan. Doesn't mean it will happen again. Especially not his so-called 'homework' assignment. No matter how long it's been since I tou—

Soft crunches sound outside my hiding place snaps my attention. My pulse quickens as I sink deeper into the tunnel's shadows, careful not to make a sound. I wait for another sound, a voice, anything to reveal the intruder, but all I hear are the dead leaves crunching as they approach the tunnel.

It's five-fifteen in the morning, this made no sense. I know I was careful when I entered the grounds, never moving through any direct light, even with the black cloak and armor. My snoozing father and I were the only ones who still remembered exactly where most of these led, trust me he's no morning person, and patrol only comes by here every four hours, otherwise, no one bothered.

Except apparently… Skylan.

His hands are clasped behind his back, his mouth is turned up in a soft grin. More than that I can't tell from where I'm melding myself into the musty darkness. Not what he's doing, or looking at, or looking for.

Geez, this guy is just everywhere…

I fight to keep my breathing under control as he steps further into the post light, closer to where I'm hiding behind the vines.

There's no way he could've seen me… right? Could he have been waiting here the whole time? No. No, that's ridiculous. That would mean that he knows I'm the Dark Warrior. Which he couldn't because no one knows. No one knows I use the tunnels for comings and goings either.

So, what the hell is he doing here?

But just as quick as he came, Skylan turns on his heel and stalks away.

What was that?

Don't think I didn't miss the little smirk when he did.

I sprint through the tunnel to my bedroom, just in case he decides to drop by unannounced, as is the typical Skylan thing to do. To my relief, no knocks came from outside my door—been a while since I've moved through the passageways in the palace walls that fast—no sarcastic texts, not a single noise other than the chirping birds outside my windows.

I lock my door before stripping out of my armor and down to my underwear, not bothering to open my curtains to let the early morning sunlight in as I drag my exhausted body into bed. The cold, three thousand thread-count sheets do wonders for a weary soul; a soothing cure for everything but my sneaking suspicion that Sky might be on to me. Again, how could he? There is no way anyone knew who I was.

Castor made sure of that the next time I hit the streets. He wouldn't have said a word, not when both of us benefited from our partnership so greatly. Not to toot my own horn but if I am to believe what the latest consensus says, as well as the overall boost in the citizens' moods, I'm helping more than a few people. Just knowing of the hooded vigilante protecting the streets has brought crime down, not by supernatural numbers, but at least some difference is being made.

Although, I can't lie… the prospect of getting caught sparks a rush of deep-rooted lust I forgot I had.

What would Skylan say?

Would he approve? Be proud of what I've already accomplished? I certainly am. Knowing Sky, he probably would be too. Or he would be furious with me putting myself in danger on a near daily basis, and insist I stop.

Not that I'm trying to win his approval, you understand, if anything he needs to win mine. He's just always been protective in that way. But for now, I'm choosing to go with the former. He'd be grinning ear to ear, taking my hand and cupping my cheek… lifting my eyes to his, my insides fluttering at his adoring gaze as he whispered, "Such a brave princess you are, my Em-Em," even if I hated the nickname.

He'd kiss me all the way down from my forehead, my cheeks, my chin, then finally my mouth. Gently caressing my lips until I fully give in to his touch and wrap my arms around his neck.

I don't know exactly why I'm doing this. Probably to prove Sky isn't all that and he in fact can't make me come as hard as he thinks, but this has been building up for so long and I needed a release. And I can't stop the fantasy weaving together piece by piece as he showed me exactly how proud he was, if he knew…

"Skylan…" My voice would come out a soft but desperate whisper.

"I'm here, darling," he'd whisper. His voice steady, and laced with desire. So crystal clear it's as if he's standing over me.

"Please," I'd plead, breathless as I'd pull him even closer.

"What do you need, Emryne?"

My body is on fire, but my fingers traveling down my bare skin are cool. Caressing my thighs, I pull up and spread them, running featherlight touches on the soft fabric covering my soaking center.

"You."

"I'm at your command, Princess. Tell me what you desire, and you will have it."

"Anything?"

"Anything."

"Kiss me."

"But of course."

His lips would touch mine again. Just once, ever so softly.

"More."

"As you wish."

He'd do as I ask. Kissing deeper, more firmly, until he leaves my lips and moves to my neck, earning a sultry moan as he hits the sensitive spot I love. The one only he has ever been able to find.

"I want you," I'd whisper again.

"Are you sure?"

"Yes," I'd whimper, arching my back and inviting him to slip my panties off.

Skylan would happily oblige, kissing his way down my body as he does so. His eyes would find mine, with that mischievous twinkle pulls the expensive fabric down—my fingers doing exactly that—and kiss further, all the way down, until he'd hook my legs over his shoulders and give a long, slow lick.

My back arches as my fingers tease the pierced, swollen bud, coating it with my wetness as I imagine his tongue working.

"Oh God."

He'd chuckle softly. *"Just Sky is fine, darling."*

I'd chuckle at the thought. Even in my fantasies he'd tease. It's been so long since he called me his darling. And I can't stop my heart melting at his words.

He'd bring my body to a fever pitch, teasing with his tongue exactly the way I wanted. Until I'd feel my orgasm steadily building, and I couldn't stand being apart any longer.

"I need you inside, now."

Who am I kidding? I want that more than anything. Wanted to for so long, and now it's just at my fingertips.

"Anything you desire."

He'd leave a final kiss, grinning wickedly as he'd prowl his way up my body and back to my neck, pressing his lips to mine as he'd caress my thigh before hooking my leg over his hip.

I'd suck in a breath as he rubs his tip along my soaking pussy, sucking his lip between his teeth as he does so.

"Is this what you want?"

"Yes," God, I'm so close. "Please."

He'd give a throaty chuckle. *"I love it when you beg for me."*

And finally, he'd push into me until he fills me completely. *"Fuck, darling. You're so tight."*

He'd pull out and push back in again. My arms would wrap around his neck, willing him closer as he fucks me.

"Feel good?"

"Yes," I'd rasp. "Please, yes. Keep going."

Our eyes would meet. And he'd smile, looking deeply into mine.

He'd push in and out again a few times, our bodies moving as they used to. Meeting each thrust perfectly. Fitting together perfectly.

But before I can come, he'd move behind me, roll me on my side and take me from behind. His fingers coming around and playing with my center then inserts a finger, no doubt feeling me tighten around him. Telling him I'm close. So, so damn close.

"Come for me, darling."

My gentle moans echo my bedroom walls as my fingers work my clit and my back arches as I come apart. My orgasm hits me like a ton of bricks, rolling through my body, all the way from my head down to my tippytoes. Sweet, sweet release leaving me a panting mess as I come down from the mental screw Skylan gave me. And as much as I despise to admit it, it's been a hell of a long time since I've experienced this a fantasy so viscerally. What's more, this *is* just a silly fantasy. Both of us are older and more experienced, if we were to sleep together… how incredible would he be now?

And from the second my fingers leave my wet folds; one thing became abundantly clear: I… am in trouble.

Very. Serious. Trouble.

Chapter 9
Skylan
Her Dirty Little Secret

When I'm right, I'm right. Of course, Emryne is the Dark Warrior. Told you I know this girl like the back of my hand. She, on the other hand, seems to have forgotten that I know the palace just as well. We've spent enough time exploring this place for me to remember every nook and cranny. Like the little old sewing room where she hid when her mother upset her, the forgotten war room we recreated what battle strategies we would've chosen to conquer our enemies, dusty, with mold growing on the walls.

And as memory served, the tunnels we used when we snuck out to Starbucks for iced coffees over weekends when she needed a break from her duties. One of several only three people remembered and the only passageway that led directly to her bedroom.

It was by pure coincidence I'd been jogging past when I heard the squeaking iron gate swing open and shut. I never used to be a morning person, but lately I've been finding less and less reason to sleep in. Definitely won't be now that I know my sweet Princess's dirty little secret. In the early morning light, I saw the bare minimum at best, and from what I saw, I was hard as a rock. I have no idea who made her armor, but it was exquisite. Imagining what it must look like up closely, I have no doubt was even better. The conversation flows easily. As usual, the all-out breakfast spread is arranged perfectly with everything from a variety of baked goods, to poached eggs, salmon fillets, to waffles and crepes, served on the finest floral China sets and polished silverware.

I haven't decided whether or not I'd confront her yet, but her positively disheveled demeanor this morning gives me all the ammunition I need. Maybe not to come straight out and ask, but to pester like only I can.

But first… She did her homework last night.

And how do I know? See, Emryne has this tell when she's had a good orgasm, a look she's only ever had with me (a hundred percent blowing my own trombone or however the fuck the saying goes). Her legs are tightly crossed at the ankles, she sits straight as a plank and never makes eye contact, and her cheeks tinted with a rosy red. Her movements are short and deliberate, and she doesn't make a single noise.

I can't stop myself from staring her down, a shit-eating grin on my lips. My eyes slowly sweep her face, humor and utter satisfaction blooming in my chest as I sip at my black coffee.

"How was your evening, Princess?" I lean forward, looping my forefinger through the ear of the light blue cup and bringing the steaming liquid to my lips.

"Fine. How was yours?" She answers tight-lipped, stirring in deliberate circles, even if I know she hates sugar in her tea.

"Can't complain. I came by and knocked on your door. You didn't answer." Which I did. And she wasn't, hence the early morning stroll.

She still avoids my smile as she reaches for an herbed croissant and says through gritted teeth, "Could it have been that I was asleep?"

"I thought so as well," I swallow a sip of coffee. "But your bed was empty when I checked."

She shrugs. "Bathroom."

I can't stop myself from chuckling, she's always been terrible at keeping secrets. How she's managed to keep her entire Parliament and her family in the dark is beyond me. "I don't think you were."

"I don't have to expl—" Finally, her eyes snap to mine. "Wait, you went in my room? Urgh, you freak! What the hell were you doing in my room?"

"I told you, looking for you," I stare her down. She can feign disgust all she wants; I know the idea of my watching her turns her on. May as well have that chat now. "You want to lean over a bit more, darling?"

"Not particularly," her tone may imply boredom, but I don't miss its curious flux. "Why?"

"So we can talk," I shrug simply, placing my cup down. "I'm sure you don't want an audience for the conversation we're about to have."

Emryne shifts, darting her eyes around the table and I follow. Everyone was too enthralled by whatever her mother was saying to pay attention to us.

Satisfied we have no prying ears, her head snaps back and she lowers her voice. "Where you there when… when I…"

"What about you, Princess Emryne?"

I hear my father's voice, but I can't hide my widening lips at her shocked expression. "You might want to answer him. Everyone's watching." She clears her throat, gently wipes her mouth with her napkin, and meets his gaze.

"Your Majesty?"

He sets his mug down and repeats his question. "Do you feel you are prepared to rule as Queen of Alorewyn?"

She considers the question, then answers with confidence. "Is anyone ever really prepared to be queen? Isn't most of it subjective, learning as you rule? My great-grandfather taught me that there are several situations no mother or father, king, or queen, can prepare you for unless you find yourself in that situation. Although why a king is such a necessity is beyond me."

"Fair," he nods and smiles knowingly at me. "You share Prince Skylan's sentiments on that matter. He'd prefer to rule Callior by himself as well."

I'd prefer *not to rule Callior at all.*

"Queen Charlotte served without King Adelio for quite some time when my father was young and created herself quite the legacy. Why should my sister and I be any different?"

I've got to hand it to Emryne. There's so much admiration and determination in her answers. She's always had this gift of knowing exactly what to say, a skill she's learned from her father, as I did from mine.

"Queen Charlotte lived over a hundred years ago, and she had no other choice. You do," her mother berates.

Emryne rolls her shoulders and straightens further. "Then I choose to rule without a king."

Her fork clatters against her porcelain place. "You will do no such thing."

"Perhaps," King Ryne interjects, taking the queen's hand, "this is a conversation best continued behind closed doors."

"Or not at all, for that matter," she avoids the daggers Emryne's blue eyes shoot at her and yanks her hand from the king's before taking a bite of salmon. I doubt Emryne missed it. She scoffs, "Of course, because Queen Lilliette cannot stand the idea of a woman ruling alone. Or me, ruling at all. Ironic, since you've been absent from Father's life for years."

"Not now, Emryne," the queen says through gritted teeth.

"Oh! And God forbid we make a scene in front of our fancy guests, right?" Emryne throws down her napkin. She pushes back her chair and stomps out of the dining hall, a vision of soft orange fury.

Sadly, this is how most of their conversations go. Emryne always says more than her words convey, and her mother ignores them. I know she's not opposed to finding a king, none of us would be here if she did, her father simply wouldn't allow it, but what she would like is her mother's support in giving her the option of choosing for herself which path she'd like to take. That's what my mother would've done.

What, as a matter of fact, she encouraged Queen Lilliette to do whenever we'd visit. To which her answer would be that she couldn't possibly understand what it's like to raise girls since she never had any. Not for a lack of trying, Mom never wanted more than one child; Maverick was the exception.

"Quite the wildcard, Lilliette," Cane's father, King Lodran, chimes, straightening his shoulders. "Whoever gave her such a ridiculous idea that a queen can rule alone?"

I swear, the day I see this man in anything other than his navy, yellow and cream white dress uniform is the day pigs fly, or dogs talk and horses tap dance. He's never in conversation appearing anything less than perfect.

His eyes are more sunken than the evening of the welcoming dinner, though.

"I wish I knew," she sighs and sips at her cup.

"I think she has a point," Allister adds from beside King Ryne. "If you won't meet her terms, then at least allow her a choice on the matter." My point exactly.

"A woman cannot rule without a king. As can a king not rule without a queen," King Lodran bites. "Though I hardly think someone like you, a divorced prince as well as a son of heathens, could possibly understand such formalities."

Cane's fork clangs against his plate. "Father."

"Don't snap at me, boy," he seethes. Lodran is about the worst example of a ruler anyone could have. I may not agree with Cane or some of his opinions, but with a father like his, I understand he didn't know any better.

This is the biggest problem with the monarchy. Some, like his father, are so set in their archaic ways they refuse to evolve with society surrounding them. Not when change would no longer butter their fragile egos and of course, Allister was targeted more than anyone for having two fathers and seeing the kingdom of Mauvrepurth ruled by two kings instead of one.

At least he has two parents.

Not to mention his marital status. We've flown together more than once; I know the seven corners of hell he's been through with his ex-wife Deana. That woman robbed him of everything but his memories, and he still holds his head high.

King Lodran swallows whatever alcohol, I can smell it from here, he had in his glass, then turns his insults to a new victim. "And what about you, Prince Skylan? How fares your cousin Maverick in Callior in the time you've been away? Where have you been?"

Not that it's any of his business but, "Peroue recently, before arriving in Alorewyn. Prince Lando was kind enough to arrange guides through the Italian countryside and French riviera. It was the most amazing experience. I don't have enough words in my vocabulary to express my gratitude." I raise my cup toward him.

"And you are welcome back any time, my friend," he returns my gesture.

King Lodran, however, has a different assessment. "Yes, well, while you were off parading around that mosh pit of sin, what has become of your kingdom? Has the Greenland separatists not opened yet another attack on Callior?" He remarks, as if it's somehow my fault.

We do what we can to keep them away, it's a battle fought daily. Technology is changing by the second and the separatists are getting smarter, adding more sophisticated weapons to their arsenals. It's already difficult enough as it is, even with Alorewyn reinforcements. This is a marathon, not a sprint, and we have my grandparents to blame. Greenland was forced to secede as part of Acadan in the early-nineteen hundreds.

My own spine straightens at his tone. "Are you accusing me of something, Your Majesty?"

"Oh no, dear boy, I wouldn't dream of it. But I must say, you cannot possibly think your absence in Callior has gone unnoticed by the nobility."

"Lodran," Dad warns from beside me.

He ignores him. "Frankly, I find it flabbergasting that you were invited to court the Gennady princesses at all, what with your... reputation among traveling tongues and the recent company your father's been keeping—"

"My father's business," I speak slowly, boring my eyes into his, "is no less mine, than it is yours. That goes for my cousin and myself as well. Frankly I find it ironic what you say about my family when it is no secret what's happened in yours," his grin disappears and turns into a venomous scowl.

His eyes flick to Cane and I continue. "You cannot begin to fathom the heartbreak my family and I have suffered in the past years, and I refuse to sit here and listen to your pathetic attempts to prompt a response. So, I would appreciate it if you kept my family's name, as well as Prince Allister's family's name, out of your mouth."

I fly from my seat, throwing my own napkin down.

"Son, where are you going?"

"To check on the Princess. Since I'm the only one who cares, apparently. No offense, Your Majesty." I bow to her father, who holds up a hand smiling, assuring me he didn't care, and follow Emryne's exit.

#

What a dick.

Who the hell is he to question the choices I've made in my life when his were nothing short of disgusting?

It's not my story to tell, but what he did to Cane was despicable. My father was on the brink of starting a war when he found out before Mom somehow talked him down. What happened in other kingdoms was none of our business, and interfering was never a wise idea unless you in fact did want a war on your hands.

Few people knew this, but I abdicated my eligibility when I left Acadan in 2019 and recommended Maverick be elected instead. Dad wasn't exactly happy with my choice, but he understood my feelings once I explained. He respected my decision, encouraged me even to explore the world and return when I was ready.

There was no way I had the capacity to rule so soon after my mother's death.

ALS is a serious disease that breaks down the nerve cells in your spine and brain and causes a complete loss of the body's ability to control muscles. Every doctor in Callior worked around the clock to figure out why and how her symptoms progressed so rapidly in such a short period of time, yet no one had answers; not even the team of experts King Omari sent from Southern Ficara.

Seeing her struggle every day, become less and less of the warmhearted, vibrant mother I knew and adored more than anything was the worst feeling in the world.

Especially knowing there was nothing I could do. Nothing I could do to stop her slurred speech, her difficulty in doing the simplest of tasks like working on the poetry she wrote so beautifully, or the excruciating pain she had in her legs every single day, the hours she spent wailing in Dad's arms out of fear of what would happen to us, nothing I could do to keep her from being in pain. Nothing I could do to keep her from leaving me when I needed her the most, when I needed her to guide me through arguably the most important time of my life: choosing a queen, and becoming king.

I love my father, he's always been there when I needed him, even more so when Mom died and he did a phenomenal job teaching and allowing me to stick to his side to learn what I needed to be as incredible a ruler as he is. But I couldn't do it.

Couldn't stand the idea of walking through those massive hallways, seeing her favorite art adorn the walls, never hearing her singing again, or her bright smile in the morning when she brought me a cup of coffee, or the creamy hot chocolate she made on arctic winter evenings. I couldn't stand it. It'd been weeks of sympathy and sorry-for-your-loss's, and I'd had enough. I had to leave.

So, I did. And I won't apologize for that.

Emryne tried to be there when she died, and even after. When I started my journey through Southern Emarica, I got off the earliest flight I could find and opened my phone to a string of text messages and missed calls, failed videocall attempts, even emails, for months on end. None of which I answered. What I am hoping to do is finally explain what happened, tell her I come in peace. If I can find her. She's always been strong, capable of swallowing her emotions except when it comes to her mother. And I'd be the dick if I didn't make sure she's alright.

I check all her usual hiding places, but she was nowhere to be found. Not in her father's study, not in the Grand Library downstairs, or the daffodil fields behind the palace, strange since they're her favorite flower. I'm about to give up looking and head back to the West Wing when I remember her open bedroom door. Considering it's the one place I haven't checked; I may as well try and make sure to knock before entering in case she was busy.

"Emryne?"

But she doesn't answer. Guessing it's safe, I poke my head in and call her, again with no answer. And it makes sense why. She's on her balcony, her radiant skin soaking up the mid-morning sunlight. Emryne has always been a vision. Smart, cunning, a sense of humor that stops for nothing, but seeing the pained expression on her beautiful face tightens my throat. As not to scare her, I knock on the balcony door, then clasp my hands behind my back.

She's untied her hair since breakfast, the loose curls pool around her shoulders in silky waves, gently blowing in the morning breeze. I swallow the urge to weave my fingers in the dark, coppery mass, and meet her faint smile, "Hey."

"Hi." Dare I ask? Emryne rarely shares her feelings openly. She's always been more of the suffer in silence type. Like me. "You okay?"

She takes a breath before answering. "Just another day in paradise. You know how she is."

"Doesn't justify her actions," I sigh, joining her on the balcony.

She shrugs. "I've hoped she'd change too many times already."

The late June sunrays heat my skin. Summer in Alorewyn could be unforgivable sometimes, but I understand her need for fresh air.

I nod. Nothing more to say. People like her mother and King Lodran never change, and it's pointless to keep hoping they will.

"What're you doing here?" she sniffles.

"Just making sure you're not contemplating leaping from your balcony."

She smooths out her gown and smiles at me. "Thank you, but I'm fine. Not like we haven't had the argument before."

"She should be on your side though."

"My mother only has one side. Hers," she states, matter of fact. "It's nothing I can't handle though. I'm used to it."

I keep my elbow perched on the warm sandstone, my body facing hers, and risk a step closer. Emryne's gaze is fixed on the gardens outside, only meeting mine when I say, "You know, you don't have to be so strong all the time."

Her brows furrow, "What do you mean?"

"It's okay to ask for help sometimes."

"Would you?" she scoffs.

"What?"

"Ask for help."

I shrug. "No."

"Then what makes you think I would?"

Okay, fine. Still. "Because you can't do it all. Trust me, I've tried," and I left for two and a half years because of it. "Sometimes it's necessary. Don't let your pride get in the way."

"It's not about pride. I don't need anyone's help or pity. I'm fine." It pains me that she's been forced to think this way. She's always been stubborn about accepting help; I understand it speaks volumes if you're able to solve a problem yourself, but that doesn't happen when you rule a kingdom. Parliaments wouldn't exist if every decision depended on a king or queen and I'm pretty sure we've established long ago why that sort of thing can't happen.

My grandparents are the perfect example. When they decided to expand Acadan into a larger empire, the speakers of government, namely Greenland, had more than a few words to say regarding my grandfather's suggestions, demands actually, and at the first sign of objection, he threw—as father put it—the temper tantrum of the century and seceded the nation from the mainland.

Greenland was already a fully sustainable country then, perfectly capable of feeding their citizens without Acadan's assistance, so what the attacks are, are nothing but a revenge vendetta. As the saying goes, even a worm will turn.

But I'll let Emryne wallow in her stubbornness. For now. "Don't need help. Got it."

She chews on her lip, tilting her head toward me. "Sky, I just mean…"

"It's okay, you don't have to explain. I get it, I know you're not the type to ask for help, all I'm saying is that it's okay if you have to. I'm always here, you know that."

I see her hesitate, but she asks anyway, "Are you?" I know exactly why, further proving I have my work cut out for me.

I raise my hand and brush my fingers over her cheek. At least she hasn't been crying. "Of course, I am. I always am."

I take another step closer. Emryne lowers her head, a stray lock of her hair falling over her shoulder. I bite down on the flesh in my cheek and swallow the saliva in case I start drooling, and push it back over her shoulder. My willpower is already riding low just from her perfume alone. Fuck, she's always looked stunning in light colors, and I swear this one is tighter than others I've seen her in recently. Whether it is to spite her conservative mother, or because she feels more confident with her body, I don't know. Neither to I care.

I fucking love it.

Her eyes close as she leans into my touch, her warm body inches from mine. I bend down to her neck, and breathe in her scent again, restraining every urge I have to taste her skin. "God you smell incredible, Em-Em."

"Sky," she whispers as her fingers wrap around my biceps, "someone could see."

"Let them."

She chuckles softly, sending all kinds of shivers down my spine. "Haven't we had this conversation before?"

"I believe so," I wrap my fingers around her forearms, and pull her into my chest. "Funny how we ended up in the same room as we are now."

"That was a long time ago."

"No reason we can't relive it."

"I can think of a few."

I raise a brow. "That we can't or shouldn't?"

"Both."

I'm further gone than I care to admit, and my curiosity has officially taken command of my control.

"You were saying something. Before we were so conveniently interrupted."

She shifts back with an awkward laugh. "Oh, you uh… you heard that?"

"It's you Emryne, I've never missed anything you said," I press my forehead to hers, lowering my voice, brushing my lips against her ear, "So, did you do your homework?"

"Are you serious?"

"Answer the question, Emryne."

Her doe eyes open, and she whispers, "Yes."

"And?"

"It was… good," she swallows.

"Just good?"

"Fine, amazing. Satisfied?"

"Getting there," I lean my head to the side, and suck her earlobe between my teeth. "Long and slow, or short and quick?"

She sucks her bottom lip and my eyes glue to her as she does. "Slow."

"Good girl," Fuck, I need to bite that lip.

She rolls her eyes, "Is it not enough for you to invade my dreams now you're invading my personal space?" and she smacks her lips shut immediately. Well, well, well…

"What dreams?" I play dumb, but there's no mistaking her words. "Why, Princess Emryne, have you been dreaming about me?"

"That's not the point," she groans. I let go of her hands, instead gripping her hips. They too are just as delicate as I remember.

She tries her best to escape, which only makes me squeeze her harder.

"Oh, yeah it is. Tell me, was it filthy? Did you wake up wet?"

"You really are full of yourself, you know that?"

"So were you once, darling. And if memory serves, you begged me not to stop."

I watch her throat bob as she swallows her lust, her hands balling into tight fists at her sides. She licks her lips and flutters her eyes to keep from closing them again. "I should drag you downstairs and beat the shit out of you for this."

"You can. But you won't. Why would I fight you when watching you fight your feelings is so much more satisfying?"

"I despise you," she moans.

Liar.

"And I you. Doesn't mean I can't let my tongue explain how badly I crave you."

She leans back to meet my eyes. "Think what you want Prince Skylan, you have no effect on me."

I squint my eyes at her, my grin widening. Man, she's stubborn. "Oh, really?"

Her breath catches as my lips finally touch her skin. I place the softest of kisses on her neck, careful to avoid her sensitive spot this time, unless we in fact did want an audience. One that could leave me without a head.

My eyes sweep her face, immediately picking up on her reddening cheeks.

"Then why are you blushing, Princess?" I bring my lips to her ear again, "Do you like the idea of what my tongue can do?" and just to prove my point,

I bend her head back, exposing her beautiful, supple neck, and trail my tongue along her skin. Softly sucking the spot just below her ear that makes her…

Finally, Emryne grips the lapels of my jacket, pushing her chest flush against me as she releases an exquisitely feminine moan.

"Emryne?" a voice call from inside her room.

She fights to release herself, but not before I whisper one last thing. "You better, because whatever your imagining, I guarantee it's three times better, darling." And I let her go.

I take a step away from her as her sister pokes her head through the balcony doors. "Princess Addylin. How are you?"

"Oh, hi Sky. Sorry, I didn't mean to…" she says and steps into the sunlight. "Is… everything okay?"

It wasn't until I followed her eyes to Emryne's that I realize why she asked. Look up 'hot and bothered'in a dictionary, and her name would be written in bold. She's barely able to keep upright. And her eyes are fixed on me.

"Emryne?" Addylin asks again.

Her voice is thick as she swallows, finally looking her sister's way. "Fine. Everything's fine." Despite the fact, I have no doubt, her panties are soaked. "Did you need something?"

"Mother is waiting for you in Father's study." Addy says, crossing her hands behind her.

Her eyes fill with relief. "Then I shouldn't keep her waiting." She turns to me and curtsies. Very un-Emryne-like. Yup, she's completely frazzled. "I'll see you later," she says in my direction but avoids eye contact, and gallops through her balcony doors.

Chapter 10
Emryne
Good Mother. *Sweet* Mother!
Understanding Mother.

How the HELL am I supposed to concentrate on speaking to my parents when I was on the brink of orgasm not two minutes earlier?

If ever there was a time to thank God for Addylin it would be now. Her interruption was the perfect excuse to exit as fast as my wobbly legs could carry me before I did something I might not be able to take back. Then I thanked God even more as Des shuffled past with a fresh pile of laundry. She must've thought I lost my mind with the speed I ran at her and wasted no time grabbing a clean, more importantly—dry, pair of panties and slipped them on while hiding between two armored statues before I reach Father's library. It was by sheer dumb luck no knights were passing at that moment, or they would've gotten a full frontal of my pierced lady parts. Something I'm not particularly eager to share with strangers.

About a year and a half ago, I walked into The Hidden Gem—the perfect name if ever I've heard one—piercing salon with every intention of getting a bellybutton ring, only to meet the owner, Mia-Tamara, and have my mind changed after the most revealing conversation I've ever shared with a woman, which included my sisters. We sat in her office, chatting the afternoon away about everything from her life, all the way to my and my mother's complicationship and my own sex life which, evidently, was as dry as hers even with her piercing, so she suggested I get my own.

I was hesitant, of course, most women were, but she explained every step of the process to a T. Almost convinced me a career change was a splendid idea; I already had all the info and probably could've passed the exam with flying colors.

A small part of me got the piercing as a last-ditch attempt to reach orgasm, but even then, nothing happened. And when it did, I wasn't thinking about them, I was thinking about Sky.

Then again, I could've been sleeping with clueless men.

That has to be it, right?

One of them came close. Alex and I met through a member of Parliament last summer. He was so sweet, and the things he did with his mouth were certainly memorable, but when it came to the actual sex… let's just say his tongue made up for what other organs lacked, always talked big game for such a… small man. Of course, I wasn't going to be a huge dick and go pointing out his shortcomings… okay, way more double-entendres than I'm intending, point is it was bad. Even more, boring. But he tried his best.

I had let him go eventually. Especially since it was only a week before our twenty-first.

It's been a wild ride. Not as wild as I'd hoped, but the year's still young. I've gotten to know so much about myself in the time I've spent with different people, all unique in their own way. All of them added valuable pieces to my puzzle, and I don't regret a thing, especially not the piercing.

Satisfied with my discreet wardrobe change, I stuff the discarded fabric into my gown's pocket, my absolute favorite detail of the dress, and continue my walk to certain confinement. After the conversation Mother and I had this morning, it's like I can smell her annoyance from here. Suffice it to say, I am not looking forward to walking through those doors.

I'm almost happy I didn't when I hear her arguing with Prime Minister Fredrick. Almost.

"No. Emryne is not ready," she says, ornery as always.

"I don't mean to undermine your decision making, Majesty, but I must respectfully disagree."

"So do I," Father chimes. I can already picture him at his desk. Leaning back in his leather chair with a tumbler of whiskey to his right, equally as bored as he is annoyed.

"Of course, you would."

"We've had this conversation before, Lil. Addylin is a wonderful girl, and she's matured into a beautiful woman, but Emryne remains Parliament's first choice to elect as queen," Father says.

"That is ridiculous, Addylin Rose is a seasoned princess. She has been training longer, and she attends her lessons as instructed. Emryne is wild and unpredictable. I'd stand behind your decision if *she* attended any of her lessons—" *And I would've taken them had they not had a giant stick up their ass.* I roll my eyes. "—instead of sneaking off to God knows where, doing God knows what and disgracing the Gennady name even more than it already is."

"Watch yourself, Lilliette. That is my daughter you're speaking of."

My heart clenches in my chest. Father will always defend me, though a part of me hates that he has to. If he could respect my wishes, why couldn't she?

"Seasoned, yes," Minister Fredrick carefully interjects. "Leader, and a strong one at that? I stand by my statement. Your subjects trust her, the latest consensus confirms that."

"Right, because being a respectable leader is the only trait to be acknowledged." *Yes, it is. Well… it should be.* "And what of the princes? Pray tell Parliament's opinion on them?" Minister Fredrich might've missed her condescension, but I hear her loud and clear. And I've just about had enough. I inch open the heavy oak door and slip through. Quiet enough that no party alerted; Mother and the Prime Minister have their backs to me, but I see the relief in Father's eyes when I smile at him. He sits taller and puts away his glass. Though I don't blame him, if I were married to a woman like my mother, I'd be driven to alcohol daily. Hourly. Minute…ly?

"They all have potential, Majesty." The minister pauses, then crosses his hands behind his back and looks to Father. "Does Princess Emryne share a connection with Prince Skylan still, Your Majesty?"

He nods. "Since childhood. Although how strong their connection is now, I couldn't be sure." *I'd say it's pretty damn strong considering our several recent R-rated encounters.* "What're you thinking, Fredrich?"

He turns to the pictures on Father's wall, specifically the one where he and King Harryson are standing in the old Alorewyn Special Forces combat fatigues. Those particular designs may have been retired since, but everyone in the world knew the legendary camos; the Red Scorpions were the most feared and expertly trained battalion to date.

"An allegiance with Callior would be greatly beneficial to Alorewyn's reputation and keep Greenland from another assault. Not to mention our paramilitary forces would triple if not quadruple in size compared to Eikenish, or the Asai Empire."

"You seem to be forgetting we still have two other visiting princes. Allister and Lando remain in the running as well. Allegiances with Mauvrepurth and Parson would be equally as beneficial as one with Callior. Although it wouldn't be necessary given my and King Harryson's friendship. We already have an allegiance."

But Mother shakes her head. "Prince Caneic is the better choice. He's charming, he's kind, intelligent. He has the makings of an excellent king."

"And Skylan has none of those traits? He has better training. He is a weathered fighter and has spent every waking hour next to his father. He is well aware of our parliamentary procedures as well as international relations." I agree. Of all the royals, Sky's been in Alorewyn almost as much as Callior. If anyone is a smart choice for king, Skylan Henry Alexandrius Dormer is at the top of that list.

Isn't that just fantastic.

Mother recoils. "And has Prince Skylan recently been included in parliamentary hearings?"

"How could he when you've attended them all? Insisted on our daughters' presence as well. The point I'm trying to make is that Skylan is not an imbecile; he's surely noticed certain details as to how Alorewyn is to be ruled."

Mother scoffs, dismissing his argument. "Caneic has a better reputation."

"You mean Lodran has a better reputation," Father rolls his eyes.

"Yes, he does. And neither Lando nor Allister would be suitable either."

"Based on what criteria?" Father barks a humorless laugh. "You barely know those boys."

"I know enough to know of Allister's history. How he dragged that poor girl's name through the mud with that horrible divorce. And Lando?" she jeers. "I'd rather not speak about Lando."

"Then what did you invite them for?" Excellent point.

"Reputation, my love. Why else? We must keep our standards high in choosing our future king."

Enough of this. "And here I thought I got to make my own decision in choosing a husband," I finally interrupt and neatly fold my hands at the waist.

Mother yelps in surprise, her hand flying to her chest to calm herself.

"There you are. What took you so long? And what are you lurking in the shadows for?"

"You would've noticed my standing here five minutes ago if you paid closer attention to your surroundings."

"I'm already being gracious about allowing you and your sister a choice, and I can just as easily take it away. Bare that in mind the next time you insult me in the presence of my guests. There will be serious consequences if you do."

Because I just couldn't resist, I say, "Really? Like what?" I challenge, widening my grin while she wears her temper on her sleeve. Her jaw is clenched so tightly her teeth might shatter. She's almost growling.

Is it completely childish of me? Yes, yes, it is. And does Mother despise when my sisters and I do this? You bet. But since she's not the violent type, despite her lovely sneer, she never did much other than take away privileges as punishment.

Father's knuckles are pressed against his mouth, fighting to contain his laughter. As for Minister Fredrich… he's gone dead quiet. Observing the way I handle the situation; *everything* I do is considered an evaluation. I make sure to extend him a deep curtsy, as Mother once instructed, and he bows his head, then join my father at his desk, kissing his cheek. He takes my hand and places it on his shoulder, smiling as he turns back to my mother.

"Is there a point to this? Despite what you might believe, I do in fact have work to do."

"And I have flirting to do," even if I had no desire to. You know, duty and all that.

Her shoulders straighten and she clears her throat, swallowing her fury. "I want you to spend more time with Prince Caneic," Mother orders, and I watch Father roll his eyes from the corner of mine. "Show him everything Alorewyn has to offer. Get used to the idea of his possibility of becoming king."

"That's not your choice," I leave him side and step around his desk to her.

"And is it so hard to accept that I'd rule better alone? It's the twenty-first century. I am perfectly capable of coping by myself. Father has," I really am pushing it now, but I'm at my whit's end.

"I'll ignore your insinuation and remind you that he is a man."

"And I can't rule alone because I'm a woman?"

Mother goes quiet and takes a single step closer, "Now, you listen to me. Whatever this ridiculous rebellion you've started against marriage, stops today. I will not hear a single word on the matter again. I mean it, Emryne."

"Lilliette!" Father bellows and flies from his seat.

But I merely hold up my palm, unbothered by her tone. It's no use fighting her, she will never change, and it's time I start accepting that. "It's alright, Father," I smile at her. "If you won't change your mind about letting me rule alone, fine. But you have no say in who I get to be with." Then turn to Minister Fredrich, still hidden in his corner.

"And if I do choose to marry Skylan, it will be because I love him. Not to forge some everlasting allegiance with Callior. Which, as my father pointed out, we already have."

#

I wasn't myself the rest of the afternoon, and I didn't find Cane either. I avoided everyone, including my father. He knocked twice, but I didn't have it in me to talk to him. There's only so much pity I could take.

By midnight I've given up falling asleep. No matter how many times I roll from one side to another, try laying on my stomach even, I'm as wide awake as I was when I got out of my bathtub. None of the essential oils Des poured in and promised would calm me down made an impact either.

I flip open my covers and grab the silk robe from its hook before opening my door and heading for the kitchen.

Most of the uneaten pastries the staff prepared for dessert was left in the fridge for disposal in the morning, and I couldn't get it out of my heart to let them throw out a perfectly good cheesecake.

Not that there was much left. A single slice, actually. Whatever Sir Stephané did to make it so moist was nothing short of magical. Won the hearts of his diners every time. And the fact that he incorporates actual Crème Bruleé into the filling?

Genius.

And apparently, I'm not the only one who thinks so. I hear approaching footsteps as I make myself comfortable on the long, cedarwood table, resting the plate on my knees.

I want to say I'm surprised that Skylan's come looking for treats of his own, but his sweet tooth is twice as big as mine.

He doesn't notice me at first, and honestly, I don't mind. In only his simple navy pajama bottoms, Sky has his back toward me as he opens the giant fridge doors, humming while he inspects the desserts. I don't recognize which song it is, but I do notice the moonlight's silvery beams defining the muscles on his back. My mouth waters at his smooth skin as he moves, his grip firm on the door, just like he had my hips earlier.

He blows out a frustrated breath as I swallow my bite, "Why is there never any cheesecake?"

"I took the last piece."

Skylan jumps at least three feet high, and pivots in my direction, "Jesus Emryne! You scared the ever-loving shit out of me!"

"Sorry," I chuckle, and angle the plate toward him. "I was hungry. Want some?"

He relaxes, smiling as he shuts the fridge door and joins me at the table, planting his giant body next to mine, then grabs the fork from my hand. "You're up late."

I shrug. "Couldn't sleep. What about you?"

He digs in and brings the piece to his lips. "Never got to try this at dinner. I was hoping to find at least half, but *someone* beat me to it," he jokes and bumps his shoulder to mine.

I wish I were in a better mood for conversation. This is exactly the reason why I avoided dinner and ate in my room. If you could call what I did eating, I barely took two bites before shoving the silver tray back in Moni's hands and asking her to leave.

Sky notices my silence immediately. I don't know how but he's always been hypersensitive in picking up social cues. Were I feeling more playful, I'd have shooed him from the kitchen by now. He sets the plate down and scoots closer. "Are you okay?"

I try to avoid his eyes. They really did have brains of their own. "Mhm."

"Emryne, talk to me," he takes my hand tenderly, tentatively weakening all the defenses I built earlier not to break down if someone pried.

I take a deep breath. No use resisting. He'd find a way to get it out of me, and I really don't feel like flirting right now. "Had a great talk with Mother earlier."

"I can't imagine you were happy about it after you left your room this morning. What happened?"

"When I got to my father's office, they were already in conversation with Minister Fredrich. Apparently, it would be in my family's best interest if I married Cane."

"What?" Sky's eyebrows furrow, his grip tightening around my hand. "You don't even know the guy."

"That's not really the point, but I guess you're right."

He swallows, his gaze searching. For what, I don't know. "Do you like him?"

"I mean, he's nice but I can't just make a decision like that based on image alone. No one in my family's had an arranged marriage, why would she think I would agree to it? We live in twenty-first century, for God's sake! How are we supposed to grow, how are we supposed to move forward, evolve, knowing the monarchy still lives with that mindset?"

Something resembling relief crosses his face, and he nods. "I get it. Mom always said elated Majesties, a thriving kingdom makes."

I hear the hurt in his voice, mentioning his mother. "Do you miss her?"

He swallows, keeping his gaze to the ground. "Every day."

I tried to be there for him when we heard she passed, but he disappeared off the face of the earth. I tried not to be angry, tried to understand that he was in pain and grieving, but after the way he left the last night we had sex, there was no stopping it. I was about to ask him where he went, maybe I'd finally get an answer, but he cut me off. "I just wish I knew what her problem was."

That makes me laugh. "If you figure it out, I'll give you a million dollars."

He chuckles quietly, tracing small circles on my hand. "I'd rather have you."

A gentle warmth spreads through my chest. Sky never ceases to amaze me. It's been such a long time since I've seen this side of him. He's always been quick with a joke and rubs off tense situations with a playful smile, daring anyone in the vicinity to challenge him. Like father like son.

Skylan wears his heart on his sleeve, but he very rarely shows his true emotions. Or rather, he knows how to control them. Especially in society's eye.

And when he did, it's like he'd let you into his head even if for a second. Like he lets you keep a piece of him, and all those pieces added up to a complex human being I'm trying to understand, but he's changed so much since my graduation. Since his mother died and he left Acadan. I guess I have a lot to learn about the new Skylan Dormer.

"How can I always understand every word you say to me?" I ask next.

His head tilts in question. "What do you mean?"

"Half the time people talk I have no idea what they're saying. Sometimes, all I hear is… noise."

"Most people never say anything worth hearing anyway. Shut them out. I do," he smiles, and tucks a lock of hair behind my ear. "This is ultimately your decision. No one can make it for you, and neither should they," he leans over and kisses my forehead. "You, Emryne Gwendolyn Charlotte Gennady, are going to make an extraordinary queen."

And he's going to make a phenomenal king. I've never been more certain of anything.

Neither of us say a word for what feels like an eternity. His eyes are on mine, mine on his, and I swear he's leaning closer and closer, until his lips are mere inches from mine. If only I leaned forward… even a little bit. Telling him it's okay. To kiss me. To touch me. To make me forget where we are, and get lost in each other like we used to. Even if just for the night.

But I cut him off instead, "You want the rest of this?" and he leans back with a rueful smile, taking the hint. I can't do this tonight. I want to, don't get me wrong, but not in this wallowing mindset.

As if the Almighty himself agreed with me, my ringtone eases the tension between us.

After eleven-forty-five all the palace's indoor lights are switched off. Other than the tiny ceiling lights shining a few inches below the roof, the palace is pitch-black. I'd completely forgotten I used the flashlight to make my way down to the kitchen so my teeth don't break my fall.

I stumble over my slippers, barely able to straighten myself when I flip the screen up and notice an unknown number.

"Who's that?"

I can't tell if he's genuinely curious or irritated by the interruption. He's shifted back into cool and calm Skylan, throwing me his signature cocky grin, and playing off the situation as if it's completely normal. Why wouldn't it be? He has no idea who I'm texting or what's going on in my life.

My thoughts grasp at the closest thing I can think of. "Pen pal," I blurt out, already halfway out the door. *Pen pal?* Even I think that's ridiculous. But I don't care. Only one person would call from an unknown number, churning the most wonderful excitement in my belly. I need this. "I have to go."

"Be careful, Em-Em," I hear Skylan call as I exit the kitchen. Not knowing his statement would come back to bite me in the ass sooner rather than later. I hit the answer button and press my phone to my ear. "What's up?"

Castor's familiar scrambled voice fills my ear. No telling what government rascals might be listening in, he always says. "You might want to get yourself down to the docks. A new shipment of Sprinkles just come in."

"Thanks, Cas." I fly through my bedroom doors, shutting them behind me and turning the lock before heading to the wall where I had a discreet keypad installed. I type in the code and the concealed shelves swing open, my black armor and rows of weapons greeting me. The locker is equipped with everything from sniper rifles to pistols (some more legal than others), grenades, barrel suppressors, and of course, the brass knuckles.

"No prob. And hey, just be careful. These guys are packing some serious heat."

Chapter 11
Emryne
Not-So-Covert Affairs

The drive down to the Grand Port of Alorewyn took much longer than expected with the amount of roadworks surrounding Downtown in full swing. And when I finally arrived… my heart sank in my chest. Castor wasn't kidding. Not a single one of these guys aren't armed with what I'm assuming is AK-47's.

There's no way I can take all of them on at once.

I don't bother stifling a sigh while adding yet *another* venture to my ever-growing list criminal activities to demolish: stricter gun laws. Why can't some of these people just wear nametags or have live pins, like tagging a location on your phone, so tracking them down isn't impossible? But it's all part of the fun, I guess.

Lurking in an abandoned building by the docks, it wasn't difficult to see none of these guys were trained fighters, clinging to their guns for dear life since it was the only way to defend themselves against a sneak attack. Which of course, would've been enough had anyone other than me infiltrated their practice, but guns are never easy to deal with, and even I know the stupidity in that. I'm ridiculously outnumbered, and there's no way I'd walk away without a bullet or two in my body. Or walk away at all for that matter.

Something I couldn't afford given I have important company to keep and didn't want anyone, especially not Mother, breathing down my neck about why I have bandages around my arm, or walking strained. May as well hand them a signed picture of me throwing peace signs while dressed in my black fighting armor.

The building is as weathered and worn as the vehicles they're unloading what look like diaper boxes from. Typical trafficker stunt. The gel pads are removed and replaced with whatever drug is being smuggled in powder form very carefully weighed as not to alert port or border patrols when vehicles or ships pass over weigh stations and discrepancies aren't noted on their transport logs.

And the patrols remain none the wiser. What possible reason would they have to question perfectly valid transport records when nothing is out of the ordinary, and a dead animal strategically placed as roadkill to distract the trained sniffer hounds in case they alert their handlers.

I told you these guys are getting smarter.

The building doesn't have much to provide in terms of lighting, the ocean spray and heavy sea breezes to thank for the rotting wood, but I do the best I can after switching my phone on silent and snapping pictures for Castor to run through Alorewyn's NCIC, National Crime Information Center, database. Hopefully some of these goons should show up if any of them are convicted felons or offenders with a record.

The lack of patrolling knights does surprise me however, even with the remote location. These docks should be kept a close eye on for this reason specifically, but calling it in now would be pointless. A venture this size would simply pack up and move to a different place, but Guard should've dispatched at least a few units of knights to cover the area regardless.

Something smells fishy… and it's definitely not the high tide.

I open a new message to Castors number he texted me the address from and select the best quality images to forward.

ME: *C, runs these through NCIC and get back to me. Can u hack the yard's entry logs to track where the shipments came from?*

I watch the three little dots jump and a green bubble pop up with his reply.

UNKNOWN: *Oki doki *rolling eyes emoji**
ME: *What, can't do it?*

I joke. Knowing full well he's perfectly capable.

UNKNOWN: *No, no I can do it. I just don't like that u automatically assume I can do it.*
ME: *Oh come on, C. U can do anything… right?*

I chuckle at the middle finger he sends as reply.

UNKNOWN: *FYI YH… going off grid. Send me the pics in the meantime & give me a couple days. Will send info when back online.*

I watch the dots jump, disappear, jump again a few times before they finally answer.

I swallow my nerves, but know better than to question his reasons for disappearing. This is what he does, how he evaded Guard catching up to him. I don't know anything about what happens in his personal life, our relationship doesn't stretch beyond being my backup, but from what I've learned about how he operates, going off grid was not unusual.

A luxury I wish I had.

Hopefully he'll be able to come up with something by the time he's back. I may not catch these bastards tonight, but rest assured, in time I will drag each and every one of them to Guard Dispatch if it's the last damn thing I do.

I clamber down the adjacent roof I used as a vantage point, luckily it's in a sturdier condition than its neighbor's, and do my best to bury my annoyance.

The black rental is parked behind a service building a few blocks from the port and blends perfectly in the dark; I picked the spot for this reason specifically. As I trudge back to the car, my combat boots sloshing in the puddles along the wet asphalt though careful not to make too much noise, I rip off the mask and huff my frustration.

Tonight was supposed to let me let off some steam. I craved the chase the second I left the palace through the tunnels, this time with no Prince Skylan in sight—yes, I'm sure—yet here I am. As bored and itchy for action as when I left. So, instead of heading home with my tail between my legs, I tuck the car keys back in my coat and decide to wander the streets a few hours longer, keeping my ears perked for the slightest disturbance. Downtown isn't the safest area, something's bound to happen.

These buildings have been standing since the nineteen-sixties. Most are old factories turned apartment buildings, but the architecture is incredible. It's supposed to fall on the queen to make sure enough funds are designated for their upkeep, but with my mother's absence these past few years, the neglect doesn't surprise me walking past and taking in the state of them. But it doesn't break my heart any less.

All of them tell a story of their own, all pieces of Alorewyn's unique history, and they're not taken care of. Walking between the seven story brick structures, I make notes on what needs upgrading, promising myself this will be my first duty as Queen. Light fixtures need repair here and there, lightbulbs need replacing and whatever can be done about the state of these alleyways certainly will be done.

Simply because it is a less affluent neighborhood was no excuse not to be maintained, especially being this close to the ocean, and the same goes for dispatching more Guard units to patrol the area. If anything, Downtown needs to be protected even more.

Looking at these homes, I find myself wondering how different life would've been if my family were normal. What kind of lives would we have led? Father would've been a knight, Chief of Guard of that much I'm sure, and Mother would undoubtedly do something that'll drive us all up the walls. Wouldn't she?

Maybe she'd be more understanding and we'd all get along like we were supposed to, rely on each other instead of my relying solely on Asa and Ophelia for advice. Maybe with the change of scenery she'd—

"No!" a scream from the alleyway up ahead shook me from my fantasy. "No, get off of me!"

"Why? This is what you want isn't it, you fucking whore!" A man screams, followed by a hard slap and another scream.

I'm going to hell for thanking God for this, aren't I?

My legs carry me on autopilot, my feet rhythmically hitting the asphalt as I close in on the scene. I bite back my temper and slow down to a brisk walk before seeing two figures struggle under the murky yellow of an outdoor floodlight. The alley is trashed with so many torn garbage bags, empty produce moving boxes and rotting food it's a miracle they're able to keep upright. Small mercy though or this situation would've been much worse.

My fingers wrap around the collar of his sweat-soaked jacket, and yank him off of her.

Pulling him away was no different than throwing the covers off your bed; the guy as all skin and bones. It astounds me how his wobbly legs kept him upright for a long as it did, but it told me enough to know he's obviously drunk. Or high. Both probably.

"Who the fuck do you think—Jesus, you're—" I don't let him finish before my fist flies into his jaw in a deafening smack. He takes a single step backward before crumbling to the filthy floor.

Turning my attention to the trembling girl, beyond a nasty bruise on her left cheek and a few cuts down her bare legs, she seems unharmed otherwise.

"Are you okay?" I reach my hand out and grip her twiggy shoulder and her body seizes up under my touch.

"Y… yes…" her voice trembles, and she falls to her knees and bows her head. Blonde gurls swallow her face. "Your Highness," my brows knit together. *Your Hi…?*

All the blood drains from my body as my fingers fly to my face. I completely forgot I pulled my mask off after leaving the port.

Shit.

SHIT! No, no, no, no, NO!

I rack my brain trying to figure out a logical explanation, but the traitorous thing keeps the secret solutions to itself.

Alright then, next best thing. "What's your name?" I hold out my gloved hand for her.

Her green eyes flood with admiration and awe, gingerly sliding her small hand in mine. "V… V… Vanessa, Highness. Vanessa McCauley."

"Vanessa, please," I plead, speaking slow enough so my words sink in. "It's very important that you keep what you saw tonight between us," she remains speechless, her eyes never leaving mine. "Can you do that? Can you keep this between us?"

"Y… yes," she swallows, then swiftly straightens her spine. "Yes, Your Highness. Your secret is safe with me."

"Thank you. Are you sure you're okay?"

"I am now," behind me, her attacker's limp body moans, fighting to bring himself back to consciousness no doubt. Her eyes turn downward, filling with sorrow. "Ironic, isn't it? He's the one sleeping around and he calls *me* a whore," she snickers.

"Boyfriend, I presume?"

"Todd," she nods, wrapping her arms around her torso. "He never used to be like this. Ever since he started using that shit it's like he's changed into a completely different person."

That perks up my ears. "Do you know what he's on?"

"I don't know much about it, but I think it's called Purple Sprinkle."

Of course, it is. Where the fuck is this shit coming from?

I stifle another sigh. "Is this the first time he's acted like this?"

Vanessa shrinks back, swallowing nervously. Of course, it isn't. It never is. But she answers, "He doesn't mean it. He's… just been stressed. And stuff."

My hand gently squeezes her shoulder. "That's no excuse for treating you like a punching bag." I bend down and grab her purse, what's left of the tattered thing anyway, along with her jacket I wrap around her bare shoulders. "Do you know who his supplier is? How long he's been using?"

She smiles as she shimmies into the fabric, zipping it up. "I wish I could say it's been long, but a few weeks at most. He used to get his stash from this guy named Rolo." Vanessa flicks her eyes to mine, filling with silent humor. "He was arrested though. I don't know who his new dealer is."

I huff a laugh, nodding my understanding. It comes as no surprise that they knew who handed him to Guard. Gossip spreads like wildfire in this frickin' kingdom. Though something isn't adding up. "This may seem like a rude question, but how can he afford it?"

"What do you mean?"

"A… friend of mine brought four pills and she paid three grand for it."

She frowns at me like I've lost my mind. "The most I've heard it sell for it forty dollars a pill. Whoever your friend is got ripped off pretty bad," *Motherfucker.* No goddamn wonder the idiot had such shit-eating grin on his face when I handed him that money, and the phone conversation in his apartment after…

"I've never seen addiction this bad though," Vanessa continues.

"What do you mean?"

"It's not easy to explain," she closes her arms over her chest.

"But it's like it sucked his body dry. He lost a crazy amount of weight, doesn't eat much and barely sleeps. And the nightmares…"

"He didn't have them before?"

"Never. Todd sleeps like a log. Or, he used to."

I make a mental note of everything she's told me. Even more clues to the puzzle. Todd groans again, telling me to wrap our little conversation up. Almost release my own remembering Castor's absence.

"I need to take him in," I tell her.

"No, no please don't, he didn't mean it, I swear! I'll take care of him; I'll make sure he stops using!"

"Vanessa, the Dark Warrior knows about this now. If someone finds out I let this slide, the public's faith in me will disappear, and I don't want that to happen. The only way he's going to get clean is if I take him in so he can get the help he needs. The program works, I've seen it." Mostly because Cameron is the one who funds it, and he'd sooner commit suicide than let Alorewyn's people suffer.

Her teary eyes drift from mine back to her boyfriend's. She takes a deep breath and finally says, "I don't want that to happen either." She turns back to me. "Are you sure he'll be okay?"

"It won't be easy, but he will eventually," I try my best at being gentle, but the reality is I'm pissed. Without Castor's moxie, I'll have to figure out how to get more information elsewhere. Starting with tracking those lovely, heavily armored goons down.

Vanessa nods, keeping her eyes trained to the ground.

I ask her to keep an eye on him while I bring the rental around, then help her get him in the back seat.

"I'm sorry I have to do this. I know it's hard," she still avoids my eyes but nods her head.

Before I'm able to get in my car, Vanessa grabs my hand. "Your Highness?"

"Yes?"

"Just so you know, we're all rooting for you for queen."

Half an hour later, I drop Todd at the Downtown Guard Precinct. Not in the least bit sorry for the message written on his stained white shirt.

I Beat My Girlfriend While High on Purple Sprinkle.

The roads are as quiet as ever when I stop on the rooftop of the multi-level garage a few blocks from where the tunnels begin and park the car in its usual spot near the fire escape. Pressing the lock button, the alarm beeps once and the lights blink. I slip the keys under the notch above the right wheel, inspecting the car one last time before I head for the stairs. Ready for a good night's rest.

"Funny. Entire battalions of Knights Guard can't find you, yet here you are."

Ice cold fear cements my spine.

This. Can not. Be happening.

I can't bring myself to turn around. The only thing my mind shouts at me is *get off the roof get off the roof get off the roof*!

This makes no sense. How long has he been following me? Did he know about Castor?

I've always been careful about maneuvering in the shadows, never to be seen or heard unless I want to. Unless I need to when someone is in danger. Then again, this is Skylan were talking about. He's no idiot, and it's exactly the damn reason I fell for him.

"Interesting that you took the high road at the docks. I'd have thought a person of your qualifications could take them down with your eyes closed."

My snicker comes out in a menacing laugh. The voice scrambler working its magic. "With a shitstorm of bullets potentially flying in my face? I'm not stupid."

"Why doubt yourself? You had enough cover to get at least a few shots in."

"Then why didn't you, whoever you are?" I challenge, tongue-in-cheek. No need to hand him my identity on a silver platter. And since he saw what I did, I know he's picking on me. Well… on the Dark Warrior. "Given you obviously had nothing better to do than follow me around. And I don't carry guns unless I absolutely need to."

Finally turning around, I make sure to keep my eyes hidden beneath the hood while stepping away from him, giving him the impression that he's, closer and closer to the fire escape's railing. I'll have to make a beeline for the foliage behind garage though; heading for the tunnels would've been a drop-dead giveaway.

"Nowhere to hide them under your hood without getting noticed, right?" His eyes are ablaze with delight as he closes the distance between us.

I don't answer. "Is there something you need, citizen? Are you in danger?"

Skylan shrugs once, keeping his gaze on the wall behind me. "Nope."

Nope? Then what was the point of this?

"Well then, you'll need to excuse me. I am terribly bus—" And just as I turn, something zings past my ear.

Making a simple sweep to the wooden notice board, barely attached to the wall, my eyes lock on the black throwing blade stuck on a help wanted flyer.

Curling my fingers around the hilt, the warped blade's jagged edges I notice immediately, a last-minute pawn shop purchase no doubt; its balance is so far off hitting that board should've been unlikely. Then again, off balance or not, warped blade or not, Sky's aim, even knowing he'd touch these monstrosities with a fifty-foot poll. Is never less than perfect.

"You want to prove how good you are?" he smirks, spinning a second knife looped around his forefinger. "Let's dance, darling."

Okay then. He wants a fight?

Fine.

Let's fight.

#

Two weeks later, and Skylan is yet to say a word about our encounter. All I've gotten was sideways smirks and a wink here and there. He's been friendly, don't get me wrong, but every time he gets close, it's like waiting for a heart attack only he knows will kill me.

What could he possibly be waiting for? Is he planning to out me in front of an audience or pester me about this for the rest of my natural life?

Since my eyes in the sky went AWOL, I'm no closer to figuring this out than I was in that club, which isn't doing wonders for my nerves, and staring at these damn walls, bored to death, I had no choice but to join Mother and Addylin with planning our annual Independence Day ball.

You think she was irritable before? Let me tell you, nothing beats the Fourth of July. With three days to spare before the upcoming festivities, the staff work around the clock to prepare the palace. Adorning the walls, pillars, and drapes with a symphony of red, white, and blue strings, ribbons and sashes hanging from every cast iron light fixture as far as the naked eye can see.

I'm halfway through finishing another party favor—an expertly weaved bamboo basket filled to the brim with chocolate coated everything, two mini bottles of Mother's favorite sparkling wine, soaps, bath bombs and is to be finished off with a bouquet of freshly cut Alorewyn roses on the evening—Mother insisted we send home with our guests, when my phone buzzes on the loveseat I'm using for my gift station next to me. I tap the answer button and Asaria's bright voice settles an instant relief in my heart.

"I'm just calling to make sure you're not dangling from your shower rod," her greets.

"Oh, you called three days too early," I joke, just as Mother yells at her lady's maid, Vivica, "No. No! I said no lilies in the ballroom! Doesn't anyone listen anymore? And for the love of God, I want the Forester plate sets on the tables not the Wessing-Ivory!" then rushes off with poor Viv trailing behind her.

"Already at it, huh?"

I tuck my legs under me and lean back on the cushions. "Since you're not here, guess who got roped into making the favors?"

Asa laughs. "Hey, you wanted to stay and do the whole queen thing. I told you to come with me to Spain after graduation, but you insisted Father needed you."

"And I stand by it," Mother barrels back in the hall and grabs the starred ribbons Moni held in her hand, then stomps off again. "God, Assy, I don't know how but it's like she's gotten worse."

"Better you than me, babe. Wait no—" Asa's voice drifts away while she gives someone orders. "—make sure it's being catalogued with the rest of them and please be very, very careful when lifting it out. And if anything happens to those femurs it's your head on the chopping block!"

Imagining the five-foot seven, dark-haired wild child Asaria Esmeray Gennady as a board-certified archaeologist digging up some dinosaur is insane to me.

Despite their differences, and there are many, the resemblance between the two of them is uncanny.

Her voice returns. "Sorry, what were you saying?"

"Just that Mother is a pain in the ass. Where are you?"

"A couple miles outside Turkey. Didn't I tell you?"

"Nope. Please, please tell me you're still coming on Wednesday?" I all but plead. Because that would be the only thing that would make this event even the least bit tolerable. And she promised when we had a group FaceTime with Ophelia and Kaleo on his birthday last month.

"I wish E, but I'm here until the end of August."

Of course, she is. "What did you find this time?" I laugh, fighting to hide my disappointment.

"Oh, just a few fossils of a new species of dinosaur dating back to the Cretaceous period!" Asa shrieks, loud enough I pull my phone away from my ear, her no doubt doing that little shimmy she did when she's happy. "Oh, you should see it, E! It's incredible!"

"I believe you," I say, feigning excitement as much as possible. All while a dull ache glows in my heart. "Did you tell Ophelia?" I know Kaleo loves history as much as she does, so he'd probably like to know.

"I tried calling, but I think they're still on their flight."

"Where to?"

"Uhm…" Asa's voice creeks. "Where are they flying to, Asaria?"

This is Emryne speaking.

On the other line, I hear papers crumbling followed by a knock and something crash, then my sister's exasperated sigh. "Shit, I really liked that vase."

I know what she's doing. Asa's always been a bad liar, and with every noise she makes in the background, she's hoping it'll distract me enough to change the subject. Unfortunately, I know my sister.

She stays quiet for the longest time while I sit glued to my seat, waiting for an answer. Even if I know I'm going to hate it. "I'm sorry, Emrie. We wanted to be there, we really did, but…"

"It's fine," I sigh, cutting her off. I don't need to hear the rest. "I'll just… hang out with Addy."

"Chin up, babe. Tell Father I love him, and send lots of pictures, okay? I'm dying to see your dress," she says, blowing a kiss before she ends our call. I slam the phone on the seat next to me.

I hate the pity in her voice. I hate that she's not here. Ophelia is on a plane, and I can't talk to her, and I hate that I have to keep making these stupid, ridiculous baskets.

Hate. Hate. Hate!

My sisters were my biggest support system after the whole Skylan fiasco, and I can't stand the idea of them not being here. Even Cameron called saying he couldn't make it since he's in Papua New-Guinea treating and monitoring a recent E-Coli outbreak, which makes this even worse. The Fourth of July ball is tradition, one we never celebrated without everyone here and only the princes and their families in tow.

And speaking of princes in tow, it's an all-out battle between the heat from another scorching day outside as the balcony doors swing open, and the cool air inside. Father enters with King Harryson and the princes behind them, bare-chested and laughing the day away.

"Christ Rynny," King Harry wipes the sweet from his forehead. "Did we have to do that outside?"

"What's the matter, Harry? Afraid of a little sun?" Father chastises. "Oh, that's right. Ice melts in the heat."

"You're a pain in my ass, you know that?" King Harryson says, snapping his towel at him. "You could've at least given me some sunscreen or something."

"Don't bother, Your Majesty," I add, coming closer to them. "My father's philosophy is that sunscreen is for the weak."

The king rolls his eyes. "So is tea, but people still drink it."

"There you are. Hello darling," Father kisses my cheek.

I take his hand and try a smile, hoping he'll buy it. "Asaria says hi."

"Will she be joining us?" his calloused thumb brushing circles on my hand.

"No. Apparently, they found a new species of dinosaur in Turkey that'll keep her busy until the end of August. So, it's just us."

He shrugs, stepping around me. "Pity. Well, there's always next year."

What the hell? Am I the only one who cares that no one will be here?

"Yep," I mumble as they go back to chatting, surprised to see Skylan keeping his distance. I'm still waiting for the ball to drop. He barely meets my eye when I look his way, leaning against the mahogany stairwell with his steel arms crossed over his chest.

I'm tired of waiting. I'm sure if I said something we could come to some sort of understanding or bargain for him to keep my secret.

But before I could, Caneic steps toward me, flashing his pearl-white teeth. "You look stunning, Your Highness."

"Oh, this old thing?" I joke, waving my hand at the flowy sleeved, off-the-shoulder yellow chiffon dress. I hear his strained laugh though. Cane's shoulders tense as he clasps his hands behind his back, shifting off his left leg.

Instinctively, despite the sweat glistening on his bronze shoulders, my hand grips his shoulder, "You look exhausted. I hope my father's not tiring you out too much."

Don't think I miss Skylan's piercing glare behind him. His eyes glue to my hand, straightening his body like a hungry lion ready to pounce.

He shrugs playfully. "I could use the exercise if I'm being honest."

Not from where I'm standing. Cane isn't much smaller than Skylan, leaner maybe, but still a body of solid muscle. Not at all unattractive, but Sky? Sky's just… ripped. With a body ready to stop a train…

Oh enough, you fool!

He places a hand on my lower back and guides me a step away from the group. "Are you busy this afternoon? I was hoping we could go for a ride?" Though not far enough it seems.

"Actually, your father was hoping you'd join us," both Cane and I turn to King Harryson. "How about it, boys? King Ryne and I are setting up a little sparring match this afternoon. Any takers?"

I try to swallow my annoyance despite my excitement. It's been a while since I took my big ole stallion out for a ride. Frolic loves galloping through the daffodil fields behind the palace. But, by the way my father is grinning at me, I guess that'll have to wait.

Allister and Lando are in apparently, so is Skylan. *Shocker.* All eyes turn to Cane, waiting for his answer. I can see it pains him, though I have no idea why, but he forces a grin to his lips and agrees.

Without another glance in my direction, the boys follow the kings downstairs.

Father steps back and leans to my ear. Cordially extending my own invite, my favorite look of familiar mischief flashing in his eyes. "Two p.m. sharp. Dress accordingly," he winks.

Chapter 12
Emryne
Sugar, Spice, and a Piece of Advice

I've never been more excited to ditch a gown for my favorite pair of black leggings and matching sports bra. The fabric fiercely accentuates my curves, hugging all the right spots to create the perfect distraction, and the mesh cutouts morphed my body into the ultimate warrior temptress. In other words, it's sexy as fuck, and wonderfully misleading.

Since she was the plait queen, Moni decided tight rope braids was the hairstyle I needed to complete today's ensemble. Not that she was impressed by the amount of skin I'm showing, but if my father taught me anything, it's that war is all about deception. And what's more deceptive than an innocent, pretty princess in tight clothing batting her eyelashes at anyone who'd look her way?

It's one-fifty-nine on the dot when I descend the spiral sandstone stairs to the training room, packed with everything from free weights, treadmills, and yoga mats, stopping short just before rounding the corner and catching the tail end of whatever gracious speech Father is giving before we take to the large rubber training mat in the center of the room.

"Sun Tzu's Art of War explains that one should know the difference between when to fight, and when not to fight," having already grabbed a pair of hand wraps, I pull back the Velcro strip keeping the heavy-duty fabric secured and release the roll, hooking the loop around my thumb and fastening it around my wrist as I've done countless times before.

"Violence," Father continues, crossing his arms over his chest, "is a situational necessity. When it can be avoided, it must. When not, and the circumstances are favorable, modify your strategy."

All eyes turn to me, a strange combination of confusion and silent outrage plastered on all but Skylan's face, then back to my father awaiting some kind of explanation.

"Your Highness?" Lando questions, taking a step toward me.

"Prince Lando," I nod to him with a megawatt grin before I stop next to Father just as he finishes.

"Wonderful. Now we're ready to begin," Father pats my shoulder, smiling down at my choice of wardrobe.

"Are you sure about this?" King Harryson asks, unconvinced at whatever plan he thinks Father cooked up.

"Oh, trust me Harry, this won't be much of a fight," as he finishes, my eyes settle on Skylan, already grinning ear to ear and as hungry for the challenge as I am.

"Beauty, gentleman, is a weapon. Same as any other, and one we will never have the privilege to experience. My daughter, however, does."

I nod my head at Sky and step onto the black rubber mat, hoping he's prepared; I have no intention of holding back. By the steady anticipation burning in his hazelnut eyes, it's obvious he won't be either.

Father pulls two fold-up chairs closer and slides one to King Harryson as he swings his around and sits with the back against his chest.

"So, who's first?"

To my surprise, Allister leaves his frozen state and grabs two pairs of boxing gloves, shoving his hands inside as he steps on the mat, handing me the other pair.

"You'll forgive me if I don't go easy on you?" He winks. I'm sure his smooth Alaristaurian accent is enough to drop panties as far as the eye can see, bad news for him because I'm the last person it'll work on.

"Don't bother," I assure him sweetly, raising my gloves to my chin. "Your move, Your Highness," he raises his gloves, and Father signals for us to begin. Allister swings a tight right hook at my jaw. I square my shoulders, pulling my hands up and blocking him.

This is Allister speaking.

Of course, he'd aim for the obvious places. Fighters usually take turns dropping their defense, leaving their chin and lower body unprotected giving the opponent the perfect opportunity to strike. All of which I block easily enough, strategically throwing my own jabs where he lacks to defend himself, and keep a close watch on how he shifts his body.

"Where have you been hiding her, Ryne?" I hear King Harryson muse. What did he think this was? A ballet recital?

"Rule number one in boxing, always keep your hands up," Father instructs. "If you don't…" Allister hesitates, darting his eyes to Father, and I jump into action. Knocking him off the mat with a simple right-left-right-uppercut combination. "Well, there you go. Next up."

Lando took all of ten seconds to take down. The poor guy's footing completely escaped him when he grabs the fencing saber, holding it at an angle I've never seen in my life and allowing me to knock it straight out of his hands, not to mention him on his ass, past my father and King Harry's heads. Not that he stepped onto the mat with a ton of confidence to begin with, but I was sure he'd last longer than that.

It's fascinating to see how sheltered life affects confidence. I know the Parsóneians rely heavily on their knights for protection, and save for the king and Cane, so does Eikenish, and see no need for their ruling monarchs to learn self-defense skills. What for when an entire staff of knights who takes care of business for them?

Obviously, my father thought differently. Boxing was the first martial art he taught us, even if Cameron and I were the only ones who paid attention. Asa and Ophelia could hold their own well enough. Then Cam left, and Addylin had no interest in battle whatsoever. Hence, I became Father's apprentice. Cane is a different story entirely.

My excitement doubles when he strides to black training spears against the wall, taking one in his hand and testing the wood's dexterity. Satisfied with his weapon of choice, Cane swings the spear in his palms, acclimating to the oak. If I had to pick a favorite weapon, it'd be the spear. About sixty-five inches in length, my father had them custom-made for training. Whatever he couldn't teach us, he'd make sure to hire the best of the best. And boy did he.

Master Tsukumo may have been a five-foot-three, all around pain in the ass as an instructor, but even I can't deny the valuable lessons he taught us. The importance of reading body language for example. By the comfort with which Cane handles the spear, his hold firm but not tight, shows me he's trained with them before. Unlike Lando's, simply put, fake-it-till-you-make-it approach.

I preferred the bamboo spears as a child, everything about them always reminded me of the Asai Empire and the tranquility and discipline with which one should fight, which reminds me to check in with Prince Zimo and see how his father is doing.

Laying a few steps to the right of the mat, I head for the spears I trained with earlier the week and never bothered to put back on the wall, and step just short of the edge, propelling it up, and catch it mid-air.

"You're not going with the oak?" Father asks in Japanese tongue.

"Bamboo suits me better. Have you heard from Prince Zimo?" I reply easily. Japanese was only one of the four languages I'm fluent in and by far the quickest I've picked up.

"Later," he waves his hand.

I eye Prince Caneic and he does the same. Not every day you hear a young princess speaking a language so easily, not to mention at all. Very few monarchs bothered to learn when translators were so readily available.

I study him closely, and notice him hesitate putting pressure on his left leg, for the second time today.

I keep to Japanese when I ask, "What's wrong with him?"

"Concentrate. I can tell Cane knows what he's doing."

"Why is he hesitating like that?"

Jaw taunt, Father swallows, answering, "His left leg is prosthetic," in a tight voice.

"What?" I snap back to English.

He hooks his spear behind my legs and sweeps my feet from under me, knocking me on my back. I'd curse myself for dropping my guard and allowing him to get close, but I'm too stunned to react.

A prosthetic leg? Why did I not know that? *How* did I not know that?

"Focus, Emryne!"

Cane uses my disorientation to his advantage, crawling up my body until he straddles by hips, securing me in a headlock with the spear underneath my chin.

His leverage beneath my chin is secure enough to force me up unto my knees. Exactly where I want him to be. Cane's so focused on pinning me down he doesn't notice me letting go of my own spear, freeing my hand.

"You may want to tap out, Princess," he rumbles from behind me.

I can already feel him cutting off my blood supply, my vision slowly dimming at its edges; he doesn't relent his grip in the slightest.

"You have something on your face."

"Pardon?"

With all his focus drawn to what I'm trying to say, I'm able to slide my ankle around him, angling my hip under his. "You have something on your face."

"What?"

"Blood." My elbow connects through his jaw.

And with my ankle around his, I use my strength to push my hip upward into him. Cane's body tilts left, and he loses his balance easily—having a prosthetic in this situation doesn't exactly help without training in weight compensation, which I can tell he hasn't got—and I push him off me and onto his back, scrambling to straddle him, and push my elbow into throat, prompting him to tap the mat, yielding.

His startled expression is enough to bring a smirk to my lips.

Almost caught me there, Princey. Almost.

I wink at him before rolling off him and into my back, then tuck my legs under me and raise my torso enough for momentum to work to my advantage when I push my legs up, and propel myself to my feet.

"Valiant effort, Caneic," Father claps his hands. "Better luck next time, son."

He groans, wiping the blood from a cut on his lip to his chin, and gets to his feet, pushing past me without so much as a glance.

I find my father's humored gaze, and shrug my shoulder. Not everyone accepts losing very well, I guess.

Finally, Sky steps onto the mat. Eyeing me with a shit-eating smirk as he strides to me. "You speak Japanese?"

I raise my head in challenge. "You don't?"

"This should be good," Father muses behind us.

"Just like old times," Sky teases, walking to the corner of the mat. "Don't make it too easy for me now, darling."

I bare my teeth at him. "Wouldn't dream of it, *darling*."

Sky raises his fits at his chin, and advances. No gloves, no weapons, just his wrapped knuckles, and a devilish smirk spread over his lips.

I revel in the freedom with him, squaring my shoulders and bringing my fists to my chin. Simply because I'm a woman is no reason for Sky to hold back, he's not the type. And he's taught me too much, including the three-punch combination I throw at his jaw, which to my irritation, he easily blocks.

"Fighting dirty, are we?" he smirks, recognizing his own teaching, and countering with two jabs and a hook of his own. Sky catches me chin, enough to disorientate me. I stagger a few steps backward, cursing inward at myself for not blocking him in time. He slips behind me with every intention of getting me to the mat, but I counter in an instant, catching his ankle in mine and knocking him on his back instead, and letting my jabs loose.

"If that's what it takes to get you to shut up, you better damn well believe it."

He chuckles, and before I had time to react, he's feet are under him, and he's hooked my ankle over his. My breath slams from my chest as he flips us, pinning me down under him.

"Was that your plan all along, darling? To get me on top of you?"

"Screw you!" I spew through gritted teeth.

Sky wiggles his eyebrows. "If so, all you had to do was ask," he winks, blowing me a kiss.

"Stop talking!" I grunt, tilting my pelvis upward, forcing Sky to lose his balance and shoot forward, then tuck my legs under me and raise my hips, the momentum propelling him forward until he slams his hands down above my head.

I study the lines on Sky's face, readying my forehead for a headbutt, but, of course, I'm an idiot thinking Sky wouldn't catch on, he'd been watching as closely as anyone.

Instead of the slam, Sky captures my wrists, and force them above my head, pinning my in place. What makes matters worse, Sky holds himself over my body at such an annoying angle my piercing keeps brushing against the fabric of my panties, stirring my arousal every time he moves, which pissing me off more.

"Give it to me!" I demand at him, thick beads of sweat running down my forehead and back, still trying, and still failing to free my wrists.

This is the last damn place I want to get wet, and with both our fathers watching no less, but of course, Sky simply takes my annoyance as encouragement to increase his relentless pestering.

"Careful what you wish for, Princess," he murmurs, flashing a snide grin.

Precisely my point.

Now, as I slam my forehead into Sky's nose, I knock him on his ass with a surprised huff. He scrambles to his feet, straight into the heel of my trainer in a turning kick, and he's back on the mat. Both of us grappling, a mess of limbs, sweat, grunts, and legs, fighting for dominance, for victory we both crave the taste of.

"Reel it in, Emryne," Sky breathes, gripping his head in defense as I pummel my fists into his head once again. "You're losing your cool. Seriously, reel it in."

Here's thing about beavers. The more twigs the little web-footed critters add to their dams, the greater the risk of collapsing under pressure, destroying all the poor thing's hard work. And my mental beaver dam, a place for every emotion and every emotion neatly weaved into an intricate pattern, has evidently had enough.

Enough of his games. Enough of his suave smiles, glistening muscles and definitely enough of his intense hazelnut eyes staring into my soul and breaking down every wall I had built up. Enough of him dancing around the truth about why he packed up everything he had, along with my heart, and he disappeared for three fucking years.

I never told him that I loved him. In retrospect maybe I should have, but I was barely nineteen years old, what on earth did I know about love? What do I know about love now? The closest reference I have to what it's supposed to look like is Ophelia and Kaleo, even if I only saw them once, maybe twice a year, but I know he loves her more than life.

Sky's only been my best friend since birth, but I don't know if I've ever loved him the same.

Enough.

I've had enough of this.

I shove to my feet, stepping away as he springs up, advancing in three determined steps.

Hands at the ready, he squares his shoulders, his wrapped fist angled at my jaw in left hook, but I catch his wrist in my palm instead and twist. The sweep quick enough, one of my favorite lessons Master Tsukumo taught, to send his body somersaulting through the air; his back slams to the mat in a heavy thud and a thunderous grunt.

I pull the small dagger, discreetly strapped to my ankle, free, and force the blade against his throat, forcing the air from his lungs with my knee in his chest. Shutting him up once and for all.

His dark chuckle rattles me to my core, sending tendrils of hushed pleasure flaring right between my legs, and he reaches up, yanking my arm hard enough for my chest to slam against his.

"You made the same move on that rooftop two weeks ago," Sky breathes, his voice barely loud enough to hear. "Hello, Dark Warrior."

All I can do is blink.

I guess if there's ever a time for the bubble to burst it would be now.

But I do my best to play if off. Last thing I want is him thinking he's getting to me. "You're full of shit," I declare, getting to my feet.

"And you will always look sexy as fuck in black, Em-Em," he bends down and picks up Cane and I's discarded spears, making a show as he straightens, his velvety voice lighting my body on fire. "What's underneath, I wonder?" He saunters away without looking back. I'm about to stomp after him, demanding he names a price for keeping this quiet, when Father appears next to me, slaps my shoulder, and closes me in a one arm hug.

"Never doubted you," his smile never falters as he extends his free hand to King Harry, wiggling his fingers. He plants a stack of fifties in his palm.

"Pleasure doing business with you."

"Smartass," King Harry rolls his eyes.

I eye him suspiciously, caught somewhere between a laugh and mortification. This is such a Father thing to do, and if there's one thing he loves, it's being underestimated. It makes proving people wrong all the more satisfying.

Success is the best revenge, he loves to point out.

"You made a bet?" I can't decide whether I'm amused or annoyed, though a smirking Skylan behind his father's shoulder definitely aids to the latter. "Since when do you gamble?"

"It was only a little one," Father muses, raising his shoulder and flashing an innocent smile. "And betting against an old friend isn't a gamble, it's an inevitability."

"Oh sure, look who's calling who old," King Harryson rolls his eyes, then smiles my way, nodding his approval. "You handed their asses to them. Well done, Princess."

"Chip off the old block, isn't she?" Father ruffles my hair, "Now go cleaned up before your mother sees. And for goodness' sake, don't be late to the fitting." He kisses my temple before heading back up the stairs.

"That would've been yours if Emryne hadn't cheated," Skylan calls from the racks where the dumbbells rest, picking up two thirty-five pounds and laying down on the bench.

Cheated! In what world?

My eyes shoot daggers at him, but he's already on his back with the weights above his head. Only he would have the urge to get a pump even after sparring. Though by the way I've been slacking with my workouts I desperately need it too.

King Harry's body shakes with deep laughter. "She most certainly did not," Thank you. "She had you in that last scuttle whether you like it or not. I think you've just lost your touch, son." He pats Sky's thigh as he walks past, following my father upstairs.

Another infamous grin flashes my way after he nods goodbye, sending all kinds of butterflies skipping through my body. All I can do is roll my eyes at him, willing the little creatures to stop their shenanigans and settle. Sky knowing who I am is a serious threat. Might not be his plan to use this against me, and blackmail isn't his thing, but I need to know what's happening in that big head of his more than anything.

"Well done, indeed," Cane saunters closer, towel in hand and wiping the sweat from his forehead. "May I request a rematch?"

"Request all you want, mate," Allister calls next to a chuckling Lando, "still won't make you better fighter."

He shrugs, ignoring him. "I've had enough time to study your strategies. I'm confident I will win the next round. Although, if you ask me, a princess shouldn't be fighting at all."

I raise an eyebrow. "Excuse me?"

"Surely battle doesn't interest you? You've whole battalions at your disposal ready to protect you. As is their duty."

I cross my arms in defense. "And what exactly about me makes you think I need protection?"

"You're a crowned princess, of course, you do," he shrugs.

My head falls back with bitter laughter. "Oh, let me guess? A princess's place is in a ballroom, smiling and waving at her people, planning high teas, bachelorette parties, and birthdays?"

Smartest thing he does is taking a step back. "What? No, that's not what I—"

"Or better yet, her place is on her king's bed with her mouth shut and her legs spread, right?"

He holds up his palms in surrender, shaking his head, "No! No, that is not what I meant at all, I was only—"

"Look, I get that your way of doing things are traditional, but you won't find those roles here. My sister might be content with smiling and waving and being a perfectly obedient princess, but let me assure you, Your Highness," I spit his title like venom, "that is not me. Nor will it ever be me. I am not the type of woman to roll over, ready at your beck call. This is my kingdom, and I want an equal, someone I can rule Alorewyn *with*, not stand behind while *he* rules. And if that's what you want, then I suggest you get out of my training room and cozy up to Addylin instead."

Was that harsh? Maybe a little. But I'm tired of listening to people explain why complacency is in my best interest. I like my independence thank you very much. And I'd like a damn drink.

About to reach for my phone and text Tory and Beth for happy hour at our favorite rooftop bar Uptown, my ringtone buzzes and I swipe to answer, not bothering to check the caller ID, hoping it's Asa.

"If you're not calling me to tell me your plans have changed, I don't—"

"It's me," Castor's muffled voice says.

I breathe a sigh of relief. "Finally."

"I know. Something came up I couldn't avoid, sorry."

Not that he's ever told me anything about himself before, and he sounds fine, but, "What happened?"

The line goes quiet. I lift my phone from my ear, checking we weren't disconnected. But Unknown still displays on my screen.

"I thought we agreed we'd keep our private lives private?" Castor finally says.

"Yes, I know. Just checking. Sue me."

He laughs. "Your concern is amiable, Your Highness, but that would be the very definition of a frivolous lawsuit."

My lips turn up. It's nice to have someone who gets my humor. God knows I need a good laugh after these last couple of days. "Did you find anything in the pictures I sent you?"

"Plenty. I forwarded the casefiles of the few I managed to find through NCIC's facial recognition, the others I'm still working on. Is your laptop nearby?" The one Castor insisted he encrypt if we were to enter a partnership. Not that it mattered to me. Everything about this made me feel like I'm in some James Bond movie. The other part wished it more than anything. At least Bond gets the villain in the end.

"It's in my room. Give me ten minutes." I don't wait for a goodbye before ending the call and tuck my phone in the side pocket of my leggings, throwing my towel over my shoulder and heading for the stairs.

"Going somewhere?" A body moves in my way.

Seriously? "Jesus."

"We've been over this, darling. Just Skylan will do," he smirks.

Really not in the mood for this. "So help me God, Skylan, if you don't get out of my way, the next place I hit won't be your face."

His cocky grin only widens as he leans in my face. "Princess, why are you so angry with me?"

"Please tell me you're not seriously asking me that," I deadpan.

"I would, but you know I don't lie."

"You keep getting in my way, that's *why*."

His eyes flick to the ceiling as he blows out a mocking breath, stepping closer as his hands clasp behind his back. "I don't think that's the reason."

"And I couldn't care less what you think, now if you'll please excuse me," I don't bother apologizing as I rush past him, shoving my shoulder against his.

#

"Well? What do you think?"

An opioid derivative. Or a synthesized version of it.

"Paranoia and hallucinations that lead to above average violent aggression and self-injury, not to mention highly addictive with more than sixty-five percent of users hooked on first injection." That was what Castor had said.

In other words, if I don't get this trash out of my kingdom, we're headed for an epidemic without a doubt. Great for Cam and his science-y brain when it comes to studying their behaviors, horrible for the rest of us. But finally, some progress.

Since Castor is yet to have luck with Markus's laptop, it's become obvious that the only way to figure this out will probably be the old-fashioned, beat down doors and break bicuspids until I find something. He explained why he couldn't get into the laptop, apparently Markus wasn't as stupid as he seemed and his security was state of the art, but I stopped listening after the picture of me and my sisters hiking in Hawaii distracted me.

What's the point of a ball without them?

Mother's excited shriek finally pulls me back to reality. "Isn't it fantastic?"

No. It's a goddamn monstrosity. A pink, sequined monstrosity with way too many of layers of lace and ruffles. The gown looks like something straight out of a Junior Miss… everything pageant.

Father's furrowed brow and wrinkled lip says even more. "She looks naked."

Naked is the subtle way to put it. "I look dead. I hate it."

"Don't say hate, Emryne," she scolds, flicking my arm. "And don't be ridiculous. It's perfect."

"Mother, I don't like pink," *which you would know if you didn't have your head stuck up your ass.*

"Oh, enough with the dramatics, you look perfect. And stop slouching. It's unattractive," Mother scurries over to Addylin modeling a gown similar to mine.

"See? Look at your sister. Absolutely beautiful," yes, because any shade of pinks looks phenomenal with her porcelain skin. I am my father's daughter, and our sun-kissed complexion can be very unforgiving at times. Which would've applied in this case, if I didn't already hate pink.

"I think she'll look better in red," Father chimes, eyeing the rows of gowns hanging on every available rack in the tailor's room in every color imaginable before he kisses my cheeks and exits with Claire behind him.

Mother gave Justine her okay and floated from the room not long after, leaving me to my turbulent thoughts. Starting with my silent sister. Addy's always been chatty, but something changed in the last few months and for the life of me I haven't been able to figure out what; she hasn't exactly been open about it either.

Her eyes are plastered to her phone while her fingers fly over the screen. If I hadn't spoken up, she probably wouldn't have known we were the only two standing here.

Addylin's gown is flattering as always. She swapped her pink for royal blue silk Mother said would suit the occasion better and made her cream-blonde hair shimmer in the afternoon sun. Why she keeps insisting on tying it in a ponytail is beyond me.

"Please tell me you're wearing your hair down for the ball?"

Her eyes finally leave her screen. "Hmm?"

"Your hair, Addy," I smile at her frowning face, "wear it down. For the ball."

She nods, but goes right back to typing. "Yeah, okay."

I climb down the pedestal, kicking the ugly fabric out from under my feet and walk to her. "What's going on with you? Feels like we haven't talked in months." She's still my sister, and I miss not seeing her.

"We're both just busy, I guess," she hesitates for a second, but picks up her gown and climbs down to me. "Remember that pen pal from Adlengn I told you about?"

Pen pal… maybe that's where I came up with it when I escaped Sky in the kitchen. "The one you send all those recordings of you singing?"

She flinches. "How did you know that?"

"You forget I can hear you from the balcony. You know I never shut the doors in summer," not that I mind at all, Addylin's voice is phenomenal.

"Oh, yeah," she winces, shaking her head.

"You really should sing more Avril, by the way. What about him?"

Addy turns on her heel, patting her phone in her palm while in thought. "I think I know who he is."

My brows furrow. I don't know how pen pals work but I'm pretty sure names are involved. "You didn't know when you first started talking?"

"No, the app we use is VIP exclusive. High-profile people looking to meet someone new without worrying about it being leaked on every social media platform in existence."

I didn't know that. "And… you're happy with who you suspect it is?"

She shrugs a petite shoulder. "I think so."

I nod. Not something I'd expect from her, Addy's never had trouble making friends, but if she's happy, "Then I'm happy for you, Adds."

"Thanks," she tucks her phone away and walks toward the door, stopping at the frame. "Hey, I'm going for a ride in a bit, feel like joining?"

I almost weep with relief. "Yes, please. Anything to get out and as far away from this frickin' eyesore as possible."

She laughs. "I think Father's right, pick something red," Addy winks before she walks out.

Mother always insists on having the dresses pulled that matched Alorewyn's red, white, and blue first, yet this year they apparently weren't good enough. Clearly the woman is blind, the dresses I'm looking at have to be some of the best I've seen.

Like Monique, Claire and Justine have been here forever, when my great-grandmother was still queen in fact, and let me tell you, those little old ladies can sew. Claire tailors Father suits while Justine and her assistants worked their magic on our gowns.

I think a part of them, despite my mother's ludicrous demands, enjoys the work even more now that they only have adults to cater to and no giggling little girls running around with pins in their dresses.

There had to be a worthy gown somewhere in this room.

"I haven't seen that many ruffles since Barbie came to your eighth birthday."

His reflection didn't surprise me at all. I'm starting to get used Skylan just appearing everywhere.

I laugh. "You did make a phenomenal Ken."

"Don't say I never did anything for you," he chuckles, shaking his head. He has no idea just how right he is. He's done more for me growing up than I care to admit.

Sky's leaning against the door frame, his big arms crossed over his chest and smiling. Every important part of my body tingled when my eyes traveled down his reflection. He's traded his workout clothes for his kingdom's colors and medals, clean shaven and his messy hair is expertly, and more important— elegantly, styled. Callior's red and white dress uniform is something of a marvel to me. I can't stop my wandering gaze even if I wanted to. More so, I can't stop the flutters in my stomach meeting his warm eyes. And I don't think I want to.

"You look nice," not sure if I said it out loud, but it's true.

He smiles politely as he makes his way over to me. "Just wanted to say goodbye before we left. My father and I are headed home."

"Why?" my excitement fizzles out and is replaced by concern. "Did something happen?"

"Mav asked us to sit in on a meeting with Parliament."

"Separatists?"

"Yeah."

"Couldn't you do it over video call?"

"You know how Dad is. He hates technology. And he'd never miss assembly even if we're in a different country. It's only about an hour and half by chopper. We'll be back in a few days."

I use my smile to hide my relief, opting for a playful flick of hair he'll hopefully believe, coyly sweeping my gaze over him as I say, "Are you flying?"

His eyes fill with that light I've come to know is excitement. If there's one thing Skylan adores, it's flying. "Naturally."

I've seen him in action. He has his own fleet of fancy fighter jets he flies with Acadan's Airforce. He'd totally put movie Maverick to shame if he were to fly against him.

Not that I know the first thing about flying, other than I love it. But I've always been Sky's biggest fan.

"So, you're still coming to the ball?"

"Wouldn't miss it," he smiles warmly, then shrugs playfully. "Dad would kick my ass if we did. The old man hates missing a party."

Something similar to curiosity crosses his eyes when he tilts his head to the side, meeting mine. And of course, like the coward I am I flick mine away from him and back at the mirror to the ugly gown.

"No offense, but pink is not your color," he grimaces.

"I know right?" I say, nearly gagging at the image in front of me. "God, doesn't the woman know me at all?"

Sky takes a step. "She is a queen."

"That's not an excuse," I dismiss him. "Even my father thinks I look like an idiot."

"Easy, I wouldn't go that far," I watch his eyes survey the gown, and his lips press together, choking on a laugh. "You kinda look like a cupcake."

"Oh yeah. Laugh it up, why don't you?" I deadpan.

"Maybe I should call you cupcake from now on," he wiggles his eyebrows behind me.

"If you value your front teeth, I suggest you not. Don't think I won't knock them out."

"So aggressive," he smirks, raising an eyebrow. "If this queen thing doesn't work out, consider a career in corrections. Maybe you should be a prison warden instead?"

"You're not funny," I leave his gaze and go back to dry heaving at the dress, pleading, "Sky, help me!"

"Okay," he chuckles, eyeing the gowns over his shoulder. "This room is filled with dresses, why not try something a little more… you?"

I would if I knew what I wanted to wear! I lost interest in this thing the second I ended that call with Asa. If he knows me so well then let him pick something. "Okay then, Joan Rivers, what do you think I should wear?"

"Eyes on the mirror while I go shopping," Sky winks and turns away. I see him smiling at me over his shoulder, my body is filled with so much excitement my toes are tingling. But that could just be from these ridiculous heels Mother is making me wear. Definitely not, despite the stilettos, that Sky still towers over me by at least five inches.

He returns in a minute or so with a look of pure satisfaction. "Ready?"

I suck my bottom lip between my teeth and nod. "Mhm."

I take a sharp breath in as Sky swings the most beautiful red chiffon gown in front of me. The dress has a semi-sweetheart neckline and minimal embellishments save for the few roses sewed at the waist, it's what I hoped for; a black trash bag would've been an improvement over this pink thing, and as red as Father and Addy suggested.

Say what you want about the guy, he has style.

"Much better," he grins.

My heart does that funny thing where it beats and flutters at the same time and I become blissfully aware of the heat of his body behind me, his deep, woody cologne ensnaring my senses.

So close, yet not close enough.

"Should I…" I swallow, breathing him in. "Should I try it on?"

"I insist," he hands me the hanger, "But, I'll wait until the ball to see you wearing it." Then leans down to whisper, "I'll be taking it off anyway." The timbre of his voice sends the most delicious shivers through my body. Right down to my aching center.

"Sky," I whisper, leaning back into his warmth. His fingertips trail down my bare arms, his warm touch and smooth voice awakening the arousal sound asleep deep inside my belly, dampening my panties in wonderful anticipation.

"I know how I make you feel, Emryne," Sky whispers, his hot breath tickling my ear. "Don't deny this. Don't deny us."

I don't want to. Every part of me wants to give in, to trust him. I want to trust him, but I just… can't…

I opened my mouth to say exactly that, but he beat me to it. "I won't touch you until you ask. But I meant what I said. I'm here for you," he leans down and softly kisses my cheek. "Enjoy your afternoon, Your Highness."

Chapter 13
Emryne
Lovely Surprises

Kill.

Me.

NOW.

Three hours into this party and I'm bored out of my skull, I'm ready to jump off the roof, and this stupid thing on my head is killing me!

Of course, Mother insisted our heaviest jeweled tiaras would be 'just so perfect' for the occasion. I don't care how amazing the diamonds complemented our dresses, if it were up to me, we'd never wear the damn things. At least she was pleased with my gown of choice; for once she didn't scold me as I descended the stairs. Granted, she didn't exactly sing her approval, a nod and something resembling half a smile was all I got, but it was still a smile. Baby steps, I guess.

There's easily three times the amount of people as the night the princes arrived, and all of them are wrapped up in the orchestra Mother hired for the occasion. I love classical music as much as the next person, which is not at all, but would it kill them to play something a little livelier?

Then again what's the point. No Cameron. No Asaria. No Ophelia. No me enjoying. Allister was the first to ask me to dance, but I declined, and he settled on one of the members of Parliament's daughters instead. If I can't dance with my siblings, I'm not dancing at all.

Mother's making her rounds, schmoozing the VIPs with Addylin tagging along behind, as bored as Father is schlumped in his throne without King Harryson to keep him company. He loved the dress by the way, and insisted walking in with him since my dress matched his tie perfectly.

Addy eyes flag mine down, and rolls her own, mouthing 'save me' just as Mother grabs her forearm and drags her in the opposite direction. She didn't want to do this anymore than I did, yet I can't for the life of me figure out why she stays by Mother's side.

Where is Skylan, you ask? Great question. I haven't heard from him since he left three days ago. It's been a while since I faced the internal struggle of whether or not to text, ask if everything's okay and if the meeting went well. I came close more than once, but chickened out every time I was about to hit send.

I have my doubts about whether or not he's coming back. Whatever Maverick needed had to trump Alorewyn's silly little ball by a long shot. Though if I knew they weren't coming back I'd have at least given him a real goodbye.

Not that I'm at all sure exactly what that goodbye would've looked like. I won't lie and say I've forgiven and forgotten what's happened between us, I still keep myself from not holding back. Like I said, filling my ears with pretty words and my mind with filthy thoughts won't make me trust him. I did that once before, and look where it got me.

Naked and alone in his bedroom in their imperial estate three hours from Alorewyn, with no note of apology saying where or why he'd gone and no way to get home since I stupidly left my phone charging in my room before my date for the evening, Keith, came to pick me up. I was running late and barely had my bearings even before Tory texted saying Sky was there. I don't know why it surprised me, Mav was his cousin after all, but it still caught me off-guard. Whatever, bygones.

Though if he wasn't planning on showing up tonight he could've at least extended me the courtesy of telling me so. I wouldn't have bothered coming if he had. And I definitely wouldn't have worn this stupid dress. Or my favorite burgundy lingerie.

Which is totally for me.

Not him. At all.

Skylan's not even here so… there.

And I don't miss him either.

"I'm not sure how these usually go, but I'm certain the crowned princess should wear a bigger smile on her beautiful lips than the one she is now," Lando's voice snaps my attention. Dressed in Parsón's national colors, the turquoise and yellow dress jacket defines his caramel skin like I've never seen before. I love yellow, but I'd look like an amateur compared to him.

I smile his way. "I guess I'm not really in a party mood."

He crosses his hands behind his back. "Something the matter?"

Oh, you know, I'm under a ridiculous amount of pressure to be perfect, someone is selling deadly, highly addictive drugs in my kingdom, my best friend is gone—again, I'm horny as hell and my world is otherwise imploding. Nothing major.

"I'll be okay," I brush off his question. Lando's nice, so is his smooth Italian accent, just not nice enough for me to share my feelings. "What about you? Enjoying yourself?"

His eyes brighten and he turns to the dancing crowd. "So far. Such lavish decorations. Although the lack of gentlemanly attention is thoroughly disheartening."

My eyebrows draw together. Lack of... wait... "You're gay?" Dammit, now I really wish Cameron was here. I know these two would've totally eaten each other out.

I said what I said.

"Was I that obvious?" Lando smiles awkwardly.

"Not at all," which is why this is the last thing I expected. In all the time we've spent together over the past four months, he's never once given me any indication that he'd prefer male companionship, but it makes my life easier. And either way my night just got a hell of a lot better.

Four princes down, three to go.

"How did I not know that?" I beam, nearly jumping out of my skin with excitement.

His shoulder picks up in a shrug. "You've seen how Allister is treated."

My arm closes around his shoulder and click my tongue. "Babe, you're in Alorewyn. We pride ourselves on equality here. Trust me, this is the last place you'll ever be judged." It's true. Emarica is among the most culturally and sexually diverse countries on Earth, alongside Alaristau, Peroue and Acadan.

It's one of the places Lando and every other member of the LGBTQ+ community could live in peace thanks to my father's zero hate tolerance. Unless you want a particularly complicated, particularly dragged-out civil suit for your foreseeable future, you'd keep your surly opinions to yourself if you had any.

"Does... anyone know?"

"My friends, they know. Mama suspects. My father, he's too busy to notice," Sounds like someone I know. "It is not easy being an only child."

"I can imagine. My sister and I have each other, but even we can't keep up. It's like, all of a sudden we're future queens, we need to act as such. You know, play the part, smile or they'll think something is wrong. Sometimes I wish I could just be normal."

"Such is the life we chose, I suppose." Lando nods solemnly. "You're not… angry?" he questions as we make our way to the dancefloor.

"Why in the world would I be angry?"

"You don't feel like I've wasted your time?" he swallows nervously.

I give his shoulder a reassuring squeeze. "Not even a little bit. If anything, you've just made my life so much easier. Seriously, this is amazing. And I insist you point out who you'd like me to introduce you to."

Hell, I'll plan every one of their weddings if it meant I get out of this. If none of the remaining princes make an impact, I'm out. Surely Mother would have to listen to me if Addy doesn't find anyone either.

I introduce Lando to our minister of agriculture, Timéon Farley's, son Kyler. It doesn't take long for the two to really hit it off before heading through the balcony doors and to the gardens outside.

Good. I will be living vicariously through Lando tonight. And I'll definitely be needing some liquid courage if I'm to endure the rest of it.

Making my way over to the open bar, careful to avoid Mother's hawk eyes in case I did in fact want to make a scene, my hand closes around the neck of a bottle of Don Julio. Of course, I forgot I had Moni and Des make sure Asa's favorite tequila was stocked for tonight. The two of them returned to the palace with enough cases to last a month. Although between the four of us, when Cam could join, we'd finish off half the bottles by the end of the week.

Being a hot mess is delicious, isn't it?

I twist open the cap and throw back the shot, welcoming the deep burn and already pouring another one.

"Thank god."

The shot is halfway to my mouth when warm hands cover my eyes and two voices appear on either side of my head. "We saw that."

No.

No way.

I shake out of their hold and spin around, straight into the elated faces of the loves of my life, my sisters Asaria and Ophelia. "Surprise!"

My excited squeals turn more than a few heads I couldn't care less about and practically leap into their arms. "You're here!"

"Of course. Think we'd miss a Fourth?" Ophelia flicks her long blonde hair over shoulder.

Uhm, I did when Asaria told me so. And I used to think she was gullible. She beams and takes my hand and spins me around. "That dress is magnificent, Emmie-Bear."

"Me? Look at you!" Ophelia's wearing the most incredible deep turquoise flowing silk gown with long-sleeves, its cape adorned with delicate crystal accents on the shoulders. Her skin was already the perfect porcelain, like Mother's, but under tonight's soft lights she looks iridescent. Her cheeks are fuller and amber eyes are glowing. Ophelia never ceases to amaze.

Neither does Asa. Although… "Black on fourth?"

Ophelia shakes her head. "I told her."

"You know what Mother's going to say, right?"

"See the worry in my eyes, babe," Asa declares. Ever the vixen, her black mermaid gown sticks to my sister's femininely slender figure like its survival depended on it. Asaria's three inches taller than I am, and never lets me forget it, with the same deep brown eyes as Mother's.

Asa takes my hands. "Seriously E, you look like a goddess."

"Thank you. Skylan picked it out," even if it pains me so say so. Who the hell am I kidding? Of course, Sky's not serious. He slept with me and got what he wanted. End of story.

"Is he taking clients?" Ophelia jokes, I think. "Because I desperately need to upgrade my wardrobe." Not from where I'm standing.

I reach over the bar top and grab two more shot glasses, filling both before handing them to my sisters.

"I didn't realize he was invited," Asa says and drags the bowl of lemon slices closer, taking one and clink our glasses before throwing hers back. "I still need to kick his ass for last time. Although if I hear correctly, you've already taken care of that," she nudges my shoulder.

I smile faintly. Pretty sure the entire world's heard about that by now.

"Well, if you can get a hold of him be my guest," I shrug, following Asa and suck the lemon before pouring another.

Ophelia's eyebrows draw together. "What do you mean?"

"He left with his father three days ago. Some important thing Maverick needed them for."

Asaria tips the bottle and pours another shot, "And they couldn't video conference?"

Exactly the question I asked. "Apparently not."

"Screw him," Ophelia hands me another glass, holding up her own. "Who needs men when you have sisters?"

"Amen to that," Asa says and we clink our glasses.

An hour later, my stomach is aching from laughter, I've forgotten all about Sky and all my stupid problems as I fill my sisters in on my life.

Maybe I'll have more success with Allister or Cane if I paid more attention to them. Both are in my line of sight, but I'm surprised to see Cane dancing with Addylin. I know I came at him pretty tough the other day, but dammit, I don't want to be treated like a fragile flower who doesn't know her left from her right. I wouldn't be the Dark Warrior if that were the case.

Whenever I wasn't under Mother's watchful eye, I was in my room studying those rap sheets. Typical crimes like robbery, aggravated assault, DUI's and outstanding bench-warrants, hell some even guilty of manslaughter and third-degree murder. All of them blend into a crowd easily and all of them the perfect spies in Alorewyn streets. Evade the knights, stick to the shadows, and only hit areas not under heavy surveillance, that way Guard, Parliament and King Ryne remains none the wiser.

Except me. Give me a couple hours, and I'm out of this puffball and up their asses with a pistol firmly shoved between their cheeks.

"Emryne," Father calls. Guess that'll have to wait. My body all but leaps over the bar top to reach for a bottle of water, and I gulp down at least half of it before hopping off the stool between my howling sisters before I head to my father. No need to inform him of my own slight intoxication.

"Yes, Father?" I reply once I've gotten my bearings and scurry over to him.

"Would you come here for a second, darling?" I smooth out my dress before taking his extended hand. Father waves at the girls and loops my hand around his forearm as he guides me in the opposite direction.

I smile at him knowingly. "You knew they were coming, didn't you?"

"Of course, I did, my love. Your daddy may be old, but he's still got it."

"Oh, Father. You're not old," I kiss his cheek. "Maybe a little gray."

"And I'm still the most handsome king on the planet." Can't argue with that. It's thanks to both our parents' immaculate features that the Gennady children look like we were molded by Aphrodite herself.

I wonder if she had a big attitude?

We're halfway to my parents' lavish thrones when a friendly face steps in front of us and opens his arms, neatly dressed in light gray from head to toe.

"King Vallian."

Remember when Mother referred to disgracing the Gennady name? Just wait.

"Princess Emryne."

Think of King Val like that one non-creepy yet disturbingly good-looking uncle who spoils his friend's children rotten regardless of if they already have everything. He was Asaria's thesis advisor at Arcadia University, one of the youngest professors there when she attended as an undergrad, and an old friend of Father's. My favorite thing about him on his visits when I was young was the rare, antique weapons he brought along from every corner of the planet. With so much knowledge in his steel blue eyes, I hung on his lips when he told Father their history, and always asking more questions than he had answers for.

I take his hands and kiss his cheeks like always. "I didn't know you were coming?"

"Last-minute trip to before I head to Egypt. I can't stay long I'm afraid, but I had to see you."

King Val's son died of the same bone cancer his wife did when he was twenty-seven. Now he mostly spends his days traveling the world collecting beautiful artifacts and turning his kingdom off the West Coast of Eikenish into museum.

"I swear to the sweet gods above you get more incredible every time we meet," he spins me around, beaming as he takes in the dress. "Congratulations on your eligibility, you will make a stellar queen, las."

I chuckle. "Thank you. I'm happy you could make it."

"So am I," he eyes the crowd over my shoulder, "though I reckon Asaria might not be particularly—"

"You have *got* to be kidding me," Asa's voice bellows from behind us. Her arms are crossed over her delicate chest, and her eyes are staring daggers at him.

He throws his hands up in outrage and turns to Father. "You see! A single sentence, and a naked blade to the throat," he flattens his lips, making a cutting motion with his forefinger.

And here comes the fun part. One evening of deliciously sweaty sex (Asa's words, I swear) led to several others, and the two of them fell in love only for her to surprise him at his vacation home in Cancun and ambush King Perfect's wife. It was quite the scandal for the time. I'm not sure exactly when they broke up but I know it wasn't pretty. And no one holds a grudge like Asaria Esmeray.

"Are you following me?" she barrels toward him.

"Of course not," he recoils.

"Then what are you doing here?"

"I came to visit my oldest friend. Is that such a crime?"

Now begins the part where they talk over each other per usual and I stop listening. I have no interest in hearing about some theodolite someone left in Camaguey, or something.

Father sighs, "I know I should be angrier that the two of them were involved, but I swear their fights get funnier and funnier every time they're in each other's faces," his arms are slung over mine and Ophelia's shoulder, grinning from ear to ear. This argument is nothing new, all of us have heard it before, though I must say today's is surprisingly civilized. Dollars to donuts because of the lack of priceless breakables readily available to throw at one another.

At least she has someone to banter with.

Their bickering catches more than one wandering ear. Including my fuming mother who's storming toward us and all but barks through gritted teeth, "What in God's name are you two blathering about!"

Fingers are pointed, and more surly names are yelled back and forth, but I stop caring. With all the attention on them, and Father and Ophelia headed for the dinner table, it's the perfect opportunity to make my escape.

Keeping my smile on my lips, I back away from the scene, eager for an extra-long bath to work off some of tension, in the water and then between my sheets, but not before sultry cologne hits my senses, and I turn straight into a solid chest.

"Hi," Skylan grins.

"Hi," I'm not sure if I said it out loud. I'm too floored to know the difference between up and down.

I hear elated voices and laughter from somewhere behind me, but my body is frozen in place. And Sky's rich eyes are all that's keeping me from shivering. Neither of us make a move other than slowly taking each other hands. Somehow, I'm the first to break the silence. "You're back," I say softly, my lips turning up in a smile.

He smirks, lowering his head. "I told you I would be."

I search his eyes for more. "I didn't hear from you. I thought you weren't coming."

His chest vibrates with a low chuckle I feel all the way from my fingers down to apex of my thighs. "Easy now, Em-Em. You'll make me think you missed me."

Oh, who am I kidding? I did miss him. Not that I'd ever say it out loud. This kingdom isn't big enough for both of our oversized egos.

"You're breathtaking," he breathes, eyeing the dress up and down.

I do my best to play off the rampant fluttering in my belly, though I'm not sure how convincing I am.

"I had an excellent stylist," I give him a playful shrug. "I think he deserves a raise."

He doesn't answer. His eyes fill with a strange synergy of wonder and bewilderment I've never quite seen before. His hands tighten on mine, and he slowly pulls me closer, despite his body stiffening as he does.

"Sky?" I watch him curiously, wondering what's going through his head. I wish now more than anything I could read his mind.

"Why are you looking at me like that?"

"It's just… I, uh…" he swallows, shaking his head, rejoining reality from wherever he went. "Nothing." He smiles. "Dance with me?"

My lips curve upward as I follow him to the dancefloor, as ladylike as I can manage without trembling like a Chihuahua. Sky pulls me close and slides his hand around my hip, firmly settling his warm palm in the small of my back.

"What in the world was that about?" he asks as I close my hand over his upper arm.

I glance over my shoulder to where Asaria and King Val are still arguing the night away and roll my eyes. "Lover's quarrel."

"Lovers?" he recoils, "But she's like…"

"Half his age? Yeah, I know. Everyone knows."

I turn my head back, watching a sly grin spread and nod his approval. "Way to go, Asaria."

"Just wait until she stomps away. He'll follow her like the puppy he is and they'll end up screwing in the back of his car as always."

His head falls back in laughter. "What is not to love about Alorewyn?" he shakes his head. "Fine wine." He lets go of my hand, spins me around, then pulls me close again. "Finer women. Win-win if you ask me."

"Oh, my God, are you always this smug?" I recoil, laughing.

"Don't need to be. I have my father's smolder," he wiggles his eyebrows, "Let me be your Prince Skylan."

"Don't you mean Prince Charming?"

"Darling, please. Look at me," Sky spins me again. This time leaning his forehead against mine when he pulls me back. I'd say he's a cocky bastard, but that much has already been established at the beginning of this story. "I have all the charming you need. And I'll give it all to you, my pretty, pretty Princess." He brings my knuckles to his lips, and presses a soft kiss. "If you'll let me."

I shake my head laughing. "Sure, Prince Skylan. You may be charming, but you also have the affinity for being a complete pain in the ass."

Sky chuckles as he pulls me close, letting me lay my head against his chest, feeling his heart beating almost as wildly as mine, and we fall in comfortable silence as we slowly sway to the orchestra.

I'm trying not to focus on how much I missed having him so close. Or how his skin reminds me of every one of my favorite memories we shared.

Our first kiss. The first time he touched me, and I begged him not to stop. Every precious moment I'll cherish forever, knowing it may never happen again.

I'm not sure why now of all times it dawns on me just how young Skylan is. How young we both are for that matter, and how we'll eventually have this colossal job of making sure entire kingdoms, millions of citizens, thriving economies, and several hundred allegiances and trade agreements survive the trials and tribulations of time.

No pressure.

"Em?" Sky eases back, finding my eyes once I lift my head.

"Yes?"

"Do you think…" he swallows, a gentle grin turning his lips upward.

"Can we maybe just start over?"

My head tilts to the side, "What do you mean?"

"Just, forget it all. Like the last few years never happened?"

"Forget?" I drop his hands and step away from him. "Forget that you broke my heart and left without so much as a single word?"

He reaches for me but I back away another step. He doesn't get to touch me. Ever again if I have my way.

"Emryne."

"Don't. You want me to forget the weeks I spent crying because I didn't know where you were or whether you were alive or not?" His eyes are full of regret as reaches for me again. "Forget that I thought you hated me and that everything that happened between us was a stupid mistake?"

"You were never a mistake," he says softly, yet his tone is determined.

I scoff, ignoring him. "No, Skylan. I will never forget that."

I turn and walk out of the ballroom, good mood over.

Chapter 14
Skylan
E for Vigilante

"Emryne!" I call, following her from the crowded ballroom and into the hallway leading to the foyer staircase.

If I had an arcade ticket for every time I've ran after a woman who clearly hated my guts, I'd get one of those tiny erasers that disappeared the first time you used it. Ipso facto, it never happened at all.

I knew Emryne in that waterfall of endless ruby would be a feast for the eyes, but fuck, I wasn't expecting her to steal the breath from my lungs the second I walked into the ballroom.

She really isn't a little girl anymore.

She's halfway to the staircase before I catch up with her, gripping her forearm and pulling her toward me before she can climb the steps. "Emryne, wait. I'm sorry."

"Sorry?" She shouts, eyes of ocean blue brimming with tears. "Sorry? That's all you have to say?"

"I was a stupid kid, what do you want from me?"

"So was I, Skylan," I hear her voice crack with her words, fighting to keep her composure. And I hate that she has to. I hate that we're here right now, knowing it's my fault. "I was eighteen years old. I was alone. And you left me there."

I don't answer. How can I when she's right?

She scoffs and yanks herself free. "Whatever."

Best I can do at this point is blink at her, and try to gulp down my nerves. Not that it works.

I know this conversation won't be easy for her to hear, but it's time we talk about it. She deserves the truth.

Neither of us spoke for seemed like an eternity, the silence a deafening curtain.

As gently as I can, I say, "I told you not to get attached," and I did. I've said the same thing to every other woman I've been with. I've never seen the appeal in a relationship, not when I was a teenager at least. I've never wanted a relationship. Or maybe I've never wanted a steady relationship before. Not until now. Because they weren't her.

"Oh, right. Like that would've stopped any girl," she climbs off the bottom step and walks around the mahogany banister to the small passageway below the stairs, and stops a few feet short of a set of heavily embellished closed double doors. "I cared about you long before we slept together."

Her confession demands a staggering halt, forcing me to swallow my guilt before speaking. "I… I didn't… I had no idea," I'm lying. I knew, but I couldn't deal with it all. It was too much at once.

"Of course, you didn't. Because I'm easily replaceable. Right?" she states.

"No! You're not." I shake my head at her. She wants to put all cards on the table? Fine. "How was I supposed to deal, Emryne? Huh? I was barely twenty years old, how was I supposed to deal with my mother's death, my father's near death in the last separatist attack, knowing I had weeks before my eligibility and dealing with every ounce of stress that went along with it *and* juggle what I felt about you? Tell me how?"

"You could've been honest with me," she answers with confidence. "I could've put my feelings aside if that's what you needed."

"Could you?" I step toward her, no longer caring about keeping a respectable distance between us. "You told me the last night we slept together that I was it for you. All you've ever wanted. Could you honestly have put your feelings aside and waited for me to come home? *If* I ever came home?"

"Yes." She answers assuredly.

I scoff. "Could you?" Not the Emryne I knew back then.

"Yes, Skylan, damn you!" she slams her palms against my chest. "Do you not know me at all? If you told me what you were going through, I would've let you go if that's what you needed. I cried for you for weeks. Weeks, Skylan! Do you have any idea what that's like?"

Again, I have no answer.

She rolls her eyes and snorts, even with the tears threatening freedom and her shaking voice. "You told me you'd always be there when I needed you."

I turn my eyes downward, unable to keep the guilt flooding my chest from seeping into my voice. "I know."

"You told me we'd always be together," she steps closer, her eyes never falter once.

And I hold mine strong. "I did."

"You told me—"

"I know what I said, Emryne. Jesus, you don't need to make me feel worse about this than I already do."

A pause, as Emryne studies me closely. Like a million words are flying around her head and she's fighting to figure out which to focus on first.

"Fine," Emryne says after a breath, crossing her arms and straightening her shoulders as she blinks the tears away. "Then let me make it easy for you. Go home."

My heart stutters in my chest, stunned at her words. That's not what I meant at all. "What?"

"Go home, and live your life, Skylan. Forget me, forget all of this. Find yourself someone you actually care about." She turns to walk away but I grab her and spin her back into my chest.

"Let go," she growls through gritted teeth, her cheeks puffing like an angry kitten. It's actually kind of cute.

"No."

"Skylan, let me go," she struggles in my hold again, but my grip tightens.

"No," I press. She can beat the living daylights out of me as much as she wants, but I refuse to leave things like this.

I feel her arm slack, and she steps right in my face. Her chest flush against mine. "Let. Go. Of. Me."

Her perfume fills my senses, and any control I've had for the last few months, snaps.

My lips crash against hers. Soft, warm, and perfect. Just like she is.

Emryne fights me at first, squeezing her lips together, sparring for dominance, but the longer our mouths battle, the more she relaxes, and the more we lose ourselves completely.

Her protests lessen, and she finally opens, allowing my tongue to dance over her own. A sweet moan escapes her, and she wraps her arms around my neck, pulling me closer and tangling her fingers in my hair.

Fuck, I've been craving this. Craving her for so damn long I feel like I've forgotten myself. Forgotten how good she feels in my arms, and how soft her lips are. Definitely forgotten with how much passion she kisses, and how well her body fits against mine.

It was only a matter of time before we eventually lost the little game we played and we both knew it. Made an even bigger one the more we challenged each other to see who would cave first.

When we finally break, lips swollen, cheeks flushed, I keep my forehead to hers. My hands cup her cheeks, wiping away her hot tears with my thumbs.

"Look, I messed up. I ran away at the first sign of feeling something. I was a coward. I know that now," I shake my head, searching for the right words. "It's… I just… with everything that was happening, my mom, Dad almost dying? I wasn't ready for anything serious yet. I wasn't ready for *you*. If he knew we were in a relationship, he never would have left my side, made me become king, and marry you. Neither of us were ready for that type of commitment, you know we weren't.

"Hell, we barely are now. There was so much I wanted to do, so much I needed to see. I needed to get my head together before making the biggest decision of my life. And I know how selfish that sounds, but I couldn't go through with something so permanent without knowing who I am, and the best way, the only way to discover that was to get away. I wouldn't have treated you the way you deserved. I wouldn't have been able to take care of you."

"How could you possibly know that?" she sniffles.

That earns her a laugh. "Emryne, how was I supposed to take care of you when I could barely take care of myself? I would've resented you. And you don't deserve that."

"Well, then are you…" she shifts, and swallows, asks with a tight voice, "Are you saying you ready now?"

"I don't know."

She had to be sure. Of course, she did. I know she didn't want to hope I'm being serious if this was just some cute speech.

So, I give her that. "But I want to try. That's why I'm here. I never lied to you when I told you I was," I take her hands, welcoming her warmth. "Emryne, the second I was made aware of your eligibility I dropped everything and accepted that invitation."

"But why?" she pushes, shaking her head.

"You think I could stand the idea of seeing you with someone else?" I answer easily, though my voice had a definite edge. The very idea of that drives me into blinding rage. "You think I could stand the thought of anyone touching you the way you let me touch you? Moan their name, came on their tongue the way you did mine? Or imagine you looking up at them with these eyes? So bright, and so beautiful, and my favorite part about you? Flattering them with this pretty, pretty smile? It made me sick."

Emryne lowers her head, a small smile tugging at her lips.

"I'm sorry for being an asshole. I swear, it wasn't my intention to hurt you." Her breath catches in her chest. My lips turn up and I nudge her chin for her to look at me. "Can we please just start over? Please?"

Impossibly blue eyes dart between mine. I know she wants to, but it'll take time. I've hurt her, deeper than I've ever imagined, and I can only hope she'll find it somewhere in her heart to give me a chance to make this right.

"I don't know, Sky. I don't know if I can forgive you."

"I'm not asking you to," I shake my head. "Not yet anyway. All I'm asking for is a chance to make this right. Please," my voice lowers, "please let me make this right?"

She swallows. "It's going to take a lot more than an apology. I'm not that forgiving teenage girl anymore." No, she's not. She's all woman. A woman I want more than anything.

I nod anyway. Relieved she's at least willing to give this a try.

"I have a lot of making up to do, I know," I need her to hear me. Now more than ever. "And if I have to spend my every waking moment proving how much you mean to me, then I will."

I watch as her eyes close. She breathes out a heavy breath, then opens them again, her bright smile warming my heart as whatever heaviness she held onto begins to disappear. "Okay."

A wonderful hope fills my body. "Okay?"

She laughs softly and nods again. "Okay." And her arms close around my neck, pressing her lips to mine in another sweet kiss. My arms wrap around her waist, pulling her even closer and backing her into the wall behind her.

For all I knew, we could've been standing like this for hours and neither of us were the wiser, until I lift my lips from hers but she shakes her head and pulls me back to her. "No. More."

Of course, I give her what she wants. I'd give her the world if it meant she'd allow me back into hers.

Our kiss is innocent at first, just to test the waters before I lose myself in the beauty that is Emryne Gennady of Alorewyn. But the longer I kiss her, the longer our tongues are locked in this virtuous tango, the quicker I realize there's nothing innocent about that mouth whatsoever. Not anymore. Taking her hands and lifting them above her head, I firmly spread my palms over her wrists, locking her in place.

On to a lighter note… there's still something I think is high time we address.

I pull back, and my lips spread in a shit-eating grin. "Em-Em…"

She grunts her annoyance. "Oh God, what is it now?"

I blink down at her, fighting to keep my laughter at bay. "You've been keeping secrets, Em-Em," I watch her brows furrow and her head tilt to the side, eyeing me curiously. "Tell me, what would the king think of your little shenanigans?"

Her smile disappears in a flash. I feel her arms tense under my hands, readying to free herself despite me having no intention to let her go. "I don't know what you're talking about."

"No?" I can't resist lowering my head down and running my tongue over her bottom lip. "Shall I inform him of my discoveries then? Tell him of you after-hour extra-curricular activities?"

Her head lifts from the wall as she challenges. "You wouldn't dare."

"Wouldn't I?" I tease, lifting my eyebrow.

She rolls her eyes. "It's not me," she can fight it all she wants, but I know what I saw, and who my opponent on that roof was.

I saw the guns when I followed her to the Port of Alorewyn two weeks ago too. And I agreed with her, interfering would've given her a one-way ticket to a shallow grave. I just couldn't resist biting her in the ass for it when I cornered her in that parking garage. And seeing her slip off the mask after climbing off the roof was icing on the cake. The black armor, the hood, the whole Xena Princess Warrior thing? Emryne written all over it.

Though a part of me is a little jealous of just how sophisticated her whole endeavor is.

I choke out a laugh. "I'm not an idiot, Emryne. I know what I saw. And you, my Princess, should pay closer attention to your surroundings."

"Wha—"

The thing I love most about Callior uniforms is its ability to conceal weapons. With so much heavy material, it's easy to find somewhere to stow something sharp. Like the old, jeweled dagger I nabbed off the wall beside her and hid under the rear lapels when my tongue was between her teeth. I let go of her wrists and rip it from behind my back with lightning speed, aiming for her throat. She catches my wrist not a split second later and redirects, spinning on the balls of her feet as she shoves me against the wall and presses the dagger into my throat.

God, it's been a while since I've been this hard.

Neither of us say a word for what feels like a millennium.

"Well," I breathe, releasing a deep chuckle, my voice barely escaping my lips while my willpower holds on by a thread. "What are you going to do now, Princess?"

Emryne's eyes dart between mine and my lips. Her own barely a few inches away. "What do you want, Skylan?"

I stare her down, taking in the ethereal beauty that is Emryne Gennady. Until I'm no longer capable of resisting the near painful erection threatening to strip the zipper on my pants.

I lower my head next to her ear, sucking her earlobe between my teeth, "I want *you*, Emryne," my voice barely a whisper as I declare, "I want to rip off that pretty dress. I want to shove you against a wall, and I want to fuck you until I my name is the only word left in your vocabulary."

Chapter 15
Emryne
A Long Time Coming

I only have split second to back out of this before I cross a line I know I won't be able to return from, but his fiery gaze keeping me in place has reawakened every fantasy I've ever had about Skylan. Some of them normal, some of them kind of messed up, and every single one ended with me screaming his name over, and over, and over again.

Our breaths tangle, eyes dart between each other's lips and my self-control snaps. The dagger drops to the ground, and I grab the lapels of his coat, pushing my breasts into his chest and crashing my lips onto his again, kissing the life out of him.

I feel his hand slide down my body and between my legs, trying to reach the one place aching for him to touch. But this dress has so many layers I don't feel a thing.

I pull back, sucking his bottom lip between my teeth. "Not here," Spinning around, I grab his hand, urging him to follow me through the heavy doors and locking it behind us once we're inside.

The music and laughter from the ball drowns out, and the gentle crackling from the lit fireplace is the only sound in the room.

Sky unbuttons his jacket and slides it from his massive shoulders, neatly draping it over the back of the faded turquoise lounger a few feet away from the fire before he walks around, surveying the room. "What is this place?"

I smile at his back. I've always loved this room. The wall-to-wall bookshelves and antique clocks, vases and porcelain sculptures remind me of the fairytales I used to love reading. Gets a little spooky in the dark though, not to mention it's one of the coldest rooms in the palace even in summer, which is exactly why I asked Des to light the fire a few hours after the ball started, just in case.

I spent hours in here as a child, holding each precious vase and ornament and studying them close, making up an origin story for each one. Like the witch who trapped her husband in the ginger jar, the pouncing tiger on it hand-painted, for a thousand years because he cheated on her. Or the red-headed lady in the painting on the wall to the right of the shelves, holding her glass orb she uses to spy on her enemies. Imagination really knew no bound when it came to this place.

But the story I'm most excited about is the one Sky and I are about to write. Something new and electrifying. Filled with twists, turns, and maybe even a few unexpected declarations of love.

"One of the informal lounges," I reply, joining him in front of the plush cushions.

Sky takes my hands and places them over his shoulders. I kick off my heels, bringing my lips to his in the softest of kisses, until I feel his hands snake around my waist, pulling me into him.

We stay locked in each other's embrace, tongues in a battle for dominance, slowly chipping away the anger I held toward him.

"Turn around," he whispers against my lips, gripping my sides.

I do as he asks, keeping my eyes glued to his and slowly spinning until I'm facing the crackling flames. Sky's fingers brush my bare shoulders before trailing down my back until he reaches the bottom of the corset lace-up, untying the bow keeping my dress secured over my body. I catch it before it falls and spin to face him, using my free hand to push at his chest. Only when he sits back into the lounger do I let the heavy material slide down my body.

I hear Skylan's breath hitch as I climb out of the gown, kicking it aside and away from the glowing embers.

His eyes fill with mischievous heat as they travel down my body, setting on the burgundy lingerie.

I decided a while ago I wouldn't be sleeping with anyone until I found the person I wanted to be with for the rest of my life. Whether that person is Skylan I have no idea, but I need this.

This is a really bad idea, but I need the release, crave it after months of repression. I need to feel again.

I did miss this. I missed *him*.

He licks his lips and takes my hand, pulling me into his lap so I straddle him. "Is this for me?" He brushes his fingertips over my, down and over my panties, an up again.

I bite my lip, slowly nodding as I slide my hands over his shoulders.

"Fuck, I love it when you do that," he rasps, shaking his head. "Lucky me," he breathes out, guiding my lips down to his. This time, I don't bother keeping my tongue to myself. I'm done holding back. So I give him everything I have with this kiss. Every fantasy. Every hope, and every desire.

"You have no idea how long I've been waiting for this," he moans. Nips, bites, all the way between my breasts, leaving the most delicious marks on my skin.

Me either. "Touch me."

His mouth leaves my chest, darting his eyes to mine. "Can I?"

"Yes," I all but moan as he runs his tongue along my jaw. "Please, Sky."

Neither of us waste any more time. My fingers work unbuttoning the perfectly ironed white dress shirt, freeing his heavily muscled body on my fingertips and my sex clenches as feel his smooth, steel chest under my palms. My hands travel down to his waist and I go to work unbuckling his belt, ripping the leather off, and finally unzipping his pants. I slip my hand into boxers, and salivating at the hits of precum already escaping his erection as I work his shaft up and down coating his cock, somehow resisting the feminine urge to lick my fingers.

"Fuck," his head rolls back for a split second before his hand grips my neck, and he pulls my lips back to his. Sparks of the purest, most delicious pleasure fills my body as I angle my hips downward and my piercing rubs against Sky's manhood.

My head falls back as a moan escapes my throat. His fingers loop around my back, unclipping the strapless bra and letting it fall to the floor.

"Fuck, Emryne," he hisses, running his fingertips over my pert nipples, sending shivers racing down my spine. He bends down, sucking one between his teeth, gently biting down, swirling his tongue around the bud. He plays, licks, and flicks it between his teeth, until I feel hints of my impending orgasm slowly starting to build.

This is a wild lust I've never quite experienced before. Every touch, every kiss, every whisper urging me to grind harder, kiss wilder, feel my final climax inch closer and closer, begging me for sweet release.

Though I can't say I'm surprised, the things Sky does with his fingers alone should be put on some kind of list.

An A-list, a wanted list, world's-most-dangerous list, I don't care, as long as it's on there.

As his fingers travel down my body and between my thighs, it dawns on my just how much things have changed since the last time he touched me. "Wait," I mumble against his lips. Before he could find my soaking center and find the unexpected, gold-studded surprise. "Wait, Sky, I have to tell you something."

"Tell me after," he moans against my mouth.

"No, I have to tell you now."

He grunts his disapproval, but leaves my lips before his tongue finds my neck again. "What is it, darling?"

"Some things have… changed since the last time we slept together."

"Mmm, I know, darling," he takes my nipple between his fore- and middle finger, and squeezes hard. He chuckles deeply as another throaty moan escapes my lips and my hand weaves in his dark hair. "You've gotten sexier."

Sky glides his hand between my thighs, this time giving my aching pussy a long, firm stroke, and the words tumble from my lips.

"I have a piecing."

Chapter 16
Skylan
The Goddess of Gold

"I have a piercing."

"Okay, cool." Why she feels the need to tell me this now I have no idea.

"No," she lifts my head. "Sky, I have a piercing."

My eyebrow lifts in confusion. I don't know if this is her stalling or her way of telling me she's backing out, but the way she was grinding against me not two seconds ago says it isn't the latter.

So, what gives? "Yeah, great. And you're telling me this now because…?"

"I just… don't want you to freak out when you see it."

"What are you talking about? Why would I freak—" My confusion disappears, my breath catches in my throat as reality barrels into me.

"You…" No… surely not. Not innocent little Emryne Gennady?…

"Emryne."

She searches my face, then let's me go. "I shouldn't have said anything. Forget it."

She shifts backward, climbing off my lap, but I reach up and grab her, spinning her around and pushing her on her back. Her perfect breasts bounce as she hits the cushions, and my fingers hook her panties, savagely greedy to see her. If she's telling me the truth. My eyes never leave hers as she lifts her hips, urging me to pull the pretty lace thing down.

She bites her lip, hesitant, but I spread her legs all the same.

And there it is, in all it's golden, pearl-studded excellence. I nearly weep at the sight of her.

On a scale of one to hell, how inappropriate would it be to sing hallelujah?

"Jesus Christ," I mutter. I have my own goddess.

The way she said it made it obvious it's freaked someone out before. What man in their right mind would?

Fucking pussies.

If this is what she thinks it takes for me to leave a room running, she clearly doesn't remember me very well. What's more, that she felt confident enough to go through with something like this? This is the hottest thing I've ever seen. Though Emryne's confidence has always been a turn on.

My eyes travel up her thighs, hooking her legs over my shoulders.

"Don't ever run from me again," I declare, my voice glutted with lust. I lower my mouth to her swollen center, rolling her piercing between my teeth before flattening my tongue.

A sudden gasp escapes her as she jerks forward, weaving her hand in my hair and pushing herself into my mouth. "Oh God… Sky…" she moans, fucking my tongue, filling my body with wild need.

Emryne is my goddess, and I desperately want to be her god. And if she was queen, I'd happily serve as king beside her. I'd rule this country with a goddamned iron fist if it meant I got to be inside her after a busy day. And if we should return home victorious, beaten and bloody from battle, it's her arms, her body, her perfectly wet pussy I'll retreat to after nursing our wounds. It's her moans I'll crave, her I'll watch come undone on my cock, knowing I'm the only man capable of making her feel this way. Holy hell. I didn't think it possible but my cock hardened even more.

There's nothing I'd love more than taking her bare, but I'm so goddamn hard for this woman I already won't last long as it is, and I want the first time I come inside her not to be on a tiny lounger in a tiny room where I can barely watch her ride me let alone enjoy her screams echoing the walls.

So, I opt for plan B. For now. "Condoms?"

"Black panther jar behind you," she mumbles, body squirming under my touch.

I chuckle, straightening and grabbing the pouncing figurine off the mantle above the roaring fireplace, and hand it to her. She unscrews the head and dumps about seven unopened wrappers on the couch next to her.

"Do I want to know why this is here?" I ask with careful intent. Preferably nothing to do with her sleeping with other men.

She raises a brow with a smirk. "Uhm, have you met Asaria?"

I shake my head laughing, and she joins me. Because we both know it's true. And we laugh, as if for the first time in months. Years. Quiet at first, then an all-together, belly-aching, deep laughter. Just like we used to. Until her head falls back, and my hand finds her neck, gently nudging her fiery blue eyes back to mine. I link my fingers in hers, pulling her upward until her gorgeously naked body is against mine.

My fingers travel down her curves, soft and gentle and beautiful, down, and down until I grip her hips.

"God, I missed you, darling."

Her eyes sparkle in the fire light, giving me another perfect smile. "I missed you too," her fingers hook around my pants and pull down, freeing my cock. She wraps her hand around my shaft, pumping me a good three or four times before I take her hand, spinning us around and sitting down, beckoning her to straddle me. As much as I love her mouth around me, I need her touch, to get lost in her like I did before.

She sucks her lip between her teeth again, taking a step toward me and climbing into my lap. She reaches next to her and grabs a condom, tearing it open, and expertly rolling it on. I can't wait any longer. I need to be inside her, to feel her around me as she rides her way to blissful release.

I settle myself under her, ready for her perfect warmth, and wrap my hand around the back of her neck, lowering her lips to mine.

"Show me the way home," I rasp, and I take her mouth as she sinks into me.

Emryne sucks in a breath, and I have no choice but to do the same in effort to keep from embarrassing myself. There's no way I'm coming before she does.

She links her fingers with mine, settling them on her butt before she wraps her hands around my shoulders, lifting and lowering herself until she finds a good rhythm, and our breaths weave together.

I've had some good sex in my twenty-three years of life, but none of them in any way compares to my Princess. God, this woman is ecstasy personified.

She continues her rocking, moaning as her orgasm builds more and more, but I grip her hips, guiding her deeper until my entire length stretches her, over, and over, and over again.

"Slow down, darling. Deep, and slow. That's where I want you."

Mark my words, there will be plenty more times to fuck the shit out of each other like old times, but tonight, all I want is to enjoy her, get to know her body again. And I want her to enjoy this as much as I am.

This moment isn't about me. It's about her, making amends for abandoning her when I should've known better. And watching her? Screaming no one's name but mine as she came around me?

Who said God never answered prayers?

Chapter 17
Emryne
Mistakes Not Twice Made,
Most of the Time

Three.

That's how many times we had sex last night, how many times Skylan came. Twice inside me, against the wall and on the lounger, and once on my ass with my hands and knees on the floor after he took me from behind.

Hell of a way to make up after an argument.

Today marks the first day since turning twenty-one I've slept in. I'm rested, relaxed, rejuvenated, I have the most delicious ache between my thighs… and I'm as confused as ever.

I ignored every part of me shouting what a stupid idea sleeping with him was, pushed it so far away until it drowned in the satisfaction my body so desperately craved, and I did it anyway.

What pissed me off to no extent is that Sky still is the only man capable of getting me off. I don't know if it's the attachment I guess I formed after he took my virginity (I'm not a psychologist, nor will I *ever* consent to seeing one), or if he is just *that* good, or maybe it was because I see an actual future with Sky that had me all hung up on him. All I know is, none one I'd been with ever came close; they either had a great mouth, and boring dick, or the other way around. Then there was Skylan, who was supernaturally phenomenal at both to this damn day. Did he unknowingly turn me into a naughty little sex machine? Based on last night alone, yes and yes.

Braden Hastings, the six-foot, blond-haired, sky blue-eyed stunner of a grandson of Prime Minister Fredrich, was the last time I'd sort of not faked my orgasm with.

Okay fine, I didn't. How could I? The guy was a carbon copy of a young James Dean. It wasn't crazy fireworks, but we had fun after the disaster that was little Alex (and we all know how that went). Hell, my father almost walked in on our steamy sexcapades more than once, but it didn't last. He'd just broken up with his girlfriend, Skylan had just left, it always would've been rebound sex and both of us knew it.

Before him was Téo DeWitt. My version of McDreamy. He was Pre-med at Alorewyn State University I met at a frat party Tory and Beth somehow convinced me to attend after a five-month dry spell, only problem was he couldn't get it up unless he was heavily under the influence. Only made that mistake once.

We never made it past pulling his shirt over his head before he passed out. Guy didn't even remember meeting me when I saw him at Beth's sorority house mixer a few weeks later, thank God.

Keith tried the night of Maverick's party, and it probably would've worked had I not been torn away, torn into by Skylan, then having my clothes ceremoniously torn *off* and fucked every which way but missionary on every visible surface of his massive bedroom, and he wasn't exactly gentle either. Neither of us were. Angry sex at its best.

And then he left. And I finally know why.

I did confess my feelings before he disappeared. But I was so wrapped up in *Skylan*, wrapped up in the moment *with* Skylan, his beauty, his masculinity, in the idea of him, and the fact I was the one he gave his undivided attention to when he had his pick of women in Alorewyn and Callior both? Combine that with the security I felt in the center of my very soul when he held me in his arms, you bet your ass fell. Hard.

Intimacy is a notorious trickster, and I'm scared the idea of him still is much prettier than the reality of him.

I'm not sure what I expected him to say after he finally told me the truth, but he surprised me when he did.

The pain he felt after losing his mother I totally get, but his father? We've always known the separatists were a problem, yet it makes no sense why King Harryson wouldn't request for reinforcements.

Hell, I would've thrown away every item of clothing I owed and worn Callior's armor for the rest of my life if I knew the situation was that bad and they needed the help.

I'm trying to keep being mad at him but… I get it. I'm not saying I agree with how he handled it, or that I in any way would've done the same, but I get it. I thrive under pressure. Mostly because I'm addicted to the adrenaline that goes along with it. He accesses the situation from every angle while I face the problem head-on. It's the one place Skylan and my personalities differ. He choked, that much was obvious. He choked and ran away.

I snuck away somewhere between three and four this morning, leaving a snoozing Sky tucked under the thick mohair throw blanket and walked straight into a steaming, twelve jet shower, cleaning myself and him off my body. And the only thing I was capable of thinking about was the images of us. How well we fit together. His heated breath in my ear, riding him slow and deep, feeling every inch of him, his lips against mine. Coming apart inside me. With me.

Three. Damn. Times.

"Oh my—Asa… Emrie. Emrie!" Ophelia calls, wiggling her eyebrows, thankfully pulling me back to reality before I soak yet another pair of underwear, leaning over Asa's open luggage and holding up the thinnest black lace G-string I've ever seen in my life. She shakes her head, twirling the material on her forefinger. "Do you wear this or use it as dental floss?"

My body shakes with laughter so wild I tumble off Asaria's bed, which only makes me laugh harder, just as my freshly showered sister pokes her head out of her bathroom and throws a wet towel at Ophelia's head. "You have absolutely no taste. For your information, those have gotten me out of three term papers, two parking tickets, *and* a DUI," she flicks her wet hair over her shoulder.

Perks of being royalty folks.

"What am I hearing!" My jaw is on the floor at her confession. I know we're all wild bunch but this is just insane. "Aren't you supposed to set an example and be a good role model?"

"Oh please, roll that model straight out the door, babe," she kicks her leg out, dramatically sweeping her hand down her thigh and slapping her butt. "I am nothing but a bad influence, and I regret nothing." Such a drama queen. And completely unapologetic about it. "Frankly, what you should be doing is taking notes."

I shake my head, sipping from my raspberry mimosa. Sparingly, mind you. Asa wasn't shy with the sparkling wine.

Ophelia tilts her glass back, but rips it away from her lips after swallowing. "Jesus, Asa. Did you have to pour both bottles in here?" "What?" she quips. "I'm about to endure two weeks with your mother, it's a miracle I haven't been in a constant state of inebriation since we got here."

After eating nothing but Skylan last night and the two hours of sleep I ended up getting before Ophelia dragged me from my sheets and to Asa's bedroom, I was starving by the time we burst through her doors with Moni and Des behind, decorating her breakfast table with enough food for a village and enough mimosas to intoxicate a… well, us. I sink back into Asaria's pillows, releasing a long breath and biting into a vanilla protein muffin.

"Someone's looking very relaxed today," Ophelia singsongs, tucking a pillow under her arm next to me.

"I agree," Asa saunters closer, combing her brush through her wet hair. "Could it possibly have something to do with you and a certain eligible prince running from the ballroom last night?"

Ophelia smirks. "Hmm… what was that about I wonder?"

"It was a conversation," I feign modesty. "Which got pretty heated, so I walked out because I didn't want to cause a scene, and he followed me."

"Oh, I bet," Asa remarks sarcastically, carefully eyeing me up and down, then crosses her arms. "Did you fight or fuck?"

Ain't that the question for the ages.

"Asaria!" Ophelia shouts outraged. I forgot my sister and swearing is like oil and water.

"Better shut your ears, dear, the adults are talking," she says and waves a hand, turning back to me. "What happened?"

"We talked about some stuff, that's all," I don't give them a straight answer, though I'm not entirely sure why. My sisters are the last people to judge, hell they'd encourage me if it wasn't Skylan at the receiving end of my tongue. But a part of me feels guilty knowing what a stupid idea it was. Not to mention breaking the law.

"Oh please, I know what a woman looks like after being dick-down," Asa says, popping a fresh donut hole in her mouth.

"And how would that be?" I challenge, though I know exactly what she's going to say.

She lifts a perfectly manicured eyebrow. "Exactly the way you are now."

"Oh my God, Emrie, you slept with him?" Ophelia chimes.

I feign an innocently lopsided grin. "It… was an accident?"

"Oh, it was an accident," Asaria claps her hands together. "Okay. So, you what? Slipped and fell onto his cock?"

I bite my lip, shrinking back in my seat and wishing the earth would swallow my whole, I'm about to explain when Ophelia holds up her hand, "Don't bother. We saw how you reacted when he showed up last night. The two of you have so much sexual tension between you I'm surprised it took this long. Just, be careful, okay? You know how you can get around Skylan."

"Which is how, exactly?"

"Like he's the one who painted the sky with stars," she replies frankly.

I shrug my shoulder, playing it off. "It's not like we're dating, we just had sex. It's not a big deal."

"I'm going to pretend that I don't know that you just broke about… what, seven laws, screwing a crowned prince and just say again, be careful. I don't want to see you like the last time he disappointed you."

"I know, okay!" I fly from her bed, and walk over to Asa, sitting down next to her on the lime green leather couch. "I know. I'm really not putting much heart into this," I think…

"That's what you say every time," Asa mumbles, emptying her glass.

I ignore her. "The sex is one thing, but Skylan wants a queen, not a porn star. He wouldn't be here if he didn't."

Not much has changed about Asa's room. No one ever uses it, or Ophelia's for that matter, other than her when she visits, so all the retro furniture, from her purple lava lamp top the shaggy, floral carpets, and the NSYNC posters are exactly where she left them before leaving for college.

"I'm pretty sure Skylan *is* a porn star," Ophelia remarks, pouring herself another glass.

Both my and Asa eyes shoot to her.

"What?"

At least she says something. I'm stunned beyond words.

"Yeah, I saw the video a couple of weeks ago," she brushes it off as if it's nothing. I'd say it's very un-Ophelia-like, but she barely speaks about her sex life. I'm impressed she actually said something.

"Since when do you watch porn?" I question.

"Since I occasionally like spicing up my and Leo's sex life," she shrugs her shoulder, as if it's the most innocent thing. It wouldn't have bothered me as much if she wasn't watching the prince with who I have a longer history than the vampires from The Twilight Saga. But it was.

"And you... saw the video?" I spoke slowly. This can't be true. She's out of her mind.

Asaria is out of her seat with her phone in her hand in a flash, ferociously tapping the screen.

Her lips turn down as she shakes her head, as if she only realized now the gravity of exactly what she just admitted. "I... uh... No. No, why would I?"

She gasps, "Oh my God, she's telling the truth," she angles the phone toward us. "Skylan has a sex tape!"

And she's not kidding. I'd recognize that smolder anywhere.

Somewhere with evergreen mountains behind them, the camera smoothly pans on Skylan in slow motion, strolling closer to a beautifully slender, dark-haired woman, naked and splayed out on a beach lounger in the sunshine next a giant swimming pool. She mumbles something I'm guessing is in Italian, the one language I never learned, and Sky goes down on his knees, pulling her closer and hooking her legs over his shoulders. She writhes under him, moaning while she grips fistfuls of his hair as the camera zooms in on his face effectively devouring her.

I half expected it to be something stupid and old-school: him dressed as pool boy, or pizza boy asking for money, but no. This is classy. It's kind of... hot. And I despise it.

It shouldn't matter, what he did with his time traveling the world should be his and his alone, but I can't stop the jealously kidnapping the oxygen reserved for my lungs.

I feel my throat tighten as she pushes him on his back, taking his length into her mouth. God, the woman looks like she's swallowing him whole.

"Oh hell, how am I supposed to compete with that?"

"I have to learn how to do that!" Asa shrieks, rewinding the video and watching her sucking him again. "Alright, Skylan," she smirks, zooming in on his fully erect penis. "Does his ass really look like that?"

Ophelia smacks her shoulder, clicking her tongue and slapping Asa's phone from her hands. "Stop looking at it! He's Emrie's boyfriend. She should be the one who learns how to do it."

I grunt. "He is not my boyfriend," That would require us entering into something monogamous, something I'm not ready for. Also, my sucking skills are just fine, thank you very much. Phenomenal, if I believe the compliments I've gotten over the years.

"And no. I already have the piercing, I don't need any fancy stuff," the words tumble out before I can stop myself, and I slap my hand over my lips. Shit.

Asa's brow lifts. "Piercing?"

"What piercing?" Ophelia sits up.

"Uh… uhm…"

"Emryne Charlotte Gwendolyn Gennady, what piercing?" Asa says, beaming with every word. And my knowing smirk answers her question.

Ophelia's lips fall slack, and they both let out a simultaneous shriek followed by a string of questions one after the other.

"Where?" Think that's kind of obvious.

"When?"

"Who?"

"What!"

"You need to spill," Asa flops down next to me and grabs my arms, shaking me from side to side. "Spill, spill!"

"One at a time!" I laugh. Geez, is this what it feels like being a kindergarten teacher? No wonder they start smoking. "It was kind of a last-ditch decision."

"I am so proud of you!" Asa claps, beaming.

And Ophelia looks at her, mortified. "Oh, my God! You put her up to this?"

"I dared her when she was like, seventeen," she deadpans. True. She mentioned she was considering it, but we never spoke about it again. "After she lost her virginity."

"You lost your virginity at *seventeen*! No one ever tells me anything!"

"Oh, we've tried, but you're too busy watching porn with your husband to care," Asa chides, eliciting another fit of giggles so hard my stomach cramps. I missed my sister a lot.

A light knocking comes from the door, then it opens, welcoming a smiling Addylin, still in her orange frilly pjs.

Well, I guess we all slept in.

"There you are," Ophelia says. "I didn't talk to you all night," she gets up and walks over, wrapping her in a tight hug.

"Please tell me there's food," she squeezes our sister tight.

Asa beckons her. "A buffet worthy of the future queens."

Addy and I share a pointed look, which she brushes off and makes her way over to the table and pouring herself a cup of tea and grinning at me. "Really, Em? Raspberry?"

"I'm a whore," I shrug playfully. "You know that." I was referring to the tart little red fruit, but now I'm not so sure anymore.

I know we've have changed in the time been apart, and usually something as trivial as a sex tape wouldn't have bothered me in the least, but it's Skylan.

The first man I gave my body and my heart to.

Fuck it. Let him have the hot Italian. If the decision wasn't easy enough already, based on what I saw today, one thing's for damn sure: it won't be happening ever, ever again.

Chapter 18
Emryne
Well...

Fuck.

He's lying in bed next to me, sheets draped over his finally complacent manhood with rows of golden abs on full display. His arms tucked behind his head with the smuggest, biggest shit-eating grin I've ever seen on his face.

Oh, you bet I thought about that stupid fucking video the whole time he was inside me. And I made sure to ride him twice as hard as the foreign woman on that lounger. He wanted to be screwed like a porn star?

Challenge accepted.

And then, per usual, it stopped being about revenge and started feeling... just so fucking good.

"Well, that didn't go as expected."

"Really? Went exactly as I expected," he flips on his side, jokingly rolling his eyes. "I mean you practically threw yourself at me."

I bark out an outraged laugh. "I did not!"

I did. I did exactly that. It's twelve-thirty-nine a.m., an hour and a half after I ran into him on my way back from the spending the day in the training room. Sometimes working out, others lying on the floor staring at the roof while listening to one of the seventeen Spotify playlists, flipping between melancholy and straight-up eighties ballads. Then when I stopped feeling sorry for myself, got my ass up off the floor and switched back to one of my workout mixes. Instead of sticking my AirPods in like I usually would, Eminem filled the space through the mounted speakers in the corners of the room. And I worked out. *Hard.* Pushed myself to the limit like I haven't done in a good while. After leaving Asa's room my mind was a mess. God knows I needed it.

I was exhausted. Drenched with sweat by the time I trudged up the staircase on wobblily legs, only to be hit by a tidal wave of need as my thoughts drifted back to the night before—I hoped I could work it off with some heavy weight lifting—to no avail. I walked straight into a bare-chested, smirking Skylan, whose body also happened to be dripping. Which I didn't bother asking where he got from but shamelessly licked it off his collarbone the second my bedroom door locked before shredding his clothes with absurd speed, and climbing him like a tree after I pushed him into the shower jets.

"Denial is not sexy, Emryne," he says, getting to his feet and striding to the mini fridge next to my desk and grabbing us each a bottle of water.

"Neither is world domination, Skylan," my world domination. I swear this was the guy's vendetta from the second he walked into this palace. Conquering me and my body like only he could.

He chucks the bottle my way and stops at the foot of my bed, twisting the cap and gulping down half of his, then throwing the bottle on the bed next to me.

"Isn't it? I am supposed to be evil, remember?" Sky smirks, lifting his pinky, sticking it in the corner of this mouth like Dr. Evil from the Austin Powers movies.

I roll my eyes, playfully tossing a decorative pillow from behind me at his stomach.

"I so resent making you watch that." Only thing remotely evil about Skylan is that mouth of his.

"Why?" he leans over, still wonderfully naked, grabbing my bedsheets and pulling them back down, his deep voice oozing with raw lust as he mumbles, "Do I make you horny, baby?"

He shimmies his shoulders, wiggling his eyebrows while speaking in the worst attempt at an English accent I've ever heard. My head falls back and my lips spread wide with laughter.

"Huh? Do I?" he asks again, grinning widely, reaching for my exposed leg and pulling me closer to him.

"Oh, yes, Prince Skylan," I drawl, fluttering my eyes and pressing my foot into his stomach. "I'm so wet right now."

"Oh yeah?" he pulls his bottom lip between his teeth, drawing my eyes to their fullness, and squeezes my calf, happily accepting the challenge. "Prove it," Sky grabs my ankles, lifting them to his press into his shoulders, and slides his forefinger over my piercing.

My body responds immediately, my hips lifting to meet his determined strokes as he slides a finger inside me, then two, slowly stroking until he falls into a steady rhythm, and a string of feverish moans leave my body.

"Well, what do you know? Her Highness tells the truth for once," he chuckles deeply. As if we didn't just have sex fifteen minutes ago. Sky pulls his finger out, sucking it into his mouth, a mischievous gleam shining in his eyes as he bends down, finally hooking my legs over his shoulders and drags his tongue over my swollen clit, plucking my piercing between his teeth and earning him another moan.

"Fuck, Sky... I whimper, weaving my fingers through his hair, encouraging him to suck harder, bringing my climax closer and closer. "Use your fingers," I urge, those calloused hands are otherworldly emperors of satisfaction in my book.

He chuckles. "As you wish."

Sky rolls me on my side and crawls over my body, settling himself behind me, sliding his fingers between my thighs where his tongue had been a second ago.

Calloused fingers work my clit, squeezing my piercing between them. My hips push backward, grinding against him, moaning louder and louder as I reach sweet oblivion.

"I adore you like this, darling," he breathes. "This feel good?"

I nod breathless, reaching behind me, wrapping my arm around his neck, willing him closer.

"Yeah?" he rasps, this thick voice sending ripples of need through my body. "Tell me, Princess."

"Amazing," I moan as my breaths deepen and feel my body begin the climb over the edge.

"I fucking bet it does," his dark chuckles rumbles against my ear, "Don't be shy, darling. Show me how good it feels."

All it takes for my orgasm to shake every fiber of my body is for Skylan to squeeze my piercing between his fingers, and stars explode in my eyes. My climax hits me a million miles an hour, screaming his name as I ride waves of pure ecstasy, turning my head and slamming my lips to his, massaging his tongue with mine. His hand tangles in my still damp hair, drawing my body closer to him. Sated, roll over into his arms, deepening the kiss. We stay like this for a good while, until he leaves my now swollen lips and I snuggle into his side as a warm comfort settles in my body.

"I could listen to those pretty little screams of yours all l day long, darling," he chuckles, running his wet finger along my lips as I'm coming down from my high, covering it with my precious juices, and seals mouth over mine once more. I could happily *live* with his fingers inside of me all day long.

I'm trying to keep myself from seeing further into this than I should, for my own protection. Sleeping with him is one thing, but letting it go beyond the physical is an exponentially disastrous idea.

"Did it hurt?" he asks eventually, stroking his hand along my thigh, lazily tangled with his.

I didn't take long to realize what he meant. "It was tricky at the beginning. The hardest part was remembering the thing every time I went to the bathroom," I shiver at the memory. "It was fine in a couple weeks. You know pain never bothered me."

"Of course, not," he grins. "My fierce warrior," pressing a kiss to my lips and sending little flutters through my heart.

Since we're asking questions, and he brought it up yesterday, "How did you know it was me?"

Sky narrows his eyes at first, but then he chuckles. "You always take a step back before you advance. I've told you before, you're strong enough, you don't need to."

We haven't seen each other in years though… "How could you possibly remember that?"

Sky eyes me knowingly, "I know you better than anyone, Emryne. I trained you, remember? Do you think that's something I'd forget?," he takes my hand, bringing my knuckles to his lips and placing a soft kiss over them, tracing his finger over the thin scar on the inside on my wrist. "Then there was your eyes."

"My eyes?"

"No woman has eyes like yours."

"Which you saw how? My face was behind the hood the whole time. And how long were you following me anyway?"

"The whole night, darling," he reaches for his bottle again, twisting open the cap and taking a drink. "It slipped back on the roof when you shoved me against the wall. Nice job with the wifebeater by the way."

I snicker. Of course, he saw that.

"I was talking about before the night on the roof," I say, sitting up and facing him while I tuck my legs under me. "I saw you that night outside the tunnels."

"So did I. I went for a run that morning and heard the gate open."

"Since when do you run?"

He grins. "Since whenever I want to run."

"That's not an answer," I deadpan.

Sky sighs, crossing his hands behind his head again. "You've been in my head since I got here. A part of me always knew. I mean, your sister gets attacked without explanation and *suddenly* there's a vigilante running around rounding up every criminal responsible?" Well, those who weren't executed that is… "I know how close you are. Doesn't take a rocket scientist to figure it out."

"My parents don't know. Or my siblings."

"That's because you're used to walking in the shadows when the situation calls for it. You have this freaky ability of blending into any crowd without them knowing who you are at first, and only when they do a double-take do they actually recognize you. But, knowing you, you'd already be gone by the time they search again."

I guess when he puts it that way. And my parents are way too preoccupied with preparing for whoever the new queen will be to concern themselves about who the vigilante is.

Especially since my mother is convinced Parliament has it handled.

Father? I'm actually not sure…

"I saw you texting someone about it that night we went to Forum," he says, "What the hell is Purple Sprinkle?"

"A very big problem," I throw my head back in frustration before facing him again, needing him to hear me. "Listen Sky, you can't tell anyone about this."

He shrugs. "I know."

"I'm serious. No one can know what's happening here."

"Emryne, I know," Sky cups my cheek and kisses my forehead. Sky finishes his water and throws the bottle into the trash next to the bedside table, then turns back to me. "The Dark Warrior does important work, and it seems like the citizens really need her. Even if they technically don't know you're a *her*." He links his fingers with mine. "I am wondering though… does the Dark Warrior need a partner, by any chance?"

"You don't think I can handle this alone?" I know he doesn't, but I tease him anyway.

"Don't put words in my mouth," he shakes his head, pushing me on my back. "I just think you could use some backup."

In truth, I never considered it until now and I'd never say it to Sky's face, but I probably could. Even with Castor in my corner, this is a gargantuan task. I'd say I don't want to share the spotlight, but let's face it, there technically is no spotlight other than the scrutiny of Parliament and if they knew was good for them, they'd let me work.

Though it annoys me knowing the amount of time his armor is going to take Castor to make. If I agree to this. There's no way I'm letting Sky go anywhere in anything less.

"I'll think about it."

Chapter 19
Skylan
The Likely Partnership

"One condition," I bend my knee, resting my arm over it as I trace my finger down a very naked Emryne's body. I have no idea where the idea came from much less the motivation, but the more I think about it, the more I like it.

I've known Emryne my entire life, and the last thing she needs is protection. It'd be an insult of epic proportions if I told her I'm doing it for that reason alone. Suggesting being her backup instead? I'd have to pat myself on the back when I'm alone. While I'm well aware of just how capable she is of taking care of herself, I'd be an ass if I didn't at least offer when I know she would've done the same thing for me were circumstances reversed. Hell, she'd do it, permission be damned.

"I can't wait to hear it," Emryne sighs, rolling her eyes and tucking her fist under her chin.

I almost lose the battle with my own eyes, keeping them from traveling down her feminine curves next to me. She was already toned from the little I saw that day in their training room, and watching her kick every single one of the other royals' asses, I had to duck behind Dad more than once to keep from completely embarrassing myself in front of her and King Ryne.

Hell of a confession that would've been. *"Hey, Your Majesty. How are ya? Your daughter is giving me a wicked hard-on, think I can grab her and fuck the shit out of her real quick? Trust me, we won't be long. Also, I broke her heart two years ago which is why she's beating the daylights out of me right now. No hard feelings, right?"* Then top it off with a one-handed thumbs-up. The man would cut my head off and shove the rest of me through a meat grinder without thinking twice.

"I am not wearing your girly stuff."

"Relax," she gets up, grabbing a hair tie from her bedside table and tying it on her head, then reaches for the gray satin robe halfway to her giant walk-in closet, smoothly sliding it over her shoulders and tightening the belt around her waist. She bites her nail and spins to face me. "Look, if we're really going to do this, I need to know you're a hundred percent in, and you're not just saying this to get me in bed."

"I meant what I said," I throw back the sheets, grabbing my boxers and pulling them on before joining her and taking her hands. "I want to help. Whatever it takes, as long as I'm next to you."

"Then we need to get started ASAP," she gives my hands a firm squeeze. She heads to a huge, black laptop, though I don't recognize the brand at all it looks sophisticated as hell, like it's straight out of a Mission Impossible movie, and she flips it open, tapping the keys with manic speed.

I'm definitely not jealous.

"Let's just get one thing straight," she straightens and steps closer, lifting a finger at me. "If you get in my way or slow me down at any point in this, I will fucking kill you."

"Yeah, yeah," I wave her off. "Is that a yes then?"

"Probationary," she says. It's a start at least. I won't look a gift horse in the mouth. "And only because I need the help."

"Ah," I tease, drawing out the sound. "Finally admitting you aren't indestructible, Em-Em?"

"Oh, shut up," she rolls her eyes, though I don't miss the smirk. "We'll need to get Claudia to take your measurements so I can send it to Castor." She says, running her hands down my arms and to my hands.

I drop my eyes to my clothes, or rather the lack there-of, and raise an eyebrow.

"Now?" Might not be the best idea to let the crowned princess's ladies' maids walk in here and seeing my flustered face and messy hair. These girls know everything, and I'd rather our affair stay between Emryne and I, at least until I can figure out where this is going.

Where *is* this going…?

"No, dick for brains. Obviously not now, but sooner rather than later. It'll take some time for him to gather what he needs to get started. Not to mention I'll have to expand the locker."

"Him who?" My brows draw together, eyeing her room. "What locker?" She already has a closet the size of a small shopping mall, what would she need a locker for?

I watch as her lips turn up, and she saunters to her wall where she lifts a hidden panel revealing a small keypad and types in a six-digit code. "Well, you'll need somewhere to hide your weapons, won't you?"

I watch in awe as two hidden doors built into her wall swing open, and I feel my erection building once again.

My jaw falls to the floor when my eyes settle on hidden weapons locker in front of me. I knew her endeavor was sophisticated, that much was clear with the way she moved when I tailed her, but this is another level.

Everything from high-velocity sniper rifles to hand grenades to pistols, hell even three sets of brass knuckles, weapons that would've taken a normal person months, years even, to master let alone own, all neatly stored I'm their velvet linings, and right there in the middle of it all, is her full black armor.

But Emryne is no ordinary person, she's the crowned Princess of Alorewyn, and her father's pride and joy; her brain is like a sponge.

"Welcome to the business, Your Highness," Emryne smirks, coming to stand next to me.

My cock is already hard as hell, which I don't bother hiding, but it takes all I have not to drool at the sight of this, or at the sight of her, especially when my eyes settle on one key set of her equipment.

I take a step closer, battling to wrap my head around what I'm seeing.

"Where the hell did you get suppressors?" My fingers stroke the cold metal, carefully lifting it from its holster and marveling at the equipment in my hand. Along with automatic weapons, they are illegal as far as I remember. Mainly because I've been trying to get my hands on them for years with no luck whatsoever, and here she is with them in her bedroom.

I reiterate, I'm not jealous.

She grins, mumbling, "Uhm… I've… uh, Ivegotaguy…" under her breath and watching as I fawn over her collection.

"What?"

"I've got a guy, okay," she playfully rolls her eyes, brushing it off, and I can't help my grin.

What twenty-one-year-old woman—oh yeah, she's all woman, all right—has 'a guy'? Seriously, I have 'a guy' too, though I use him for parts for the jets.

And he's perfectly legal, I can assure you of that.

"It's not much, but it's mine," she shrugs.

Not much? It's every assassin's wet dream.

"Titanium?"

She sucks her bottom lip between her teeth, and nods. A woman of quality.

Like she'd settle for anything less.

"I never get to use them though."

My eyes bug from my head. "You can't be serious? What's the point in having all this then?"

"Well," she shrugs. "I'd rather have it and not need it, then need it and not have it. Fortune favors the prepared." Touché. "Besides, the paperwork accompanied with discharging any of these is a fucking nightmare. So yeah, I'm good with knives and knuckles."

Of course, clever girl.

Although… "I'm not sure whether this makes you sexier or twice as terrifying." My eyes narrow, but a slow smile spread over my lips.

She strides closer and wraps her hands around my neck. "I vote for the former."

I grip her sides, whispering, "I'm inclined to agree, my princess," and press my lips to hers, kissing her tenderly. She never ceases to amaze me.

"You really thought this through, haven't you?" I ask, holding her close, and adoring the way she melts into me.

"I have no choice but to. This way I'm prepared for every situation. And we've got some serious work to do."

"Catch me up," I give her ass a squeeze before letting her go, and we move to her desk.

Over the next forty-five minutes, I sit at her side in awe of just how much work both her and whoever this Castor person is have put into this as she fills me in on everything she knows so far, right down to handing me the rap sheets she'd printed out.

No wonder she kept disappearing at Forum, she was chasing down one of her leads. Which she ultimately handed to Guard after getting the information she needed. Not that I'm pleased she cornered some drug mule where anyone could've seen her at any point in time, regardless of how much she convinces me she was careful. That would've been an entirely different disaster. One that would implicate more than just her reputation, but her father's as well.

At least this way I get to provide support in whatever way she needs and I wouldn't feel like an extra in the Grease movie, only showing up when there's a big dance number and performing behind John Travolta and Jeff Conaway, which in my case is Emryne and her 'Castor' and I'm honored to be a part of it. Even if only on probation.

#

Breakfast this morning is oddly civilized. The room is filled with floaty conversation by the time we sit down. Even King Lodran keeps his mouth shut while he ate, his eyes weirdly glossy and emptier than usual, even his skin appears greyer, add the fact he barely spoke a word almost has me thinking something was up.

Not that I care. I stopped paying attention the second I set my sights on the blue-eyed beauty next me—her irises seemed even darker with the forest green floral blouse and black jeans she wearing for some shopping date she has with her friends later—who couldn't keep her gaze or her smile to herself either.

Dad stayed in his room to pack while I headed upstairs to meet her outside her door before we came here. Not exactly the way I wanted to kiss her good morning, but it'd do for now.

"You two are very civil this morning," beside her father, Asaria smirks and picks up her teacup. "Finally kiss and make up?"

My eyes never leave Emryne's. "Something like that."

She smiles, rolling her eyes as she lifts her cup to ger lips and takes a small sip. "Oh yeah, we totally… worked it out."

"That is good news indeed," Queen Lilliette adds. "The last thing we need is more body parts being ruined."

A wicked grin spreads over Emryne lips, and I already know what she's going to say… "Oh, they're getting ruined alright."

Queen Ophelia chokes on her water and Asaria burst out laughing. The ideal comeback if ever I've heard it given mine would've been profoundly dirtier.

Luckily it seems like the four of us were the only ones to catch her joke. Thank God.

I can't for the life of me begin to identify the expression on her father's face as he surveys the situation.

"What time does your father's flight leave, Prince Skylan?" King Ryne asks after our laughter settles down. "I don't want to miss saying goodbye."

"He still has about an hour before take-off, Your Majesty. And I don't think he'd forgive you if you didn't," I tell him politely.

"Oh, I am so excited for cousin, Prince Skylan. A doctoral degree and a king?" the queen says, oddly chipper even for her. Did someone sneak some kind of relaxation mix into everyone's tea this morning?

"He seems to be handling the separatist situation very well."

"I agree. He's working on some major peace treaties he'd like to instate, but I know he wants to wait until after he's crowned to set the meeting with the president."

From the corner of my eye, I see Emryne frown.

Shit. Did I forget to mention I abdicated before leaving? I swear it was on my to-do list, after explaining the situation and kissing the hell out of her, followed by some R-rated making up.

I nod to her, extending a silent promise that I'd tell her everything once were alone again. She returns my nod and goes back to snacking on the bowl of raspberries and yogurt before her.

"Will you be leaving as well?" her mother asks.

"Not this time, Your Majesty," my eyes met a hopeful Emryne's once again. That's right, I meant what I said. "I think I'm right where I'm supposed to be."

"Excellent news. You know we love having you here," the king says.

I'm blessed with one more genuine smile before Emryne hops up and excuses herself. She squeezes her mother's shoulder, kisses her father cheek, then returns to her seat to grab her coat and purse. As her longing eyes settle in mine, it wasn't impossible to imagine she'd have loved to give me a real goodbye. A perfect Emryne hug, and a few soft kisses. I wanted nothing more either, but we couldn't risk it. None the less, my eyes convey what I couldn't say out loud.

Me too, darling. Me too.

So, I smile and give her a nod, and she left the breakfast room with her phone in her hand.

Not a split second later and my phone buzzed in my pocket. I smile when I open the message to about twenty kissy face emojis and a message saying.

EMRYNE: *Have a date with Victoria Secret today…*
Followed by,
EMRYNE: *My room. Midnight.*

And my body already responds, so much I had to adjust the zipper of my beige slacks under the table as discreetly as I could with all these faces around me.

Didn't have to tell me twice.

The conversation shifts back to Callior and Maverick after she left. The whole reason we traveled before the ball was because Dad wanted to see how Mav's handling Greenland by himself. Needless to say, he was more than pleased when we arrived and saw how at ease Parliament was with his performance.

He even goes as far as to tell me he's almost drafted the finalized version of the treaties which he's excited to discuss with Greenland when Dad gets home on our I call after lunch.

"It's under control," Maverick assures me.

King Ryne decided that today was the perfect day for a hunt. He flew from his seat after got a call from a member of Parliament claiming two foxes were spotted on the hunting grounds outside the palace. He ushered Cane, Allister and me to the stables, slung his spare hunting rifles on each of our shoulders and off we went.

As much as I hate riding, I've never been so entertained watching Emryne's father hunt for foxes. At least her horse was the most level-headed of the herd of the twenty-four other members of Parliament who joined as well, despite being a giant stallion, though I've never seen an animal gobble down gourmet raspberry treats as vigorously as Frolic did. I wonder whose horse he is…

"Any more incidents?" I lean back on the dark gray velvet couch after getting back from the hunt.

"Few stray kittens slipped through border patrols but they were flagged down pretty quick," music to my ears. We saw the solid state of the border when we were there, I'm surprised they managed to slip through. "I appreciate you coming to the meeting on such short notice."

"Of course, man. You know your uncle," I say.

"I also know my cousin," he smirks, leaning back in the office chair. Something about seeing him in Dad's old digs just sits right. Especially since he got rid of those God awful, bejeweled bull skulls Dad liked to collect. I'll swear up and down those damn corridors I heard something huffing every time I worked in there. Still gives me the creeps just thinking about it.

"Didn't like the idea of leaving her, did you?"

I don't answer. What do I say? *No, I didn't like it, I hated it. We needed so badly to hash things out, but my family and my country will always come first.* Were Maverick the one who said it, I never would've believed him.

Mav chuckles and shakes his head. "Dude, you're completely pussy-whipped."

"Yes, I know," I won't bother denying it because it's true. And when it comes to Emryne I always will be, even if she broke it off when she got home tonight. "If you felt what I did, so would you be," and, frankly, all of this scares the fuck out of me.

We just got back… together… Were we ever together? Are we even together now? Point is, it freaks me out just how willing I already am to drop everything and stay with her if that's what she needed. Though, I guess a part of me has always been willing.

This is a totally new feeling and I can't decide whether I like it or not, much less why.

And as if to prove his point further, Mav smirks and says, "I've seen the bikini shots. Are you offering?"

I can't stop my lips from straightening into a thin line even if I try, and my fingers curling into a tight fist is just icing on the cake.

He lifts his hands in defense, an all-too-satisfied grin on his face. "Easy tiger, just a joke."

"See me laughing?" I deadpan. I should be laughing, but I'm not. And if this is how I'm reacting to my cousin making joke from five hundred miles away, how the hell am I going to keep my emotions in check when she's with her friends, partying the night way at some club where every guy in Alorewyn can ogle her. Or when she's with Cane. Or Allister.

Knowing she's supposed to be seeing both of them, that one of them could be king in a few months…

Oh, fuck me.

"You would have if you weren't so damn pussy-whipped."

Tell me about it.

I roll my eyes, and continue filling him in on life so far—narrowly avoiding the whole Emryne/Dark Warrior thing even if it almost slipped out more than once—and he does the same.

It's been a while since I've been this excited, both about watching her in action and knowing we're doing our best to make a difference.

And it makes me feel a hell of a lot better knowing I have something else to keep my mind busy other than thinking about the next king of Alorewyn touching my girl.

Chapter 20
Emryne
A Single Princely Kiss

"You slept with him?" A very shocked, very caffeinated Tory shrieks.

I cringe right down into my very soul, "Shhh!" pressing my hands against her mouth. "Do you want this entire block to hear you?"

At least she lowers her voice before speaking this time. "Sorry. But did you?" I roll my eyes and smile at her, and she shrieks again, clapping her hands together like a hungry seal. "I am so happy for you, E!"

Two things here.

One, the problem with having bloodhounds for friends is that they fish out the truth, regardless of how convincingly I deny the allegations or divert the conversation topic to something a little more vanilla, so there really wasn't any point in hiding it.

Two, I missed my bloodhound friends.

And apparently all of Alorewyn's elite missed Café Del Mar as well. Their interior has always blown me away. Nothing in the restaurant wasn't alive: the throngs of vibrant green ivy thriving on the walls, the bright tropical fish floating aimlessly around the tank spanning virtually the entire restaurant, even the Blushing Brides draped around the warm yellow chandeliers, all alive and beyond breathtaking.

Today was the ideal morning to crowd into the famous three Michelin-Star restaurant for their midweek brunch headliner: cinnamon brioche fresh toast with a creamy coffee liqueur sauce, and after several selfies and few autographs, we finally get to our table. Not the brightest idea bringing Tory here since we've already had two double caramel frappés while raiding the shelves of every store in this fashion complex. And adding alcohol to the mix was just as dumb.

It's not that I don't want to see them but with Beth getting promoted to the new head of marketing at the design firm she works at on the west coast and Tory following her mother around like a puppy, learning precisely what to and what not to do when managing multi-million-dollar trust funds, and we all know what I've been roped into, none of us have time to relax as it is let alone get together. And it'll only get worse.

Adding Skylan to team Dark Warrior isn't a relaxing, lavender-scented bubble bath either. I still haven't sorted through the realization of what exactly I've gotten myself into by letting him join, but knowing the gigantic pain in my ass as well as I do, he wouldn't have dropped it anyway. Even if I shoved one of Father's antique swords down his throat and wiggled it around, ghost Skylan wouldn't leave me alone either.

The guy's already possessing every inch of my body, giving him access to haunt me with cocky grins and random phantom gropes for the rest of my life?

Ha. I don't think so.

Of course, I couldn't keep the whole Skylan situation from them, a blind person could tell I'm more relaxed I've been in months, which naturally Tory was the first of the two to notice. Especially with the floral blouse I left the palace with when I barely wore anything with a flower on in to begin with. But it was cute and went perfectly with the black leather jeans so I'm not complaining; I practically ran out of there when Des held up the emerald tiara Moni suggested I wear, but pretended I didn't see it. Big ass no.

Beth remained her typical analytical, take-it-all-in-and-never-say-a-word-until-I-have-all-the-facts self throughout explaining what happened after we talked about the fourth, which she wasn't happy about not being able to attend.

And as soon as she does, the third-degree begins.

"Was it hate fucking, or good fucking?" Beth asks.

I raise an eyebrow. "There's a difference?"

"Let me get this straight, five months ago you couldn't stand to be in the same room as him, and now you're bumping beauties?" she leans back, finishing her glass of Rosé.

Tory frowns, recoiling. "Don't you mean uglies?"

"Honey, look at her," Beth reaches in her purse to pull out her phone and opened Sky's Instagram account to a picture of a bare-chested prince on a beach. "Now look at him. Ain't nothing ugly about either of them."

I mean when she puts it like that. It's not by accident that he has one of the largest followings in the world.

I'm still convinced the girl should've gone to the knight's academy with her supernatural ability to snuff out the truth. Back in high school, someone stole Tory's limited-addition Alice in Wonderland Prada tote she'd spent months, not to mention a small fortune, trying to get her hands on. Turned out to be our science teacher looking to make a few extra bucks to support his coke addiction. Surprisingly, I'm not talking about the drug.

Beth has a knack for discovering the truth and Tory has knack for finding anything Alice related, and I mean anything. Skincare products (regardless of the chemical burns she had on her face for weeks from the cheap ingredients), accessories, hair clips, high-fashion labels with themed clothing, anything. Better believe the girl seeks them out like a highly trained sniffer-dog.

As for me, I prefer my authors' hands fetish-free, mostly, and not neck-deep in some freaky fascination with little girls.

"Are you sure this is a good idea?" Beth grips her glass and turns to me. "I mean, we all remember what happened the last time you ended up in bed with him."

"Yes, but," I hold up a finger, "the last time I had no idea where his head was at. Now I do."

"And you're just gonna believe him?" she deadpans. My lips straighten into a thin line while I blink my eyes in derision. "I'm just saying E, some guys will say and do anything to get in your pants, you know they will. Especially since you're the princess."

"Usually, I'd agree with you, but this isn't some guy. This is Skylan." The hell is up her butt?

"Which is exactly my point, babe," she raises her brows, holding up her empty glass.

Our waiter heads over to refill our glasses, and as if the universe wants to add insult to injury, my own phone buzzes next to me.

ASA: *Headed back to Turkey. I know you probably don't want to hear this, but I still don't think this thing with Skylan is a good idea. But you're a grown-ass woman so I'll say again: please just be careful. I can't see you heartbroken again, Emrie. Love ya. And don't touch my Don! Xxx*

I throw my phone in my purse and turn back to the girls. I'll deal with her later.

"Look, I get where everyone is coming from and I thoroughly appreciate the lack of faith in my judgement, but I have this under control. I've already had a conversation with myself not to get carried away like I did last time. Besides," I reach for my filled glass and state matter-of-factly, "there still are two other princes in contention for king here."

"True. But we all know they're not Skylan," Tory mumbles, smirking innocently.

I open my mouth, to say… what can I say? She's right. They're all just going to have to trust that my guard is up.

It has to be.

"Just, keep your eyes open, okay?" Beth kisses my cheek and heads to the ladies' room.

I chew on my words for a second before turning to Tory, who's more reserved than usual. "What do you really think?"

"About Sky?" she leans her elbows on the table.

I nod. I know there's something she's not saying, and I'd very much like to know what it is. "Since my sisters are evidently not on board, and Beth doesn't make any major life decisions without a bullion flow-chart, what do you think I should do?"

I prepare myself for the worst when she takes my hands, cementing her green eyes in mine. "You really want my advice?"

"Begging for it."

Then again, this is Tory. "Just have fun. Geez, everyone's acting as if Prince Skylan freaking Dormer is the end-all-be-all of major decisions. But there's history here, Emrie. You know it. I know it. And they know it too. Which is why we're all being a pain in the ass about this. Don't think we've forgotten the way he used to look at you. Honestly, I'm surprised it took you two this long."

She squeezes once, "Look, I know as well as all of them that you'll probably be married and crowned queen by the end of the year. Isn't the whole point of this to see who the best candidate for king will be?"

I swallow. "I mean, yeah."

"Exactly, so just take it easy. My God, you're going on—hell, everyone's going on as if you absolutely have to choose Skylan for king. That's not true.

Sure, I don't want to see you heartbroken either, but it's all part of the experience. How the hell else are you supposed to learn what you want and what you don't? My advice? Enjoy yourself. Worry about the other stuff when crunch-time comes. God knows I wish I could."

"You still haven't talked to your parents?"

She snorts. "Of course, not. How do you tell your severely homophobic parents your gay? Spring it on them at Sunday dinner with Pastor Johannesen sitting next to Dad?"

Being a woman used to speaking her mind, I hate that she's forced to hide a part of who she is from her parents. And while Alorewyn may be a safe haven, it doesn't stop people from being real assholes. Most, like her parents, have mastered the art of quiet hatred.

I want her to be free. I don't want her to be anyone but who she is.

"Maybe ripping off the band-aid won't be a bad idea. They probably should know, T."

"No, they don't," she protests, leaning back in the stool and throwing her head back in frustration.

"If it's keeping you from being happy then yes, they do."

Tory grunts. "I know. I know, okay? Just, let them retire first. At least if Dad has a heart attack he'll already be sitting in his favorite chair."

This time it's my turn to take her hand. "Have you told her yet?"

She raises her head, looking at me as if I've lost my mind. "Tell your best friend you've been in love with her since junior year of high school? I don't think so."

She takes her hands back as Beth sits down. "Please tell me you're not having revelations without me?" Beth sighs, flicking her curled hair over her shoulder.

"Nope. Just some bestest friendly advice," she swallows nervously. Yeah, you guessed it. Sweet as sugar Victory is head over heels in love with Beth. And I hate that she has to hide it.

"Only revelation I'm having is that I'm starving," I say. Forty-five minutes after we placed our order, and after Beth nearly bit the poor waiter's head off when he explained they'd already sent the last order out, then threw my name around like it's a Dungeons and Dragons healing potion, our French toast finally arrives and we finish brunch in peace.

We pay the check and dive right back into emptying the fashion houses in the complex when Tory taps my shoulder right as we're closing in on Victoria's Secret, smiling and pointing over to two pigtailed little girls running toward us hand in hand with their panting mother behind them.

"Hello Princess Emryne," Their bright smiles greet in unison.

My lips turn up, and I bend down to take them into my arms. "Oh, hi girls. Don't you two look gorgeous."

It's been a while since I've seen tiny people in baby pink and dark blue sparkly gowns so poofy they can barely move in them. I'd say it makes me miss that part of childhood, but what I rather miss is chasing my sisters through the muddy fields behind the palace after late-afternoon thunderstorms drenched the paddocks the horses grazed in, then get scolded by Mother for ruining perfectly fine dresses after we waddled back; riding piggyback with Asa, and Ophelia holding Addy's hand so she doesn't slip.

Those were good times.

"She likes my dress!" The little dark-haired one beams and shakes her sister as they jump up and down, squealing with excitement.

"Can we get a picture with you?" The one with the ginger hair asks sweetly.

"Of course, you can," who am I to deny these little rosy cheeks?

I hand Tory my purse and shopping bags, and kneel between them, pulling them close as their happy giggles float down the walkway.

"I am so sorry to bother you, Your Highness," the mom starts with a deep bow after she tucks her phone away. She has the same ginger hair as her daughter, but it's easy to see which one of them takes after her the most. "The girls saw you and wanted to say hi. I told them not to trouble you but they ran over here before I could stop them," she puffs, still gasping for air. "And I think I need a new gym membership," she chuckles.

"It's no trouble at all. Did they choose their own outfits this morning?"

"However did you know?" she teases, giggling once she catches her breath. "I wish I could say they wear regular clothing but that would be a big, fat lie," I join her as she laughs.

"Who needs normal clothes when dresses are so much better?" I wink the girls' way and say with a pinch of sugar.

"That's what I told Mama this morning!" The ginger girl beams. I shake my head, smiling. Of course, that's what she said.

I lean down, taking their hands. "Well, since you two already know my name, I think it's only fair that I know yours?"

"This is Hadley," Mom gestures to the taller ginger girl, "and her sister Mina," then little dark-haired one.

"Where's Prince Skylan?" Hadley asks, head inclining to the left as she flutters her long lashes.

I choke on a laugh. "He's… probably back at the palace doing some very important things with King Ryne."

"I like him," Mina chimes. "He's so dreamy. And he has huge muscles."

"Mina!"

"What? He does!"

I can't help but laugh. Part of me is contemplating whether or not to actually tell him about this little exchange. No need to inflate his parade balloon sized ego any more than it already is, but it's nice knowing someone else is rooting for him though.

"I really, really want him to be king," Hadley sighs, leaning into her mother's side.

"I like him too," Mina says again. "Especially when he helped all those people in India last year. That was very brave," I didn't know about that. I barely kept up with his travels.

Okay fine, I sort of did. There was a mudslide in Mumbai a few months before my birthday and he volunteered on the rescue squads. But that's all, okay?

I didn't stalk him at all after that. Get off my ass!

"He is a good person, isn't he?" I smile, my heart fluttering with excitement. Interesting to see where her priorities lie, even at… nine? Ten years old?

"Can you tell him we said hi?" She asks, her eyes pleading with mine.

"You bet," I wink at Hadley.

They wave goodbye in unison as she thanks me again and pulls the girls back the other way, happily skipping and giggling as the do. "We love you princess!"

Tory smiles and hands me back my purse. "I forgot how amazing you are with kids."

"Did you see those cheeks? How was I supposed to ignore that?" More so, public exchange is the pinnacle of any royal's career. The world needs to see us having fun. Hanging out and laughing like normal people, interacting with everyone from children to adults is vital, it's how we're humanized. Just because we wear crowns, get chauffeured around in bulletproof vehicles and are referred to as Your Highness or Majesty, doesn't mean we're above the law. Sure, it comes with a few perks, but whatever doubt my grandparents created in our citizens minds changed when Father was crowned. He said so himself in his keynote address before coronation. And that is a legacy I, and whoever the future king is, have to endorse until we have children of our own to keep that legacy going.

Oh, God...

"What's changed?" Beth's voice chimes from behind the models in Burberry, after we all but emptied Victoria's Secret.

My brows furrow. "About kissing ass?"

"About sleeping with Sky?" Oh, for goodness' sake, we're still on this? "I have no idea." I raise a shoulder. "It kind of just happened."

"So, goody-two-shoes Emryne, who cannot fathom the idea of doing something wrong, broke *the* cardinal rule against fornication between eligible parties and slept with a crowned prince?" She asks. I already broke that rule when I shoved my virginity in his hands, what difference does it make now?

I shrug my shoulder, trying and failing to concentrate on shopping.

"My, how the tables have turned," Tory singsongs over her shoulder.

Beth sucks on her teeth. "So unfair. You get the young, hot guys while I'm stuck with the finance geeks."

Tory and I share a look. "What finance geeks?"

"You know, all the squints behind their desks," Beth explains as if we're supposed to know what she means. I do, but hounding her is just too funny. Especially since we've had this conversation before. Many, many times.

Tory smirks. "Why do I get the feeling this is less of a 'them'," she adds in air quotes, "and more of a 'he'?"

"Please," Beth snorts. "There is no he. You two would know if there was a he." Would we?

"Are you still feuding with that Kenwick guy?" Tory asks.

"Keithwin," she corrects almost immediately. Well... there's your answer.

Although... my brows draw together. "What the hell is a Keithwin?" I ask through risky mirth.

"He's the new CFO at my company," she answers with a dismissing wave. "He goes by Keith—it doesn't matter! He's a pain in the neck is the point I'm trying to make."

"Oh," Tory closes her arm around Beth's shoulder, pulling her close. "I'm sure he's perfectly… formidable."

"Oh, formidable my ass. And don't patronize me! The guy's a fossil."

"He is not," Tory laughs.

My eyes dart between the two of them. "Okay, why did I not know about this?"

"Because you've been too busy getting dicked down to answer your phone!" she says annoyed. Beth's face falls blank. "Last week, he made me send him email ahead of schedule if we have any late meetings just in case it overlaps with his mahjong nights. Sometimes he doesn't even show up."

"I mean… he's a CFO, doesn't he get to make his own rules?" I have no idea how stuff like that works. Now I'm curious though. "Please tell me you have a picture of him?"

She sighs, pulls out her phone and opens the company webpage. And there, in all his salt-and-pepper glory, is the fresh face of one Mr. Keithwin Rogers, CFO of Delaney & DeMartino Marketing. Round, honey-brown eyes, full lips, smooth skin, defined muscles. He's not bad looking for a guy in his early forties.

"I think he's cute," Tory shrugs.

"Puppies are cute. But they don't exactly make stellar husbands," she flings her purse in the front seat of her car after we finished our spree, and leans against the doors. "We can't all have sex gods for lovers."

Just a second… "Husband?" Both Tory and my gazes shoot to each other.

Beth turns away, grunting into the early evening. "Mom thinks it's time I settle down," she snorts. "I barely even know the guy."

"Do you want to?" Tory jumps ahead.

That's a good question given how she's reacting to the—wait. Beth's eyes flick to the ground to her left. Oh, yes. "B, have you slept with him?" I ask. To which her answer is her sucking her lip between her teeth and squeezing her eyes shut, confirming my suspicion.

"Oh my God," I choke on a laugh and my jaw falls to the floor, "Eww."

Tory eyes bug out of her skull, and she blinks slowly. "What?"

She bites the perfectly manicured nail on her forefinger and shrugs. "What?"

"Eww, B! He's like twice your age!"

She throws her hands in the air, outraged, "Which is exactly why I didn't say anything, you assholes! I knew you would react like this!"

"React like what?" I sing-song. "Like you aren't totally banging your boss?" Risqué even for Beth. And she's done some wild things, some more legal than others, and if I hadn't been sworn to secrecy, I'd totally tell you the whole story. What I will say is that it involved a Harley, a heavily tattooed, heavily muscled biker, a bottle of caramel sauce and a case of Red Bull.

I'll leave the rest to your capable imagination.

I am thoroughly impressed though. Her mother is a bigger pain in the ass than mine, only difference is she smiles a lot more, and her not knowing about this little affair is like Beth playing with wildfire. A nightmare waiting to happen.

"And you're on my ass about my sexcapades," I deadpan.

"We need to meet this guy so I can be jealous another one of my friends is getting more ass than I am," Tory says.

"You shouldn't be. He's crazy."

I take her phone and study his picture again. "If you mean crazy hot, yeah."

#

"I'm so sorry we haven't been able to see more of each other."

Cane laughs. "It does seem that every person wants a piece of you lately."

"You have no idea," I laugh, stating matter-of-factly. Lately? It never stops. "Well, now that you have me, what are you planning to do with me, I wonder?" I joke, batting my lashes at him.

"Certainly nothing of that kind," he chuckles. "I am, first and foremost, a gentleman."

I'm aware. But sometimes I wish he wouldn't be. Cane's stiff shoulders, calculated smiles and all business responses are clear signs of hesitance. Everything about how he carries himself, the way he speaks? I understand Adlengn people are all about being polite, hell some of them would give the Acadans a run for their money, but this feels a little too rehearsed. But I'll go with it. For now.

"And a gentleman knows when to ask for forgiveness."

"For…?" I eye him curiously.

"How I acted toward you in your training room. I apologize for offending you."

"I should be the one apologizing," I say, linking our arms together. "I was upset about something that had nothing to do with you and I should've known better than to snap at you. That was rude."

"I understand the pressure you're under. I'd have lost my wits long ago where I in your shoes."

"I'm not far off," I laugh. "Trust me."

After being thwarted at almost every occasion, we finally get to spend some time together, and in this short hour and a half, I've already learned so much about His Royal Highness Prince Caneic Hadrian Magnusius Loundry III.

After a quick shower and fresh make-up, Des finished my hair, a high knot she somehow perfected in under ten minutes, and I changed into one of my favorite dove gray tulle gowns with a simple cherry red belt and a few rosy embellishments along the sleeves and neckline. The light, off-the-shoulder fabric is perfect for an evening outside in one of the more private rotundas I asked Moni to set up and where we've been dining for the past hour while he tells be about his younger sister, Amaranda, who's a princess by day and metalcore base guitar player by night, whatever that means. DiDi, he and their grandmother call her, but never Mandy. She hates, no despises, the nickname.

His mother passed away not long after Skylan's. He doesn't say how or why, and I don't press him either. Not hard to tell he wasn't comfortable sharing any details.

He went to undergrad at Cambridge, majored in art philosophy and graduated with highest honors, though he hasn't picked up a brush since he's been here, something I plan to remedy as soon as I walk through those white French doors.

We finish dessert, and decide to make a relaxed beeline for the greenhouse Ophelia's wild orchid garden is thriving when he kneels next to a black and white spotted flower. For the first time since we sat down, he rolls his sleeves up to his elbows, studying the flowers. And I didn't realize why he chose a long-sleeve white dress shirt to wear in the middle of summer until I saw the rows of white scars on the sides of his arms.

Scars I know can only be made by a small blade, and my heart seizes in my chest.

His eyes give nothing away as he asks politely, "Would you mind if I take a photo?"

I shake myself out of it, and smile, hoping he didn't notice me staring.

"Not at all. The only thing my sister loves more than her husband is her flowers."

He nods, turning back to the flowers. "Extraordinary," he says, snaping a picture. "I never seen this species thrive outside of the Asai Empire."

I nod. I don't know anything about orchids in general, other than they're fucking expensive—Father's words, not mine.

"Is that where they're from?" I ask, bending down next to him.

"If I recall correctly, yes," he straightens and tucks his phone away then crosses his arms behind his back as we continue our walk. "Mum would've loved these. She was a botanist, you see. Always made me send her samples if I came across a rare or new species she hadn't had in her collection. She was fascinated by orchids. And now, it seems, Amaranda has taken up the hobby herself."

"Orchids too?" I ask.

"Carnivorous plants," he muses, gazing at the stars before turning to me. "Hardly little things. They suit her personality quite well."

If Cane were Skylan, he'd have walked straight into a dirty joke about eating ass or something ridiculous along those lines, but with Cane, I've learned not to bother. Apparently not everyone gets sarcasm.

So, I nod and laugh quietly, agreeing whatever analysis he made, and change the subject. "How often did you travel?"

"Depending on the time of year and place I was stationed on deployment, fairly frequently."

My eyes widen. "You were enlisted?"

A humble smile plays at his lips as he nods thoughtfully. "Tradition in the Loundry family. Father was partial to the Royal Marines. Mum, on the other hand, insisted the Special Air Service would be more to my liking."

I stop in my tracks, gripping his forearm. "Shut up. You were in the SAS?"

He chuckles. "What is it you Emaricans like to say?" he eyes me coyly and smiles. "Strictly need to know."

"Oh, come on, I hardly count as just another citizen," I step closer to him, beaming. "Those guys are legendary. You have to have some good stories! Tell!"

"Matter of national security, I'm afraid," he winks playfully.

My shoulder gives a playful shrug. "Fine then. Keep your secrets," I saunter a step away. "Although, if we get married, technically your secrets will be my secrets."

That has him laughing deep and hard, and oddly lyrical. I like it. "Oh, you are a little minx, aren't you?"

I smile. I have no idea what a minx is, but it sounds cute so… sure.

"Is that how you lost your leg?" I ask, facing him again.

Something changed in him just then. Whatever humor he carried in his eyes disappeared, replaced by what I can only describe as mixture between horror and embarrassment. He takes a step away, keeping his eyes downcast, and rubs his neck.

"I'm sorry, I didn't mean to intrude," I try, keeping my voice gentle. Not wanting him to have whatever battle is going on in his head, so I explain. "My father mentioned it a while back, I was just curious, I guess."

He still keeps his gaze off of mine, then chuckles softly. Yet all I hear is sadness. "I suppose it was only a matter of time before someone asked."

Great. Now I feel like an ass. It's been sitting in the back of my mind since Father said it. I guess I shouldn't have assumed it happened on duty, especially if it was something he was self-conscious about.

"It's alright," his eyes filled with a new kind of grief when he finally lifts them to mine, and he blew out a pained breath. "No, it wasn't an accident," he says quietly.

"You don't have to say anything," I take a few careful steps closer and place my hand on his forearm, painfully aware my fingers are inches away from those roughly healed cutmarks. Whatever happened, for him to be reacting like this? It had to be awful.

"You're incredibly brave for surviving something like that." Something in my head saw beyond the words he was saying out loud. If it wasn't an accident, it was inflicted. Which already woke my temper from its fluffy, red California king bed deep in pit of my stomach.

But I don't have time to think… well, anything, because the next thing I know, Cane closes the distance between us, and crashes his lips against mine.

And all I can think is… what do I do with my hands? Do I wrap them around his neck? Is that too intimate?

Intimate is good though, right?

Though, at the same time, I guess this is fine. Mother did say I needed to spend time with him, and I am. Tory's right, none of this is set in stone yet so may as well let go, and try something new.

New is fun. New is good, new is… boring.

Boring and empty.

The longer his lips are on mine, the more I'm trying to feel something, to keep myself present long enough *to* feel something, and lose myself in him the way I do Skylan but, nothing.

I feel nothing.

Cane's lips rip from mine, and he takes a step back. "I'm… I…"

"Mhm," is all I can muster through tightly pressed lips. Both of us are too stunned to speak.

His shocked expression turns apologetic in a flash. "I'm not entirely sure what came over me."

"It's okay," I try a smile. "It was… uhm, nice," it was as empty as a can of devoured Pringles after a reckless night of binge drinking cheap alcohol. Not that he needs to know that.

He chuckles softly, shaking his head. "Nice. Of course. The words every young man dreams of hear—"

Cane's sentence is cut short by a pained grunt. He steps back, wincing as he grabs his left thigh and his breaths quicken. This had to have something to do with his amputation.

What the hell happened to this guy?

"Cane?" I reach for his hands immediately, steadying him as he struggles to stay upright, and the clammy feeling of his skin on my fingers isn't exactly doing wonders for my nerves either. I have no idea what to do and I hate it. "Are you okay?"

"I'll be fine in a minute," he grits out, a thin layer perspiration forms on his forehead.

"You don't look fine. Let me call someone—"

"No!" He tenses and grips my hand tight, his tone even as he straightens, "I apologize, Your Highness. It wasn't my intention to bark. No, that really won't be necessary. I'm alright," then straightens, smoothing out his jacket.

His pained gaze stays glued to the ground when he says, "Would you excuse me?" and leaves the greenhouse without another word.

#

ME: *Things serious w B & this Keith guy?*

TORY: *Dunno. U know her though. It's a miracle she said anything in the first place.*

ME: *U ok?*

TORY: *It is what it is.*

I watch her text bubbles jump, then she sends, *I'll figure it out.*

I want it figured out. I want her to be happy and thriving, not worry about competing with other people for the attention she deserves. But that's her journey, I guess.

ME: *Well, I'm here if u need me.*

She sends three x's.

TORY: *So how was dinner w His Godliness?*

I release a heavy sigh.

ME: *Fine. At first.*

TORY: *Spill that tea E* 😏

ME: *Well, we were talking, things got a little weird and then he kissed me.*

TORY: *Rawr. {smirking emoji} Look at u. How was it?*

No reason not to answer honestly.

ME: *It was… ok…*

TORY: *But not Skylan. I get it. Are u gonna tell him about this?*

ME: *Probably… I don't know yet…*

TORY: *Do you think Princy is as good in bed as Sky?*

ME: *At this point, I don't even think it matters. U know Sky's the only one who makes me come. Regardless of whether Cane's good in bed, I never felt a thing kissing him. But Sky? He does everything with so much care, and attention… I don't know…*

TORY: *So, what ur saying is, when u feel loved.*

That stops me in my tracks.

ME: *What?*

TORY: *Come on, E. Skylan made u feel loved. This isn't as complicated as ur making it out to be.*

ME: *Don't be ridiculous. I don't love him.*

TORY: *Not what I said. I said he makes u feel loved. Cared for, instead of used. I get it. Like I said, just have fun. Worry abt the other stuff l8r. <3 u!*

I smile, ignoring her ridiculous comment about love and sending back a dozen more hugs and kisses before pressing the lock button and tucking my phone in my gown's pocket while I walk to Cane's bedroom with a bag of brushes and paint I found in Ophelia's room. Playing back tonight's events, I decide to read up as much as I can about phantom limb syndrome in the short period before heading to his room to make sure he's okay.

The princes are rooming in the West Wing of the palace and only takes me a few minutes to reach his door. Mother thought our guests would be most comfortable in one of the newly refurbished rooms we mostly used for diplomats.

I knock on his door and call out twice, but he doesn't answer, so I lean the bag of supplies against the frame. Almost knock a third time, but decide against it.

I don't blame him for being embarrassed, but I don't want him to be. Especially since the pain is beyond his control.

Just have fun.

Okay, I can do this.

I kick off my heels when I walk through my bedroom door with Tory's words in mind, and turn into a shirtless, pacing Prince of Callior, phone pressed against his ear and a deeply concerned frown on his face.

I'd jump his bones after what just happened for a little much-needed stress relief if he didn't scowl like he was about to punch a hole through a wall.

"What time was that?" he paces, dragging his hand through his hair. "And it's already gotten that far? How many acres have been destroyed?" Paces more.

"I've been looking at it all day!" Still pacing. "That's not good enough and you know it. Why aren't the choppers in the air right now?"

I take a careful step toward him. All I can make out his father saying is something about bad visibility but not much else. "Dad, please. The palace is an hour away. Just let me help."

He finally stops, and looks my way. I give him a small smile and a wave. "Then make sure Bouchard has at least six Bambi buckets filled by the time the sun rises," Sky reaches for my cheek, softly caressing my skin as I lean into his touch, his shoulders slowly loosening.

"Alright, keep me updated," he ends the call. Then blows out a frustrated breath. "Hey."

"Hi," I stand on my tiptoes to give him a quick kiss. "Is everything okay?"

Sky turns and takes the remote from the lounger at the foot of my bed, turning on the TV to CNN reporting on a forest fire in Acadan, and sinks into my sofa.

"Oh my God, Sky," my heart is in my throat as I sit next to him, taking his hand. "Separatists?"

He nods, "Dad says it under control," and snorts out a laugh. "What part of that looks under control to you?"

"Do they need help?" my throat tightens just thinking about him leaving again.

"I asked that exact question about twelve times in the last half an hour. I asked if he needed me in a chopper helping to extinguish the flames but every time I do, he insists they're fine and that I stay here."

"Sky," I don't want him to but, "if you need to help then you should. Don't stay because of me."

He squeezes my hand and raises his eyes to mine. Pained, but thoughtfully. Then he shakes his head.

"Maverick's watched too closely. I won't be helping his performance if I show up without invitation." Sky slides his phone on the coffee table, then gets up and throws himself on my bed with a grunt.

"You're the crowned prince, I hardly think they'll see it as interference," I say, draping my arm over the back and face him. "Do you think he can handle it?"

He chuckles softly. "You know how stubborn Mav is. He won't let just anything get the better of him." He links his arms behind his head and looks down to me, "Like someone else I know," and winks, warming my heart. He sighs as I turn the flatscreen back off. "Say something to cheer me up, please. How was your day?"

Deciding to start with a safer subject then unfamiliar lips pressed against mine, I opt for more of a play-by-play answer when I sit down on the bed next to him. "Well, I met the cutest little girls at lunch today."

His eyes close and his arm falls over them. "Yeah? I saw the Instagram posts."

"Mhm. They were all over me at first but I'm pretty sure it was just to ask about you."

"Me?" That has him leaning on his elbows as he waits for me to go on.

"Apparently you're sooo dreamy, and you have huge muscles," I smile, playfully batting my eyelashes at him.

He laughs, "Well, well. Little ladies know what's up," saying with a cocky grin, "You totally agree with them, don't you?"

I reach behind me and grab a deco cushion, swinging it down on his dumb, way too satisfied face. "How was the hunt, Prince Dreamy?"

"Too long," he scoots backward until he hits the pillows. "Honestly, I've never seen so many horses freak out at once. Frolic stayed surprisingly level-headed through it all."

I cross my legs, turning to him fully while I lean back on my hands. "I told you he'd take care of you. No one calls Sir Perciville Dominicus Albundy Royalé anything but a cool cucumber."

"No one's got the time, darling," he rolls his eyes and tucks a pillow under his arm. "Where've you been by the way? I've been here for like an hour."

"Dinner with Cane," I say, reaching up to pull the first of about ten thousand pins out of my hair.

"How'd that go?" he asks tightly. "As dry and boring as Mr. Suave himself, I'm guessing."

"Well, it started off fine. We were talking, and walking, and then he kissed me."

Chapter 21
Skylan
First Times for Everything. Literally

I sit up, making sure I heard her right. "He… kissed you?"

"Yes."

"On the lips?"

"No, on the ass," she rolls her eyes. "Yes, on the lips."

"Interesting," I chew on my words as I climb off her bed, getting some much-needed space between us.

Kissed her… Not exactly the news I wanted to hear from her given my kingdom nearly burning to ash.

"And you didn't think to check in with me if I'm okay with that?"

Emryne's brows draw together. "I didn't need to. Last time I checked you're still a friend, a term I use in the loosest way possible just FYI, and not my keeper." She follows me from her seat and crosses her arms. "Technically, I'm not supposed to say a word to you at all. The only reason I am is because I didn't want you finding out some other way."

I bark out an unfriendly laugh, my visions steadily blurring. "How else would I have found out? When I find you two making out in the gardens, riding off in the sunset on the back of his perfect horse? Or when he's shoving you against your bedroom wall fucking you while you're screaming his name when you come?"

"Stop it, Skylan."

I throw my hands in the air. "Hey, I'd be a dick if I didn't at least mention it."

"You're being a dick either way, what difference does it make?" she casts her eyes downward, wringing her thumb in her palm like she always does when she feels guilty.

I hate that look in her eyes. She doesn't have anything to feel bad about.

I'm the one being an asshole. Why, I'm not sure, but I'm definitely not happy.

"You have no right to be angry," she says quietly. She's right. I'm perfectly aware of that, but I am. Sue me.

Emryne sighs, lifting her eyes to mine again. "Would it make you feel better if I told you I didn't feel anything?"

"No."

I'm sulking. A kindergartener could see that. But it doesn't stop me from taking in her words. Emryne's never lied about anything. I've never seen the girl break a rule so of course, I believe her. Still, I don't like idea of someone other than me touching her.

Cane's not a bad guy in any way, but she's mine. And I'll be damned if I let him anywhere near her.

I sigh, burying my face with my hands with a grunt, "Yes," then finally meet her assuring gaze. "Nothing at all?"

She shakes her head once. "Nope."

"Not even a little bit? I mean the tiniest, little…"

"No, Prince Skylan. I didn't feel anything at all when Prince Caneic kissed me."

Best I can manage is a small nod.

She crosses the distance between us and takes my hands. "You knew this wasn't going to be easy," she says, craning her neck to look at me, her eyes so damn blue I almost can't stand it. "You knew what you signed up for when you came. Sure, we have our wild nights, but you need to realize this has to go further than just the physical. So, we'll probably need to hold off on the sex for now."

"Completely?"

"Mhmm."

I did know that. Just fine. I swallow, rolling my shoulders and searching her eyes. "Is that what you want?"

Her mouth opens, then closes, taking a second to consider her words. "I mean… yeah. We have to at least try. How else will we now if we work together or not?"

"Oh, we work together just fine, darling, and you know it." I link my fingers in hers and watch as a genuine smile spreads over her perfect lips. Lips no one gets to kiss but me. Ever.

She's right, the least I could do is try. And if it doesn't work out, it doesn't work out.

But I... want it to. "Okay."

"Okay?" I slowly nod my head, taking this all in.

"I'll try harder," well, I guess I'm—we're really doing this. "Tomorrow. You and me. Dinner."

#

SKY: *On a scale of kale salad to I-can-eat-an-entire-wildebeest, how hungry r u?*

ME: *Somewhere between a warthog and a gazelle* 😊

SKY: *Music to my ears.*

Toothpaste was invented by some dentist named Peabody in 1824. He was the first person who thought to add soap to what they used then called tooth cream or tooth powder. Then in 1850, a Mr. John Harris added chalk, and so the toothpaste empire began.

And while you're only supposed to be brushing once at a time, just once, using about a penny-sized amount... How many times have I brushed my teeth?

Three. Three times. And I'm very seriously considering brushing a fourth.

And while you are only supposed to be using said penny-sized amount, here I'm standing.

At the sink.

In my bathroom.

Coming to a world-altering, life-changing revelation: I need new toothpaste.

I think it's obvious from this whole endeavor that I've never been this nervous in my life, and while it is completely new, and kind of exciting, I'm now pacing the hallway outside Emryne's bedroom like I'm about to enter a senatorial debate, and I don't know why. I was fine when I texted her, confident, relaxed even, now? When she opens her door and walks out in a vision of turquoise silk, with flowing three-quarter sleeves and her hair tied high on her head… I'm in severe trouble.

Fuck, I've got to brush my teeth!

"Hey," she smiles brightly. "You look nice."

I'm not entirely sure what's happening to my face, but I'm guessing I'm gawking at her in the stupidest way possible. "Ready?" she asks when I don't say anything.

She looks like a queen. Future queen. And I could be future king… Oh hell, I'm not wearing enough deodorant. And I have to brush my teeth! And I'm going on a date with Princess Emryne. I've never even been on a date… what am I supposed to do?

What do I say? How many complements should I give her without sounding creepy?

Why does this keep happening to me?

"Sky?" she frowns, quiet concern in her voice.

I shake my head. Shit, did I check my hair before leaving? "Yes," I clear my throat and smooth out my dark gray suit jacket, and I've never been so happy I opted for two-piece instead of three. "Yes, all good here. You?"

"I think so," she smooths out her dress. "Does it look okay?" I don't know how she's able to breathe in the skintight fabric, and I don't care either.

She looks amazing. Though how I'm supposed to keep my eyes off the deep V-slit all the way down to her stomach, showing off just enough of her breasts for my mouth to water, I'm yet to figure out.

"Perfect," I reply, finally composed enough for a grin, even if all I can picture is my tongue between her legs. "You look perfect," she always does.

"So do you, Your Highness. Very dashing," she winks and straightens out my black tie, then hooks her arm around mine. By some miracle, my nerves gradually settle and I'm able to breathe a little easier.

We chat about nothing in particular as we make our way to the small dining room I spent most of the afternoon setting up, with a little help from a well-trusted source.

Towers of chocolate truffles and bouquets of daffodils line the walls. I made sure to have the chef make her favorite recipe of Tuscan chicken for dinner, no doubt waiting under the silver cloches on the medium-sized, round dining table in the center of the room. The space is lit with so many candles it's a fire hazard waiting to happen, but all in all, quiet and romantic. Exactly what I was going for. By the mused look on Emryne's face though I guess I may have gone a little overboard.

"Is it okay?" I stop next to her.

"It's… something alright," I watch as she takes a few steps forward, scanning the room. "You did this for me?"

I nod. "Cosmopolitan said this was the perfect date," obviously not perfect enough.

"I'm sorry, did you say Cosmopolitan?" she chokes on a laugh.

"Yes."

"As in… the magazine?" she raises an eyebrow.

"Yes. What's wrong with it?" I throw a once-over to the setup. It looks fine to me.

"Nothing," I can see she's still fighting to keep her laugh in, though I have no idea why. This took me hours to come up with. "It's… really nice."

I scratch the back of my head. "The article said that girls like flowers and chocolates and when you smell nice and wear fancy clothes."

This time she does giggle. "How old are the Cosmos you're reading?"

"I don't know, Monique found them for me."

A tiny smile of admiration turns her lips upward. "You asked Moni for help?"

"I had to," the little old lady jumped at the chance, believe you me. "It's better than what GQ said which was to take you to my apartment, tie you up and drip candle wax all over you," I scratch my head, "Although, now that I think about it, that was probably an exposé on BDSM," then turn back to her. "Oh hell, was that what I was supposed to do?"

"No!" she giggles, holding her hand up. "No, God no."

I couldn't keep the cocky smirk off my lips even if I wanted to. Which I didn't. "I mean, I totally could. I'd love to, in fact, but we're supposed to be holding off on sex, so…"

Emryne steps closer and cups my cheeks. "It's wonderful. Thank you." She reaches up and kisses me tenderly. The second her lips find mine my arms wrap around her body, pulling her closer, deepening the kiss.

I have to force myself to let her go. Much as I didn't want to, but we're here for a reason. "Maybe we should take it easy."

She steps back, and my body immediately misses her warmth. Her eyes sparkle in the candlelight when she meets mine, equally as flustered. "Yeah."

Night's still young, so I swallow my craving to lift her onto the table and lick my way to heaven, and I pull out her chair—yes, I know how to be a gentleman—and take her hand as she sits down, then walk around the table to my own seat.

"So," I link my fingers together on the table. "You have a lot more experience with this than I do. What do we do now?"

"Small talk," she raises her delicate shoulder. "Getting to know each other and what we like. Treat it like a real first date."

"Technically it is a real first date," I smile at her.

"Which is why it's supposed to be fun," a jolt of electricity shoots through my body when she reaches for my clasped hands, and squeezes. "Just have fun."

I nod. I can do that. "Okay then," I clear my throat with new determination. "So, tell me a little more about yourself Elize."

She grins, catching my drift. "It's Emryne."

"Right, sorry. Weird name for a girl." I reach over to the corked red wine, pouring us each generous amount in the crystal wine glasses, and take a long, well-deserved drink after we clinked our glasses.

"It was my mother's idea to combine my grandmother's and my father's name. So, Emarise and Loryne became Emryne," she tells me. "Middle names are my great and great-great-grandmother's."

I sit back in the chair, caught off-guard. "I actually didn't know that."

"And what about you?" Emryne leans her elbows on the table. "What do you do for a living Simon?"

I smirk, loving this little game. "It's Skylan."

"Right, my bad," she winks, sipping from her wine.

"I'll forgive you for now," I straighten, and lean forward mimicking her. "Officially, I'm the crowned prince of the kingdom of Callior."

"A prince, huh?" she singsongs. "And what about unofficially?"

"Unofficially?"

"Uh huh."

"Unofficially, I'm just a guy, siting in front of a girl, on a first date, trying to charm her into a few goodnight kisses with my mesmerizing eyes and fierce good looks."

Her head falls back in laughter. "Well, aren't I just the luckiest girl in the world?"

"I'd say I'm the lucky one here," even in the candlelight, her piercing blue eyes sparkle in a way I haven't seen before, and it's becoming severely difficult to breathe, tugging on heart strings I never knew I had. Mav might not have been far off with the whole pussy-whipped thing.

"What about you?"

"Well, I'm a crowned princess of Alorewyn. Currently running for queen. And I'm supposed to be dating these two other guys to see who I'll get along enough to become the next king."

"So, your life is pretty easy-going then?" I joke.

"Oh, yeah. No stress at all. Like, ever," she reaches for her glass and takes another sip. "So, when did you decide to abdicate? Weren't you excited about becoming king?"

I blow out a long breath, sending any remaining nerves along with it. "Oh, I don't know, after the… fourth panic attack?"

Her glass is back on the table before she even had the chance to swallow. "Oh my God, Sky."

"I was excited. Really. Then Mom happened, and the separatist attacks became more frequent, and after the fifth one made me hyperventilate so bad it knocked me unconscious for almost two days, something had to change."

"That's awful. I'm so sorry you had to go through that," she eyes me thoughtfully. "You should've told me."

"It wasn't your burden to bear," I shrug my shoulder. "It's my own fault for trying to do too much at once. You know how bad it can be."

She nods and we finally we tuck into dinner, and I feel like I haven't eaten in weeks. Between obsessing over the dish's creaminess and nearly falling out of our seats from laughter, I think it's safe to say this is going pretty well.

As the conversation flows from this to that, I lean forward and refill our glasses. "Your drive, where do think it comes from?"

"What do you mean?"

"Well, of all the years watching you, and now the whole Dark Warrior thing, I've never really seen anyone with determination like you have." Honestly, it's a trait I sometimes wish I had. Sure, I know my way around diplomacy, but Emryne's on another level entirely.

"I'm guessing I can take that as a compliment," she swallows her wine and smiles. "My great-grandfather said it's because I was kissed by the sun."

"What does that mean?" Sounds like something Mom would've said and had like a hundred different meanings.

"Beats me. He died before I could ask, but I'm guessing it had something to do with confidence. He could be very cryptic sometimes."

"You two were pretty close right?"

She nods, "Gramps was my best friend. Other than you, of course," I laugh, reaching for her hand and give it a squeeze. Her great-grandfather was a cool guy when his Alzheimer's allowed him his memories even for a few hours. Both mine died before I was born so I the only relationship I had was with my uncle. I don't remember much about him other than he was an avid baseball cap collector.

Though I have no idea what happened to them.

Still, doesn't make the loss any easier.

"I'm sorry."

"Thank you," she smiles softly, squeezing back. "I wish he was here. He was so excited to see who would become queen. But, it's just the way the world works, I guess."

My eyes drift to her hand, soft and delicate in mine. Her touch is warm, welcoming. And for the first time, it crosses my mind how strange it is sitting here with a woman and not wanting to run for the hills. Maybe it's because Emryne isn't the type to push, specifically since she also happens to be at a weird stage in her life. Before she knew who she was and what she wanted, yes, and then having her heart broken, her trust destroyed, which was entirely my fault.

But she's different now.

Although, knowing exactly what future awaits forces you to grow up pretty fast. Some, like Emryne, thrive under that pressure, and others feel trapped with no hope for a stress-free future. Like me, I guess.

"What if it wasn't?" I know I'm taking a leap here, but I'm curious to know how she'd react if asked.

She narrows her eyes. "Wasn't what?"

"How it worked. I mean, we're technically not forced to take over from our parents. It's a responsibility we accepted," when she doesn't say anything, I take it to keep going. "Hear me out. Normal people don't have any of this to worry about. They live their lives day by day, travel when they want to, sleep when they want to, with who they want to, just be people. No royals, crowned princes, or princesses performing like circus monkeys for the throne, just… them. Why couldn't we do the same?"

She takes a second to mull over my words, but then she shakes her head.

"Not everyone is like us, Skylan. It's not that I don't think about it, I do, but quitting now would end in chaos. I'm happy you got to clear your mind if that's what you needed, but this is the life I chose, and I stand by it."

Fine. But still, "Would be worth it for me. I'd be able to fuck you up and down the streets if I wanted to," I wiggle my eyebrows at her.

She rolls her eyes, smiling and shaking her head. "Must you be so crude?"

"We could be happy, Emryne. That's all I'm saying." I know it's a leap assuming she isn't happy, but it didn't keep me from saying it. Once she has time to take it in, and those wheels start turning in her busy head, she'll see the logic, I know she will. It's who she is. Though, whether or not she'd agree with me I can't say.

Emryne casts her eyes to our hands, gently rubbing circles along my skin and sending sparks of heat through my body, then closes her other hand over mine. "I know it's kind of a sore spot, but, what about your mom? Think she would've approved of this?"

Of me being here? Definitely. Everything else… "Maybe not at first, but she was pretty special. All she wanted was for Mav and me have the lives we always wanted. But I think she'd be happy with how things turned out. She's always loved you."

She smiles. "Do you miss her?"

"Every day. But, like you said," I shrug. "It's just the way our world works."

Isn't that just the saddest sentence you've ever heard?

"I still have the poem she wrote me, you know."

I frown. "Poem?" I didn't know about a poem. She wrote every day if she could hold her pen long enough, but wasn't exactly one to share her work with anyone but Dad and me. I shoot forward. "What does it say?"

She sits up, taking her hand back, and I immediately miss her. "I'm not telling you. It's mine," she shrugs her shoulder. "It doesn't make all that much sense anyway."

That has me laughing. "Yeah, that sounds like her. She loved hiding messages in her poems. Figuring them out is all part of the fun." Her words always spoke more than anything said on paper. Just like Emryne.

Though I really am surprised she shared it with her, even more that this is the first time I'm hearing about it. "I could help you figure it out if you let me see it?"

"Nope," she states with a massive grin.

"Why?"

"Why do you want to see it?"

"Because I want to."

Her eyes dart from the roof to the table, then back to mine as she taps her forefinger against her lip. "Nope."

And now I need to know what she said. Remind me to make her come like never before then ransack her room while she's passed out later, will you?

We fall into comfortable conversation when Emryne's in the middle of telling me about the disastrous date she had with the H2O-obessessed Prince Herwin when actual tears run down both our cheeks.

All throughout the conversation it dawns on me just how tough it must be for her spending so much time with men she doesn't know. It's never made more sense why she's been fighting to rule alone. I'd have done the same thing if I were in her shoes, and I've never admired her more than I am now.

At least she can still keep a sense of humor about it all. "Get out. No way," I say between gasps of air.

"Yes way!" She reaches for a truffle—yes, I made sure the filling was raspberry—and takes a bite before continuing. All the while my eyes glue to her mouth. "Seriously, he wouldn't shut up about it for like half an hour."

Enjoying listening to her beautiful stomach-fulls, I add a little dazzle, anything really to keep her smiling like she is now. "Oh man, could you imagine sweet ole Ronny as king?"

A statement so outrageous it has her laughing harder, "Oh—oh no. Please no!"

Not that I like thinking of anyone of these guys being king. Or looking at her. Especially not touching her. Thank God most of them are gone.

"Kid probably tucks his bottled water in bed and sing them lullaby's every night—oh, wait, glass. Save the sea turtles and all that," I laugh shaking my head, mimicking cradling a baby. "Hush little water, don't you spill. You're totally not being held against your will."

My heart does a funny kind of flip as I watch her wipe her tears with a delicate forefinger, reveling in knowing I'm the one brining that smile to her face. "Stop, Sky, please… I really can't breathe!"

"Please tell me I'm more entertaining than that?" I finish the last of my wine and reach for a chocolate of my own. When I bite down, I get her obsession with the tiny red fruit. Or it's Sir Stéph working his freaky-deaky food magic again. Probably both. Either way it's incredible. Tart yet sweet enough not to overbear, hardy outside, but perfectly soft on the inside once you break through that tough exterior.

Exactly like someone else I know.

"Don't worry, Prince Simon," she grins when she finally caught her breath and pats my hand. "You are much more fun to be around."

"Well, thank you," I bow my head, then lean closer. "And it's Prince Skylan."

"Of course, silly me."

After we finish dinner, Emryne somehow convinces me she needs a piggyback back to her room, and happily jumps on my back as we make our way out of the dining room. The woman may have some solid muscle on her, but I swear it's like carrying a toddler. And I don't mean that offensively. This just so happens to be another thing she loved doing when were kids. And playing outside until who knows what time at night, chasing each other through the sprinklers on hot summer afternoons, falling asleep in puffy sleeping bags on the cinema floor while watching Monsters Inc for the thousandth time.

Man, how times have changed.

And through all this, I can easily say I'm relaxed for once. Not having to worry about being perfect, or having your every move watched and judged by a Parliament who isn't our peers. Just being.

I could get used to this.

I stop outside her door while she's in the middle of telling me about some chick movie, *Dumplin',* she feels is thoroughly underrated, especially the Dolly Parton song at the end credits, when I decide to pick some more fun at her.

Hell, I'd do anything to hear her laugh again. "Dolly who now?"

"Parton?" She jumps down and steps around me, looking at me like I've lost my mind. "She's like the queen of country?"

I shake my head, somehow convincing her I have no idea who she's talking about.

"Oh, you know! *Tumble outta bed and I stumble to the kitchen, pour myself a cup of ambition, and yawn and stretch and try to come alive… * Nothing?"

Man, I've never had to fight back laughter this hard in my life. I press my lips together and shake my head again. "Nope."

She rolls her eyes and keeps going, "*Working nine to five, what a way to make a livin', barely gettin' by, it's all taking and no givin'…*" her little shoulder shimmies break my control and I set the quiet laughter free.

When her eyes find mine, my shoulders are shaking. "What's funny?"

"I know who Dolly Parton is, Emryne," I say though a stomach full. "I just really wanted to hear you sing that."

She clicks her tongue and smacks my side. "Jerk." Which only makes me laugh harder. She joins me, and steps forward, pulling me into a hug as she wraps her arms around my neck.

"Tonight was incredible. Thank you," she says against my cheek. Her perfume circles my nose with flirtatious whisps, making my heart hammer so damn fast I barely hear her sister's door fly open and an obviously distressed Addylin sprinting from her room with one arm in her purple robe and the other struggling to find the other sleeve.

"No. No. No. No!" She mumbles as she storms by us.

"Addy?" Emryne asks after we share a look of concern.

"Medical kit," she says as she rips open a door to what I'm assuming is a storage closet besides the stairwell, frantically rummaging through the contents.

"Where are the fucking medical kits!"

"Bottom rack, next to the—" she barely replies, and before either of us can ask, she has a little red bag in in her hand and slams the door shut, slippers slapping against the marble floors as she takes off down the stairs.

I'd ask how Emryne knew that, but it'd be as useless as asking why the sun shines when I know her extracurriculars likely required more than one band aid.

"Do we ask?" I turn back to Emryne, easily as confused as I am.

"Nope," she shakes her head. "I'll talk to her in the morning."

Shaking off the weird event, I turn my eyes back to my princess. "So, can we rule tonight as a successful first date?"

She smiles, returning to me, "Not that we're supposed to be keeping count, but yes. A plus for effort."

I nod, satisfied. "Good," score one for Prince Skylan. I watch as she leans against her door, tucking her hands behind her. Her breaths deepen, eyes darkening with need, drawing my own to her bottom lip she sucks between her teeth.

"I mean it. It was great."

"I'm glad to hear it."

I can't keep my eyes off her. I know we're supposed to be taking it slow, seeing where this goes, but surely sex has to be part of the experience, right?

And the way her gaze is effectively devouring me, undressing me right in the middle of this damn hallway…

I step closer, caging her between my arms. "Emryne?" I all but whisper, reaching to cup her cheek and running my thumb along her bottom lip.

"Yes?" she whispers, and fuck if it isn't the sexiest thing I've ever heard.

My fingers curl around the back of her neck as her hands grips the lapels of my jacket, pulling me down to her.

"You have no idea how badly I need to kiss you right now."

Her breaths become heavier. "We shouldn't," her eyes fluttering shut as I lower my head to her ear.

"Do you want me to stop?" *Say no. Say no. Say no. I don't have it in me to stop anymore.*

She pulls me into her, pressing her lips to mine. Warm, and welcoming, the greatest fucking feeling in the world.

Are we risking a hell of a lot making out in a dimply lit hallway outside her door for her entire family to see? Yes. Yes, we are. And I don't give a shit. After everything I learned about her tonight, with everything she shared… God, I want this woman like never before.

"I'll take that as a no," I mumble against her silky lips. She opens her mouth, allowing my tongue access, massaging mine with her own.

She moans against my mouth, "Take it as a hell no."

I couldn't tell you what day it is even if I wanted to. All I know is Emryne. All I want is Emryne. All I need is my fingers inside her, her soft body over mine, her gorgeous breasts in my hands, teasing her nipples as she rides me to orgasm, begging for her own release. And I won't be coming until I'm inside her.

Trailing my fingers down the slit in her dress, and she whimpers beneath my touch as I push my near painful erection into her. Her small moan brings a smile to my lips as her body angles toward mine, urging me to keep going.

I want to lift her in my arms, wrap her legs around me and—

"Ehem."

My blood runs cold at the voice coming from behind me. Both of us fly out of reach with such guilty speed it's a miracle I'm still alive, though I push her behind me all the same.

"Father," she clears her throat, smoothing out her hair then stepping before me to keep the very obvious bulge in my pants from assaulting the ruler of Alorewyn's eyes.

King Ryne crosses his hands behind his back, smirking as he looks between us. "Pleasant evening?"

"Mhm," she chokes on a laugh, pressing her lips together to keep from laughing. Glad she thinks this is so funny when I'm a few blinks away from an early death. Or horrific public mutilation. Don't think anyone's forgotten about that.

"I'm guessing the knuckle sandwich had something to do with this?" he gestures between us with his forefinger. Emryne doesn't answer, but her uncomfortable shift speaks volumes.

"Your Majesty, I can explain," I start, figuring this will go over easier if it comes from me.

But he simply holds up a hand. "Don't bother. I was twenty years old once too."

He surprises the hell out of me when he steps between us and wraps his arms around our shoulders, pulling us into his sides, "Dears, you think you're so slick keeping this between you. Let me tell you, you ain't foolin' no one," then pats our shoulders, looking from one of his youngest daughters, "We'll talk in the morning." kissing her temple.

To me, "And I'll meet you on the airfield at eleven a.m. Sharp."

Chapter 22
Skylan
Houston... I Have SO Many Problems

I've been up since the ass-crack of dawn, not that I slept, pacing my bedroom like I did in the hallway before the date last night. I've already changed my shirt twice, and for the first time in my life, I understand why people use drugs. This would've been the ideal moment to roll a joint and light it so it can take this godforsaken edge off.

If Emryne and I were anything other than royals, getting caught wouldn't be as bad as I'm making it out to be, but the problem is—we are. King Ryne's not stupid, he made that clear with the whole 'knuckle sandwich' statement, and him knowing we slept together spells out a fuck ton of issues for me, my family, and my kingdom.

Sure, it's all hot and sweaty, fine and dandy in the moment, but after? Relationship gets complicated, someone's heart gets broken and decides to get even.

How do you spell war? S-E-X. That's how.

It's ten twenty-three a.m. and my nerves are so completely shot I just about shit myself when my laptop pings with an incoming videocall from Dad, his voice cheery as always. "And? Are you coping?"

Wonderfully. I'm about to be executed by your best friend, I'm enjoying being under sex suspension and I can't stop thinking about burying my cock so deep inside her—"Yes, fine. Doing just fine."

"You look like you're about to throw up," Dad raises a concerned eyebrow. "Talk to me. What's going through that head of yours?"

I take a few seconds to consider my answer. He's seen me panic more than once, and it both warms my heart and infuriates me that it still happens when I thought I'd gotten it under control. Hence the three-year sabbatical.

"Just… I really don't want to mess this up," and I really can't.

"Mess what up? You're being awfully cryptic, Sky," Dad pushes.

I don't bother replying. Not when I have no clue where King Ryne's heads at, definitely not when I've come so far in rebuilding her trust. I mean, he walked in on me seconds away from defiling his daughter in the filthiest way I ever have. Three times, in fact, if I had my way.

But I'd didn't. And I'd rather know what the hell's waiting for me sooner rather than later.

"What's the penalty for pre-marital fornication again?" I ask through pinched eyes. I don't think I have it in me to look at Dad as he's about to give me to lay down the law.

"Traditionally? Stripping of any titles pertinent to the crown and banishment of both parties who participated in sexual acts outlawed by the principality in which they're accused in after several court hearings, major fines, even possible jailtime," he leans forward on his elbows. "Now? No one really gives a shit. Why? What did you do?"

Most of that is true, yes. In Callior.

Here? I have no idea what laws they still uphold. King Ryne's a pretty laidback guy. About everything but his family.

"Something bad, I think."

"You think or you know?" he lifts an eyebrow. There really isn't much difference. "Should I expect a call from His Majesty?"

He watches me open and close my mouth while my leg dances to a beat of its own. I'm trying to find the right words to convey to my father why my execution is imminent, but I'm drawing blanks. At the same time as Emryne's father about to draw his weapons.

And use them.

And now I'm terrified all over again.

"Skylan," Dad's voice turns grave, sending a different kind of shiver running along my spine. "What. Did. You. Do?"

Finally deciding on the least obscene explanation, I raise my head ready to answer, only to be interrupted by a knock on my door.

"I'll talk to you later," and slam the screen shut before I can hear his reply.

Guessing it's one of the lady's maids, I'm glad I had the sense to change into one of my flight suits I packed before I'm supposed to leave. Granted, the green fatigues have Callior's red and white colors sewn along the sleeves and legs as well as our flag embroidered on the chest, but even with the inordinate anxiety, I wear my kingdom's colors proudly. No matter how close death's dancing at my door.

I grab my jacket from the sofa on my way to the door, pleasantly surprised when I swing the heavy oak open and Emryne's radiant smile greets me, her skin shimmering in the mid-morning sunlight. I'm not sure whether I'm supposed to be relieved or twice as terrified that she's standing here, but I'm happy either way.

She's dressed in a simple dark gray skirt that hugs her body down to her knees, accentuating her curves in all my favorite places, and a silky white blouse with a pair of white high heels; her kingdom's red, white, and blue sash tied elegantly on her right shoulder.

If ever there was a time for her to remind me just how phenomenal her body is, I wish it wasn't now.

"A tiara?" I tease, noticing the intricate diamond piece on her head, which I know she despises wearing.

She rolls her eyes. "Don't remind me," I watch her gaze drift down my body. I'm sure she had every intention of being more subtle with checking me out, or maybe she didn't, but she's failing. And for some reason it's making me feel better.

"What's the occasion?" I ask, closing the door behind me and taking her hand in mine.

"I'm standing in for my father at today's assembly," she falls into step beside me as we make our way to the foyer, curling her fingers around my bicep.

"How're you feeling?"

"Oh, you know. Like your father caught me seconds away from making you scream my name and at the same time I don't know if I should throw up or pass out," I roll my neck, trying and failing to relieve some tension.

She stops me by taking my other hand and turning her body to mine. "Trust me, it'll be fine. If something was wrong, he wouldn't have asked you to meet him today, and sent you packing. You know how much he likes you."

Yes, I'm aware. But it still doesn't make me feel any better.

"I'm sure I can handle it." Lies.

"Of course, you can," Emryne steps closer, leaning her head back with a sweet smile. "I'll miss you." Her gentle as her touch warms every inch of my body, calming my erratic heartbeat at the same time as encouraging it to beat even faster.

"Come, Emryne!" Her mother bellows past the wall leading to the assembly chambers and disappears as quick as she appeared.

"Good luck," I smile at her annoyed eyeroll. "I'll miss you too," I whisper, leaning my forehead against hers. And I mean it. Spending time with her is beyond intoxicating and watching her smile is very quickly becoming my favorite past-time.

"Breathe. You'll do great," her lips press against mine in a tender kiss, and her touch gives me a reassurance I never realized I needed.

Her delicate fingers wrap around my neck, deepening our kiss, and it's all the invitation I need to close her in my arms. I have no idea who needed this more, and we could've been standing here for a month and I wouldn't care. What I do know is that I don't want it to end.

I don't want to leave her to her mother, or have her face Parliament without backup. Yes, she can handle it, but I want to be next to her. I should be next to her.

All too soon, her beautiful lips leave mine, swollen and glistening, and she pushes me toward the door and winks, leaving my own wonderfully swollen, and starving for more. Her hand lingers in mine for the longest time before she steps away, finally letting go. Smiling as she turns to face the music in her father's place. "Go or you'll be late."

Breathe, she said. Sure.

Am I overreacting?

I'm not overreacting, am I?

He's going to kill me. I know he is.

"Good morning!" King Ryne's cheery voice calls. I find our assigned F-16 between the brigade jets easily enough when I arrived at the tarmac at exactly ten fifty-three and my body resumed pacing, while I run through the speech I've prepared to explain the situation; everything from our first kiss to me leaving her at our estate. Though how exactly I'm going to break it to her father that I took her virginity I have no fucking idea.

Glad he's so happy, because I can't feel my… anything anymore.

"You're shaking, Prince Skylan," he muses, eyeing me up and down with furrowed brows and a teeth-baring grin.

Of course, I am, what did he expect? Me skipping around throwing daises over my shoulder singing Cum Ba Yaa to anyone who'd listen?

I don't waste any more time, this is killing me. "Your Majesty, please let me—"

He holds up a hand, "Fly now, talk later." He pats my shoulder, and climbs up the steps and into the copilot seat.

They finish fueling the jet, and relief floods in my core when ground control signals we're clear for take-off, and we're in the air before long.

Seven years of flying, and I've never felt this calm in the skies before. I remember climbing into the copilot seat of a Douglas CF-18 Hornet with Colonel Bouchard like it was yesterday, thinking I knew what freedom was from learning to dance with Mom, holding her hands and stepping on her toes, earning me more than a few rounds of tickles and deep laughter. Or sparring with Dad when he shooed a hovering Prime Minister Levesque so he could spend time with me, or chasing Maverick through the gardens blanketed with fluffy snow, but no. The second we hit the air, and Bouchard hit the first barrel roll, it was a different gratification entirely.

Gratification only attainable thirty-three thousand feet in the air. Same place I went when I think about Emryne and how being with her is a different kind of freedom, one I don't think I ever want to give up. And I swear, once I get the chance, I plan to tell her father exactly that.

When we touch down two hours later, and even though I'm breathing a little easier, my nerves still aren't fully settled.

"Better?" The king asks, sipping at his water we grab in the hanger and handing me a bottle.

"Somewhat," I flash him an awkward grin.

"Good. I thought it might help. Let's take a walk."

I follow him through the rows of fighter jets, choppers, cargo planes and oily workstations, all the way out the building and through the palace Guard building. All the while he doesn't say a word other than flashing friendly smiles and nods as we're greeted by the passing knights, taking his surroundings in with a gentle curve of his lips. I hate that I can't read him. I've gulped down half my water by the time we reach the pathways to the gardens leading back to the palace when he finally breaks the silence. "Quite the symbiosis between you two, wouldn't you agree?"

My eyes meet his, and I'm surprised to see a softness in them I haven't seen before.

And now I'm more confused than ever.

"Between… me and Emryne?" I ask, forming a frown on my brows.

"Who else, Ace?" he grins, admiring the flock of wild lovebirds chattering in a Japanese Maple to our right. "Saw it the day you sparred. Your father saw the same."

I haven't exactly given it as much thought as he obviously has but, "I guess so," I finally turn to him fully, needing to get these godforsaken jitters under control. "About what you saw last night, Your Majesty—"

"I need to know how serious you are about my daughter, Skylan."

He crosses his hands behind his back and shifts his gaze back to mine, studying me closely. "Despite the fact that I can, and frankly I should have both of your heads for blatantly disregarding the law, it's the twenty-first century, and you aren't the only party involved. Emryne's already given you a beat down, and I don't think she'd ever forgive me if laid a finger on you. You have my and your father's long-standing friendship to thank for that."

I nod, swallowing my guilt. "Are you… angry?"

"I'm certainly not happy, I won't lie about that. But I am relieved she's getting used to the idea of ruling with a partner. She wouldn't be spending time with any of you if she didn't. And my daughter's happiness comes before everything else."

I nod my understanding. I don't want her spending time with anyone but me, period. But I know where he's coming from.

"Do you think she's ready, Your Majesty?"

"I know she is," he replies assuredly. "In fact, she's been ready for some time now. Unfortunately, my opinion isn't he only one that matters." He might not say it, but I know what he's getting at. Emryne's mother isn't an easy woman to please, and while Fredrich Hastings is a nice enough guy, neither is he nor any members of Alorewyn's Parliament for that matter. Dad's complained about them having their heads up their asses enough times for me to believe him.

I straighten my shoulders, ready to admit what's been in my mind for a while. "I care about Emryne, Sir, and I only want what's best for her. I guess I haven't gone as far as telling her that much, but I do. What I don't know is if she still cares."

"Ace, my daughter mastered the art of using her words at a very young age. But a good old-fashioned slobber-knocker? You know as perfectly well as I do, she wouldn't lift a finger unless she truly cared," he stops to grip my shoulder. "Emryne is not a little girl anymore. She is a grown woman. Strong and wise beyond her years, on the verge of ruling a kingdom. And while I don't know what happened between you, neither do I want to, I do remember the tears, and I don't want that for her. Ever again. You hear me?"

I don't want that either, which is why I'm putting so much effort into this. I care about her. "I understand, Your Majesty."

"I need you to understand something else. A few months from now, if Parliament is satisfied with her performance and her numbers remain in the green, Emryne will be queen. Capable as she is, and did the decision lay solely on my shoulders of course, I'd let her, but she cannot rule without a king. Which is the point of this endeavor. I understand our emotions run away sometimes, we're all human, myself included, but what she needs is the match of a lifetime. I will not have what's happening between her mother and I be repeated.

"You two have chemistry. Real chemistry I haven't seen since the day Ophelia met Kaleo. I think you would be a perfect match, and I see a prosperous future for both of you, and Alorewyn. But if you aren't ready, then I'm asking you not as the king of Alorewyn, but as a father, not to drag my daughter through this if it's temporary. She needs a life partner, not a fling," his fingers squeeze my shoulder, making sure I hear his words. "I just want you to really think about it."

He straightens his shoulders and continues walking. "That being said, it's quite a lot to take in at once. This shouldn't be an easy decision in the least, so take some time thinking about it, and when you feel you're ready, then I will begin integrating you into more formal procedures."

"When… will I know?" I swallow, letting his words sink deep.

He pats my back in that typical fatherly manner, "Trust me, Ace, you'll know the second you do," and leaves me with a wink and a spinning head as he walks up the steps and into the palace.

I feel like I'm about to pass out.

A lot was said in our short walk back. Things I should've been more aware of when I accepted the invitation. And knowing five other guys received the same fancy envelope had me racing toward Alorewyn like never before? Just thinking about her with them makes me sick to my stomach. Not when she truly let me into her head for the first time. Yes, I've known her since birth but our old conversations never stretched past the platonic. Definitely not something as serious as becoming king. Or marriage for that matter.

Then again, I've been gone for three years. Three years since I've had to worry about my own future. But it's here now, standing in front of me. With seven thousand windows, forty-four bedrooms, twelve dining rooms, five ballrooms, and one Emryne Gennady.

Brightening my day with magnificent smiles when we're together, warming my heart with soft laugher, giving her all to prove herself to her family and her people when we're not, allowing me to worship her body when the urge hits, and it hits hard.

It's all becoming very real, very quick.

Leaning against the sandstone banister outside the French double doors safely housing the diamond of Alorewyn inside its steadfast walls, I'm faced with the same issues I did when I was running for my own crown, which is why I've been so hesitant in the first place.

Issue #1: I'll have to rule an entire kingdom alone.

No, I won't. Emryne will be next to me every day, doing her part, which is much bigger than mine in all honesty. Not to mention Parliament and both our fathers close by for guidance if needed. Alright, fine.

Issue #2: *I* will be alone.

No, I won't. I'll have my best friend and the love of my life right next to me the entire time, supporting me and my choices, making her own and challenging others with her ideas. She'll have her own jobs to do, and we'll divide and conquer like the monarchs we were raised to be.

Easy as that.

Then what's the problem?

The problem is I can't control the future and it hate it. I hate that I can't see what'll happen to my kingdom in the coming months, especially with the meeting with President Sørensen nearing, and if my cousin will be able to handle it. Yes, I've abdicated, and yes Maverick is the new king, but it doesn't leave me less concerned.

I let my head fall back and close my eyes, soaking up the afternoon sunshine, and try a few deep breaths.

Day by day. That's all I have to do. Take it day by day, step by step, and this will all work out.

It has to. There is no backing out, no running away anymore.

Wait… the love of…

Chapter 23
Emryne
Vengeance is Mine, Sayeth the Hormones

Oh, a visibly nervous Skylan.

What a rarity.

Guess after being caught in the act is what it takes for Mr. Cool, Calm and Collected not to be so calm anymore, and it was most adorable thing I've ever seen. What I admire most about Skylan to this day is his unwillingness to back down. He never ran away from taking responsibility when he was the one who made a mistake.

Though I can't say I didn't share his nerves either. Not from walking into the assembly with forty-two eyes hawk-eyed members of Parliament watching my every move—nerves that would've been justified given Addylin was nowhere to be found when she also should've been here—but rather from wishing I knew what Father is planning to say to Sky.

I tried to concentrating, I really did, but all I could think about is Sky and our kiss this morning. How much I hated letting him go. I get where he came from last night, I really do. Living a normal life is something I've fantasized about several times even before Sky came back into my life, what it would look like, where I would live. I'd have enlisted in Knight Academy if that world included a kingdom, maybe a different branch of intelligence. And yes, those fantasies occasionally included Sky. We'd be regular people, pay regular taxes, and live in a regular home. Nothing special.

But I'm not. I am the crowned princess of the kingdom of Alorewyn and proud to be. I represented my father in assembly, spoke up when an opinion called for challenge, vetoing the ones who made unnecessary or unreasonable changes, and by the encouraging shoulder squeezes and nods of approval, I think I did pretty damn well. I've already risked too much to step back now, especially in terms of the midnight marauding. Even if he's the only one who knows about it.

"These are the changes we discussed today," Minister Fredrich hands me the stack of papers when we're back upstairs in Father's office two and a half dull hours after assembly adjourned.

"If you're satisfied, Your Highness, date, initial and sign the bottom of every page. Mark anything you feel needs further review with a red asterisk and get it back to me by end of day so I can discuss them with His Majesty in the morning."

I nod, scanning the first few pages when my eyes settle on the word vigil, and I couldn't help the question bubbling up. "Prime Minister?"

"Highness?" he asks patiently.

"I was wondering, has there been any more information regarding the Dark Warrior or their identity?" Funny how it seems everyone's gone radio silent.

"Other than the two punks he dropped off at Dispatch a few weeks ago, nothing so far," with more to come, trust me. "But we do have a few suspects under consideration and the knights are working to uncover their identity."

"Suspects?" he makes me sound like a criminal. "Wouldn't it make more sense if they were just a good Samaritan trying to help?"

"I suppose," he nods slowly. "But we have an entire force of Knights Guard for a reason."

Yeah, an entire Knights Guard yet to get a handle on this. "And has anyone mentioned something called Purple Sprinkle?"

His bushy eyebrows wrinkle. "Not to my knowledge," he answers, and I stifle a heavy sigh. *You cannot be serious.* "But I can check with the Chief of Guard if it's important?"

"No," I shrug. "Just curious."

"Alright," he smiles, patting the doorframe he's halfway crossed. "I'm impressed you're taking interest."

I straighten my shoulders. "The only thing I care about is my kingdom, Prime Minister. I'll do anything in my power to make sure it stays safe."

"Duly noted," he says smiling, "I'll be in my office if you need me," and leaves me with a nod.

The tiara and sash were the first thing to go when at I sit down at Father's desk, though it didn't bother me nearly as much as before. And if I'm being honest, the precious jewels weaved into the delicate silver spikes has to be one of my favorites. Even if it is uncomfortable. And looking the amount of ink typed on these pages, knowing I'll be sitting here most of the day is even worse. So, I pull open Father's top drawer, and I take out the spare set of headphones I keep just in case, plug them into my phone and put one of my playlists on shuffle.

Forty-five minutes into reviewing and I'm ready to pull my hair out. I blow out a frustrated breath and push back the heavy leather chair, raising my hands above my head and stretching my tight muscles, relieving some tension I had built up. I'm trying my best to stay focused, but every time I do, he longer the melody plays, the more my music shifts my thoughts back to Skylan and our kiss. The kiss that lulled every worry in my body, flooded my mind with peaceful images of us.

Wrapped in each other's arms morning, noon, and night… It's all I can think about. And our date… Sure it ended with my cock-blocking father—who had nothing to say about last night other than he's happy for me—but the effort he put in intricate details, from the food right down the chocolates and daffodils, melted my heart. Add taking charge the way he did? Stepping up instead of bitching about me kissing a man that wasn't him? I like decisive Skylan. Decisive Skylan is good. Decisive Skylan is hot.

Even through all this, through every action in the past few weeks, I'm beginning to see Skylan as something other than just a friend and I think I like it. The probability of keeping my hands off decisive Skylan for the rest of the week is not particularly high either, and he needs to get inside me before my raging hormones set this office on fire. My bare ass on these pages would definitely be an apt representation of my feelings toward the rejected changes.

I am technically supposed to be having fun, right?

A light knock taps from the door, and a smiling Moni walks through carrying a tray with a steaming pot of tea.

As I'm working through the charity funds with what little concentration I have left, I notice something strange. Over half a million dollars' worth of unallocated funds strange. I page back and scan over the policies one more time in case I missed something, but everything is set in specific terms of exactly what percentage of taxes is divvied among various stipulated charities. Nothing is mentioned about where the money is going to. Every penny is supposed to be helping families in need.

I mark the section with an asterisk in the reddest pen I can find, thoroughly annoyed at yet another subject Queenzilla has been neglecting.

"Your Highness?" she draws my attention.

"Yes, Moni?" I finally raise my eyes into those of a smiling Monique patiently waiting.

She sets the tray down on the coffee table and straightens, linking her fingers at her waist. "You requested I inform you when His Majesty returns."

"They're back already?" I glance at the clock on Father's wall as she nods.

That was quick. Part of me hoped they'd keep each other busy long enough for me to finish this paperwork, but knowing a flight suit-wearing Skylan I almost regret not jumping at his door is walking around like sex on a stick? This is perfect.

She nods. "He just walked through the dining room doors with Her Majesty and Minister Fredrich."

"And Prince Skylan?"

"Passed him by the terrace on my way here," she recalls.

"Please call him for me?" She curtsies and hurries through the door.

I'm out of my father's chair and at the door at the exact moment Sky walks through.

"Hey."

"Hi gorgeous," he grins, taking his sunglasses off, and I slam my mouth to his, reaching behind him and locking the door.

No more interruptions.

"How was the flight?" I ask between kisses, not that I'm remotely interested in anything other than his dick inside me.

Sky is surprised at first, but the longer my tongue moves against his, the tighter he wraps his arms around my waist, filling my body with even more lust as I pull him further into the room.

"Pretty good," he says against my mouth. "Your father likes me. Your mother will probably need a little more convincing. You should've seen the look she gave me when I walked through the doors."

"He's always liked you. And I don't give a shit what she thinks," I spin, facing the desk and shove the brass figurines and file holders out of the way, sending the items crashing to the ground. Sky's eyes flash with hunger watching me hike my skirt up around my hips and pull my panties down.

"You should," he says, not that I in any way believe he's hearing a word coming out of his mouth by the way he's staring at me. "I kinda need her approval if we're—"

I clamp my hand over his mouth, "Sky, please just stop talking and fuck me," then hop on the edge, wrapping my legs around him. A throaty chuckle vibrates from his chest, hitting me straight in my soaking center.

I crave his body against mine, pulsing around him as he thrusts inside me, filling me up with his come, so much it's become unbearable. I'm so ready for him to touch me. To be feel him inside me.

"Right here? Right now?"

I spread my legs slowly, a shiver of pleasure running through by body as the cold air hits my pussy, bare and ready for him. "Right here right now."

His lips turn up in a devilish smirk. "Yes, ma'am."

My fingers find his suit's buttons, working swiftly to free his chest, then pull his boxers down with voracious speed, finally wrapping my fingers around him and stroking his hard length.

"Fuck, darling… I'm not gonna last if you keep doing that," Sky's head falls back and he releases a sigh, hissing as I brush my forefinger over his silky, wet tip. "Emryne, I'm serious."

I laugh, bringing my finger to my mouth and sucking. "Maybe I don't want you to."

"Where are the fucking condoms?" he growls, tightening his grip on my thighs.

"I have an IUD."

"Is that supposed to be some kind of 'you're the bomb' joke?"

I roll my eyes, smiling. "No, dumbass. A birth-control device."

Sinful realization fills his eyes the second my words hit home and he bares his teeth. "Soo… what're you're saying is… we don't need them?"

"Mhmm," I suck my bottom lip between my teeth, nodding as my eyes glue to his swollen lips.

"Turn around," he demands, dropping my thighs and stepping back before taking my hand to pull me down. "Hands on the desk, ass out to me."

My lips turn up in a lusty smile as I spin around and I plant my palms on the hard wood. I feel Sky's heat against my back as he steps closer, hiking up my skirt as he positions me on the desk below him.

"So ready for me, darling," he groans, dragging his finger over my piercing and down to my entrance. I whimper as he repeats the motion before circling my clit with a featherlight touch.

His warm breath against my ear sends shivers down my body. "I've never wanted another woman as much as I want you," I push my bare butt into him, rocking against his erection, aching to feel him inside me. He wraps a solid arm around my waist, holding me close to his iron chest. Nipping at my ear, earning an intense moan as he teases my piercing with his tip, wetting himself with my eagerness.

"Fuck, I want you," he moans. The deepest sense of satisfaction settles in my soul when he finally pushes into me. Deep, and raw, his breath hitching as he stretches me.

"This it?" he growls. "Is this what you want?"

"Yes…" I breathe, moving with him, rocking my hips against him while matching every one of his thrusts, slowly releasing every bit of tension in our bodies and pouring our every breath into each other.

"I'm sorry," Sky chuckles, and slows down, before he pulls out of me completely. "I didn't hear that," he leans down, wrapping his hand around my neck and turning my head to him as he teases me with his tip, earning him a shaky moan. "Is. This. What. You. Want?"

"Yes!" I moan, desperation seeping from my pores. His dark chuckle rocks me to my core. He forces me forward again, and pushes into me with a gluttonous grunt.

"Look at you," he rasps through gritted teeth. "So beautiful." And his thrusts get deeper, slower, dragging in and out of me, clearly in no rush for this to end anytime soon. "You take my cock like a fucking queen, darling."

I do. I am a queen. I'm Skylan's queen.

"Fuuuck! *Fuckfuckfuck,*" I moan as he pushes into me again. "Sky…"

"I know darling, I know," his hand squeezes my stomach tighter. "Emryne, I don't think I can… I'm gonna…"

"Come," my fingers grip his neck tightly, wrapping his free hand around my neck and turning my head to his and nodding as my orgasm teeters on the edge of final, blissful release. "Come with me. Inside me. Please, Skylan."

Sky's hand snakes from my hip down between my legs, rubbing my clit in circles, freeing a different wildfire inside me entirely, pushing me further and further over the edge, until my climax slams into me with the force of a brick wall, rolling waves of long overdue pleasure through my body as I ride the high with Sky inside me. His thrusts quicken and pushes into me a final time, falling over the edge with me as my walls clench around him, demanding every ounce of his release inside me, and nowhere else as he frees a gluttonous moan into the cool air.

He shifts his hand, letting me go with ragged breaths. "Damn, darling."

I turn to face him, wrap my arms around his neck and pull him to my lips. "Yeah."

Sky finally opens his eyes, deliciously sated with sex, and he leans down to give me another tender kiss. "That was one hell of a hello," he says against my forehead.

"I'm sorry," I laugh, just as breathless. "I've been waiting all day for that."

"Never be sorry. If sex is what you need, I'm happy to comply," he grins, closing me in his arms. "Though I thought we're holding off for now?"

"Changed my mind," I shrug. If he wasn't holding me up against him, I'd sink to the floor. And the second his tongue slides between my teeth when I press my lips to his, I'm ready for round two. "And you better be prepared, because I'm nowhere close to being done with you, Your Highness."

#

"You know, what's kinda funny," Sky mumbles against my lips.

With newly arisen fervor not ten minutes after we buttoned up his flight suit, I yanked him out the door and up the stairs. And on our way out of my father's christened office, the idiot's lips turned up in the goofiest grin and thought it would be the greatest idea to refuse giving me my panties back, and instead decided to pull them his over his head, my family members be damned, and carry me through my bedroom door bridal style.

"Give me those!" I tried reaching for them after he put me down, but he simply swatted my hand away. "Skylan, you look like an idiot," I said as he kicked the door shut.

He grinned, linked his fingers in mine and pulled me against his chest.

"Your idiot," then brought his lips to mine.

Yeah. He is. "Am I ever going to get those back?"

"Hmm…" he pulled back and darted his eyes over my room, obviously pretending to think it over, even if I already knew what he was going to say.

"Nope," and he kissed me again. "You're gonna have to fight for them, Your Highness," he declared and threw me over his shoulder, giving my ass a good spank before dropping me between my plushy pillows while an elated shriek left my lips.

I reached behind me flung one at his face he dodged it easily enough, but took the opportunity to close the distance between us.

"Don't… tempt me," I threatened, fisting the suits material in my hand.

To which his answer was to push me down, and grip my cheeks between his fingers. "Shut up and give me that mouth."

And here we are. Buck ass naked on my bed, with me on top of him.

My panties are still there by the way.

"I've always hated my name. Never liked the way it felt on my tongue."

I lay my palm on his chest and push him on his back. "You're out of your mind, Skylan is awesome. And I fucking love your tongue," proving my point, I lower my chest to his, letting my nipples brush warm skin and plunge my tongue between his lips.

"Yeah?" he flips me on my back and kisses his way down my body until he hooks my legs over his shoulders and drags his tongue over my piercing. "Tell me how much."

"So much," I moan into his touch, weaving my hand through his thick hair.

Sky glues his eyes to mine, "Beg me," and he lowers his mouth again.

I'll kick my ass for obeying later, right now I'm too far gone to give a shit.

"Please, Sky…" I gasp as his tongue licks my clit, gripping at the pillow behind me as not to tear Skylan's hair clean out of his skull. "Please, oh God."

His deep chuckle rattles my soul as he continues, bringing another orgasm closer and closer. "I think I like you like this, darling. Begging for my touch," his lips leave my soaked pussy, and he shifts back, torturing me with his forefinger instead, then his middle finger, sliding it all over my pussy and around my entrance, then back to my clit, working in agonizingly slow circles until I'm squirming under his touch.

"Begging me to make you come," he rasps as I buck my hips upward, grinding against his fingers, hoping to gain more friction, but the asshole pulls his fingers away completely.

I groan my frustration. "Sky, what are you doing? Don't stop."

I watch as his eyes change from humored to dark, scorched with vicious lust. "Do you deserve it, darling?"

I try forming coherent words, but I have no idea how to respond to that.

He, no one, has asked me anything like this before. I should be more freaked out, but I'm not.

It's hot.

He's so fucking hot.

"I… I do…"

"Do you want it?"

"Yes," I breathe out with an unsteady voice. "Please."

Sky chuckles again, flips us back over, and beckons me on top of him with his forefinger. "Up you go then, baby girl."

I all but scramble to my knees before swinging my leg over, straddling him. I reach between us, fisting his hard length and giving him a good few pumps before I position him under my soaked opening, starving with need to take every inch of him inside.

When I sink into him, Sky releases a strained, "Fuuuck. You feel like heaven, darling," and slides his fingers around my ass, urging me to ride him deep and hard. "Fucking heaven."

And of course, because of the sick prank the universe keeps playing, I'd just gotten into a good rhythm when my ringtone blares on my side table. I reach over with a frustrated grunt and bring the screen to my face.

Seriously. Now?

"It's Castor," I say annoyed, and watch as Sky's lips turn up in a cocky grin, moving my hips against him.

"Answer it," that devilish grin is all over his lips again.

But I freeze. "Uhm… you're inside me right now?"

He leans back and tucks his hands behind his head. "Answer it. I dare you," he challenges, biting his lower lip.

I roll my eyes. Does he not know me at all?

I hit answer, never taking my eyes off his, and clear my throat.

"Hey, what's up?" I say with great determination to keep my voice steady. Then the asshole underneath me picks that exact moment to start moving again.

"Hey, I finally got Millman's laptop to spill all her delicious secrets," Castor's muffled voice comes through after I hit speaker. "You're going to want to hear see this."

Sky bucks his hips upward, making sure my piercing rubs against his rough skin. I can't stop my moan no matter how hard I tried. "Oh God…"

"Yep, it's interesting to say the least. The emails are pretty incriminating. I can forward them to Guard Dispatch if you want? It'll be good if they have this." I'm only listening with half an ear as my hips continue to grind. That incredible bubbling builds low in my stomach and I know I won't hold out for much longer. And by Sky's own heated moans, I know he won't either.

"Yes," I answer eventually. Though it's more a moan than anything.

"Which," he speaks slowly. It doesn't take a rocket scientist to recognize the confusion in his voice. Everything about this situation is so hysterical, my head falls back with breathy laughter. "I don't need to tell you could play… are you busy right now?"

My orgasm is so fucking close, all I need is Skylan's thumb taking control. So, I grab his hand, putting it exactly where I need him to be.

"Atta girl," his deep, approving chuckle vibrates ever cell in my body the second he starts moving. I know I'm heading into one of the hardest orgasms I've ever had in my life, and I don't want anyone to hear it but him.

"Can I… uhm… call you back in like five minutes?"

Sky shoots upright and grabs my hip, thumb still working the golden stud in steady, deliberate circles.

"Thirty," he rasps, and I hear everything I need to know he's just as close as I am.

"Thirty…" I nod. Even if just Sky can see. "Thirty minutes?"

"Uh… yeah, that's—"

"Hang up the fucking phone, Emryne!" Sky demands with a hoarse voice as I feel him tighten inside me. I don't bother saying goodbye before hanging up and throwing the phone next to me. And not a second too soon, he thrusts upward one final time, groaning as his release slams into him, and it's not long before my own orgasm rips itself free, tumbling through my body in intense, turbulent waves.

No longer able to keep upright, I drop to Sky's chest a sweaty mess. And this is how we stay, gasping for air, while he runs his fingers over my back.

"Jesus," he pants, both of our bodies covered in a thin layer of sweat.

"I know, right?" I answer with a lazy grin.

After a brisk shower, with cold water on Skylan's pestilent insistence, Castor's masked face pops up on my laptop screen with his hands over his eyes.

"Are you decent?"

"Physically, yes. Morally? Debatable," I joke. Though I'm not exactly sure it was a joke.

I tried pulling another chair closer, but the bare-chested beast of a man whose lap I'm sitting in absolutely refused. Refused even more when I began drying my hair and purposely yanked the towel from my hands, insisting he do it himself. I'd make a fuss, but meeting his sweet gaze when he began drying squeezed my heart in all the right places and warmed my body from the freezing water after we sat down.

Castor drops his hands, blowing out a breath. "You know, we've been partners for over a year, the least you could do is send me an uplink so I can watch," he muses, sitting back and crossing his arms.

"Oh, you think you're funny, don't you?" Sky shoots him an annoyed glaze.

"According to the comedy club I frequent, very."

I laugh. "I thought we agreed to keep our private lives private?" I sing-song, throwing his words back at him. I've tried connecting believe me, but the guy is as tight-lipped as a CIA agent.

"That was before you answered the phone with someone inside you," he deadpans.

I roll my eyes and lean my head back so Sky can reach my scalp. "Sky, Castor. Castor, Prince Skylan Dormer of Callior, our newest recruit."

"What's up man?" Sky nods his head.

"You, apparently. Seriously, that was actually kind of hot. I'm disappointed you hung up the phone when you did. Would've been nice to hear the grand finale," Castor sighs dramatically.

"Watch it," Sky points his forefinger at him. "That's my girl you're talking about."

"I'm not talking about her; I'm talking about you." Castor deadpans.

"Oh." That shuts him up, but then he smirks. "*Oh.*" Just like his father, Skylan is a shameless flirt. Men, women, doesn't matter as long as he's desired.

I watch the two stare each other down, somewhat annoyed yet pleased this is going well. Obviously, I wasn't expecting Castor to call. He wasn't particularly happy about the new addition to our weird little family, but after some pointed convincing and heavy-handed schmoozing, he eventually came onboard. Reluctantly.

"Would you two like me to leave you alone?" I chime in, humorously eyeing them having their little moment.

"Actually, yes, that'd be great," Castor jokes. I think.

"In that case, watch it. He's my man," I say, wrapping my arm around his shoulder and pulling him close.

My heart flutters at the light that fills Sky's eyes and the smile he meets me with. "Yeah?"

I bite my lower lip, bringing my lips to his, "Yeah."

"Oh, yes," Castor claps his hands together. "Now this is what I'm talking about. Rip his towel off, Your Highness."

"Alright, take it easy," Sky holds up his hand, shrugging him off. "What've you got, Cas?"

He clicks his tongue and sits up. "You two are no fun. Like I said before I was so sexually interrupted, I finally got into Millman's laptop. Motherfucker had some serious security on that thing. Which told me plenty from the get-go."

"Could you find anything in his emails?"

"Content-wise, plenty. Other than the copious amounts of Indian porn, and I'm talking hot curry and fancy painted elephants Indian, and several folders of mac and cheese recipes, he was telling the truth about the orders. No names, no faces and the mails are never consistent. Every three or four days, sometimes five, he'd order a new supply and they'd simply respond with a time to pick up the product. That's it as far as communication goes."

"It sells out that fast?" I ask astonished, pulling a pen and notepad closer and making sure to take down everything Castor's saying.

"Apparently."

"Could you trace the IP's?" Skylan adds next to me. "Find any other dealers they supply to?"

Castor shakes his head. "I tried to, but it's been blocked."

Sky and I share a look. "Blocked by who?" I ask.

"Someone from way up high it seems. Like, a member of Parliament, high."

Interesting. "Is there no way to see who blocked it?"

"Not unless you want me to hack the government," he answers with a raised shoulder.

Not the best idea given Castor's twenty-four computer fraud inditements already hovering over his head. No need to add a twenty-fifth, unless conditions absolutely necessitate.

"All I could find was a routing number for the bank payments are made from, but even that was a wild goose chase."

I note it down. "From which bank?"

"One authorization came from First National Bank of Alorewyn but that's where it gets kinda fuzzy. I was able to trace the transactions to an offshore account in the Maldives, which boomerangs to a bunch of corporate shell-companies with P.O. Boxes in Adlengn."

"Adlengn?" Of all the countries on the world I expected this to come from, Caneic's home definitely wasn't one of them.

"Mhm."

"Was there an address attached to the emails?" I ask. He nods, and I take down the exact coordinates.

Thirty minutes after we hang up, I make Sky hide in the bathroom while I call Moni to bring dinner up. It takes her all of fifteen minutes to set up the coffee table family style and us digging in as if the world was our oyster.

"This is huge, Em-Em," Sky shakes his head and releases a long breath before he bites into his burger. We took the better part of waiting for our food to go over what Castor said, trying to put some pieces together, but ultimately failing. This whole damn thing feels like it's all over the place.

"I know. Why do you think I'm absent most evenings?" I reply, taking a bite of steaming porcini risotto.

"Don't you think we should tell someone about this? I'm sure your father would understand the situation if you talked to him?"

"My father already has enough on his plate as it is," I put down my fork. "This is our business now, and we're handling it. No need to worry him." Sky smiles, clearly satisfied with my answer.

Then another one drifts into my head. "How did *your* talk with my father go, by the way?" I incline my head, eyeing him thoughtfully.

He shrugs and digs into his fries. "Pretty good, I think."

I raise my eyebrows, waiting for him to continue. But of course, to my utter frustration, he doesn't say a word.

"Oh, come on!" I reach over and throw my napkin at him. "Are you not going to tell me?"

"Are you not going to tell me what's in my mother's poem?" he bites back smirking.

Touché, Your Highness.

"No," I recoil. Crossing my arms. Why does he want to know anyway? I've had the thing for over five years. If I can't figure it out, he definitely won't be able to.

"Then you have your answer," Sky winks and drips his finger into the whipped cream next to our slices of Oreo cheesecake, then dabs it on the tip of my nose, smiling.

"Hey!" I laugh, swatting his hand away and wipe the cream off my nose.

"But I will say this," he says, leaning in close as he sucks his finger into his mouth and drawing my eyes to his puckered lips, wishing it was my finger he's sucking instead. "He made me see it was high time to open my eyes."

"About what?"

"Something very important." Sky beams.

Chapter 24
Emryne
One Giant Leap for Alorewyn

Thanksgiving is three weeks away, and Skylan and I are stronger than ever. Father has never been happier seeing the two us close again. Whatever he said to His Highness must've made a surefire difference in the way Sky went about me still having to entertain Allister and Cane. He hasn't said anything specifically, and I know from the pained glances when we saw me with them, he wasn't exactly happy seeing it, but he's putting up with it. What I love most is the effort he's been putting into us when we aren't hanging out as a group.

From three a.m. sneak-aways to the kitchen to make pancakes, laughing our faces off between trying to decipher Sir Steph's atrocious handwriting, and heated kisses when we do, to which the morning staff would be as confused as ever at the amount of flour and batter smeared all over the place since neither of us knew how to use an electric mixer, and his insistence on taking full advantage of November's frosty temperatures in our indoor pool when no one was around, it's been amazing. And when we didn't, Sky, Allister and I bunched into the heated water on more than one occasion when the sun barely kissed the glass even in midday, mostly with Cane and Addylin watching us from the cushy loveseats next to the pool, something I found extremely strange given she used to love water.

Cane made sense for obvious reasons. I don't know what the protocol for prosthetics and water is, specifically since it's salted not chlorinated, but I'm guessing he stayed away in case anyone saw, made even more of an effort to avoid us being alone, though he and Addy seems to have grown pretty close. Which I don't mind at all. And if I'm being honest the two of them… actually look good together.

It's just a little after five in the afternoon when Castor's blocked number pops up on my phone. I walk through Sky's door freshly showered after a rigorous workout, with an oversized t-shirt over my otherwise naked body and my favorite body lotion I stuck under my arm.

Castor's on speaker with highly anticipated news, excitement bubbling in my belly as I leap into his open arms. "I have a gift for you."

"Darling," Sky's bare chest and lowriding tailored slacks greets me with a tender kiss. "Your virginity was enough. I don't need anything else," he reaches behind me and gives my ass a good spank.

"Dumbass," I roll my eyes smiling. "You want to tell him?"

Castor's muffled laugh comes through the line, "Your armor is finished, Your Highness."

I don't think I've ever seen Castor as excited at the day he heard I was sequestering his expert sewing skills for Sky's armor. Guy jumped, and I literally mean jumped, at the chance to get started. Even went as far as to upgrade my own, and though I have no idea how useful a cape will be but apparently it was a non-negotiable addition to the ensembles.

"You're the man, Cas," Sky's elated grin warms my heart, pumping his fist in the air. It's taken forever, but we're finally able to start kicking some serious ass.

"It'll be in the P.O. Box in Midtown, and you better send pics once it's on. I shall like to look upon the fruits of my brilliance."

"Alright, Picasso."

"Is there anything else?"

"I think we're good for now. Keep working on those emails and let us know if you find anything."

"Gotcha," he clicks off.

My gaze falls on Sky's unkept bed. Since we mostly spend time wrecking my sheets, I've only been back in any of the West Wing's rooms once before renovations when I helped Mother pick out the new interiors. While Cane's room was sleek and modern, I decided on something a little more rustic for this room given the old oakwood fixtures, exposed brick (a feature not often seen in palaces but I absolutely love), and the intricate wooden headboard behind the four-poster bed. Add a rugged, broad-shouldered, unshaven Skylan to the mix and it becomes every woman's wet dreams. It didn't involve satin though.

"Who gave you satin sheets?" I ask genuinely curious, running my hands along his mattress. All while the feminine urge to feel the soft, midnight black fabric caressing my bare body has never been stronger.

"I did," Sky shrugs, not at all seeing what the problem is. "You know how much I hate cotton."

That I do. He never let me hear the end of it the first time he fell asleep in my bed and woke up with an ugly red rash on his butt. I thought it was funny, but the amount of eczema cream he went through in that week alone wasn't funny to him at all, and is also why he never stays beyond our many, many orgasms. Although the thought of waking up next to a sated, sleepy-voiced Skylan makes my heart beat in somersaults.

Sky shakes his head laughing. "You two have got a great thing going by the way."

I nod, knowing he's referring to Castor. "It's nice to have an eye in the sky, I agree. Crazy how this is the most we've ever spoken."

"How did you meet anyway?" He sinks into his navy couches, beckoning me to him. "And what's with the mask?"

I leave his bed and my filthy fantasies between the sheets for now and take his extended hand, letting him pull me into his lap. "Wanna hear the long version or the short version?"

He clicks his tongue. "You know don't like short things. Except you, of course," he says wiggling his eyebrows.

"I'm not that short," I recoil, playfully slapping his stomach.

"I like it," he leans his head back, sweeping my hair over my exposed shoulder where the t-shirt has fallen away and place a soft kiss on my skin. I open the cap, ready to work the grapefruit scent into my skin when Sky reaches for the bottle, "Let me."

"Really?" I smile, giddy at the thought of his strong fingers sensually massaging the lotion into my skin.

He winks, squeezing a good amount in his palm and begins rubbing along my calves. "Tell me the story, Em-Em."

I would protest, I would, but those fingers of his are magic. Inside and outside of me.

"About a year ago, I got tipped off that someone was stealing knight's armor and selling it on the black market. Castor hacked into the Guard database and accessed the retirement records of discharged knights so his accomplice could steal the armor."

"Was he wearing a mask like he did the other day?" he asks and scoots us forward, "Up, I need to get your thighs."

I swing my legs down and stand in front of him, gripping his shoulders as he moves his lotioned fingers all the way from my ankles and up my thighs.

"He was," I continue, trying not to focus on how close he is to the apex of my thighs. I sure know how to pick a day not to wear panties. "He always is. I have no idea what he really sounds like, or looks like, or what his real name is, much less why he wears it. And I don't really care, not when he's gotten me out of more than one sticky situation. When I caught up to him, we made an arrangement. Instead of me handing him over, he'd become my inside-man. And we've been partners ever since."

"Well, color me jealous," he comments, the calloused pads of his fingers finally kneading my aching muscles, and him a deeply satisfied groan. Sky smirks, fingers still working my calves. "Feel good?"

"Heavenly," I suck my bottom lip between my teeth, allowing my head to roll backward as I lean further into his magnificent touch.

"You're very tense, darling," he chides, moving to my thighs. "When's the last time you had a massage?"

"I don't know, a couple of months maybe?"

"Naughty Princess," he tsks, giving me a disapproving shake of his head. "Not taking care of herself like she should."

"I have you for that now, don't I?" I tease, moaning as his finger brushes over my naked sex, sending a whisper of desire through my body.

"That you do, gorgeous," he winks, pressing languid kisses inside my thigh.

I roll my head to the side, eyeing his empty plates on the black marble coffee table behind me. "You ate already?"

"Mhmm," Sky hooks his hands behind my knees and pulls me closer. "But I haven't had dessert yet."

"Isn't that raspberry cheesecake right—"

"I'm not talking about cake, darling," he cuts me off, hooking my leg over his shoulder as I watch his eyes fill with heat. "Would you look at what we have here," A sinful grin turns his lips upward as he leans down and grabs the spoon, digging into the whipped cream and lifting it right between my legs, dragging the chilled metal over my throbbing center.

"Well, I never," he drawls, wiggling his eyebrows in that typical Skylan manor. A subtle gasp escapes me as my hand latches onto his massive shoulder, while the other caresses the back of his head, encouraging him to continue his teasing.

"Mmm," his tongue lapping up every bit of whipped cream, sending pulses of sweet pleasure rippling through my body. "Lips like sugar."

My head rolls back in laughter.

"You and your shamelessly filthy mouth," I say, weaving my hand his hair, then bend down to place soft kisses on his lips. Sky parts his lips, allowing me to sweep my tongue over his, savoring the taste of the sugary cream in his mouth. Just as he settles his fingers between my legs, my ringtone blares next to him. He grabs my phone, holding it up and showing me the caller ID.

This is unexpected.

He swipes the answer button. "Cassy, what's shaking?"

"Twice in one day, this has to be a new record."

"If you've imprinted on us like a baby duck, I'm sorry to tell you this but we're not ready to be parents yet," Sky jokes.

And all too soon it seems. "A new email just came through. Massive shipment is heading for that warehouse."

My fight instinct shifts into gear as anticipation bubbles in my veins. I drop my leg from Sky's shoulder and grab the phone, sitting next to him. "How? They should know Markus was arrested by now."

"It's probably under auto CC or BCC. I'm running a diagnostic to trace the IP, but either way it's happening today."

Sky and I share a look. "How much time do we have?" he asks.

"It'll arrive in the next hour."

My head snaps over my shoulder, settling on the afternoon sunrays shining through the massive windows. Less than ideal circumstances for covert operations.

"Infiltrate a drug ring in broad daylight?" I deadpan. "Are you out of your mind?"

"Dispatch is blowing their radios up, Your Highness. Their planning on raiding the place, so either go get some answers or let them handle it."

My eyes find Sky's tense expression. This wasn't exactly how I wanted our first day as partners to go down, but I guess we have to get out there at some point. This problem isn't going to solve itself and it could be our one chance to get these guys once and for all.

"Up to you, darling."

Let's weigh our options here. Number one, jump into action and get ahead of this thing now, kick some hard ass all while risking getting discovered or number two, leave it to the authorities to solve despite months of work stalking and spying, ultimately for nothing.

I can't see the latter ever going over well in my head, so. Risk getting discovered it is.

"We'll have to get there before traffic starts," I pace, "Though I have no idea how. Not like we can maneuver the streets in our armor."

"Let me handle that. Just get yourselves to the P.O. Box, I've got transport."

"Volunteering to be our getaway driver, Cas?" Sky smirks.

"Don't be ridiculous," he deadpans. "I'm your eye in the sky, and I will be nursing the beginning of what I have no doubt will be a museum-quality hangover from the comfort of this basement."

Interesting, this isn't the first time he's said something similar. I've asked him to do the driving a few times, and every time he'd come up with some fabulous reason why he definitely won't be doing that, add the fact that he probably never leaves his house, I could be wrong but I'm guessing he's agoraphobic. Another piece I'll be adding to Castor's personality puzzle.

Dressed in simple gym clothes and ready to take some names half an hour after we traversed the tunnels to the parking garage where the rental car was waiting, Sky and I arrive at the PO Box. The well-kept building surprises me every time given its barely used since mail is delivered directly home, but it's been a key factor in sending things back and forth between Castor and I, especially since no one's ever here and the CCTV cameras no longer work (accidental misfire, I swear).

Navigating the librarian rows of empty boxes, we reach the back of the building near the emergency exit we're using to make our escape.

Without wasting another second, I hand Sky the key. He unlocks the metal door and pulls out the gray suitcase safely housing his armor, and yanks the zipper back.

He reaches in and pulls off his gray t-shirt as he takes out the black Lycron undershirt, a fabric combination of Castor's creation—blended high-grade cotton with Lycra which he designed to absorb sweat—and puts it on. Since we don't have time nor would it make sense to head back to the palace to change, I threw my own armor in a duffle bag and begin changing.

"Think I can get this guy's detail? This is phenomenal," Sky says once he's secured the bulletproof vest over his chest.

I do the same, and fasten the mask around my neck. "Sorry. He's mine," I smile at him, testing the scrambler as I always do and watch as Sky gives me a much too amused look.

"Does mine do that too?"

My eyebrow raises. "It does indeed, Your Highness. The whole point is not to give our identities away."

He chuckles, shaking his head and securing his own over his face. He hits the button and does a few tests on his own.

"Sweet," as with mine, Sky's natural tone is lowered by at least two octaves as he speaks. "So does this… whoa, trippy… hey, check it out—"

I rip mine off and hold up a finger. Those mischievous eyes give away more than he knows. "Skylan, I swear, if you so much as think of saying the words 'I Am Your Father', I will beat you with your own fist." At least the scrambler works.

"Do you have to suck the fun out of everything, Em-Em?" he chastises with a grunt, pulling his mask back down.

"Considering my kingdom is on its way to an epidemic, yes."

He rolls his eyes. "Fine, put it like that."

We fasten the new capes around our necks, and lace up the black combat boots.

"Well, what do you think?" Sky asks once he's fully dressed.

Suffice it to say I'm not often rendered speechless, but now? Admiring a blacked-out Skylan, with every part of his armor fitting like a glove, my legs move before I have a second to think about it and my hands wrap around his neck, pulling him down to my lips for another breathtaking kisses.

Castor never messes around when it comes to armor, and neither do I, particularly since we have no idea what we're heading into once we leave these four walls. Even knights didn't have uniforms as sophisticated as this.

I snap a few pics of a posing Skylan and hit send, and got "Imma freaking genius!" a few seconds later as a reply. If that isn't the gospel truth, I don't know what is.

Six rhythmic knocks let us know our ride's ready and the coast is clear, and I swing the door open, checking the area before we sprint to a crusty old delivery truck and hop in the back, hunkering down between the crates of organic vegetables stacked inside. Sky knocks on the canopy twice, and the truck starts moving.

"Ready?" he says, resting his elbows on his knees.

"As much as to be expected, I guess. Most of the time I just wing it." Key word being 'most'. While I do end up playing the scenarios off by ear, having another body to worry about complicates things a little. But I have faith Prince Skylan will pull through. At least they won't only be aiming for my head this time.

"What about you?"

He considers the question. "I'm happy you won't be alone, that's for sure."

"You think I can't handle it?" I tease.

"No, no I have no doubt you'll be fine. But if what Castor's saying about this shipment is true you know as well as I do this won't be easy. As in, double the firepower then the docks."

Of course, I considered that. I'm not the fan of making noise when I'm working, "Which is exactly why I brought the smoke grenades."

"What if this is mob related?" Sky then asks, tapping his chin.

"We can't discredit anything at this point," which is true, on the other hand… "But you saw those mugshots. None of them exactly spelled out capos to me. And add the fact that Adlengn is somehow involved? I'm guessing no."

Sky nods. "Would be kind of cool though, don't you think?"

"What?"

"Me and you, taking down an entire mafia," he wiggles his eyebrows, earning a laugh from me. "They'd be idiots not to make you queen."

And start a war with organized crime lords, something neither of us have the time nor I the desire for.

"Easy tiger," I shake my head. "But you're right. That would be one for the record books."

I'm pretty sure no vigilante princesses have ever done anything like this. Well, no princesses have ever given much thought to being a vigilante in the first place I'm guessing.

"Like totally Godfather style. Kind of have to respect it," Sky nods slowly, flashing that boyish grin he usually does when he likes the idea of something.

He smiles. "You have to let me take you to Italy someday. I know where all the good pizza places are. And the gelato? It's like heaven in your mouth."

My humor expeditiously vanishes. Yeah. Right. Italy. The place where he made a sex tape with the bodacious brunette.

"No thanks, I'm good," call me a child all you want, it's going to take a hot minute to get over this. I would've, in fact, eventually forgotten all about it had he not brought up the first place. I yank my phone from the utility pocket on my cargo pants and redial Castor with new determination.

"Darling?" I hear the frown in his voice, but I ignore it.

The only person who gets to see Sky naked for the foreseeable future is me.

He picks up on the second ring. "Three times in one day, aren't I lucky?"

"I'm sending you link to a video I need you to take down."

"Sounds juicy," he says. I almost laugh at the accuracy of his sentence. Almost. "What is it?"

"Prince Skylan's sex tape."

My eyes glue to him and I watch every emotion from laughter, to shock, to embarrassment on his chiseled features, until it finally turns apologetic as he tries moving next to me. But I simply hold up my finger.

"Only if I get to watch it. Just once. Please?" Usually, I'd laugh at the silly desperation in Castor's voice, even if it is scrambled, but nothing about it is funny. In fact, it pisses me off even more than I already am.

"No. Get rid of it."

At least he takes the hint and clears his throat. Back to business. "Yes, Your Highness."

Chapter 25
Skylan
Two Takes for the Team

"It was a favor for a friend. She was a film student. It's not a big deal."

"No big deal?" Emryne deadpans. "It's all over the damn internet, Skylan."

I have to give it to the guy. Castor's ability to build quality armor is unprecedented. The Kevlar is snug, yet comfortable, and easy to maneuver in. I'd be very much naked right now were it not for him, and there is no way in hell I'd have let her do this alone.

How Castor pulled transport off I'll have to ask the next time we talk. Old-school, but effective. If this is the universe's way of telling me to cut out sugar and up my vegetable intake, unfortunately it's not working. Although, if my princess always tastes as sweet as she does, I don't think I'd ever need it again.

Unfortunately, that sugary side has bittered now. How she got a hold of the video I'd love to know. Loved to leave this conversation alone also, but by the way Emryne's eyes are propelling daggers at mine I can see that won't be happening. Nowhere to escape to now given we're hunkered down in a produce vehicle on our way to probable injury.

"Well, I didn't know that. Where did you find it anyway?"

She lifts an eyebrow. "You're kidding, right?"

"Not even a little bit, darling," smirking probably wasn't the best idea given the fuming princess in front of me, still didn't stop my lips from turning up.

"It's. All. Over. The internet. Skylan!" she bellows, crossing her arms. "Aren't you… ashamed?"

Well, that is news to me. Last time I spoke to Careyna was almost a year ago, and had I known her intention was to release it I probably wouldn't have agreed. Then again, I was on sabbatical and walking a flimsy tightrope between drunk and tipsy most of the time. I have nothing to hide. And I can't see why she's making such a big deal out of this either.

I simply shrug. "First of all, I had no idea it was released." Truth. "Second, why would I be? I'd already abdicated by then so who was I upsetting? Besides, did you see my ass in that? Phenomenal, right?"

She snorts and turns her eyes away. "Of course, you wouldn't see the problem."

I study her closely, coming to a fascinating conclusion. Not that it could be possible, this is Emryne we're talking about, but, "You're not jealous, are you Em-Em?"

"No," she says all too promptly. "And stop calling me that!"

I scoot closer, giving her a toothy smirk as I say, "Would it make you feel better if *we* make a sex tape?" Which I obviously mean as a joke. Although the idea of her naked on camera is… strangely appealing.

She still doesn't look my way, so I reach for her gloved hand, squeezing gently. "Hey, what is it?"

"Nothing," she tries taking her hand back only for me to hold her tighter and pull her closer.

"I can't read minds, darling," I speak gently, letting go and bending a finger under her chin, lifting her to look at me. "Talk to me."

She doesn't say anything but her silence speaks volumes.

"If you're worried about Careyna, don't be. Trust me, that was a one-time thing." And it was. She's married to the director of that video now, according to her Instagram account anyway. Apparently, all it took was seeing her sleeping with a man of my caliber to wake the idiot up. Not that I'm in any way happy about being used as revenge. But, bygones. Sort of.

When she finally lifts her gaze, I see more worry that I'd care to admit, and I hate it. "If you slept with a woman like that, what can I possibly bring to the table?"

I swallow, my heart tightening in my chest. That's what she's worried about?

"Careyna was pretty," I nod. "And she did everything I wanted."

The truck's brakes screech to a halt, and I hear the driver's door swing open.

She rolls her eyes, shrugging out of my grip, turns away and shoots upward, heading for the exit. "Precisely."

I follow her to the door, and my hands catch her upper arm, pulling her flush against my chest. "Want to know the problem though?"

"What?" she says flatly.

"Exactly that. She did everything I wanted," I tell her. Her eyes narrow, not entirely catching my drift, so I keep going. "She didn't push back, make any sassy comments, and she can't suck a dick for shit. I've never been so bored in my life."

The smile I hoped for didn't return. In fact, her eyes were staring to water. "You still came though."

"Of course, I did. If you were a man with a naked woman on her knees in front of you, so would you." I say, knowing perfectly well my princess responds to logic. More so, she responds to action.

If she needs me to prove my point, I will. "Difference is, darling, she wasn't you. And I'll prove it to you," I grab her face, and pull her lips to mine, kissing the hell out of her.

Her arms close over my shoulders, and my hands snake around her waist, pulling her closer to me.

This right here, this is what I'm talking about. This feeling, this bond we've always had, it's something no woman can replace. I kiss her, and I feel everything. I feel her soul, her kindness, her determination. I feel it like a second heartbeat, or a fresh perspective. A dream I somehow got lucky enough to become a part of. No one else can give that to me.

No one.

I deepen our kiss even more as her body slowly leans into mine, my hand curling around her armored ass. My fingers brushing the smoke grenades she clipped to her belt, and a new rush of thrill hits my senses.

We're really doing this.

When my lips leave hers, I still haven't opened my eyes yet. I lean my forehead to hers, whisper in a heavy breath, "Yeah, definitely not you," and place a tender kiss above her brows. "There's only you. I promise."

A hint of a smile turns her beautiful lips upward, just in time for the two knocks against the doors, and the lock clicks open.

I follow her as she drops to her haunches and swings open the doors, careful not to bang it against the canopy, and we hop down, making a run for the warehouse. While I wasn't sure what to expect about the condition of the place, it definitely wasn't a well-kept red brick building in the middle of what

I'm guessing is Downtown, right between a chocolate factory and a Persian carpet wholesaler.

"You know, when you become king, we'll have to make sure that thing is never sees the light of day," Emryne says as we hunker down next to an emergency exit.

This is where we begin to weigh out options carefully. With most buildings like this one, emergency exits are rigged with alarms directly linked to Guard Dispatch. Door opens, alarm blares, goodbye speedy resolution. And unless I'm missing them, what I find strange is the lack of security cameras when I survey the door and the top corners they'd usually be, which means there had to be some kind of silent fail-safe.

Plan B it is.

"Fire escape," I point upward to the metal stairs leading to what I'm guessing would be the second floor.

Thinking over what she said as we climb the steps, I know what she means. But it doesn't keep me from stopping in my tracks.

Interesting choice of words back there. "When?" I turn back to her, smirking.

She shrugs awkwardly. I'm guessing she wasn't paying much attention either. "Would you... I don't know... would you want to be king?"

"Why Emryne Charlotte Gwendolyn Gennady, are you asking me to marry you?" I tease.

"What? No!" she snorts, but don't miss that hopeful gleam in her eyes. "If anything, you're going to ask me to marry you."

"You sound very sure."

Reaching the window, she pushes past me, and slides it open soundlessly. The reek of burning chemicals is the first thing to hit my nose when clambering through the window.

The same organized exterior can't be compared to the inside. The hallway is a mess of scattered paper, broken glass, cracked walls and used syringes. We slide our masks in place, already making breathing easier, and hit the scramble button—out of this world, really—then pull the hoods over our heads. She turns back. "You... you wouldn't ask me to marry you?" Her voice comes through somewhat rough as her eyes focus on mine. That is a question neither of us are not ready to have answered yet. And honestly, it blows my mind even thinking about it.

We look at each other a second longer, and both chuckle. "Maybe we should talk about something else," I say which thankfully earns me a nod.

We move further into the building and kneel behind a wall, surveying the room. I count six guys unloading boxes from what looks like a cargo truck. The floor below is lined with workbenches, all covered in remnants of white powder I'm assuming is Sprinkle. Though who knows in a place like this.

"You know, I do find it ironic that—Behind you!"

The dull blade of an axe narrowly misses Emryne's head before I wrap my hand around her wrist and yank her into my chest, and we stumble backwards.

With her hand still in mine, she spins on her heels and propels the ball of her foot into our attacker's knee, sending him scrambling down the stairs with a heel to his jaw.

Two more appear from the stairs behind him, as scraggly and fuming as the first, jumping over the body descending the iron stairs face first. Emryne pushes me further into the hall, and the tail of her cape jerks backward.

She stumbles into red flannelled arms closing over her chest, crying out her surprise when he cages her between the wall and an overturned desk chair near the landing, prompting me into action.

I've made it all but two steps toward them when a fist grips my hair, searing pain flares from my scalp all the way to my shoulders as I'm dragged backward.

I slam my heel into his toes before we reach the landing and force my head straight into the bridge of the guy's nose.

With a mighty grunt, he finally stumbles back, just far enough for me kick his feet from under him before forcing him upright by the collar of his shirt.

"Hey, darling!"

Her head whips to me after she kicks against the wall, freeing herself as they tumble over the leather chair and she's able to free herself. Her legs propel her upward, and she's on her feet.

"Cock-shot!" I yell. She rushes over kicks him straight in the balls.

He shrieks as he knees give in, doubling over in agony before I let him go, and he slumps forward, curling into a ball on the floor before us.

"Okay. That's it," she tears hers off, followed by mine, and chucks it against the wall, her breaths deep and heavy. "No more capes!"

With the hallway momentarily clear, we creep toward the stairs, keeping a close eye.

"That was easy enough."

You know that thing doctors say about *not* mentioning how quiet it is?

I don't hear the trigger being pulled, but the little shrill of the suppressor stuns me all the same when I push her out of the way.

My breath is knocked out of me completely as the room spins over my head. The pain radiating from my sternum is something I'm at a loss of putting into words.

Dull and throbbing. Stark and aching. If I hadn't looked up at that exact moment and tackled Emryne to the ground, that bullet would've pierced her head instead of the Kevlar currently strapped for my chest.

But she's safe.

The blood pounding in my ears clouds the commotion around me, but I know I'm being pulled somewhere.

When her face fills my vision again, she's shouting, "Are you okay?" above, frantically working her fingers over my chest and digging the bullet out of the Kevlar. "Sky! Look at me!"

I sincerely hope Castor knows how fucking incredible his designs are. Without this vest, I'd be as good as dead.

"Fine," I cough, fighting and failing to catch my breath. She, on the other hand is breathing so rapidly I'm surprised she hasn't passed out.

"Emryne, I'm fine. Really," I reassure her. Not the first time I've been shot, and won't be the last, though I'm not excited for the handsome black bruise I'll have come tomorrow.

"That was supposed to be for me."

"Not if I could help it. Which I did. Besides, your chest is worth a lot more than mine, darling," I wink at her, my chuckle soon turning into a cough as I fight to catch my breath. She narrows her eyes and shakes her head, spinning three-sixty with her firsts at the ready.

Only… the goons stopped coming.

Once I recover enough to push myself upward and survey our surroundings, Emryne's pulled us behind rows of empty crates stacked high on cargo carts for easy transportation, the lack of noise is the first thing I notice after she settles next to me.

Besides the idiots we've just given a beatdown rolling around on the floor, barely conscious, the silence is acutely disconcerting.

Where the hell did everyone run off to?

"That's it?" In a building this size? "There's no way. Where's the rest of them?"

Her head whirls, noticing the same thing I did, and she gets to her feet.

"Something's off," she murmurs, "Stay here."

"Like hell, darling," I scoff, readying myself to get up, despite the ache still in my chest. If she thinks I'm leaving her to whatever pandemonium I have no doubt we're about to walk into, she's got another thing coming.

"Just take a minute to catch your breath. I'll be f—"

I'm up on my feet before she finishes. "You're not going anywhere alone."

Backs together as we round the crates, the surge of rickety rifles pointed at us the second we face forward makes me question my position in life.

All of us are locked in the staring contest of the millennia.

"Oh, shit," Emryne barely has her words out before the billow of bullets

hit the concrete where our heads were before he hit the floor and scramble behind the crates for cover.

"You know," I yell over the shots still blasting, showering us in plaster dust from hitting the walls, "in retrospect, we probably should've thought this through."

"Just shut it and take the two on the right, I've got the other three."

"Oh, sure. Upstage me on the first day," I roll my eyes.

"Excuse me, you're still on probation, sir."

She unclips a smoke grenade and pulls out the pin before throwing it over the crates behind us. The canister hits the floor, and a hiss of thick smoke fills the room, all while panicked voices shout commands left and right.

"Sir?" I raise my eyebrow at her.

"Oh, my—is sex all you think about?"

"Around you? Yes. Say it again, I beg you."

"Nope," she blinks and jumps into action. I'm right behind her, two men, one with faded green and the other with a stripped, sweat-stained gray shirts, already grabbing them by the collars and knocking their heads together.

Emryne's detained a black-haired guy, half the age of the two I dealt with, his right arm painfully locked behind his back, forcing him to drop his rifle before driving him into his compatriot, both slamming into the ground from the impact. The third, she kicks her boot into his stomach, propelling him into me, and I lock my arms around him, allowing her another agonizing kick to the balls, and with a heavy grunt he slumps to the ground.

Would it be completely insane if I fucked her right in front of these idiots and make them watch?

It is?

Yeah, it is.

I'd still do it though…

"Oh, come on, darling. Just once?" I call, joining her.

"No!"

The air within the warehouse smells like sweat, blood and ocean water, and fuck, I've never felt a rush like this before.

Side by side, fighting our way through this mess of uncoordinated bodies, Emryne and I are unstoppable. Where her fists staggers, mine knocks unconscious.

Where I drive heels into stomachs, she finishes with blows to the jaws.

She pushes, I pull.

I pull, she pushes. A perfectly choreographed team, and I fucking live for it.

And she's done this.

She discovered the shit these idiots had the gall to think they'd get away with. But this is Emryne were talking about. She doesn't miss a single thing.

Ever.

Alorewyn is one lucky goddamn kingdom.

We continue fighting through the mass of unfortunate souls, until finally, all that's left is a great mess of groaning bodies. One by one, we line the various conscious and unconscious bodies against an empty wall, fastening thick, industrial cable-ties around every wrist, tightly, as the final tendrils of smoke clear the space.

Someone must've seen the smoke by now. Heard the shouts, definitely the shooting. It won't be long before Guard rains seven types of hell on this place.

"Let's get going, I don't think we have much more to do here," I say, checking the area one last time for any unwanted surprises.

Emryne nods, and walks to a work bench near the cargo doors, littered with all kinds of paper I can't make out from where I'm standing.

"Hey, look at this."

I step closer, still keeping my eye on the goons scattered against the wall. "What is it?"

"I've seen these before when the armor thief was caught. They're wire transfer instructions. Soon as the supplier has proof of successful delivery of whatever goods being transported, the money is paid into an offshore account."

"You can tell their offshore?"

"It's how traffickers operate. Those accounts are untraceable and tax free. Any transfers or direct deposits larger than ten grand is flagged by banks and reported to the IRS."

Of course. Everyone has to pay their part, specifically larger numbers, and every cent of that goes into helping the less fortunate. At least it's supposed to.

"Take it. We'll get Cas to trace the routing numbers," I say over my shoulder, walking straight to the blond with the faded green shirt and yanking him upright. He's bleeding from his nose and a cut above his left eye where he must've hit his head against a jagged edge.

Once again, I could kiss Castor for the mask's voice scrambler, "Got a name, pretty boy?"

"Show me yours and I'll show you mine." He bares his bloody teeth.

"It's something with an L, isn't it?" I don't bother waiting for an answer. "I want to know where this shit is coming from. Who are working for?" He grumbles something I have no way of hearing as my hand tightens against his throat; my fist smacks his jaw not long after.

"Spit it out!"

"Fuck you!" he shrieks through bloody, gritted teeth. Definitely an English accent. A thick one.

"You think you're so slick? You're in over your heads, the two of ya. He knows who you are," he chuckles, spitting a mouthful of blood at our feet before his lips turn up in a sneer. "And he's coming for you."

He?

"I'd like to see him try," Emryne deadpans, and knocks him out. And not a minute too soon if the fast-approaching blaring sirens are any indication that we need to hall ass if we want to be far enough away for the raid.

I settle blondie against the wall as Emryne pulls the cap off a black Sharpie and lifts a wrinkled piece of paper in front of her, writing 'You're Welcome' in block letters and sticks it under another guy's arm, then zips it back in the pocket. I open the cargo door before we head for the emergency exit, checking the cable-ties one last time then follow her through the door and to the alleyway where Castor made sure the rental would be waiting, and a soft snap draws my attention backward.

"Oh, you can't be serious," she mumbles, flipping her long hair back.

I zip open the utility pocket on my thigh and pull my wallet out, taking a spare tie and hand it to her. "Here."

Emryne takes the elastic between her thumb and forefinger, slowly sweeping her blue eyes to mine. "How did…?" she trials off.

"Because I know you, Em-Em," all too well in fact. I chuckle. "You never leave the palace with enough of them, and you wear them until they snap. I'm always packing."

Her eyes are fixed on me, and I all but lose myself watching those stunning sapphires dart between mine. I don't know whether or not it's the excitement, or possibly just the light, but I've never seen them so gentle, or so comforting, and I have no idea what do with myself anymore.

"Em?" I ask with furrowed brows. I've never seen her look at me like this. "Are you okay?"

"Oh. Yeah. Yeah. I'm fine," she shakes her head, snapping herself back to reality, smiling warmly. "Thank you."

"You're welcome."

Waiting for the coast to clear, we stick to the shadows as we make our way to the black Chev once the street is empty. Guard has stormed the building by the time we close our doors, and we watch a chopper light up the scene from above.

I turn the ignition and shift the sedan in reverse, pressing my foot against the accelerator and back us up the alley and away from the scene.

"Well, that was pretty fantastic!" I cheer as we make our way through the backroads back to the palace. I've never felt this alive. "I mean, the way you took out those two with the rifles? Screw sex tapes, *that* should be on the internet."

"Yeah," she says with a soft voice, much to my confusion. "Pretty fantastic."

"Emryne?" My head snaps between watching the road and watching her. Despite the dark, I can tell something's up. "Darling, what is it?"

"I… I don't know…" Her head falls forward as she reaches for her side. "Something's… something's wrong…" she lifts her hand into the light, and my blood turns arctic when I see crimson coating her fingers.

"Oh God." Of course, she'd only feel it now given her subsided adrenaline.

I run over the fights again, trying to remember when, and more importantly who, got her, but I come up with nothing. Fighting upward of fifty tweaking idiots in a cloud of gray smoke doesn't exactly leave much room for notice, especially with their clammy arms wrapped around your neck.

I don't bother keeping to the speed limit and press my foot down harder.

Yes, it's irresponsible, I know, but until I see the wound for myself, I'm not taking any chances.

"Watch out for the cameras on the garage," she mumbles as I pull up behind the building.

"You're the one bleeding out and you're telling me to watch out?" I try to keep my voice even as I unbuckle my seatbelt and fly out the car to her side. I don't like how light hers sound.

"I thought you said these things are indestructible?"

"I'm not bleeding out, Sky, and I never said that," she fights back, which I take as an excellent sign. I wrap my arms under her legs and around her back, lifting her from out. I'll worry about moving the car off the road later, no one checks these back roads that regularly anyway, and make a beeline toward to the tunnels with Emryne in my secure in my arms.

She pulls down the iron light fixture that controls the door once we reach her room and it swings open. I push the heavy bricks out of the way and set her down on the leather couch in her bathroom, grabbing a towel from the rack behind her door and fling it over my shoulder before I kneel next to her and get to work unstrapping her armor, starting with the vest then hook my fingers under her undershirt and pull it over her head.

As the material frees her body, a sensual chuckle leaves Emryne's lips, drawing my eyes to hers.

"What could possibly be funny?" I deadpan. There's nothing even remotely humorous about a cut this deep, though it is another promising sign.

"If you wanted to get me out of my clothes, all you had to do was ask," she smirks.

"Don't tempt me, Princess," I say in a husky voice as a crooked smile turns my lips upward. I rip the towel off my shoulder, and wrap it around her body as tightly as I can manage.

"Do *not* take the pressure off before I get back, you hear me?" I command before spinning on my heel.

"Uh huh," she mumbles, waving me off with her free hand.

I'm pretty sure this is the fastest I've sprinted through these halls, and that includes the time we ate too much chewing gum and got runny stomachs from when she was twelve, but I'm in West Wing and through my bedroom door with what I'd say is faster than the speed of light. I yank my luggage zipper open and pull my medical bag free. Regardless of where I go, since the last separatist incident, I never travel without one.

"Is it deep? How bad is it?" I all but scream when I'm back in my Princess's bathroom.

"Wanna slow down there, speedy? she chuckles softly." "Pretty sure it's just a flesh wound, Your Highness. Really not that big a deal."

Glad she's keeping a smile on her face, but the towel is soaked in blood and she's paling, and we're right back to bad.

"No, it is most certainly not fine." I zip open the red bag and take out a pair of latex gloves and antibacterial wipes, getting to work disinfecting the area around her so I can set the supplies down. I sink to a kneel, and inspect the wound more closely.

Her cut is deep and raw, a few inches wide. At least I have enough knowledge of the body to know the knife missed anything major. Somewhat allowing me to breathe a sigh of relief, however small. "I have good news and bad news."

She shrugs. "Okay, let's go with good news."

"It's just a flesh wound so you'll be fine," I confirm.

"Like I said," she smiles. "That is good news."

"But, unless you want an ugly scar, you're going to need stitches," I tell her, reaching in the bag for the small bottle of rubbing alcohol and a few large cotton swabs.

"Is that the bad news?" She frowns.

I shake my head. "I wish it was."

"Just tell me, Skylan."

Sighing heavily, I'm ready to kick myself in the ass for not being prepared. "The bad news is you're going to need stitches and the only thing I have in this medical bag is this bottle of rubbing alcohol and a tube of numbing cream. I don't have an anesthetic to give you."

Whatever color was left in her face drains, and she swallows nervously. "So…"

"So, I'll have to stitch you up… with nothing to numb the pain." Which won't be fun.

For either of us. I can do the stiches just fine, but every other time I've had to do this I'd been assisting actual medical personnel, and they had anesthesia.

A lightbulb flashes in my head and I shoot upward, undoing the buckle on my belt and pull it out of the loops. Best I can do, and it's better than nothing.

"Here."

She flashes a look of derision, corners of her lips turning up. "You don't need to tie me up, Sky. I'm not going to punch you for trying to help."

I shake my head, grinning. "It's for you to bite on."

"Smart," she nods.

But I flash her a smirk either way. "We'll revisit the idea of me tying you up later. I do think I'd enjoy that immensely." And by the way her eyes are sparking, despite the blood loss, she might enjoy that even more.

I grab the unused drinking glass from her sink next to the faucet and empty the alcohol into the glass. Starting with the dried blood around the cut, I pull the larger alcohol-free wipes closer and clean her skin as best I can, careful to avoid the open wound.

Despite the nerves running marathons in my stomach my hands are steady. Just another day on the battlefield.

"On a scale of couldn't care less to irreplaceable, how attached are you to this belt?" She asks, flicking the leather in her hands.

"Easily replaceable," I smile at her. Worldly attachments aren't my thing and she knows it. "But you, my Princess, aren't."

Disposing the bloody wipes in the trash, I switch my gloves out for a fresh set before reaching for a cotton swab, thoroughly soaking it in the alcohol, and make sure to look her in the eyes before breathing out.

"This will sting," I warn, curling my free hand around her thigh. "I'm so sorry Emryne, but I need you to try and stay as still as you can. It's best if I do it quickly and without remorse."

She nods. "Not my first rodeo, Your Highness, and it won't be the last."

I make her count down from three with me, and I begin working the cotton over the cut as gently as I can. Emryne's hand slams down on my shoulder, and she squeezes the life out me, trying to stay still.

"That may be, darling, but I'm pretty sure this'll be your first rodeo without an anesthetic. Bite down if you need to," I remind her.

"I'm fine, just get it over with," she grits out, fighting not to writhe with the pain.

After the second or third swab, the stinging usually subsides, not by much, but it gives her some control over her convulsions.

"Where did you learn to do this?" She asks through gritted teeth.

I smile at the memories, recalling them. "Dad and I volunteer in the medical wing whenever they're short-staffed. I sewed my first suture when I was thirteen after the last war with Greenland. Neither he nor any of the doctors on-call would let me treat the more severely injured knights since I was so young and they thought I didn't need to see any of that, so they put me to work with minor injuries and stitches."

"That must've been very difficult. You were only thirteen."

I shrug. "I learned invaluable lessons during those days. In war, at least in my father's mind, there is no rank. His knights looked to him for guidance, sure, but he never let his status inflate his ego." I throw the blood-soaked swab away and take a clean one. "Dad's worked in every division of his military. Everything from administration to the palace blacksmiths, and he used the time to study them closely. Pick up whatever skill he could, however small."

"Your father is a remarkable king," she cups my cheek. "And so will you be."

I lean into her touch, letting her both warm and calm my heart. Only for it to go right back to a rattling coin-filled tin can when I breathe out, closing my eyes and reaching for the sterile suture kit and peeling the plastic lid back, allowing me access to the tools.

I'd feel a hell of a lot better about cutting into her skin with the Adson forceps if I remembered to pack the goddamn anesthesia, but I try my best to detach from the situation, just like the nurses taught me. I don't want her to have a scar. Even if she'd love it.

"It might be more tolerable if you lay down." Though not by much. At least if she needs to pass out, she can without hurting herself more. Before switching to another set of fresh gloves, I move the supplies out of the way and grip her head at her neck, gently helping her on her back. She settles with a shaky breath and closes her eyes.

"I'll try to be as gentle as I can," I say, taking the needle with the nylon suture from the wrapper and grip it between the teeth of the steel clamps, ready to start arguably the most important procedure I'll ever do in my life.

She reaches for my belt next to her and holds it to her lips, taking a deep breath then closing her eyes again. Preparing herself for the torture to come.

"Bite," I say. Her eyes are flooded with anxiety, but she takes the leather firmly between her teeth. "Don't fight passing out. This is going hurt like hell." I shake my head, blinking back my own tears.

I hate this. I hate that I don't have anything but stupid numbing cream in this stupid bag.

"Ready?" She nods, just as a small tear escapes her eye.

She spends the next fifteen minutes either screaming or on the brink of blacking out, and I've never been more relieved when she eventually she does, though I'm thoroughly impressed she held out until I was about done.

Still, every time that needle pierced her skin, I made sure to keep a clear line of communication open so she knows it's coming, even if she didn't hear. And if I'm honest, I mostly did it for myself so I didn't abandon suturing and pull her into my arms. I didn't stop the tears galloping down my cheeks either. Seeing her in pain was the worst feeling I've ever experienced, but at least it's over. And watching the gentle rise and fall of her chest fills my body with a tidal wave of relief knowing she'll be okay.

After getting rid of the rest of her clothes and cleaning her sweat-soaked body with a wet cloth and warm water, I change her into a fresh set of pajamas, working as quietly as I can so I wouldn't wake her up.

I tie off the trash bag with the bloody evidence and shove it back under her sink before thoroughly scrubbing my hands and under my nails. A soft moan leaves Emryne's chest as I lift her in my arms and carry her to her bed, settling her between the open covers, and tuck her into the soft sheets.

Just as I straighten, Emryne's hand tightens on my forearm. "No. Stay," she says through her exhaustion and gently pulls me onto the bed with her.

I should let her rest. Being operated on while awake and feeling every damn pinch takes a hell of a lot out of you, and she needs to sleep this off. I should leave her, but I just… can't. Not like this.

"Are you sure?"

She nods and snuggles into her pillows.

I lean down and place a soft kiss on her forehead. "Let me take a quick shower and I'm yours."

"Promise?" she whispers.

I smile and give her lips a gentle kiss. "On my life, darling."

I'm in and out of the jets and at her side all in under ten minutes. Not before I stride past her mirror and I'm bitch-slapped by a bruise from the bullet I shoved her away from.

Fucking hell.

If I wasn't wearing that armor, I'd be dead.

Lying in bed next to her, I should feel… fuck, scared? Shocked? Suffering from some kind of survivor's guilt, maybe? I don't know. But I'm not.

All I feel is exhilarated.

Tonight was exhilarating. Watching her work was exhilarating.

And watching her tough it out with that needle was beyond anything I've ever seen. Emryne is a ridiculously tough woman, tougher than I've ever imagined, and I don't think this kingdom is fully prepared for the shape it's about to whipped into once she's queen. And she'll need a king to do that.

She'll need *me*.

Emryne turns on her side, away from her stitches, and snuggles into me, breathing out a soft, "Thank you."

"For what?"

"Taking care of me."

My fingers find her hair, gently running through its coppery silk. "I'd do anything for you, darling. You know that." Even take a bullet. I'd take a thousand if I get to have her in my arms.

"Sky?" She mumbles, though I don't know how she could possibly still be awake.

"I'm here," I rub her back, snuggling her closer.

She lays her hand on my chest and whispers, "I forgive you. For everything."

That funny fluttering fills my chest again as I close my eyes and release a heavy breath. God, I've been waiting so damn long to hear her say that. I've been waiting to so long for the relief that came with her forgiveness. I'd half expected her never to say it and having to move on without knowing, but now? This is beyond anything I could've hoped for.

So, I lean in close, and whisper a confession of my own. "I'm not unfaithful, darling. I've plenty of faults but I'm very faithful. You'll be sick of me I'm so faithful."

Mom loved that quote. Hemmingway was a weirdo, but the man knew how to write.

Her eyes are closed, but her brows still draw together. "What does that mean?"

I chuckle, "Sleep, darling," and place another kiss on her temple, covering her bare shoulder with the puffy duvet and snuggling her closer to me. God, I could do this forever.

"It means," I kiss her forehead and take a deep breath. "I'm think I'm falling in love with you."

And I know what I need to do.

King Ryne is already in his office by the time I knock on his door the following morning. His newspaper lowers, and eyes me curiously. "Ace?"

Hard not to focus on the fact that we were bent over this desk a few weeks ago. But I swallow those images as I step toward my future.

"I'm ready, Your Majesty."

Chapter 26
Emryne
How to Dominate a Prince 101

Urgh.

So, this is what it feels like to be hit by a freight train.

I blink my eyes a few times, despite my blacked-out bedroom, trying and failing to get my bearings. At least I know I'm in my bedroom. Mostly because of the crisp smell of the Pink Champagne atmosphere diffusers haphazardly placed on the bookshelf, my desk, on the coffee table, everywhere I need to be intoxicated by the heavenly scent.

My limbs are jelly, my head is even worse, and I'd like to know what time it is; love to know what day it is. Sitting up was a slow endeavor, and swallowing even more so. Whose bright idea was it to rub sandpaper over my throat?

I only notice I'd been sleeping on my stomach when I finally muster enough energy to reach for my phone with a hefty grunt, followed by a heftier cry when I stretch too quick and my stitched-up skin pulls against the bandage Sky stuck on to keep the area clean. I have to force a few shallow breaths before pulling my arm back, hissing like a sun-exposed vampire when the screen's brightness waterboards my irises, finally adjusting when I blink a few more times and I'm able make out actual words.

Two missed calls from Father and a text asking if I was alright and why I skipped breakfast. A few messages from Tory and Beth asking my opinion on their dress choices for the Thanksgiving ball, then going on to talk between them on the group chat, but nothing much of interest. I'll text them back later.

That's when I notice these notifications were from yesterday. All except Skylan's, which were from a few hours ago.

Damn. Twenty-four straight hours of sleep? What has the world come to?

Pain.

Right.

Pain from not seeing that idiot's knife before it sliced my skin. Pain like Prince Skylan is about to be in for taking that goddamn bullet for me.

I had my doubts about letting him in on this, and all of them were confirmed the second he hit the ground in that warehouse. And the first time I've ever felt genuine fear while working. I was both aggravated and relieved when he stood up and shook himself off—yep, Castor's definitely getting a giant Christmas bonus this year—and went on pestering me like only he could, but my uneasiness was still there. I'd never forgive myself if anything happened to him, but my bullet is my bullet, my knife is my knife, and if we're going to keep working together, he needs to learn what happens when he gets in my way.

Don't get me wrong, I am beyond grateful he patched me up. I would've had a particularly nasty scar if he didn't, but you know what they say: revenge is a dish best served torturously.

After a quick shower and fresh make-up, smokey and smoldering, I tie my hair in a soft knot and change the bandage for a fresh one from the little pile Sky left on my sink, then head to my closet.

Tonight's ensemble included a black velvet balconette corseted bra, and just about the shortest leather skirt I own. Black suspenders I clip to the lace-accented sheer nylons caressing my mid-thigh, and a cozy trench coat to tie it all together.

Nope. No panties tonight.

Walking past the floor-to-ceiling mirror on my way out of my room, I'd pat myself on the back for pulling off the whole warrior-temptress look if I was the type, even with the ugly white bandage breaking the goddess-like illusion, but then again… who doesn't love a good battle scar?

Christian Louboutin embrace my feet and I'm out my door, striding to his bedroom in the midnight hour. Standing at the crossroads of this delicious impasse, it seems the place of interest is in fact the edge of a cliff, and I have every intention of pushing my prince off the edge, then falling with him.

Better pay attention, class is officially in session.

My fingers tap against his door. He calls out for a second, and a bare-chested Sky opens the door.

His face floods with such joyous relief my heart squeezes in my chest, filling my stomach with little butterflies when he takes my hands. "You're up."

"I am," I smile, giving him a squeeze.

He opens wider and lets me through, closing and locking the door behind him when I reach the edge of his bed.

"How are you feeling?" he asks when he reaches his couch.

"Like I've been stabbed and operated on without anesthesia," I shrug. Of course, I'm downplaying it and he's probably fully aware. Getting those stitches had to be the worst pain of my life, and that included dislocating my shoulder while playing volleyball sophomore year of high school, falling off Frolic when he spooked, and the piercing. "But you know what they say. Pain is a virtue."

Sky chuckles, shaking his head, "You have some pretty messed up virtues then if pain is one of them."

"If you think my virtues are bad, my fantasies are even worse," I flash my teeth at him.

"Do tell, Your Highness," he says, leaning against the sofa and crossing his ankles over each other, then his massive arms over his chiseled chest. "We should probably take it easy though. I do need you healthy if I'm to continue boinking you."

"Boinking?" I flash playfully disgusted smile at him. How old is this kid?

"Don't like it?" he says, biting his lip. "Hmm… Sleeping with? Sexually satisfying?"

I step closer and stop in front of him. Sky weaves his hands around my waist and pulls me to his chest, kissing the exposed skin on my neck, and lowers his voice. "Fucking?"

A breathy chuckle leaves my lips as my head falls backward, leaning my body into his heated touch.

"A little overdressed for talking, aren't we darling?" his fingers find the knot at my waist.

Sky's just about undone the knot when I stop him. "What do you think you're doing?" I tease, stepping out of his reach.

"Waiting to see what's underneath that coat of yours," he says. "Lucky for you, I am patient, and that is in fact a virtue."

"You won't be lifting a finger," I run my eyes over his body, licking my lips. "You're in trouble, Sir."

He swallows, gripping the couch again. "I am?"

"Mhmm," I step backward until my butt hits his bed again. "Since you've decided to disobey a direct order, when I told you not to get in my way, tonight… you're facing the consequences," I say, finally letting the coat pool at my feet, the cool silk hitting my bare butt when I sit down on the edge of his bed, sending sparks of desire through my body.

A strained moan leaves his lips. "That is what you wanted me to call you, right?" And his electric gaze is glued to mine, lust seeping from the corners of his mouth. "Sir."

"What is happening right now?" His voice comes out a breathless whisper, but a happy one.

"Your punishment, darling," I throw his little pet name back at him. Not that I don't adore it. I do, more than anything.

My lips turn up in a lascivious grin, slowly, slowly spreading my legs and revealing my bare pussy to him.

"Sweet Jesus," is all he says. I shift back until my back is against his pillows, still wearing those expensive black stilettos I have no intention of taking off, then my hand snakes to my inner thigh, my fingers running across my soft skin as I taunt him.

"Oh, God damn," he breathes out.

"You think I need protection, Your Highness?" My voice is barely audible, just loud enough for him to hear. He hisses, then blows out a breath as I slide my finger along my slick clit, gasping as the sudden roughness of my fingers. "You're thoroughly mistaken."

Sky strides closer, gripping the iron bedframe, so tight the metal screaks as his muscles strain, and I don't stop teasing myself, or him. "And because you thought to protect me," I continue. "Even when I explicitly told you not to. You—" my fingers circle the golden piercing, sending the most incredible shivers through my body, and I speak slowly, deliberately—"are going to watch me come all over these satin sheets."

"Yes," his voice leaves his chest in another breathless whisper.

"Yes?" I say, teasing my opening with my fingers.

"Oh, fuck yes," he growls, lust raging in his eyes.

I flash my teeth, running my eyes down his body and reveling in the fact that he is oh so wonderfully hard.

This is going to be fun.

"Rules are, you aren't allowed to touch. If you do, I'll stop. Nod if you understand." Naturally, he does as asked, making me chuckle. Who's a little bitch now?

He gives one slow nod, tracing his eyes down my body and to my fingers, and settles, waiting for me to continue.

"Want me to go on?"

"Please."

With a deep laugh, I keep going. Stroking my swollen clit while the hunger illuminating his eyes increases with every move, every moan.

I slide a finger inside, then two, pull back out, stroking my soaking folds again, glistening with my wetness, all while Skylan watches every move, flexing his muscles as his hold on the frame hardens. So much he's close to shaking, and his breathing has become ragged.

"You make me want to do bad things," my fingers never stop moving, in fact, I begin stroking harder, "You make me want to be yours. All yours," curling my toes as I feel my orgasm build up deep in my stomach.

"You are mine, darling," he rasps. "All. Fucking. Mine." A deep moan escapes my throat as I rock against my fingers, about to let my eyes flutter closed as my orgasm builds, when I see Sky's hand sliding into the waistband of his gray sweatpants, palming his dick, and I lift my fingers away.

"Uh, uh, uh," I lift my fingers, shaking my head at him. "No touching."

He grunts his disapproval, yanking out his hand. "Oh, come on, darling. None at all?"

"None at all."

"You're not playing fair, Your Highness."

"Who said anything about fair?" I bite my lip, shaking my head. "That's what you get for being a bad boy, Prince Skylan."

"Mmm, say it again," He licks his lips. "Say my name again."

"Prince Skylan."

"One more time," he leaves the frame and leans down, taking fistfuls of black satin in his hands as he grips the edge of the bed.

"Prince," I begin, moving my fingers again, "Skylan," and stroking harder, "Henry," slower, "Alexandrius," more deliberate, "Dormer."

"Oh, fuck me," he drops his head. "Keep going."

My orgasm is closer than ever. I plunge my fingers inside, slowly stroking my G-spot before I pull them out again, squeezing my piercing between my fingers and rock my hips until I know I'm on the edge. "Oh God, I'm going… I'm going to… Fuck, Sky…"

"Come, darling. Come for me," Sky pleads. Pleads, of all things. "I want you to watch you come for me," I move my fingers faster, squeezing harder as my eyes fall shut and I all but lose myself in this moment.

Seeing him practically drooling over watching me pleasure myself was enough for my climax to slam into me. And I'd let it. If Skylan hadn't chosen that moment to lean his head back and reach for his cock.

"Skylan," his head snaps up as I call his name, annoyed of being denied release as I lift my fingers from my pussy and beckon him onto the bed. A devilish smirk plays at the corners of my lips as I bore my gaze into his.

Slowly, he lifts him leg to climb on the mattress, but I stop him, flicking my eyes to his sweatpants. "Off."

He hooks his thumbs in the waistband, chuckling deeply as he pulls down, finally letting his hard gorgeous cock spring free.

He climbs on the bed, his brown eyes doused with lust, breathing heavily as he settles on his back.

"Remind me of what I just said?"

Sky swallows, watching as I climb over his body with hooded eyes. "I'm not allowed to touch."

"Why?" I lift my chin higher.

"Punishment," he moans as I run my fingertips up his thighs.

"For what?"

"For taking a bullet for you."

His tip is already beaded with moisture, and he sucks in a breath as I let him disappear in the warmth of my mouth. All the way to the back of my throat, and back out again.

"Oh, fuck…"

He's watching my every move, returning grunt and whispered moan, until my hand drift down my stomach, between my legs and I tug at my piercing, gasping at the steady sensations as I work my fingers around my clit, and his hard cock slides into my mouth. And his eyes never leave mine. "Jesus, Emryne…"

Sky's growl is it's all it takes. "My queen," And my orgasm slams into me, and I don't care who's listening when I scream his name. Over and over and over again as those delicious ripples of pure ecstasy possess every inch of my being.

I don't relent on his dick, swallowing him down deeper while keeping my pace, hollowing my cheeks when I pull him back out.

Sky reaches down, yanking out the tie, and wrapping my hair in his fist.

He moans deeper, "Fuck, darling, keep going. Just like that," hissing as I brush my tongue over his head, licking him all the way down his shaft before sucking him into my mouth again.

"Fucking hell," he drags out, throwing his head back as he grips my hair tighter, "Fuck, Emryne… I'm gonna—Jesus Christ."

Sky comes. Hard. I lift my eyes to meet his, and I wink, letting him spill down my throat, and I swallow. Every. Damn. Drop.

"You might look and act like an angel, darling," Sky shakes his head when he finally has some control over his breathing, with a lazy grin on his lips. "But there is absolutely nothing holy about that mouth of yours."

I laugh, my breaths hard and rapid. Sky flashes a devilish grin as he sits up, closing his arms around me before flipping me on my back. Soon as his body covers mine, I slide my finger between us, dragging it through my wetness, and into his mouth, and he sucks. Hard.

"So fucking sweet," he moans, taking my hand back down and bring it to my lips for me to taste myself.

And he calls me unholy?

I pull his lips to mine, kissing him slow, then I push him back so I straddle him again. I grip his chin in my hand, cementing my gaze to his. "Don't. Ever. Take a bullet. For me again."

He swallows. "Yes ma—"

My hand clamps over his mouth. There's only one thing I want to hear from him now.

"You're answer is 'Yes, my queen', and nothing else."

Sky swallows, and nods when I let him go, "Yes, my queen."

And that, ladies, gentleman, and every other human alike, concludes today's class on How to Dominate a Prince 101.

"Good boy," my fingers curl around the back of his neck and bring his lips to mine, kissing him deeply before pulling back and looking in his eyes with a devilish grin.

"Now fuck me."

#

"Where in hell did that come from last night?"

In our usual seats at the breakfast table, Sky's rested eyes flash with wonder as he leans his elbows on the table the morning after our blissfully uninterrupted evening of breathless moans, steamy kisses, and many, many orgasms.

I cast my eyes around the table in case of wandering ears, only turning back when I'm satisfied their attention is elsewhere, then lower my voice anyway. "You really want to talk about this now?"

"Yes, I do," he replies with shit-eating grin plastered on his lips, still swollen from the shower we took before heading to breakfast. Sky inspected his work before securing a fresh bandage over the stitches and placing kiss after kiss over it. As heated as last night was, his touch was gentle this morning, so caring, almost like he was afraid I'd break.

It was both sweet, and confusing. If anything, stitching me up should've proved to him that I wasn't fragile, but the way he looked at me when our eyes met, and the deep, soul-shattering kiss he gave me after told me something much different. Maybe I'm reading it wrong, and maybe I'm grasping for hope which probably wasn't there, but everything about the way he touched me, is touching me now with his hand securely rested on my thigh, something inside me feels this is… more. More than it's ever been before. And I want it to be so, so much more.

"I'm not sure," I smile when I meet his eyes. Warm, and welcoming, and adoring. "I had to think of something besides beating the shit out of you." I'm telling the truth. I really don't know. But watching Skylan, watching my every move was… exhilarating, and being in complete control and adored by every part of him made the whole thing so much more satisfying.

He nods. "I do prefer this alternative. That right hook of yours is no joke."

I laugh with a nod, agreeing with him. He shakes his head, beaming with a pride I've never seen in his eyes before. "God, I couldn't take eyes off of you."

"That was kind of the idea," I smile, wrapping my hand around his thigh.

"I don't know why but you drive me crazy. I guess seeing that savage hunger in your eyes just fueled the fire." I say, and reach for my cup of tea. "You really liked it?"

"I loved it." Sky takes a piece of blueberry muffin in his mouth, and chews before saying, "You will be doing that every night for the foreseeable future, just so you know."

"Punishing you?" That's an intriguing idea. I'm not opposed to it. I raise my eyebrow waiting for his answer with a smirk.

"Yeah," he swallows, shaking his head. "On second thought, maybe you should leave the fuckery to me," he sips from his coffee. As he sets his cup back down, he drapes his arm over my chair. "Without it I have nothing to bring to this relationship."

"So, we're in a relationship now?" I ask nonchalant.

"You're right," he chews on his words. "Flirtationship?"

"Cute. Very cute."

"Cute? That's something you say about a puppy," he taps his finger against his chin, "Complicationship?"

"Could work. Or," I reach for his hand. "How about we don't label anything and just go with it for now?" Though why I said that is beyond me. I want more. With Skylan. God, I've wanted it for so long. What I don't know is if he wants the same.

"That's a good idea," he nods. "Or we could talk about—"

Mother clears her throat, drawing our eyes to hers. "Would you two care to join the conversation?"

Not particularly. But we turn to her anyway.

"Right, now," Mother begins. "I need everyone—"

The dining room doors swing open, and a winded Minister Hastings bursts through. "Pardon the intrusion, but you really need to see this," he says, lifting the slim black iPad and placing it in my father's hands.

"What is it Fredrich?" Father asks concerned.

"Seems the Dark Warrior has employed an assistant, Your Majesty," the minister says, finger tapping on the screen.

So, there were surveillance cameras after all. Not that I'm the least bit worried, both of our masks were over our faces, and we had the smoke cover. Whatever he's watching, it couldn't be the best quality.

Still, I laugh inward seeing the silent displeasure Skylan has on his face. He was no assistant; he was an ally. Sky knew it, I knew it. Whether he took that bullet for me or not.

"Poor quality," Father comments. Thank God. State of the art probably isn't on their to-do list given the temporary locations, hence the lack of perimeter cameras. "There's no one at Guard who can enhance this?"

"I'm working on it," the minister says. "We should have something either later today or early in the morning."

Whatever he's watching has him smirking. "Oddly… symbiotic," his eyes sweep to me, then to Skylan. "Send me copy of this, will you?" The Minster nods.

"Any word on their identities?"

"Nothing yet, Majesty."

"And what were they after?"

"I have no idea," The Minster says. "When Guard raided the warehouse, they found a couple hundred bricks of some kind of drug. Forensics are running tests as we speak."

I swallow my nerves, and risk a glance at Sky, who doesn't seem worried in the least. I have to ask him how he does that.

"You two wouldn't happen to know anything about this?" Father asks, raising a curious eyebrow. "Would you?"

I hate lying to my father, but the less he knows the better. Sky and I have got this handled. "I don't see how. I was reviewing labor laws. I think I found a loophole in Farrow Farms contract that might entitle fieldworkers to a higher minimum wage," Which I did, Farrow Farms is the palace's main supplier of fresh produce, the day my father whisked Sky away for their air play, of course.

Father kept my gaze, smiling proudly, then settles on Skylan with the same expectant smile.

He simply shrugs. "Nothing at all, Your Majesty."

"Handle it later then," Mother says, waving a hand. "I don't have time for this."

I roll my eyes and sit back. My hand finds Skylan's thigh again, and frankly, I need the connection. I fix my eyes to hers, and wait for her to continue as the minister sits down next to Father, just as Sky's hand closes over mine, linking our fingers.

"As I was saying, I need everyone on their best behavior for Thanksgiving. I've invited your families as well as the most senior members of your Parliaments to attend as well," Mother grins, and that's when she sweeps her eyes first over Addylin, then me. "Hopefully, our princesses will have made up their minds by then, and new celebrations can begin." She claps her hands.

Addy's eyes find mine. She smiles, however weakly, and shrinks back in her seat. Since I'm all but glued to Skylan's side, I leave Mother and an inquisitive Allister to chat, and pull my phone out of my back pocket, opening a new message to my sister.

ME: *U okay?*

Her phone vibrates on the table. She reaches for it, and leans back in her seat again, hiding the screen under the table.

ADDYLIN: *I really don't want to do this, E.*

My brows crease as I read over her message. Again, and again, as if the words will change, before raising my eyes to her with confusion, then back down to the screen.

ME: *Since when?*

ADDYLIN: *Some things have… changed.*

ME: *Changed how?*

I frown as I watch the three little bubbles jump, but lock my phone when Skylan's ringtone pulls my attention from my surroundings, and the unknown number flashing on the screen my attention away from my sister. Only one person that could be.

Sky swipes to answer, and tells him to hang on. We share a look, and he points over his shoulder before we both rise from the table.

"Everything okay?" Father asks as we're about leave.

Not to either of us specifically, but I answer anyway. "Maverick… has some girl problems and he needs my opinion on something." What else was I supposed to say?

"Maverick has a woman in his life?" Father asks, surprised. Which I get, his aversion to dating was even worse than mine, don't think no one knows it. I haven't seen him speaking to a woman since his twenty-sixth birthday, and he never shares anything resembling sparkling eyes with breasts on his Instagram, other some of his favorite roasted chicken pasta recipes.

Then again, it has been three years, almost four considering this one is nearing its end.

"Apparently," I shrug with a grin.

"How wonderful!" Mother chimes. "Please do extend his invitation for Thanksgiving, Prince Skylan. I would be thrilled if the new King of Callior could attend. Even better if he brings her along as well."

Sky's amused demeanor settles on mine, and he smiles. "Of course, Your Majesty," he replies, placing his hand on my lower back and urging me to exit. Father calls after us to say hi, and we're out the door and into one of the informal lounges a few rooms down.

"Nice one," Sky says as I walk to a creamy, heavily embroidered couch and sit. We switch to videocall as Sky sinks down next to me. "He's absolutely going to love hearing about this."

"Hey," I say to Castor, lifting the phone between us. Whatever he called about has to be good news, or some news at the very least.

"She lives," Castor's masked face flashes on the screen, leaning back and clapping his hands. "Heard you got stabbed. That's pretty hardcore. But I'm glad you're okay, you're the only friends I have."

"Awe, thanks Cassie," I smile sweetly. "That's probably the nicest thing you've ever said to me."

"I wasn't being nice. I was just stating a fact. You're the only people I know who neither have the emotional dexterity of a wet slice of bread nor the overall intelligence of bag of rocks. And I don't have the capacity or the time or patience to make new friends, so you two are gonna have to last."

I stare at him blankly, replying with a dry, "Oh my heart," and roll my eyes. "What did you find?"

"I don't know how, let alone why, but every time I trace these mails back, it comes from a secure server in Buckingham Palace. You might want to get Prince Dreamy alone and ask him some questions."

Sky frowns, leaning back and crossing his arms. "I'm Prince Dreamy."

"No, you're Prince Steamy. There's a difference," he replies, to which Sky smirks satisfied. There really is no point arguing that. "Thanks for letting me watch the video by the way. Hot stuff, Your Highness," Castor says, at the same time as Sky sinks away and waves his hands on the camera beside me, then collapses his head in his hands and he blows out a frustrated breath.

I glance between the two, not sure whether or not I'm to believe my ears. "What."

"Oh, shit," Castor drags his hand through his hair. "Was I not supposed to mention that, or that Indie Film Award it was nominated for?"

Indie f—It's a fucking sex tape!

I look over at Sky, who's still shaking his head, then back to our masked quote-unquote friend.

"How did you get Skylan's number?" I frown at him.

"Have we met?" He deadpans. Meaning: hacker extraordinaire. Duh.

I turn back to Sky, who stares blankly, then smiles. "This isn't going to end well for me, is it?"

And I reply almost immediately, "This isn't going to end well for you at all, no."

"Well," Sky sits back in the couch and crosses his hands behind his head, and his ankle over his knee. "If my punishment is anything like last night, I'm totally game."

My lips thin into a straight line as I shrug. "Or I could just withhold all together."

He blinks at me at few times, then drops his smile once he realizes I'm not kidding.

"Mhm," I assure him, lips still thin.

"Okay, I'm sorry! I'm sorry!" he pleads, turning to Castor with a pointed, "Bad Castor! Bad!"

Castor's hand flies to his chest, outraged at the accusation, "What did I do?"

Annoyed enough, I steer the conversation back to the emails. "Is there no way to get around whatever security this server has?"

"Not without raising some serious red flags, no," he leans back in his chair. "Seems we've reached an impasse."

There has to be something we're missing. Castor's right, only way to be sure was to ask.

Guess it's time to make another date with Prince Caneic.

Chapter 27
Emryne
Crumbling Façades

Once again, our palace is reduced to a cesspool of shouts, sweat and anxiety.

It's finally Thanksgiving, and the snow has made its annual return. A little early, my father said, but the millions of tiny diamonds sparkling on the lawns are too beautiful for me to question it.

Same with South Piedmont Gardens where Allister and I are enjoying the mid-morning sun, though what little snow there was had already melted. At least we picked a morning free of an arctic breeze, and after the slew of paparazzi snapping pictures, adoring children, and blushing teenage girls, we're finally able to hang out in peace.

Bruno Mars's *Locked Out of Heaven* blasts in the black headset on my ears as I weather another guess at a mouthing Allister.

"Jerry Springer has a sandwich for sale," I give him my answer.

He's laughing so hard he folds in half, and I do the same. I guess that wasn't it.

What'd Ya Say was my sisters, Cameron and my favorite game growing up. The sentences became progressively dirtier the older we got. It's one of the best icebreakers.

Allister finally gets his laughter under control and shakes his head no.

"What! There's no sandwich?" I'm sure I saw that. "I was really confident about the sandwich," he tries again, mouthing each word carefully, but all I keep seeing is the sandwich.

I watch his lips closely, and finally say, "Scary Spice has secret agenda." He gives me a thumbs-up, and I pull off the headphones and reach for my phone to stop the music.

"Legend," he says, slapping a high-five on my palm.

"Is Scary Spice's secret agenda the sandwich Jerry Springer has for sale?"

"I'm not telling," he raises a shoulder. "Couldn't even if I wanted to. That's the whole point of a secret agenda."

I help him fold up our blanket and pack it and the headphones in my tote. We decide on one last walk around the park before heading back to the palace to get ready for tonight.

"Touché," I smile, weaving my hand around his arm.

"I enjoyed that a lot. Thank you," he closes his hand around mine and squeezes.

"Me too," I squeeze back. "What'd Ya Say is a timeless classic."

"Which one of you came up with that?" He asks as we walk down the steps heading to the big pond. A new wave of smiles, waves and snapping cameras pass us as we reach the edge of the water, but the knights my father assigned for our protection detail make quick work of pushing them back once they got their pictures. Not that I was particularly happy he excluded me from the decision, and I'm still not over him declaring security non-optional. But he is my father, so I went with it.

"My brother, Cameron," I say. "Trust me, it gets even funnier when we've all had a few drinks in us."

"Oh, I'd pay big money to see that," Allister chuckles, and I join him.

"Are you ready for tonight?" I ask, waving at a group of kids giggling on the playground.

Allister follows my gaze and smiles. "Somewhat."

"You've been gone for so long. Your fathers must be excited to see you."

"They are. We kept in touch. But King Ezrah's awfully attached to his son, he never wanted me to come. You know how parents are," I laugh. Can't disagree with that. His smile slowly disappears. "They like to tell me how lucky I am I even got invited."

"Why?" I ask with a deep frown.

"You know what people say about my family." Allister pauses, keeping his eyes on the ground, then lets out a snort. "I'm lucky you're even talking to me."

"Why on earth would you say that?" I've met his fathers and they're incredible. King Warrin is a little stoic at times, but King Ezrah is an angel, bright, handsome, and funny. They truly bring out the best in each other, and their marriage brought monumental changes in the LGBTQ+ community and their rights all over the globe.

"Are you kidding? Look at me. Don't let the muscles fool you, I still look like a basic white boy with blond hair," he pouts, fluttering his eyes. I laugh, slapping his side.

"You do not. You're very handsome. Anyone would be lucky to have you," I assure him. And he is. Another trait he inherited from King Ezrah. He's not really my type, like a certain brown-eyed pain-in-my-butt I grew up with back at the palace, but still attractive. And I'm pretty sure Allister doesn't have the devil as his wingman, whispering filthy things in his ear.

"Thanks for saying that," he winks, bumping my shoulder.

We continue our stroll in comfortable silence until were a few feet away from where our car is waiting when Allister turns his head to me.

I watch his mouth open and close a few times, before he finally says, "Do you…" but then he shakes his head. "Never mind."

I smile. "No, tell me."

"Listen," his chest lifts as he takes a deep breath. "Your mum said it herself, it's almost the end of the year so I have to ask, do you see this going anywhere serious?"

A fresh breeze of relief flicks my loose hair off my shoulders, applauding me in my wise choice of grabbing my wool coat before Allister and I came to the park.

I tighten the coat around my body and open my mouth to answer, barely able to form legitimate syllables. "I… uhm…"

Allister seems pensive, distressed almost when I lift my gaze to find his. I know that look. And while I don't think he bats for Lando's team, it's the same look he had before he told me he was gay.

Which makes me stop in my tracks. "Allister, if there is someone else, please don't think you have to stay and entertain me."

His Adam's apple bobs as he swallows nervously. "Are you sure?"

"Of course. I'd be a grade-A asshole if I kept you from someone you love."

We stop at the armored Rolls Royce, and he leans over to open my door. "I wouldn't say love quite yet, but I do care about her."

"Do I know her?" I ask after he hopped in next to me and closed his door.

"Nah," he shakes his head, and we fasten our seatbelts. "She's old friend of mine. We went to private school together and… recently reconnected," he says. "You're not angry, are you?" Seriously? Does everyone think I'm a walking bag of ferocity?

"No, of course, not," I grip his shoulder. "I'm happy for you. Is she nice?"

"Yeah, she's great," he says, leaning over with a boyish smile on his lips. "But just… out of curiosity, did I ever have a chance?"

I shrug. "I was supposed to give every prince a fair shot. So, yes. At first at least. And I've loved all the time we got to spend together, really." I grip his forearm.

"But I'm no Skylan," he nods his head, chuckling quietly. "I get it. I see the way he looks at you."

"You have?"

"You haven't? It's like his entire world begins and ends with you."

No, that couldn't be right… Could it? "I mean, I wouldn't go that far."

"No, I'm serious, Your Highness. I've never seen a man look at woman the way he looks at you. It's sickening."

We laugh and spend the ride home chatting about nothing in particular. His brother's love for heavy metal, Asaria's love for ancient metal, and bid our goodbyes when we arrive at the back at the veranda, where a relaxed Prince Caneic is already waiting.

"Cane," I greet him.

"I hope I'm not interrupting," He smiles and kicks off the wall.

"Not at all," Allister says and turns to me. "Up for What'd Ya Say round 2 later?"

"It's a date," he kisses my cheek and leaves me with Prince Dream—Cane.

Cane inclines his head curiously. "What'd Ya Say?"

"It's this game we used to play when I was a kid. It's hysterical, you should join."

"Sounds like fun," he smiles.

That's when I see the bouquet of roses. "Are those for me?"

"They are. I saw them and thought of you," he says, and hands them to me.

"That's very kind of you," even if I can't stand the sight of them. I accept them anyway. Their sickeningly sweet smell fills my senses, and immediately I'm thinking about how Skylan would never get me roses. Not when he knows how much I love daffodils.

Oh hell. Now I'm comparing them.

Because you're in love with him and you know it.

Quiet you.

"Are you up for a ride?" He holds out his arm, though it's more a subtle demand than a friendly request. I hook mine in his and we walk toward the stables.

"That sounds wonderful," a hack in the fields would be nice. And Frolic loves outrides. Mostly because he gets to show off to the mares in the surrounding paddocks.

The enormous, dappled gray's head is sticking over his stable door, waiting for his usual nose scratches and a handful of sugar cubes when I say hello.

Since it's a Saturday afternoon on a national holiday, the usual bustling around the horses is reduced to a few stray whinnies from the paddocks outside, and the classical music Mother insists be played twenty-four-seven, thankfully turned off. We walk through the barn doors and head to the horses, greeting Addylin's bay, One and Only Maraschino, though we just call him Chino, who's already tacked by the time we arrive. Not a haybale, saddle or bridle out of place, and not a fly in sight. Demand number eight-hundred-and-twelve from Her Majesty the Queen.

Frolic's groom, Marcia, knows not to bother fussing when I decide on a ride. Tacking my stallion is one of the few times I get to bond with him since I don't get to see him as much lately, and I miss his floppy ears. He nips at my side for another sugar cube, and of course, his lordship will have whatever he wants.

"This is Frolic," I introduce them, patting his neck as he nips up the sugar, the neatly trimmed hairs on his muzzle tickling my palm instantly bringing such joy to my heart.

"Frolic?" Cane laughs.

I cross my arms and lean against his stable, giving Cane a smile. "Well, his full name is Sir Perciville Dominicus Albundy Royalé, and I'm definitely not calling him that."

He nods. "Frolic it is," Cane lifts his hand to pet him, and Frolic's ears snap against his neck.

"Careful," I grab is hand just before Frolic's teeth took a hefty bite out of him. "He's not a big fan of people touching his face."

Chino's groom, Charles, learned that the hard way when he came just a little too close to his stable and had a chuck of his cheek taken out. Which is why I suggested he be moved to a stable closest to the wall and away from the barn doors where situations like this could be avoided when newcomers walked in. I wish I could say I knew what happened to him when we bought him from someone we thought was a reputable breeder in Spain, but by the weird scars on his hind legs and his tendency to nip at me when I doing up his saddle's girth too fast, it couldn't have been good.

It took months for the poor thing to relax, and when he did, I was relieved to be blessed with a big ole goofball who had no idea just how big he in fact was.

"Right," he says, backing away. "Addylin mentioned something like that." My lips turn up. Knowing she's been looking after him makes me feel a little better. Not much, he is my horse, but let's just say my attention has been pulled… elsewhere lately.

Namely in the shape of a brown-eyed, broad-shouldered, horse-hating prince.

I give Frolic a quick brush, finishing tacking him up as we make small talk, and the two of us are mounted on the stallions. Cane takes the lead galloping to an open field closest to the forest line. He slows Chino down to a trot, then a walk, and he stops near an even clearing free of rocks and dried branches.

A smile curves my lips upward when my feet are back on the ground and I notice the cozy blanket before me decorated with just about every snack imaginable, all the way from mini cucumber sandwiches to raspberry truffles. My jaw is on the floor when I turn back to Cane, hands in his pockets and watching me closely with a gentle curve of his lips.

Which turns into a full-on smile, "Do you like it?"

How can I not? All this without thinking twice about it, having to ask someone for advice or worrying about how to do it 'the right way'? Just effortless romance. That's what makes this so special to me. Something about Cane that would've had me obsessed with him had our connection been deeper. And I wish I could point a finger at why it wasn't.

"It's amazing," I say as he takes a seat next to me. I contemplated holding out my hand to make the endeavor easier for him, but he surprises the heck out of me when he sits down with ease.

"My way of apologizing for my actions the other night," he says, tucking his ankle over the other and leaning back on his hands. "I had no intention of running off the way I did."

I really didn't care anymore. Not when I got to ride Skylan's face after… which is the worst thought to infiltrate my mind since my sex clenches with a wave of anticipation at the memory.

Cane. Cane. Cane. Cane.

"It's okay," I assure him, taking a chocolate-covered strawberry. "And don't be. If anything, I think it should be apologizing to you for being so insensitive about what you've been through."

His eyes tense as he casts them to the palace before us, bathed in the last of the afternoon sunrays.

"Thank you for saying that," he winces, reaching for sandwich and taking a bite, swallowing before he continues. "It's quite a long and despondent story. One I don't particularly like telling."

"I get it," I nod, turning to him and giving him a cocky grin. "Just let me know if I need to kick someone's ass. It's been a while and I've got a real hankering," I joke. Kind of. Beating up people is like second nature. Bad people, of course, I'm not a sadist. And whoever did this to him is the worst kind of scumbag who deserves to be in chains.

Cane chuckles. "I hope you don't mind me saying this, but you're quite an enigma for a princess."

"I will take that as a compliment," I say, pouring us each a glass of water and handing him one.

"Please do," his lips turn upward. Cane takes a long sip before he squares his shoulders and takes a deep breath. "It's referred to as phantom limb syndrome," he explains. "It happens when someone has lost a limb and the brain sends neurons to the part of the body that was amputated. And as you saw, it causes an incredible amount of pain."

My heart squeezes at this gentle voice, taking his comfort as confirmation to continue. "I remember reading about it. Does it happen often?"

"At the most random and acutely inconvenient times," he wrings his eyes with his finger. "Some days are worse than others."

"Is there any kind of medication you can take to help relieve the pain?"

He raises his shoulder, "I already am, along with about every kind of sleeping pill and antidepressant imaginable."

I know he doesn't want sympathy, I do, I wouldn't either, but that still doesn't stop my hand from closing over his shoulder. "Cane, I'm so—"

"Distraction work the best," he cuts me off. And I let him. "High days are high, low days are getting lower. And the trouble comes on those low days when I have nothing to pull myself back. Or when I see a way to make it out. But, if I'm being completely honest with myself, I found the very best kind of distraction. It's why I arranged our afternoon together," he reaches for my hand, and grips it tightly. "Listen, Emryne. I think you are an incredible woman who deserves only the very best," he trails off. "And, well, it's… I don't… I just don't think…"

My body lights up with amusement. "Why, Prince Caneic, are you letting me down easy?" I say, smiling widely. Guess Mother was right about us making up our minds.

"I… suppose I am," he laughs awkwardly. "But I have no choice. The feelings I have for Addylin, they're serious."

I pat his hand. "Well then, the most important thing is that you're happy."

"I am," he nods assuredly.

"And she's happy?"

"She is."

"Then I'm happy that you're happy," and that's all that matters. Though it still doesn't answer those text messages she sent…

I lean back on my hands. "Just take care of her, will you? You've seen what I'm able to do with bamboo. Imagine what I can do with serrated steal."

"Duly noted," he chuckles, bowing his head with a grin.

We spend some time catching up on everything. The time he's been spending with Addy, Sky and me reconnecting and his need to dominate my every thought, much like Addylin does his, when Castor's muffled voice pops in my head, biding a friendly reminder about who exactly is sitting and laughing beside me.

I lower what was my third glass of wine and turn to him. "I know this may seem kind of out of nowhere, but have you heard of something called Purple Sprinkle?"

"The drug?" he asks, sitting up and reaching for a grape and popping it into his mouth. "Yeah, it's has quite the nasty reputation in Eikenish."

Interesting how everything keeps coming back to Adlengn. "Any guesses where it started?" I ask with a frown.

"Not a clue. But it's absolutely ghastly. The worst kind of narcotic anyone could be addicted to. Our Prime Minister, Tarron Hiddleston, has brought it under my father's attention numerous times, though I'm afraid his warnings have fallen on deaf ears."

Cane's father. King Lodran.

Who seems to have disappeared without a trace.

#

"A picnic? Really? Could he be more cliché?" Skylan howls with laughter.

I didn't find it funny at all. "I liked it," I say with a shrug. "It was romantic."

I'm freshly showered and wrapped in a fluffy towel by the time Skylan walked into my room and threw himself on the plushy, cream-colored lounger inside my closet while I'm waiting for Moni and Des to get back from dinner so we can get started with my hair and make-up.

His laughter fades, and his expression turns somewhat serious. "Is that what you want?"

"Not all the time. But a little romance would be nice," I shrug, working a towel through my hair.

"I can do better. I can top whatever lover-boy does threefold," he proclaims, sitting up.

My eyebrows draw together. "No, Skylan. If you do something romantic it has to be genuine. Because you want to. Not because of your incessant need to constantly one-up everyone around you."

"It's just a date, Emryne, why are you getting so worked up about it?"

"I'm not *getting* anything," I protest. "I'm just saying I liked the effortlessness."

"Of a picnic outside, in a field, in the cold, surrounded by flies and a bunch of horses running around next to you?"

I can't believe what I'm hearing. I pause, blowing out a heavy breath. "Of being thought about without having to ask, Skylan. Of being someone's first priority for once."

He swallows, taking a step forward and reaching for my hands, "You are my priority." but I walk around him and take a seat at my vanity instead.

Sky crosses his arms over his chest. "What is this really about, Emryne? Did Cane do something? Did he touch you?"

285

I throw my hands up with a heavy grunt, infuriated with this entire conversation. "No, Skylan. He was a perfect gentleman."

We stare each other down for what feels like eternity, sizing up which party walk away the winner, but I huff out a frustrated sigh, waving the conversation off.

"Forget it. It's stupid anyway."

"Emryne," Sky walks to me, gently taking my hand.

I step away, in no mood to hear it whatever excuse he's cooked up in his head that obviously makes sense to him.

"I have to get ready for the ball. I'll see you later, okay?" I say, and walk back into my bathroom without another word.

Idiot. Of course, Skylan isn't interested in the romantic stuff. He got off, and that's that. What infuriates me is that he *still* doesn't get it.

I wanted so badly to tell him that I'm officially free, that if he wants to be together, we can be. I want that. More than anything. Every conversation, every thought I've had in the last few months all comes back to Skylan, and our possible future. More importantly, forgetting our past. And forgiving him about it. Yes, I was half asleep when I said it, didn't make it any less true.

All those things he's done over these past few months, all the progress I thought we made only to go back to this?

I try to stop the tears, swallow them like I always would, but I don't bother. And when my bedroom door closes, I let them flow. They've been held hostage for long enough.

Chapter 28
Skylan
The Secret Lies in Parental Minds

Here's the thing about Emryne, a detail I conveniently keep forgetting: when going against her after she explicitly explained why she's right, she doesn't get angry, or upset. There's absolutely no logic in that.

She? Gets even. Just like she did that night in my bedroom. And fuck if it didn't make me fall even more in love with her then I already am.

The vixen I can handle, very well as a matter of fact. The ball-buster who's answer to conflict involves a mouthful of knuckles too. But lovey-dovey Emryne?

I've never seen this side of her before, neither have I been challenged to be this type of person for someone before her, and I want to be.

I'm in love with her. I want to be everything she needs and more, I just don't know how. And like always, me and my idiot mouth screw things up just as they get good. Which is exactly why I'm on the phone with Maverick, trying to figure this out.

"And what were you doing when she was breaking up with her other boyfriends?" Maverick asks.

"They're not her boyfriends," I spit. "No one gets to touch her but me."

He smirks, leaning back in his desk chair. "Obviously. But that still doesn't answer my question."

Where have I been? At her father's side while he discussed the Purple Sprinkle situation with Minister Hastings and what their plan of action will be should an epidemic break out. During which I had to bite my tongue and take a few seconds to weave acceptable answers without revealing either my or Emryne's involvement. Even if I still think it would've been better if King Ryne knew what we knew.

"I spent the afternoon working with her father," I say.

Mav's lips thin and he nods. "So, you are taking this seriously, then."

"No shit, that's what I've pretty much been telling you I've been doing since I got here," I roll my eyes. "How's Dad?"

"You mean after you called to admit you've been sleeping with his best friend's daughter? Fine. He mostly just hangs out with Colonel Bouchard now."

"Chardy's still flying?" I ask. It's been a while since I've seen my old instructor.

"Sure is. He tried to convince me to take up the family hobby." I laugh at that. Maverick hates flying.

"Is he mad?"

"Here's an idea. Maybe call him and ask him yourself."

"I'll talk to him tonight. He's still coming right?"

"He's already on his way," Mav says, then reaches for a stack of papers. "I should be able to head over as soon as I finished reviewing the final treaty drafts, but it still be a couple hours."

That was quick. Apparently, the meeting with Greenland's president went slightly better than horrible, and all parties were able to come to a relatively amicable agreement regarding restitution. Which will take years, but at least the conflict is somewhat over.

There is one just detail I'm confused on... "None of this surprises you?"

"What?" He raises an eyebrow.

I scratch my head. "I mean, Emryne and me..."

"Nope," he shrugs. "You two have been like magnets since the second your parents put you in the same playpen."

So, he saw it too then.

I snort out a laugh. "If we're so fucking star-crossed, why do I keep screwing up?"

"Tell me what happened again," He squints, raising an eyebrow.

A heave out a grunt, and lean my elbows on my knees, repeating the conversation yet again. "She went on a date with Cane, got back and yelled at me that I wasn't romantic enough and that she isn't a priority." Which is ridiculous. She's the only priority I'll ever have. Regardless of if she's crowned or not.

"Why would she think she's not a priority?"

"How should I know? It's not like I've been ignoring her, or not sleeping with her every chance we get."

"I don't think sex is what she's talking about, cousin."

"Then what is she talking about?"

"Effort, dumbass. Assurance, reassurance. She's a woman. She wants to know you care about her."

I throw my head in my hands, huffing as I run through Mav's words.

"It's not like I do it on purpose. I care about her more than anything, but what does she want me to do? Dress up like Romeo and proclaim my undying love for her?" I mean, if me wearing tights is what she wants I'll do it, but I'd prefer an alternative.

"Whoa there, Casanova," Mav chuckles, shaking his head. "And no, that's too simple anyway. You need to do something bigger. Much, much bigger. Something she'll love more than fancy words or picnics and dinner dates."

I fall back on the couch with a frustrated grunt, well aware of the magnitude of his words, but it still begs the question of *what* exactly that is.

That's when my eyes settle on my messy luggage and I notice a small red tussle peeking out from one of the corners. I leave a typing Maverick and walk over, flipping the bag open to see what caught my attention.

Callior's crest is woven into the navy cotton tightly wrapped around something heavy. I take my time rolling the object out, and I'm pleasantly surprised when her worn notebook falls into my hands.

Typical. Mom always knew what to do.

"Is that your mother's poetry book?" he asks with a surprised frown.

"Yeah," I reply, turning the worn leather journal over in my hands. "I completely forgot I brought it."

My throat tightens as I flip open the cover, pushing aside the memories linked to this little book, careful not to damage the dried lily Dad gave her she hid between the cover pages, and flip through the mass of poems she wrote every day while laughing and smiling at his side, just as enthralled by her bewitching words as I was.

Mom loved telling people I was the reason she wrote so well, and how she used to make up elaborate stories when she was younger, but the second I was born, it was like a river sluice opened in her mind, and she couldn't stop the words stringing together no matter what she did. Saying I missed her is the understatement of the millennium.

"You okay?" Mav asks as I wipe away a stray tear.

"Yeah," I breathe out, smiling as I read over some of my favorite pieces. Her earlier work is much happier than the last months before she died, it's obvious when you compare her handwriting, didn't make them any less brilliant.

Not all of the pages are filled from top to bottom. Some have bits and pieces she wrote down I'm guessing were supposed to have become part of something bigger, but never did since she could barely sit up straight the final two weeks of her life. I stop halfway through a torn page, hooking my finger around the paper with every intention to turn it over to keep searching, though for what I have no idea.

Then I find exactly what I need.

A single serenade whispers a lifetime of prosperity.
Choose wisely whose ears are blessed.

My lips turn up in smile. Of course. Why didn't I think of that before?

"Mav, I'll call you later," I say, closing the book, carefully wrapping her scarf around it again.

"Please don't. If this bright idea of yours works I really don't want to see my cousin naked."

I flip him off and end the call, scrambling to grab my phone and head to the music room with whatever time I have left before taking the most important step in my life.

Chapter 29
Emryne
Happy Thanksgiving

"Whoever did this, did a beautiful job." My brother nods, impressed. "You'll only have a tiny scar."

I smile. Yes, he did, even if I wish *I* could stick a needle in him.

Cameron actually came to a family event. No wonder the snow is falling in full force. And he made it just in time before the puffy gray clouds released the season's couture flakes on the kingdom of Alorewyn. Addylin and I nearly broke his arms when we flew into his chest, hugging the heck out of our oldest brother.

Ten months apart, and I'd forgotten just how handsome Cameron is. His sandy blond hair resembles Addy's the closest, but her cream-blonde stays an enigma if ever I've seen one.

Since I had no intention of having Prince Skylan see me naked for a while, Cam was my next best choice to get the stitches out since it's already been more than three weeks and the wound had closed up by now.

"Want to tell me how this happened?" he asks as he carefully cuts the nylon and removes them with forceps. Though I wish he kept his questions to himself.

I shrug. "Frolic threw me. I landed on a rock."

Cam frowns, looking up through his unfairly thick eyelashes. "Uhm, a rock wouldn't have—"

"It was a rock, okay?" I cut him off. Flashing my eyes at him not to ask. Regardless of it being Dark Warrior affiliated, I really had no interest in talking about Skylan right now.

"Okay. Sure. A rock," Cam rolls his eyes, and he goes back to removing the knots. "Ready for tonight?"

"Yes and no," I reply. He'd already changed into his dress uniform with his medals pinned to his chest, jingling as he straightens himself. "But I'm glad you're here."

"You'll do great," he smiles. "Much better than I or Asa would've done. Even Ophelia." Both of which will also be attending. What a night this is going to be.

"I would've said you'd make a great king, but…" I shrug with a playful smile.

"Please don't insult me, I'm begging you," he shakes his head. Dr. Cameron Emeric Andréus Gennady is right where he's supposed to be, and everyone knows it.

"You still came though," I say as he finishes and throws the latex gloves in the trash.

"It's Mother," he deadpans. "If the queen says jump, you say, 'Of course, Your Majesty. How high?'" he rolls his eyes. "But I was in the area anyway. May as well spend some time with my annoying sisters."

I laugh. "At least you didn't come alone this time. Connor is very handsome." I reiterate… no wonder it's snowing.

Cam smiles. "Yeah, he's nice. He's a great doctor."

"And is he great in bed?" I smirk.

"If you repeat this to anyone, I'll kill you, but I don't know," he leans against the wall, crossing his arms. "We… haven't slept together yet."

Cam came out to our parents long before Addy and I were born, in a time don't ask don't tell was in full swing; Mother has never gotten over it, and probably never will. Father? As long as Cam was happy, he was happy.

Love is love. No matter who you are or what you look like.

"I'd say no rush, but you don't really move at anything other than a glacial pace, so," I say, rolling my eyes.

Cameron clicks his tongue, "Smartass," then wraps me in a hug and kisses my temple. "You're good, Emerhino. See you downstairs. And *maybe* you'll meet Corner Store."

"I better," I laugh. Cam's ability to come up with the weirdest nicknames for people never ceased to amaze.

He cleans up the last of the medical supplies and leaves me to finish getting ready. Moni and Des are at my side in a flash, putting the last of their magical touches on my hair and make-up before helping me into my gown.

My God these woman can sew. The pointed, asymmetrical neckline once again fits my body perfectly. I chose this design with the specific intention to appear as queen-like as possible without looking like my mother's carbon copy. So I decided on a plum purple tule for the skirt and bodice with careful intention, and a string of delicate orange pearls that ties around my waist as a belt.

I slip my feet into the black heels and lower my head for Moni to place the tiara on my head, which this gown would be absolutely nothing without, and give each of them a tight hug after Des ties the red, white, and blue sash over my shoulder and hands me the pearl teardrop locket I fasten around my neck.

I meet my radiant twin in the hallway, never more pleased she chose Ophelia's design for the burnt orange satin gown she's wearing. The purple pearls around her waist resemble my dress, as mine does hers and I still smile at my idea. Never a better time for twinning like Thanksgiving.

"Oh my God, girls," Ophelia, dressed in a formfitting velvet navy dress accented with silver jewels along the puffed off-the-shoulder sleeves and thigh slit, chokes on her words as we reach the bottom of the stairs, and she takes our hands, beaming like only a proud sister could.

"Our sister is a genius," I say, pulling her into a tight hug.

"Are you all waiting for a red carpet to be rolled out?" Mother barges past us. "Get inside, people are waiting."

We share a look before she follows her through into the ballroom, packed with our esteemed members of Parliament, foreign dignitaries, their families, and my two beaming beast friends I see hovering by the door. I blow out a breath and shake my head, waving to them in their turquoise and yellow dresses before smoothing out my own gown's skirt before heading for the double doors, casting my gaze backward when I see Addylin's still frozen in place.

"Addy?" I turn to her.

"Emryne, I can't," she takes a step back, shaking her head. "I don't…"

"Don't?"

"I don't think I can do this," she says quietly.

"The ball?" I frown.

"No," she shakes her head again. "No, I'm mean be queen."

"What do you mean?"

"I just," she shifts and swallows, then takes a deep breath. "I'm going to tell Mother I'm abdicating."

I close the distance between us and take her hands in mine. "Addylin, what is going on? I've never seen you like this, and you're scaring the hell out of me."

A hundred different emotions swim in her eyes before she shakes her head. "This whole spotlight thing. I hate it. I hate having to play the part. The speeches, the assemblies, and being perfect all the time? I can't do it."

"Addy, you have to have more faith in yourself."

"I know, I know. I've just been… it's just been a crazy few months and… urgh. I don't know. I'm just, tired. And sore and I… Oh, God," she rips her hands free and her palm flies over her mouth as she takes off into the small bathroom a few doors down from the ballroom.

She doesn't bother closing the door before I hear the toilet seat slam open and my twin sister throwing up, paralyzing me with fear.

Addylin never gets sick. Ever. This isn't normal, and if someone's done something to my sister, I swear I will slit the throats of every goddamn human in that goddamn ballroom until I find the person responsible and bury them so deep under the motherfucking ground Satan himself wouldn't hear them weep.

I'm at her side in a flash with a glass of water and a towel. "Better?"

"A little," she nods after emptying the glass and wiping her mouth. "Just nerves I guess."

I wrap my arm around her shoulder and take her hand as we walk back to the ballroom, doing my best to comfort her. "Have you talked to Father about how you're feeling?"

At least the color has finally returned to her cheeks, when we stop outside the doors.

"Not yet. But I'm going to. Soon. I can't see myself doing this. I don't even want to go to this thing," she gestures to the ballroom.

I link her arm in mine, and we enter the brightly lit room with fake smiles plastered on our faces, turning every eye in room in our direction as we do.

"Find Cane," I lean closer as Father makes his way to us, speaking through gritted teeth, "Try and have some fun while I keep Parliament busy. I'll check on you as soon as I can," and close my arm around my father's elbow, and Addy takes the other side.

"Everything alright girls?"

"Yup," I say, and Addylin nods. "Let the schmoozing begin."

He introduces us to the crowd and thanks the guest for attending, wishing everyone a happy Thanksgiving while raising a glass. The festivities return to relaxed chats and laughter as the orchestra begin their next song. One I recognize for once.

"Drink," Asaria appears at my side holding a glass of what I'm assuming is… actually I have no idea what the orangey-pink drink is, to me with a lazy smile on her plumped red lips, for once elegantly dresses in a simple off-the-shoulder flowy silver gown. "I think you're going to need it."

But I hold my hand up. "Not tonight."

"Why on earth not?" she asks, recoiling as if I slapped her in the face. So does Ophelia when she left Kaleo's side to join us. "This is like the one night of the year we should be drinking."

Strange as this sounds coming from me but, "I have to make rounds." *Still in the running for queen here sis…*

"Oh, what!" Asa protests. "We're not just gonna get drunk and dance until four like always?"

"No. I have Parliament members to impress."

"Is everything okay?" Ophelia asks beside her, taking my hand.

"Fine," I shrug out of her hold and find Mother waiting.

"Finally," she says, and begin our stroll through the crowd of enthralled guests—all admiring the red and brown maple leaves, orange pumpkins, nutmeg candles, and the tiny wooden turkeys the staff adorned the walls and dinner tables with—smiling and greeting every member of Parliament, their families, and their guests as we go. A few handshakes, *my, how you've grown*'s, a series of well-wishes and early Merry Christmas's later, and Mother, for once pleased with my performance, heads to Minister Fredrich's wife, Audelia's, side and the two make their way to the grand table where the royal family dines, and leaves me to my friends.

"That looked like hell," Tory closes me in her arms, squeezing tight.

"Pretty much," I reply, hugging Beth next.

"And where might Prince Steamy be?" she asks, eyeing the crowd over her shoulder.

I watch as Tory's lips turn up in a smirk. She grabs Beth's hand and pulls her into her side. "Standing behind her in the gorgeous shape of—"

Of course, if Mrs. Hastings is here, that means…

"God, I'm an idiot," Brayden's here. Though he rarely went anywhere without his grandparents.

I turn to him with a smile, reveling in just how little he's changed. He's lost weight, that much is clear, from the last time I saw him at Minister Fredrich's birthday party in December last year. What I do find strange is how dull and empty his usual lively ice-blue eyes seem. Like a firecracker has ultimately burned itself out.

"Now why do you say that?" I ask playfully.

"For letting you go when I did," he states, white teeth on fully display as he makes his way over to me with two glasses in his hand. He shakes his head, and sweeps his eyes over me. "You look…"

"Like a queen?" I keep a flirty tone, despite how annoyed I am about barely getting a sentence in with my friends. Who wave as they saunter to Asa and Ophelia at the bar.

"I'll say," Brayden smiles. "Man, oh man, was I an idiot."

I laugh, giving him a quick hug. "How are you?"

"Regretful," he muses. "But otherwise fine. What about you? Coping with the whole future queen thing?"

"Barely," I nod. "But getting there."

He joins me in a laugh and holds the other glass out to me. "Want one? I don't know exactly what they are but your sister insisted."

Knowing Asaria there could be any number of liquors mixed into that. In other words, it's your late evening spent hugging the porcelain thrown puking up coral-colored vomit, followed by a malicious hangover stalking you the next morning.

I glance over my shoulder at a smirking Asa, who raises her glass in my direction and downs what's left in hers. Typical.

I roll my eyes, turning back to Braden. "I really shouldn't…"

"It tastes like raspberries," he tilts his head, lips forming a lop-sided grin.

Coral puke it is. "… Have more than one," I finish my sentence and take the glass.

"Still a fan I see," Braden chuckles and drinks from his glass. "Though I agree with you. I don't think I have the capacity to drink more than one of these."

"Wise choice," I nod, clenching my stomach as I tip my own glass back, getting hit with a wave of sugared rum and raspberries. "Oh hey, I read your article on the impact of modern technology on early Ficaran tribes. I loved it." Yes, that's right people. I am a constant surprise. And while Brayden may be old news, he's still a talented writer.

"Thanks," he smiles sincerely. "Not my best work, but the relationships I formed with the tribesman in Namibia is something I'd never replace with anything. I could've done without the beetle salads, but they were the nicest people I've ever met. And so welcoming."

And strange. His departure was so sudden I couldn't tell him goodbye. Brayden is a cultural anthropology major at Arcadia, so overseas travels weren't foreign to him. Still, in the time we did spend together he'd always stop in to say goodbye, mostly to his grandfather, and a lesser extent me, but then he left for Ficara he went completely radio silent.

"Speaking of relationships," I say after taking another sip, and instantly regretting it. "Did you ever reconnect with Yamina?" The ex he never got over. She was the reason he broke up with me after all.

He shakes his head, "She got married a couple months after we broke up," he says. Up until the day she left him for his best friend, Brayden was convinced Yamina was the one. No wonder he left. "Which is kind of part of why I came to find you," he takes my glass and reaches for my hands after placing it on a table behind him.

"Look, I know I'm not anything close to a prince, but I've been thinking about it for a while and I don't know, maybe we could give us another chance? And I'm not just saying that because you're about to become queen. Don't make a face," he squints at my grimace, smiling. "You're a shoo-in and you know it. I'm being genuine here. I miss you. I miss hanging out with you."

Tempting. I probably would've considered if it weren't for Skylan, even if I am pissed at him. And Brayden is just too cute, like a miniature poodle infatuated with his seventy-year-old owner who smells like cookies and roses cute. But even with the anger, getting to know a mature, and I use the term loosely, Skylan over these past few months couldn't have meant nothing.

Yes, I'm angry, and yes, he's a dumbass sometimes, but he means well. Add to the fact that he's been the only man on my mind this entire year... I could totally see myself falling for Skylan.

Oh, who am I kidding? I already fell for him the second he called me his queen, repeatedly. Sure, it was in the middle of arguably the best sex we've ever had, but I still remember that look in his eyes when he said it. Even if he'd deny it. I reach for his shoulder and give him a gentle squeeze. "That's really nice, Brayden, but—"

Firm hands weave around my waist, and Sky's voice floats from behind me, pulling me into his chest.

"She's seeing someone," the heat of his body penetrates mine, and I fight the urge to lean back into his embrace and breathe him in.

When I turn and sweep my eyes to his, Sky's not focused on anything but me. Not a lick of anger or jealously in his eyes either. Just, intense focus with a gentle smile on his lips.

"Your Highness," Brayden bows his head deeply, both shock and awe in his eyes once he straightens.

Yeah, Brayden's cute in a poodle kind of way. But Sky?

"Mr. Hastings. I appreciate you keeping my Princess company. I'll take it from here."

Sky's hot in a sex god kind of way. A sex god who makes my heart beat faster and slower at the same time, and the one I know I'll never be able to live without no matter how much he drives me up the walls.

He nods Brayden's way, "If you would excuse us," then leads me away, spinning me into him as we reach the dance floor, and he pulls me close.

"*Am* I seeing someone?" I ask, tilting my head.

"Of course, you are," his smile is steadfast, nothing but pure conviction in his eyes. "What makes you think I would ever let you go, darling?" Sky lowers his head and whispers in my ear, weaving his arm around me.

His touch is warm, steady, and a few words later, and I'm lost in him once again.

Heart to heart, hand in hand, I'm putty in his embrace as he spins me around the dancefloor, and his warm eyes never leaving mine once, and the world around us fades into nothing, and the melody of the symphony is the only thing guiding us. Our every breath and every step in sync. Like we've been rehearsing for days. Weeks. Months.

Exactly the same way we did when we fought side by side in that warehouse.

"I fucked up," he eventually says, lowering his forehead to mine. "You were trying to communicate your feelings and I ignored it. I'm sorry."

"It's okay. I overreacted anyway, I know you're trying the best you know how and I appreciate it. I really do. Fights or not, it doesn't mean I don't care about you." My lips turn up, and I wrap my hand around his neck as he holds the other against his chest.

Sky sweeps his gaze over the dress, closing them as he breathes in my perfume, and every part of my body lights up when he whispers, "How are you so perfect?"

"You," I say, resting my hand over his heart, only lifting my eyes to his when he closes his hand over mine. "You make me feel perfect."

"I thought you didn't like purple? And a tiara? What has the world come to?" His eyes travel to the golden locket, and his breath catches. "That's not... Is that...?"

"The dress would be nothing without it. And you love purple," I beam at him. "Do I look okay?"

"Like a queen," Sky stops. His hazelnut eyes glue to my lips, and a gentle smile turns his upward. "My queen," he says, cupping my cheek with his hand and pulling me closer.

Wild surprise flashes in my mind the second I realize what he's about to do. "Wait," I stop him. "People can see."

"Let them," Sky beams, leaning in even closer, and my pulse rockets to the milky way as his lips near mine.

I search his eyes for the slightest hesitation. "Are you sure?"

Sky's lips are inches away from mine, and he breathes, "Kiss me, Princess."

And I bring his lips down to mine.

Chapter 30
Skylan
Forever Starts Today

If heaven is a place, Emryne's lips would be it. Her smiles, her giggles, her eyes... She would be it.

I don't care that we're in the middle of a crowded dancefloor, or that her family or my father is watching, maybe blondie... a little, but I wasn't waiting any longer. And when my lips closed over hers, every doubt I had before walking into this ballroom disappeared from existence.

My lips didn't leave hers when I took her in my arms and spun her around, declaring her off-limits to every man in this place who had their eyes glued to my princess when she walked through those doors at her father's side.

Neither did they when I hear Dad shout, "Finally!" over my shoulder, bringing a smile to her lips as she wrapped her arms around my neck.

"Cough it up," is the next thing I hear, followed by a slap on a palm. What is it with our fathers and bets?

And only when her feet touch the ground and I whisper, "Come with me," against her perfect lips, do we let each other go.

I weave my fingers through hers and lead her out of the ballroom and up the foyer steps, through the doors of the music room in the East Wing.

"Why are we in the music room?" she asks with a chuckle when I let her hand go, closing the door behind her.

My back is still toward her when I walk to the piano and open the lid, running my fingers over the keys before turning to a curious Emryne and taking a deep breath.

"If this is going where I hope it is, we need to get better at this communication thing," I say.

She shrugs. "Couples fight. It's normal. Even if we aren't technically—"

"I want us to be," I cut her off.

I watch as her mouth opens, closes, and opens again. So much surprise in her eyes I could've knocked her over with a feather. "You… what?"

"I'm serious, Emryne," I say and close the distance between us, taking her hands in mine. "I know I may not always get it right, but I want us to be together. I want to be with you."

Her jaw is just about on the floor, her voice hitching as she says, "Sky… are you asking me…"

"I love you," I gently cup her cheeks, cementing my eyes on those impossible blues of hers. "I'm so completely, without a doubt in love with you. And I won't hold it in a minute longer. I'm in love with you, Emryne."

Her breath catches in her throat, gaze never wavering from mine when she shakes her head, smiling.

But I stop her before she can reply. "Don't say anything yet, just listen."

I pull the bench away and take a seat, reaching for Emryne's hand and settling her in my lap so she faces me, before scooting us forward so my feet reach the pedals.

"Sky, you really don't have to—"

"Shh," I kiss her temple, closing my eyes and letting every memory, old and new, happy and unhappy, flow through my mind and into the lyrics as my fingers move over the black and white keys.

From the second I put that black armor on, and fought beside her in that warehouse. Amazed at how far her skills have progressed and watching her put them to good use.

The selfies we took in the kitchen when we were making pancakes in the middle of the night.

Following her to the docks that first time, even when she punched me in the face the day I arrived.

The pearl heirloom necklace I gave her for sixteenth birthday she only wears on special occasions, the same one she's wearing tonight. The one she fought tooth and nail that she didn't deserve, but goddammit, she deserved the world.

The time we carved our initials into just about every tree on the palace grounds so the world would know we were best friends and one of the single greatest moments we shared.

I couldn't tell you in which one of those moments I loved her more.

I may not have had the words or the courage to say them then, but I will say them now. The words that fell from my mouth before I realized the gravity of what I was saying, that it was coming from *me*, when I never thought I'd say it out loud much less want to but it's true. I love her. And I'll say them as long as it takes, as loud as I can, for her to hear me.

The lyrics finish, and my fingers leave the keys. And only when I open my eyes, seeing Emryne's cheeks wet with tears and her lips tremble when she takes my hand, do I realize this was probably as stupid idea.

"Oh, God. You hated it," I was so sure this would work. "I sounded like an injured screech owl, didn't I?"

"No," she says almost immediately, letting me breathe a sigh of relief, and wipes her tears. "No, you were perfect. They're happy tears," she laughs, cupping my cheeks and bringing my lips to hers, her salty kisses making me smile.

"I loved it," she says through another string of kisses, fits of happy giggles bubbling from her chest, settling my nerves.

"I love you."

My eyes snap open. I pull my head back and blink a few times, just to make sure I'm awake and that I heard her right. This would be the worst day of my life knowing this was a dream. I weave her fingers in mine and I lean my forehead to hers, and this is real, and all of my troubles, my insecurities, meant nothing.

I'm awake, and I feel her. Warm, and kind, and so damn beautiful. I'm awake, and I love her. And she loves me.

"You do?" The only reason I ask is so I can hear her say it again. And again. And again. Until the day I die.

"Yes," she nods, eyes watering with fresh tears again.

"You love me?" I breathe out, choking down my own tears.

"I love you," she says, wrapping her arms around my neck, "I love you," and crashes her lips to mine again, "I love you. I love you. I love you."

"I love you too," I say against her mouth, weaving my arms around her waist and holding her tight. I couldn't tell you where my body began and hers ended, and it didn't matter either.

I'm in love with Emryne and I'll do whatever it takes to make her happy. No more comparing myself with others, no more doubting my feelings of decisions. Our life together has just begun.

"I swear to Christ, if blondie comes near you again, I'll have him beheaded."

#

ME: *Don't make plans for New Year's. We're going on a little adventure. No work, no worries. Just us.*
DARLING: *After the day I had, sounds like heaven! Where r we going?*
ME: *It's a surprise. For our one-month anniversary.*
DARLING: *Tell me! :D :D :D :D*
ME: *Well, that would ruin the surprise now wouldn't it?*
DARLING: *U better not be taking me to some underground orgy.*
ME: *Like I'd share u with other people.*
ME: *Just shut up and trust me. Marina @ 4pm. Don't be late;)*

Like she ever is.

Much like me, ill-mannered tardiness was whooped out of her at very young age, couldn't risk smearing our parents' names through the proverbial mud now can we. And with what I have planned for my princess, I wouldn't want to be late either.

And as intriguing as an orgy sounds, at least based on how she reacted with the video, I'd think twice before letting other people worship her body the way she lets me.

Harmony Islands are the ultimate super rich, ritzy tourist destination. I couldn't think of a better time to get away from this freezing weather and Emryne's hovering mother, who was everywhere to be seen at the least wanted times. Hovering which seems to have tripled since our very public announcement at the Thanksgiving ball about the change in our relationship, yet neither her actions for her facial expressions gave anything away about whether she's pleased or not. Or accepts us or not. She did pawn her off to Caneic after all.

At least he won one princess.

Frankly, we both need this knowing the responsibility hell storm waiting by the time we reach Alorewyn on Sunday night.

Our fathers were ecstatic. Emryne's about having another son, mine about finally having a daughter, then the two grown-ass men elated they're officially

303

family, as if their nearly fifty-five-year friendship made them anything but, to which Emryne and I exchanged more than one lingering glance. Her blue eyes were filled with so much love it was hard not to drop to my knee then and there. Which should scare the shit out of me, but all I keep feeling when my mind drifts, is excitement.

Especially when seeing her walk out onto the balcony overlooking the marina where I'm waiting, rows of shimmering white yachts hibernating in the winter waves. All but our own, ready for our next adventure.

I'm tucked in a corner when she walks past me, gifting me the greatest view of her butt in the royal blue silk hugging her curves in all my favorite places. I catch up to her just in time so she doesn't see her surprise, pull her against my chest, covering her eyes. Her warm hands curl over mine, and I feel her cheeks turn up.

"Guess who?" I whisper, leaning down next to her ear and pressing featherlight kiss to her temple.

"My prince in shiny medals?" she spins around, my hands still covering her eyes, and her radiant smile sends flutters through my body.

"Guess again."

"Hmm… my wildest fantasies in human form?"

"One more time," though I love hearing that.

Her soft hands wrap around my wrists, her warm skin sending sparks through my body. "My best friend and the love of my life?" she says sweetly, and I lift my hands off of her eyes, "Hi."

I'm trying my best to take her words with a pinch of sugar, in-the-moment and all, but the longer they echo in my head, the better they sound. Sometimes it's hard to believe I get to call her mine. "Hi, darling."

She takes my hands and takes a step back for me to admire her. "This what you had in mind?"

My eyes fall back on the dress I had delivered to her bedroom. Every part of her beauty is accentuated in the mid-afternoon sunlight, even has a small part of me wondering if her daughter would have the same wildly blue eyes and dark, thick, and coppery hair like she does.

I'd love nothing more than having another Emryne running around, especially if she calls me Daddy…

I swallow hard, taking her hand and spinning her around, pulling her into my chest once her sparkling eyes meet mine.

"Breathtaking as always darling," I say, lowering my lips to hers and closing her in my arms. "I love you," I whisper, squeezing her in a tight hug.

She smiles, pressing a string of kisses on my cheeks, forehead and finally my lips. "I love you. Can I have my surprise now?"

"Ever my impatient princess," I chuckle, spinning her around and covering her eyes again as I lead her to the edge of the balcony. "We are sailing south for the winter."

"Sailing?" she questions, then slams her hands on mine as she gasps. I beam at her excitement, and lift my hands, revealing the one thing I know she's always wanted to do. "What!" she squeals, jumping into his arms. "Oh my God, you remembered?"

"I've been wanting to do this since the day I got back," I kiss her lips. "But being alone on here is such a drag," I say with a playfully roll of my eyes, swooping her into my arms and carrying her up the gangplank and onto the yacht bridal style. She wraps her arms around my neck, holding on as if I'm her lifeline, and fits of her elated giggles float into my ear and heads straight for my heart. After finally making peace with the fact he'd met the greatest love of his life on an island not too far from here, the same one we're sailing to, my grandparents gave The Gilliana as wedding gift to my parents. It's also where their generosity toward them began and ended since they weren't in favor of their relationship given Mom wasn't from a royal family.

I never met them, but apparently the cold shoulder they gave Mom finally melted when they heard she was pregnant with me, relieved my parents would be having a son to keep the Dormer name in the throne.

We don't use the super yacht much since the gargantuan thing is a pain in the ass to maneuver in general, let alone from Callior to Alorewyn during winter, but knowing the megawatt smiles, kisses, and warm hugs waiting for me when Emryne saw it, I couldn't be happier knowing she made it the distance so I could make my princess's day.

The captain, Wes Grundy, and crew greet us as we walk on board. He signals that we're ready to set sail as soon as we're settled with a quick bow just as the few crew members on board dispersed to their duties, and the chief mate, Maggie, shows us to the main deck.

This is only the second time I met Wes since he only started a few months ago after Whinston Moseby retired, but my father trusted him, and he's done an exquisite job of keeping the boat pristine.

Fresh fruit platters and two glasses of champagne are already waiting by the time we sat down on the oval, cream velveteen loungers surrounding the built-in firepit, embers gently crackling and warming the crisp sky around us, adorned in a vibrant blend of the pinks and oranges from the setting sun. The stairs to the lower decks are to the left of the bar, just a few steps from the hot tub (Mav's insistence for exactly an occasion like today—winter with a view), and the stainless-steel railings overlooking the ocean.

"Happy?" I hand Emryne her glass as I lean back on the lounger, wrapping my arm around her shoulder.

"That I get you alone for an entire weekend?" she leans closer and lowers her voice. "You have no idea, Your Highness," she says, pressing a soft kiss against my lips. I chuckle, reaching for a strawberry and bringing it to her lips as she says, "What are we going to do with ourselves?"

Her eyes glue to mine as she puckers her lips and takes a slow bite, smirking as she chews on the delicate fruit. "Harmony Island are full of possibilities, my darling," I say, giving her a wink.

Oh, she's thinking wild thoughts, that much is obvious. And I'm fully planning on satisfying every inch of our bodies as many times as we can handle.

"How do you know about this place?" she asks, throwing her legs over my lap and snuggling closer.

"I'm the Prince of Callior, darling, I have contacts in the least expected places," I tell her, linking our fingers.

"So, you bring your other girls on here too?" Emryne jokes, but I catch the side-eye.

Can't say it hasn't crossed my mind, but, "Nope. Dad's holy about this thing. You're the first woman on the main deck since Mom died. She used to love coming here for Sunday morning brunch."

"To the islands? With all the romance?"

"Especially with the romance," I lean forward and grab another strawberry. "Despite being a notorious ladies' man, Dad's the king of romance. I saw how he treated her."

"Oh good," she releases a teasing breath, "for a second there I was expecting you to tell me about other princesses with eyes like mine."

"No one is like you," I assure her. And no one will ever be. Everything she does is breathtaking. Her smile, her kisses, the way her blue eyes shimmer in the sunlight, her ability to kick a man's ass. God, I love this woman.

"Is that why you've always been so hesitant about dating? You thought she wouldn't approve?"

I sway my head from side to side. "Yes and no. As her ALS got more severe, it was hard maintaining most of my friendships. I hardly left the palace in the few months before she died. Dad couldn't do everything by himself and she didn't want anyone but us around her. I didn't want to make promises I couldn't keep because she needed me."

I swallow hard, pushing the tears back down. Her funeral was the last time I cried, and I'd rather not spoil of getaway with my somber waterworks.

"I would've given any part of my body in exchange for hers if it meant her suffering would stop."

Emryne's eyes soften, and she pulls me into for a gentle kiss. "You were an amazing son her, Sky. She would be so proud of who you are today," she cups my cheek. "I know I am," she kisses me again, and again. Each one more reassuring than the previous.

"I know were supposed to be relaxing this weekend, but how's your keynote prep going?" I ask, taking a berry of my own, something she'd need reassurance of her own.

Coronation day is inching closer and her national address is nine days away. And based on her performance, Alorewyn will very soon have a new queen. Knowing how anxious she gets about public speeches, it's important to me hearing where her head's at. Sitting in on assemblies occasionally voicing an opinion is one thing, but delivering a life-altering keynote in front of an entire kingdom is entirely different. Even in school I'd make her practice her speeches in front of her mirror so many times she knew it by heart. This won't be any different.

"It's... going," she stammers, reaching for fresh raspberry and taking a bite. "I had to bribe Addylin with, not one, but four boxes of double-stuffed Oreos so she could distract Mother long enough for me to slip away."

"You feeling okay about it though?"

"Am I feeling okay about the fact that I'm a week away from making arguably the most important speech of my life that technically will *decide* my entire life based solely on the words aptly strung together by the woman who'd rather see a cybernetically enhanced bear instead of me become the new queen?" She tilts her glass back and downs the alcohol. "Yeah, no pressure at all."

She throws her head against my shoulder, breathing out a frustrated sigh.

We've never exactly talked about it but, "What happens if you don't get elected?"

She pauses, slowly raising her head and meeting my eyes after taking a deep breath. "Addylin's abdicating."

My brows draw together. "I didn't know that," This definitely changes things.

"Neither did I until Thanksgiving. So, it's me or I'm stuck in limbo for God knows how long until Parliament makes up their minds."

Even if she's the running alone, Parliament could extent her performance review by two years if they thought she needed longer evaluation. Which I highly doubt is the case, nearly every conversation King Ryne included me in at the ball were glowing compliments from senior members, some of which encouraged me to pursue her, like I needed it, so I can't see why they wouldn't choose her.

And I make a point to tell her exactly that. "I don't think you have much to worry about. Parliament's happy."

Her lips turn up and she straightens, "They are?"

"From what I heard, yeah."

"Where did you hear that?" she asks with a frown.

I shrug. "At the ball while blondie was feeling you up."

"He was not feeling me up," she rolls her eyes. "He just being nice."

"Yeah," I scoff, "Nicely eyeing your body before downing three shots of whatever the hell he had in those glasses before he plastered on the charm." I still get the creeps just thinking about it.

The way they spoke made it clear they had some kind of history, but I had no interest in knowing to what extent. All I knew was I needed to get her as far away from him as possible.

"No way in hell I was letting whatever that was happen," I say, cupping her cheek and bringing her lips to mind, kissing her softly. "You're mine, darling."

"Of course, I am, Casanova," she chuckles, pressing her lips to mine again before she continues. "Alorewyn deserves a queen who will put her own needs aside and serve. Someone they can trust. Someone they will listen to," she says, settling back into my side. "My mother hasn't exactly been setting a stellar example, and she might still be with my father, but he's ruled alone since Addylin and I were born. Sure, she had the title, but that was it."

"So blind obedience isn't what it takes to be a good queen after all," I comment, running my hand over her back.

"Funny, it's almost like times have changed," she says, but I catch the meaning. That might work for King Lodran and his perfectatious son, but definitely not for us.

Yes, I'm perfectly aware there is no such word, but tell me it doesn't fit.

"Pardon the interruption," Maggie's light voice and freckled face appears from below deck and stop just short of the lounger. "Dinner is ready, Your Highness."

"Perfect," I swing her legs down and get to my feet, holding out my hand. Emryne eyes me curiously, gingerly sliding her fingers into my palm. "Where are we going?"

"Patience, darling," I wink. Leaving the couch, I weave my fingers through hers as we follow Maggie a deck below where the main bedroom is. The small dining room table on the balcony is set up with a feast. As we step outside, I'm happily surprised the floor-to-ceiling heaters are on full blast, barely giving the impression of winter despite the cool breeze blowing.

Cords of tiny twinkling lights brighten the early evening as sun disappears behind the horizon.

"And here I thought you didn't know romance," she gapes at decor. The sunny daffodils' fresh scent fills the air around us, and my grin widens at her marveled expression.

For her, I'd do anything. Even become king.

"Funny," I say, pulling out her chair and taking her hand as she sits down. Maggie bids us a good evening and let us know she's on call should we need anything, then closes the bedroom door behind her.

"A year ago, I wouldn't have been within five feet of considering wearing a crown. All this pressure to be perfect, perform, and maintain this image of righteousness and lawfulness, both in society and front of Parliament?" I say, pouring us each a glass of wine. "Why do you think I walked away in the first place?"

"Parliament and perfection I can handle," she mumbles, cementing her eyes on mine as she leans forward. "But, what about now?"

My grin broadens, already knowing what's going through her mind. "Now, I'm exactly where I want to be," I say, reaching for her hand and giving her reassuring squeeze. "You'll be fine."

Her hand is still in mine when she leans back, brow furrowed. I feel her tense up as she says, "This is my last chance to show Parliament what I've got, what happens if I screw up?" she swallows, lifting her head.

"Why on earth would you think that?" Sounds to me like she has it all together.

"I don't know. Part of me just feels like… like I'm not ready."

"Then we'll do whatever it takes to get you ready. We'll practice day and night if that's what you need. Just like we did in school," I give her another squeeze, making sure she's listening. "You've always known the difference between duty and obligation, Emryne. You are perfectly aware that you're under no obligation to become queen, yet you still see it as your duty. To both yourself and your kingdom. You're always ready to take on whatever life throws. It's one of the things I admire so much about you."

Her body relaxes, and her lips turn up in a small. "What about you?"

"What about me?"

"What do you want?"

"You," I answer, easiest one I've ever given. "Whatever you need, tell me. I'm here. Always. And if I wasn't, I'd never be able to go to sleep at night knowing the infants your mother invited who'd try to make you come have no goddamn idea how you need to be touched."

"Interesting," she says, playfully narrowing her eyes. She pushes back her chair and saunters over, and leans down, closing her mouth over mine before she settles herself in my lap. Her lips leave mine, pools of deep blue light by body on fire as she sucks my bottom lip between her teeth, effectively sending all blood rushing to my dick as her hand slides down my chest and settles over my heart.

"And how do I need to be touched, Prince Skylan?" She murmurs, and presses her lips to mine again.

I let out a groan, gripping her hip before I lift us from the chair. "Well, why don't you get your ass on the bed and I'll show you, darling."

I would've let her walk, but hearing her elated yelp when I throw her over my shoulder and carry her to the bed, dropping her between the sheets, is much too precious to miss.

The second her head hits the pillows, my body covers hers, and my lips are on her. Gently at first, neither of us in a rush for the finish line, not today.

Her lips part, allowing my tongue access to hers, massaging her until she moans into my touch.

It doesn't take long for our clothing to find the floor, and we're between the sheets, back in each other's arms. This might be the first time since we've slept together that she's letting me take her while she's on her back.

Today, I plan on savoring every precious inch of her while she's still my princess. Before she becomes my queen.

And she will be Queen.

"You can do this, Emryne. Alorewyn needs you," I say quietly, stroking her cheek. "I've watched you work your ass off to be where you are today. I know, beyond a shadow of a doubt, you are going to be the most incredible queen this country has ever seen."

"Not alone. Promise me. Please, please promise me this isn't temporary. That you won't disappear again," she says, her eyes of wildest blue darting between mine. "I want you next to me, Sky. There's no one else I want to be king."

My hand cups her cheek, and I lower my forehead to hers. "You aren't just another girl, Emryne. You're home. You're my everything. And I'll be by your side for the rest out lives if that's what you want."

I watch as tears well in her eyes, and she grips my neck. "I love you so much, Sky," she whispers. Then her eyes meet mine and I know. I've never been sure about anything in my life, but today I am. Emryne Gennady is my end, my beginning, my in-between.

The world around us ceased to exist. There is no crime, no wars or race toward coronation. Just, us. Us and this moment. The moment she became my everything. My breath, my smile, my tears, my success... my life. The love of my life.

“I love you, Emryne. And I swear I will, until the day I take my final breath.”

Because I'm here, and she's in my arms. Forever.

Chapter 31
Emryne
Dear Princess, I Told You So

Okay, so maybe missionary isn't as bad as I thought. I've never exactly had the desire to have anyone on top of me, not like I did Skylan on that gigantic ship.

Extravagant, doesn't even begin to describe that thing. I've been craving to get on it since I was old enough to remember, and there was no better way to have started off 2022 then wrapped in the silky sheets with Skylan next to me. This is the Skylan I've been waiting for. I knew he was in there somewhere; he just needed a little reminder of how amazing he is.

When we somehow found a way to keep our hands off each other for longer than five minutes, he made me practice my speech until I was blue in the face.

My cotton sheets changed to satin, and Sky's spent every night since we got back waking up next to me, sometimes inside me; I think I like sleepy sex even better than shower sex.

And now I'm here. Minutes away from possibly outranking my mother.

As Addylin finishes, she leaves the balcony and earns a single nod from Mother for her performance. While she may have made some solid points, it didn't take an imbecile to notice she didn't believe a single word she was saying. But she did it, word for word exactly as expected, and not a single hair on her head is left out of place.

I, on the other hand, feel like I'm about to pass out. I've always hated giving speeches, but I have a duty to fulfill.

So, I close my eyes, repeating Sky's words in a quiet voice, the same ones he made me say every time I made a formal appearance. *It's just a few silly words. No big deal.* I love him so much.

Addylin walks through the palace front doors, and they close behind her almost immediately, leaving the two of us alone in the foyer.

She picks up on my pacing when she catches up to me and takes my hands in hers. "You're going to be amazing," she beams, glowing more than usual in the mid-morning sunlight streaming through the windows.

My eyes find her forest green irises, and give her hands a squeeze. "Are you sure this is what you want?"

"Oh, come on," she says, untying her sash and draping it over the mahogany stairwell banister before closing me in a hug. "We both know you were made for this."

"Did you talk to Father yet?" I ask, hugging her tightly.

"We're meeting in his office after."

"What will you do?" I ask, trying to swallow the lump in my throat.

"I'm not sure yet," she raises her shoulder. Her smile never faltering once. "But I'll figure it out."

I hear the minister announce my name, and I check my make-up in the mirror a final time, straighten my sash and smooth out the simple dove gray, knee-length, long-sleeve dress and check that my tiara's behaving appropriately before I walk through the doors and to the veranda overlooking the masses. All gathered on the gravel roadway leading to the palace.

The podium awaits.

I step behind the row of microphones as the applauding crowed finally hushes, and clip the speech on the board below, ready to conquer.

It's just a few silly words. No big deal.

"Good afternoon, everyone. To His Majesty the King and Her Majesty the Queen, our esteemed members of Parliament. And Skylan."

The crowd chuckles as he leans back in his seat and crossed his hands behind his head with a shit-eating grin while he wiggles his eyebrows me.

Typical idiot. Yet my nerves are already melting away.

Especially giving a quick glance to the crowd gathered at the bottom of the steps, and my eyes settling on a familiar face.

Vanessa McCauley. And a much healthier looking Todd next to her.

She gives me a small wave, bringing a warm smile to my face, before settling into Todd's side.

"Today officially marks a year after my eligibility to become your next queen was announced, alongside my sister, Addylin. It marks a year of several journeys taken…"

But I trail off, gazing at the flashing cameras, the people of Alorewyn, proudly waving the red, white, and blue.

My people, people like Vanessa and Todd, regardless of whether I'm elected or not, who all deserve better than me spewing a bunch of crap someone else made up.

"You know what? Screw it," if I'm going to do this, may as well go out with a bang. So, I crumble the robotic words and promptly toss it over my shoulder. Let's see how pissed she is after this.

"I hate birds. I hate them, I always have. Can't stand the fact that those weird little pupils dilate more in thirty seconds then I breathe in a single minute. It's creepy. But the more I think about it the more I realize now that reason I hate the beady-eyed little creatures has, in fact, got nothing to do their pupils or the fact that they have no teeth, but the fact that they can fly.

"It's nothing new that several people have openly stated that man was not supposed to fly when the Wright Brothers built the first airplane. Same thing was said about going to the moon, even the bottom of the ocean. Those people were mocked, criticized, and ridiculed for their ambitions. Ambitions humanity had no idea would change life as we know it. And despite the judgement, every one of them said screw it and screw you, I'll do exactly that in spite of all of you. Why? Because there is freedom in flying. There is freedom in exploration, and there's freedom in knowledge.

"My father strived for a kingdom where education is not limited to a single class of citizen. In fact, he strived for a kingdom that encourages its citizens to expand their horizons. To meet fascinating foreigners and have never-ending conversations until all-hours of the night, instead of fear what they don't know, or who they don't know. He strived for a kingdom free of fear, of judgment, scrutiny and corruption and built a home for all of us, ensuring and assuring that no one, ever, goes to sleep feeling anywhere but at home with where they are. None of them feel anxiety about where they're supposed to head next because they feel unsafe, or that they don't belong, because none of you deserve that feeling.

"You, all of you, are the essence of Alorewyn. Without you, there is no kingdom, which is why you deserve a future that is certain. A kingdom that is safe for you and for your children, and you deserve a queen who will look in the face of adversity, and laugh. Someone who will stare adversity down and encourage it to hit her with its best shot because she will not back down regardless of the challenge.

"I've seen first-hand what our streets look like, and I know I have a lot of work ahead of me, but I promise, to the best of my ability, I will see Alorewyn streets safe again. I will see every citizen have a roof over their heads, hot food on their tables, and running water in their faucets.

"And I will see to a future that guarantees its citizens, alongside their rulers, a place to spread their wings and soar among clouds."

A quiet breath, two, three… and the crowd erupts in a symphony of ear-shattering cheers.

Father is about to cry… actually, no, he is crying. Mother's looking over the crowd's elated faces, but I already know what's waiting for me the second those daggers plunge into mine.

And I don't care.

I leave that podium feeling a three-thousand-pound weight has been lifted off my chest. Today was the first time in my life I was able to string together real sentences in front my entire kingdom without feeling like I'm about have heart attack. I felt free to voice my opinions like I wanted, show the difference I truly wanted to make as Alorewyn's next queen.

I did what I could, the rest is up to Parliament.

When I find Addy standing at the stairwell, she's staring at her phone like she's like she's seen a ghost. I'm halfway to where she's gaping at her screen, when he moves in my way.

And now, Sky is all I see. The only person I care about.

"So, what did you think?"

"What did I think?" He shouts, wrapping me in his arms and spinning me. "I am so proud of you, Emryne!"

I laugh, wrapping my hands around his neck. The second my feet touches the marble floor again, I pull his lips down to mine. "I couldn't have done any of it without you, Sky. None of this. Today was mind-blowing, and I've never felt so empowered and… wait, where are you going?"

Sky's bright smile never leaves his handsome face as he begins to back away. "I have to get something. Stay here, I won't be long!" He gives me another quick kiss and runs upstairs to the West Wing. For what, I have absolutely no idea.

"Uhm, okay?" Are the only words I can think of. Not exactly how I expected him to react, especially not after making the best speech I ever have in my life, which he helped me get through, even if I'd did technically wing it. Still staring at Skylan's disappearing figure, Father appears beside me with the Minster and a few other senior Parliament members, chattering away as they head for Fredrich's office. He takes my hand as he wraps the other around my shoulder as we head to his office and await the verdict.

"You did it, kiddo!" He beams, patting my shoulder. "I can't believe you got through an entire speech without a single stutter."

"Skylan's a great teacher," I smile.

"That he is. Where did he run off to?" he asks as we climb the last steps toward his office.

"No idea. All he said was he was going to get something and then took off to the West Wing."

"Ah, never mind then. I'm sure he has a perfectly valid reason for disappearing. We'll see him soon enough." Father squeezes my shoulder, a coy smile playing at the corner of his lips.

I wouldn't put it past them to cook up some elaborate gift to shove in my hands.

Unfortunately, Sky will have to wait, seeing as how my usually fuming mother is already waiting in Father's office with Cane and Addy standing beside her when we walk through the doors.

"Why is it, Emryne, that every damn time you open your mouth, you deliberately undermine the work I've put into you and your future?" Mother's hands ball into tight fists at her side, about to foam at the mouth. "And why didn't you tell me our daughter was planning to abdicate?" She shoves her forefinger at Father.

"Mother please, I'm sorry—" Addy steps forward.

"I'll deal with you in a minute," she snaps, turning back to me. "What in god's name were you thinking? Pulling a stunt like that on a day this important? It is disrespectful toward me, it's disrespectful toward Parliament, and to your father."

"Don't bring me into this, Lilliette, Emryne did a phenomenal job," Father says, fighting with all his might to keep his temper at bay. "You have nothing to apologize for, Addylin."

Old me would've put up a fight, defend myself in any way that I can. New me? She's prepared for her this time. "Disrespectful?" I recoil, crossing my arms over my chest.

"Did you not hear a single word I said?"

"She spoke her mind perfectly, Lilliette, I don't understand—"

"It's all right, Father," I stop him. I've had enough. Being able to speak my mind without her micromanagement and constant minute corrections freed me from her oppressive thumb once and for all. No more of him fighting my battles for me.

"Nothing I do will ever be good enough for you, will it?" I scoff, closing the distance between us. "I'm sorry, Mother. I am so sorry that I'm such a fucking disappointment."

"Language!" she grumbles again.

Before, I would've backed down from her reddening cheeks, not anymore.

"I'm sorry I don't handle tasks your way, and instead do it the way I think it should be handled," I say, this time getting right in her face. "And I am sorry that I'm so bad at following your rules, but the reality is, your rules need to change."

"That is not your decision to make, dearest."

"Neither is it yours. And the fact of the matter, dear, is that it will soon," Father says, walking around his desk and pulls out his chair. "Parliament was quite captivated with her… albeit improvised keynote, but the reaction it gained from the citizens as well as the recent polls the ballad counters tallied before the address, speaks for itself," he says, sitting down, then linking his fingers. "Their decision will be made soon, Lilliette."

Mother lets out a bitter laugh, turning even my own mood sour. "Right. You expect me to believe Fredrich is allowing her to rule with a king she doesn't yet have?" she deadpans, turning to Cane. "Let me guess, that's the reason you're here?"

"It is, Your Majesty," Cane says, however slowly, but whatever angst he had when Mother made the comment, disappeared the instant he took my sister's hand. "But Emryne isn't the princess I'm here for."

#

My heart is beating a million miles a minute by the time we leave my arguing parents in the office and head back into the main hall. I've never seen my sister this happy, and it's the most rewarding feeling in the world knowing she's found the man she wants to spend the rest of her life with.

Just as I've found mine. And I can't wait to tell him the good news.

"I'm glad you took my advice," I say as the three of us walk down the staircase, my beaming, teary-eyed sister gripping his forearm.

"What advice?" she wipes away another tear.

"Oh, you know," I raise a shoulder, playing coy. "Just to find himself his perfect princess. You should be thanking me, Adds. I technically set you up when I kicked his ass."

She stops dead at the bottom of the steps, "You never told me that!" Addy giggles.

Cane clears his throat and scratches the back of his head, "Right, well, it was quite the draw, if ever I've seen."

"If you mean blood, then yes," I say over my shoulder, sauntering a step away with crossed arms.

"Emryne!" she shouts with a laugh.

"What? I'm a lean, mean, fighting machine. How else am I supposed knock these entitled dumbasses down a peg?" I joke, ruffling Cane's hair.

"You're so stupid," she mumbles, wrapping her arms around me. "I'm proud of you. You're going to be an amazing queen."

I squeeze her tighter. "So will you."

"Alright, let me go before I wet myself," she says, letting me go and heads for the bathroom, but not before stopping and giving me an exaggerated bow.

"Your Majesty."

"You alright, sweetness?" Cane asks, concern hinting in his tone.

"Just have to pee. I'll be fine," she turns around, pointing her forefinger at me. "And no more making my fiancé bleed, okay?"

"I make no such promises," I call while Cane laughs as the door closes behind her. "I'm beyond happy for you two."

"Your sister is an extraordinary woman. Not unlike yourself," he says, playfully bumping my shoulder as we laugh.

There is one thing I need to say. "Do me a favor though?"

"Of course," he smiles thoughtfully.

"Please take care her. We may not always see eye to eye, but she deserves the best."

He reaches for my shoulder, giving it a light squeeze, "She won't spend a day in Eikenish without a smile. I'll make sure of it."

I have no doubt about that at all. The second he got down on one knee, my heart caught in my throat. I knew from what he'd said the last day we spent together they were close, but imagine my surprise when he pulled out that gigantic rock. Addylin's smile was infectious. Seeing my twin thriving and in love was all that mattered.

And as I watched, my thoughts drifted to Sky; what he would say the day he decided to propose. Would he do it like Cane? Make sure both my parents were in the room to give their consent?

Doubt it. He'd probably make it some kind of elaborate prank or something. Or maybe he'd do the same thing he did when we first said I love you.

That would be a dream come true.

Though, it's one of the reasons why I was so anxious about the keynote. I want him. I want Skylan to serve beside me as king.

And the more I think about it, the more I conclude I have no reason not to take the first leap. It's not uncommon for a woman to ask a man to marry her, why can't I do the same?

And I would, if said prince hadn't disappeared a while ago.

Cane and Addylin leave through the veranda doors to the gardens just as I begin climbing the steps to West Wing, hoping he'd be in his bedroom when I knock on the door. But there was no answer.

"I saw him head outside, Your Highness," Monique says when I catch her and Des heading toward the kitchens. "You might want to hurry," she adds, "He seemed awfully distressed."

I take the steps down, and that's when I spot him through the massive windows in the grand foyer, walking toward one of the palace's armored vehicles.

"Sky!" I catch up to him, taking his hands and linking my fingers in his. "Oh my God, you're not going to believe this! Cane just—"

"I heard what Cane said," he cuts me off, yanking his hand back and throwing another suitcase in the trunk.

His luggage?

"Where are you going?"

"Home, Emryne. I have a flight to catch," he answers gruff, not bothering to face me. I can hear the anger in his voice in those few words alone.

"A flight?" I recoil. "Is everything okay?" There's no way he'd leave this abruptly unless it has something to do with the kingdom. "Did something happen in Callior?"

"No."

Something's not right. Sky's usual smile, laidback and chipper demeanor has vanished. Now, he's more hostile than I've ever seen him.

"Talk to me? What happened?"

He turns to me with a smile that doesn't reach his eyes. "I never figured you the type to string someone along for your own amusement. You're a great actress, by the way."

"Okay?" I draw out as my brows furrow. "I have no idea what that means. Why don't we go inside and—"

"Didn't I give you everything you wanted?" he asks, finally meeting my eyes with cold fury alight in his irises. So cold, I take a step away from him. "All the dates, kissing your father's ass, fucking you? For God's sake, Emryne, I took a bullet for you!"

"Sky, where is this coming from?" I step toward him before he attracts unwanted ears. I've never been more confused before. What possibly have changed from his telling me he's proud of me to... this? "Just talk to me. Please. I love you," I say quietly.

But he doesn't answer. All he does is shake his head, choking out another bitter laugh.

If this it, if this is the way we end, then I want to hear him say it. I want to hear him say exactly what's been in the back of my mind since the day he walked back into this palace. I'd rather hear him say it now and get over with.

"Tell me you don't love me. Tell me all this was all a joke to you."

"You thought I loved you?" he jeers. "Well, I didn't. I was here for the crown. Not you. Grow up, little girl."

He yanks open the door, lifting his leg to slide onto the seat, but barges back out instead. "You know, for a second there I really thought we had something. I was so ready to move forward, that you were willing to accept every part of me. Obviously, I was wrong. I hope he gives you everything you deserve. I would have."

He finally gets in and slams the door shut. All I'm left doing is standing on the gravel, watching the armored Rolls Royce speed away without him saying another word, or a single glance backward. Disappearing in the distance, an old, empty memory and taking the time we spent together with him. Time I was convinced we had plenty of.

Jokes on me, I guess.

I can't tell you how I ended up in my father's office, or how long it took me to get there. I can't tell you if anyone spoke to me, and if they did who they were or what they said, and I don't have a syllable left to give.

The only word left echoing in my mind is *why*.

As soon as Father sees me, the laughing stops abruptly, and he's at my side in a flash. "Emryne, what is it?"

What do I say?

Skylan broke my heart, again?

He called me those two words he promised he'd never say again?

I'm a stupid fucking idiot?

D—All of the above.

"Out," he demands. "Everyone out, now."

Feet scuttle from the room as Father wraps his arms around me, encasing me in a hug so tight it cuts off my oxygen supply.

My legs are no longer able to keep me upright, so I let them rest, and sink to the floor, finally allowing the tears threatening to drown me flow in long, hard streams as sobs roll from my lips.

"Sweet girl," he whispers, rocking me against his chest. "Daddy's here. Daddy's got you."

I thought I knew pain the day my great-grandfather died. I thought that would be the worst heartache I'd have to experience when I lost him. Turns out it was nowhere close. Not when the spewed hatred of Sky's words ripped my heart apart piece by piece.

All I keep thinking is how I'm supposed to recover from this. If I'll recover from this.

I must've looked a mess when I swung my bedroom door open after hours of crying in my father's arms, then in Addylin's when she heard of my distress probably from our lady's maids, unpleasantly surprised to see it was my mother who knocked later that evening.

Neither of us spoke then. She opens, closes, opens her mouth, but remains speechless.

Until I couldn't take it anymore. "Satisfied?"

"Emryne," her voice cracks. This is the first time in my life I've ever seen her say anything without a scowl on her face. I hate it.

I want her to go away. "Your favorite daughter gets to be queen. Just like you wanted. I'll talk to Father about abdicating. And I'll get out of your hair. You won't ever have to look at me again."

She reaches out to take my hands, but I step back. "No, Emryne, please let me—"

Her judgement is the last thing I need.

"I have nothing to say to you," I slammed the door shut.

I haven't bothered leaving my room since. In what I'm sure has been days. Days that have turned into weeks, and I'm still left with questions I know I'll never get answers to, no matter how hard I wish for them. The torture of checking my texts every few hours only to find an empty mailbox has become an addiction.

When I turn to the light streaming in through the door sometime after the sun set, I have no idea what day it is, or when they arrived, Asa and Ophelia's small, wistful smiles greet me. "Sweety, it's been weeks," Asa gently says, "you have to get up."

"Can you please not say I told you so?" I can't be sure, but I think I say it out loud as she and Ophelia pull open my covers and climb in next to me. "Please?"

"You sure?" she says, pulling me into her chest. "I think it'll make you feel better."

Ophelia giggles, rubbing my back, bringing a tiny smile to my own lips.

But it doesn't last long. I don't want to laugh.

"What did I do?" I'm barely able to speak. My hand clutches my chest as the tears I thought would've been dried up by today, but somehow keep streaming down my cheeks. "What did I do?"

"Nothing, Emrie. You didn't do anything," Asa says through her own tears while gently stroking my hair. "Skylan Dormer is an asshole. He never deserved you."

His name sears my ears like a white-hot fire poker, scorching whatever scars had already begun their healing, however little.

And now that throbbing pain in my chest decided to make a comeback. "Please go."

"Emryne," she says gently.

"I have no more fight left in me, Asaria," I shrug out of her hold, slamming my head against my pillows away from her, allowing the sobs their freedom once again. "Please. Please, just go."

"Is that really what you want?" Ophelia leans down, taking my hands and pulling me into her lap.

I want answers. That's what I want.

I want this godforsaken pain to go away.

I want to know what the hell could've gotten into him from finishing my keynote until he left.

Stupid of me to hope I'd ever get them.

"I'm here for you, E," Asa says, as she shimmies down, wrapping her arms around my torso.

"We're not going anywhere."

"It hurts," I force out, my throat completely raw from crying.

"We know, honey. We know." Ophelia chokes out, snuggling closer.

As much as I want to be alone right now, having my sisters here means more than I have the words to explain, even better when Addylin joined, carrying a tray of double-stuffed Oreos and fresh raspberry ice cream.

I don't do much but cry.

And cry. And cry. Until it the sun rises on yet another hollow day.

And we all fell asleep sometime that night.

Chapter 32
Skylan
Fool Me All This Time

She's the single, greatest love of my life…
She healed me when I couldn't do so myself…
I can't live, I can't breathe without her, Your Majesty…
Marry me…

Those words plague my dreams every damn time I close my eyes. On my flight home, the drive from the airport back to the palace, whenever I try to get a minute of fucking rest, I'm tortured.

My bedroom hasn't been touched. The forest green walls are still as bleak as I remember.

All my old sailing trophies, Mom insisted I give a try even if I climbed into a cockpit directly after, still lined the shelves on my walls, surrounded by my favorite family portraits, flight qualification certificates and awards, and couple of posters of Deadpool's funniest quotes, none of which I find funny anymore. Only difference is my usually made-up bed. The white silk barely ever left the ground lately.

Three years away from home and I never thought I'd miss this place as much as I did. Probably because life was simpler away from Callior. No drama, no hovering parents, no expectations, and no lies. Two weeks between these walls, and I still can't believe how damn stupid I've been.

How could she do this? Did she think I wouldn't find out she was using me in this pathetic soap opera she calls her life? What was the point of it any of it?

I thought I was angry before, but the more I stare at her pictures on the wall, the ones we'd taken over the years at the happiest moments of our lives, birthdays, summer vacations, graduation… that anger turned into silent rage. Dad knocked on my door several times and tried to get me to talk through it.

Maverick, whose bulked up a ton since I saw him last—good ole Dormer genes—tried. But I have no interest in talking.

For once in my goddamn life, I wish my family would just let me be pissed. Pissed off at Cane. Pissed off at Emryne for stringing me along. But most of all, I'm pissed off with myself. Every word Cane said to her is what *I* should've said to her. Pissed off about not giving her all the things I should've given her when I had the chance. And I had so, so many of them.

And now look.

Yet through all this, my masochistic mind keeps trying to convince me that this isn't something Emryne would do at all, not unless she was forced.

Maybe her mother did end up getting to her. Maybe this was all part her plan from the get-go and I was only invited to keep the peace between Alorewyn and Callior.

Oh, God. That makes this even more fucked up, and now I'm pissed off all over again.

The morning room is quieter than usual. Mostly because of Dad and Colonel Bouchard's resumed bromance since he and King Loryne haven't exactly been on speaking terms. And the two of them are up at the crack of dawn and outside until the sun sets. Doing what, I have no idea, but at least it keeps him out of trouble. And more importantly, from asking too many questions.

Maverick's on the white velvet couches opposite me, with his ankle lazily draped over his knee, and the sunlight peeking through the clouds and into the floor-to-ceiling windows overlooking the gardens still blanketed with a heavy layer of snow.

"I'm bored," I throw my unfinished muffin at his chest. "Let's do something." Of all the fruits to throw in the batter today they just had to pick raspberries.

"Can't," he throws it on his empty plate. "I have assembly at eleven and then I need to leave for an… event…" he trials off, finishing the last of his cappuccino before brushing the crumbs off his shirt.

"What event? Can I come?" I sit up, hoping he'd elaborate. Anything but sit in my room again, staring at her face all day.

"No, you most certainly cannot. I am King of Callior, I go to plenty of events," he says nonchalant.

Not that I was questioning him. "Why did you say it weird?"

"Say what weird?" he frowns.

"You paused before saying event." Mav rolls his eyes, and just because I feel like, I tease him even more. "Is it a hot date?"

"No."

"It's a hot date, isn't it?"

"No, it is not a date, Skylan," Mav bites, releasing a heavy sigh before sitting up. "You've been here two weeks. We'll have plenty of time to hang out since you'll be wallowing with that pity dick in your mouth."

"I do not have a pity dick in my mouth," I protest, crossing my arms.

"Yes, you do. You've been moping around this place ever since you got back. Here's a thought, why don't you just talk to her? Whatever she did, I'm sure you've done worse at some point in knowing her."

"Of course, I fucking haven't! I'd never do that to anyone."

He scoots forward, leaning his elbows on his knees. "Come on, kid. I get you might not want to go into details with your father, but it's me. I promise to temporarily reserve the harshest of judgement if you just tell me what happened between you two."

"It doesn't matter, Maverick. Let it go."

Mav gives me a pointed stare, then shakes his head. "I don't understand you. A month ago, you were hopelessly in love with her. What could she possibly have done to ruin that?" The last thing I ever expected her to do, choose rules and regulations over me. I still avoid the question.

"You need to talk about this, Skylan. If it really is over, you need to start getting over her and move on before it destroys you," Mav's voice grows concerned.

It's already destroyed me. I'm fine. I hardly see what difference talking about it would do.

I lean back with a huff. "Maybe we should just get married?"

Mav freezes, deadpans with furrowed brows, "What?"

I shrug. "It's not like it hasn't been done before, Ricky. A lot of monarchs make their children marry cousins." Obviously, this would never happen, but watching a flummoxed Maverick trying to wrap his head around the concept brings some humor back in my life. God knows I need it.

His head dips to the side, this time raising his eyebrows. "Skylan, I mean this in the most aggressive way possible, if you ever come near me with any part of your body, I'll shove you through a woodchipper."

I laugh. Hard, belly-aching laughter. It's the medicine I never knew I needed.

See? Talking is for wimps.

"Besides, you think I'd let you use me for rebound sex? No way. I have a shit ton more self-respect than that, thank you very much while you're up. And you should too."

"Oh, come on. You know you can't resist this face. Best seat in the house, baby," I grin, wiggling my eyebrows.

"Okay, I will not be dignifying that with a response," he says in a monotonous tone. "Just talk to her already. Be an adult, and work it out."

My smile disappears. "No. It's done. I'm fucking done."

Mav blinks at me for a few seconds, then gets up, walking to the doors. "Okay. While I'll be waiting patiently for you to get your head out of your ass, take a fucking shower in the meantime," he says, hesitating at the door. "And if you ever call me Ricky again, I'll cut your heart out and show it to you."

"Love you Ricky," I throw him finger guns as he exits.

"Skylan!"

#

Dr. Maverick Augustus Dormer has a pretty good ring to it I have to admit.

Dad decided it a necessity to throw Mav a graduation party after his dissertation was accepted, and he's been up and down these halls planning the get-together ever since. Not that I know why, the extend of lavish décor begins and ends with the tablecloths embroidered with Callior's crest—a maple leaf held in a beaver's paw.

Most of Maverick's friends are the sons and daughters of members of Parliament he went to college with, some of them I know, others I've met in passing. None of which I have feel an inkling of desire to interact with. I'm happy for my cousin, I am. I'm just not in a party mood. I haven't been in months. Only after the five-thousandth time Dad knocked on my door did I agree to come.

And I'm perfectly comfortable in the corner I'm in by the hors d'oeuvres, thank you very much.

Maverick and Dad on the other hand, given the tray of tequila shots heading for them, have different ideas.

He throws the alcohol back, then slaps Dad's shoulder, chuckling at whatever he said, then meets my eyes and makes his way over, holding a flute of champagne.

Champagne. Right. Emryne loves champagne.

"Are we finally going to talk about what happened?" he asks, draping his arm around my shoulder.

No. And the more you pester me about it the more I feel like punching you in the face.

"Crack open that bottle of Glenfiddich 1914 you fail to hide in Dad's old office and I might consider it," I feign a smile and bump his side. "How much longer are we going to be here? Can't we go do something?" Anything to get out of these damn walls.

Mav shakes his head with a laugh, "Relax. Mingle. Laugh a little. Seriously, you're moping around like a lonely housewife, it's not attractive."

"Attraction is the last thing on my mind," I grumble, rolling my eyes. Human interaction in the last thing on my mind.

"Well maybe it could be if you—"

"A king and an educated man?" A flirty voice drifts from behind us. "I guess Callior really is on its way to greatness."

Mav's usual laidback demeanor shifts and he freezes, a strange combination of disbelief and unbridled joy playing in his eyes.

He spins in her direction. He says softly, "Saphy."

A slow smile creeps over her lips. "Hi Maverick."

This is the first time in my life I've seen my cousin resemble a lovesick puppy, and I don't know whether to laugh or gag. If I looked anything like this, I'm cutting myself off alcohol for the evening in case most of it ends up on the floor.

His bewildered eyes blink at the girl. "You came."

"You asked me to," she shrugs a delicate shoulder. "And my father insisted." Both heads turn in the direction of our beaming Prime Minister Bastien Girard and he sends them a wink, raising his glass.

Mav shakes his head and turns back to her. "You look… so beautiful."

"Thank you."

I roll my eyes.

My cousin clears his throat, snapping himself back, and she looks my way. Whatever the spell was between them broke, and she bows deeply.

"Right. You remember Sapphire Girard, Minister Bastien's daughter?"

"It's wonderful to see you again, Prince Skylan," she inclines her head with a polite smile.

I've only met Sapphire once or twice, neither of which I'd spent much time studying her emerald green eyes she settles in mine, interesting juxtaposition given her name, sweet, warm and too gentle, and I can't keep myself drifting to the fiery, and in fact, sapphires eyes of *hers*.

I swallow the thought. "You too. You went to Harvada with Maverick, right?"

"Go Ravens," she beams, pumping her fist. I'm guessing she's referring to the polo team. "Aren't you supposed to be in Alorewyn with Princess Emryne right now?" She asks with furrowed brows. "My friends and I watched her keynote on YouTube like a thousand times. She's going to make an amazing queen."

I my lips tighten into a grin. "Things didn't quite work out, unfortunately."

"Oh no," her brows furrow in sympathy. "Well, if I've learned anything from my past relationships it's how important good communication is. Talking it out makes everything better."

I fix my eyes to hers and with a heavy sigh I lift my glass and swallow the last of the champagne, giving her another tight smile and head to the liquor stand.

"Did I say something?" I hear her say as I pour myself a healthy glass of whiskey.

"Nah, he's just being a stubborn pain in the ass as usual."

Stubborn has nothing to with it.

If anyone mentions talking something out one more fucking time, I'm going to lose my damn mind.

Chapter 33
Emryne
Six Months Later

"Are you really not coming today?"

It's finally Addy's wedding day. Tying the knot with the love of her life. I'm overjoyed.

Genuinely.

Can't say I don't wonder what that feels like. Being loved unconditionally.

Love I thought I had with Skylan. And all the time he made me believe he was all in, only to make yet another inexplicable exit I should've been prepared for from the day he set foot back in Alorewyn. Not that I believed a single word he said when he left, but it still hurt.

What aggravates me to this day is that I fell for it, just like I promised myself I wouldn't, so really, this is my fault. The sex was one thing, but letting him into my heart? I never should have let him get as close as he had. But I won't be stupid. Ever again.

I know my worth.

And whatever crawled up his ass that day? I hope it rots.

"I want to, Addy. But I have back-to-back assemblies the whole day." Partly. Mostly because I don't think I'll be able to make it through the ceremony.

And I hate that. Partly because of the vows Caneic recited to me a few times last week, then apologized when I broke down in tears, and partly because I'm supposed to be shadowing my father. Not that I need to, I already have a firm handle on what's expected of me. At least it's saved me from conversations with Mother, but my schedule is already ridiculously busy as it is. There's coronation day coming up, then I'm headed to the Asai Empire to meet with King Zimo, his father unfortunately didn't make it, about our kingdom's updated trade agreements, then to Ficara with Cameron to expand on the water schemes he's funded in Sierra Leone, Alaristau for Allister's wedding…

I hardly have a day to myself for the foreseeable future as it is.

Mother's marriage law was finally overruled, allowing me the crown without a king by my side.

Her work was done the day Parliament officially announced me the new queen of Alorewyn.

Usually, that would've been big news, but my nerve endings were completely shot after Skylan's departure. Everything I did from that point forward—the assemblies, the birthday parties, and private audiences with some of Alorewyn's largest charities—I did on autopilot.

Six months of grieving, of picking myself up and putting my thoughts back together one by one, and I'm finally starting to feel like myself again.

Having had enough of my woeful wallows, I texted Father to meet me in the training room this morning, and we had a grueling workout.

And every time I beat my fist against a punching bag, I forced the tears away.

Turn it off. I shouldn't be this devastated, right?

Turn it off.

This is my dream.

Turn it off.

This is everything I've worked for my entire life.

Yet the tears spilled when Father pulled me into a tight hug.

Turn it off.

Turn it off.

TURN. IT. OFF.

Word for word, I opened up to him more as we flowed through the exercises, finally able to explain what happened with Skylan. Even if I still had no goddamn idea what he was talking about, or who.

He insisted he call King Harryson and get him to talk some sense into his youngest, to which I asked countless times what good it would do, and he ignored the countless video and phone calls attempts King Harry made, and it broke my heart he had to cut off his childhood best friend over something as ridiculous as their bickering children.

Needless to say, I'm back.

But I still can't see today through. At least not the ceremony.

She takes my hands, a sad smile on her lips. "Will you at least help me get ready?"

"Of course, I will. But only if you do it here," I say, and she nods as I close her in a hug.

"I know I don't say it enough, but I love you, Emrie," Addy says, rubbing my back.

"I don't think you've ever said it," I joke, letting my hands drop, but for whatever reason, Addylin squeezes tighter.

"I'm so, so sorry he hurt you," she whispers.

So am I. "It's okay, I deserved it," for letting him in, and for letting myself feel when I knew better.

When she finally let go, she grips my forearms instead. "No, you didn't. Don't say that! I'm the one who's hasn't been there for you when you needed me the most. I'm the one who doesn't deserve this," she says through a sob, tears streaming down her cheeks. "God, Emrie, I'm so sorry."

Has she lost her mind? "Stop. Of course, you deserve this, Addy. You deserve this more than anything. Caneic loves you, a blind man can see that, and I know you love him."

She smiles through her watery eyes. "I do."

"Good. If anything good is to come from Mother's incessant micromanaging, it has to be this. One of us should get our fairytale ending."

"You'll find your perfect prince someday. I know you will."

That's the thing, isn't it? I thought I already had.

Lesson learned.

My door bursts open, making us both jump, and I can't help but chuckle at my sisters.

Only after prying her off me with a metaphorical spatula did Asaria go back to sleeping in her own bedroom a few days after they arrived, but I'll always be thankful Father called them. Ophelia insisted she stay as well, but I wouldn't keep her from her husband more than I already had, so she's been traveling back and forth a few times when I needed her.

Bridesmaid dresses—blushing peach sweethearts made with the lightest chiffon—already on and make-up done to perfection, they skip into my room, Addy's wedding dress in Ophelia's arms she insisted she design, stitch, and sew together herself, and naturally, alcohol in Asaria's.

Both stop short when they see the state of us. I still hadn't changed out of my gym clothes, and I need a shower.

"There you are! What's with the heaviness, sisters?" Asaria says, setting the bottles down and pouring us each a glass of champagne before shoving them in our hands. "You're getting married in an hour; we're supposed to be getting ready!"

"I'm fine," Addylin says with a laugh, placing her glass on my vanity.

Ophelia beams, typing away at her phone. "I think some Cher is in order."

Addy and Asaria clap, obviously all for it, but I protest. Especially since it isn't about me, "No, not today."

"Oh, come on! She's your favorite! She'll make you feel better, Queenie," Asa says. "Still can't believe another one of my sisters is a bold ruler," she playfully rolls her eyes. "While I use my mind for math."

"You look better with dirt under your fingernails than glitter nail polish anyway," I say and she knows it. I step to the edge of my bed, plopping down.

"I don't think any amount of Cher could make me feel better anyway."

Her hand slams on her chest as she gasps. "Blasphemy! Cher is the cure to everything," she states, pulling back up again and shoving me in the direction of my bathroom, "Get in the shower. You smell like a gym locker," then takes Addy's hand. "You, sit. And let the pampering begin! Ophelia!"

"Already on it," she empties my make-up bags on the table, cupping Addy's cheek as she digs through the contents and inspecting her, deciding how she'll bedazzle her skin, and starts with the primer.

Believe blasts through the speaker a few seconds later, and I laugh as Addylin is pulled into the vanity chair, Asaria stepping up behind her and pulling a comb through her hair.

"Up or down?" Asa asks her, pulling a bowl of hair clips closer.

"Down," Ophelia and I answer unison before I head into the shower. I might not join them today, but I had an assembly to get to, and I hardly think Parliament would be accepting of a sweaty, sulking queen in their presence. I couldn't care less, but my shirt is sticking to my back now, and it's itchy.

Ten minutes in the shower, and I brand new. Ready to take on a new day, and new issues begging to be solved.

Addy's hair is curled in soft waves when I walk past and into my closet and grab a simple pair of black jeans and a flattering turquoise jersey to match. I'm opting for comfort given I have no idea the amount, let alone duration, of today's assemblies will be when Addylin calls my name, "Em! I think your phone's ringing!"

"Be there in a second," I pop my head out, yelling over the music, pulling my arms through the sleeves after squeezing the last water drops from my hair as I walk toward her.

Only two people would call so randomly.

One, I have no interest to speak to ever again. Two, I haven't heard from since previously stated person and I sent him those wire transfer records. Don't think I didn't call, video call or email, I did. Incessantly, yet no reply. Until the second I pick up, and his scrambled voice breaks through. "Hey, sorry I've been MIA, but—"

"MIA? It's been six months, where the fuck have you been?" I'm trying to keep my voice even and as quiet as possible, but I'm failing. A little heads-up about his disappearance would've been nice. He did it before, why couldn't he do it again?

"I know! I know, look, I had a break in and got my equipment stolen. Needed to travel to find replacements for irreplaceable parts," he says annoyed.

Great. And now I feel like an ass. I blow out a heavy sigh. "Are you alright? Were you attacked?"

I hear my sisters laugh, drawing my attention. Really not the best place to be having this conversation right now.

"What's going on, Emrie?" Ophelia asks with a smile.

I wave her off as Castor continues, but I didn't catch his first words. "… had to move locations and step up security from a ten to an eighty-five. They beat up me pretty bad, but the painkillers are really helping."

Shit. "Do you think it was deliberate?" I press. For Castor to have a target painted on his back like this either means he found something, or he's on the right path.

"Undoubtedly. They walked away with nearly every piece of equipment I had. But like every underground scoundrel, of course, I backed up my files to a few externals hidden around my apartment. So, unless they have a… well, me, employed, I doubt they've made any leeway getting into those hard drives."

"Does that mean you found something?"

"Bet your ass I did."

I hear my name again, this time from Addylin. I need to get somewhere we can talk freely. "Can I call you back? I'm not alone right—"

But he cuts me off almost immediately. "Usually, I'd say fine, but you're gonna want to hear this, Your Highness," I almost laugh. The public hasn't been made aware of my status change yet after the whole Skylan disaster and Father decided to hold off on the announcement until after Addy's wedding. Still funny how that's one of the last times I'll be hearing the old title though.

I glance toward my sisters, luckily back to giggling about whatever, and they've since moved onto getting her dress on. "Shoot."

"I checked those records like you asked. Turns out missing five-hundred grand you had me looking into last year was used to rent a warehouse."

Interesting. "The one that was raided last year?"

"Yup."

"Who was it being leased to?"

"Apparently, someone within the palace rented the space under the queen's name for King Lodran as interim storage."

Well, I'll be damned.

Though I can't for the life of me believe my mother had anything to do with this, she's no conniving criminal, so it's more likely she trusted King Lodran's word that the space wouldn't be used for nefarious purposes. And I finally have the answer I've been craving for months.

"Is there any activity at the warehouse now?"

"Not the one that was raided, but there's another abandon building a few blocks over that looks like it's got some movement."

"Send me the address, yeah?" No time to waste. Not anymore.

"Sure thing. And uhm… One thing more, though…"

"What?"

Castor's sigh tells me all I need to know. I can't decide whether or not to have a panic attack now, or when I officially bust them, either way panic will ensue.

"They know who you are, Your Highness," he answers, defeated.

And my heart still drops to my stomach. "H—how did they…"

"By shoving a shotgun with sawed off barrels directly into my mouth."

"Jesus," I breathe out, letting my head fall backward. "Are you alright?"

"Yes and no. I kicked up my therapy sessions again. But I… uh…" He stammers with a sniffle, and it's not hard to tell he's getting choked up. "I'm so sorry, Emryne. I didn't mean to. It's just… that thing was—was so freaking big and… and…"

"Stop. Don't think twice about it, Cas. You did what you had to do. I would've done the same thing."

I know he wasn't acting intentionally. If the kid had the training I did, he never would've squealed, but I expected nothing less.

"Has anything been released yet?" If my identity has been discovered, I'd rather know about it sooner than later, just in case I needed to prep for a slew of uncomfortable public appearances.

"No, nothing. I've been watching news channels closely. My resources are limited right now, but I'll do what I can in terms of information control should someone run their mouths."

I breathe out a sigh of relief as I head to the pad on my wall, but I drop my hand before I reach the keys. "Thanks, Castor. For everything, and I mean it."

Because I don't say it enough, and he deserves it. None of this would be possible without his help. I just wish I could give him a hug I'm sure we both so desperately need.

"Of course. And hey, get rid of your laptop. I'll send you a new one. Oh, add an extra kick to the bastard's ass for stealing my stuff when you find him, okay?"

"It'll be my pleasure," I say before ending the call. Whether or not these assholes know who I am, this *will* end today.

I waste no time pushing past my sisters, all tearing up over Addy's dress, and head to the keypad typing in the four-digit code. The doors swing open, freeing the black armor once again, and I yank the turquoise back over my head before reaching for a Lycron top neatly folded in the rack above my combat boots, yanking them out and pulling it on. With my cover blown, time is of the essence.

"You guys will have to carry on without me," I say to my giggling sisters over my shoulder. Giggling that evidently have stopped when I catch their eyes, jaws just about dragging on the floor as all three of them stalk toward me with white-hot shock.

"Uhm…" Addylin starts. "What the…?"

"What is going on?" Ophelia asks next as I reach for the Kevlar vest and secure it over my chest. "What in God's name… Emryne, what is this?"

"I'm sorry Ophelia, but I really don't have time to explain now," I say, turning to Addylin. "Addy, I'm going to ask you a question and I need you to answer me honestly," I step forward. "Did you know about Cane's father's drug addiction?"

She had to, right? With his scraggly looks, sunken eyes, not to mention completely falling off the face of the earth, I damn-well should've known.

I'm not entirely sure what I answer I expect, but it definitely isn't, "Yes," or the guilty swallow preceding it.

I can already feel that rage meter slowly creeping toward red. "How? When did you find out?"

I watch as her head falls back and she breathes out a heavy sigh. "We were taken a few weeks ago—"

"You were WHAT?" Asa shrieks.

Rage meter's dangerously close to red… "What the fuck, Addylin! Why didn't you say anything!"

"How the hell was I supposed to know you're the Dark Warrior? Mother's absolutely going to have a cow when she finds out!"

"No, she's not. Because she's not going to find out. And we're not talking about her. You still should've told me, or Father for that matter!"

"After the last time one of us almost died? Not likely. It didn't seem like it mattered anyway, we were already back by then. Cane talked him down and they let us go and—"

I hold up a hand, recoiling. "Wait, what do you mean let you go?"

"Cane got him to let us go," she shrugs a delicate shoulder.

"Which he did how exactly?" I pressed, taking another step toward her. "Last time I checked maniacs don't just let hostages go."

She goes quiet, swallowing as she shifts nervously.

"Addy?"

Addylin's eyes close, and she takes another deep breath. "I'm pregnant."

None of us move for a moment, none of us ever expected to hear her say those words either, but the quiet is short-lived the second Ophelia and Asa's elated screams fill my bedroom. Oh sure, they can be as happy as they want, all this news does is pisses me off more.

Now, I want blood. This asshole is done fucking me.

"Addylin," my voice turns grave. "Listen to me very carefully, I want you to tell me where he is."

She swallows nervously. "I don't know. It was already dark when I woke up."

"What about the building? What can you remember about the building?" Anything I can give Castor to narrow the search in case they were taken to a different location.

"Uhm…"

"Anything. Regardless of the minute detail."

She backs up into the living room couch and sits, racking her brain.

"Seagulls," she meets my eyes again. "I remember seagulls. And it… smelled."

Oh, no. No. No. No. No. "Smelled like what?"

She zones out again, this time closing her eyes, "Gasoline… I think? A bunch of chemicals. And sweat. Clammy, like seawater."

I'm at her side in a flash, taking her hand in mine and squeezing tightly, searching her eyes. Please God, she better not have breathed in any of that filth.

"Are you alright?"

"I'm fine, Emrie," her voice is gentle. "I just really want to get married today."

"Cane's the father?"

"Obviously," she says, gripping my hands.

"And you're sure he's happy about this?"

"Of course, he is," she says as her smile returns. "Why would you think he isn't?"

"Just checking whether or not to break his neck now or later," my shoulders lower but an inch, but the tensity is still there. "He better take care of you, Addylin."

"Well, he helped me get over my fear of water and I stopped him from committing suicide, so I think it's safe to say he's here to stay."

"What? What fear of water?" Ophelia chimes.

"I'm sorry, suicide?" Asa joins.

Her lips turn up in a shy smile, "It's… been a rough couple of years for both of us."

I shake my head, "Okay, you need to fill your sisters in on some details I expect to hear later, but right now, I have ass to kick." Either way I close her in another tight hug and kiss her forehead before walking back to the locker for the rest of my gear.

But stop short and turn back to her. "He was the pen pal, wasn't he?"

She nods in earnest, tucking a lock of hair behind her ear. Talk about a match made in heaven.

I didn't notice Asa next to me until she spoke, surprising the hell out of me. "Where the hell did you get suppressors?" I wasn't aware she knew what they were.

"I have a guy," I reply, shutting the doors with my mask in hand. Probably won't make much difference since they already knew who I was, but it couldn't hurt taking it.

"Oh my God, you're the Dark Warrior," Ophelia exclaims, closing a hand over her mouth.

I turn back to her with a raised eyebrow, strapping the hood over my shoulders and a pistol to my thigh.

"Pretty sure we established that five minutes ago. And half of it anyway. Skylan was…" but I stop myself. I sweep my gaze over the locker as every unwelcome memory of us comes flooding back in my mind. When he got shot. Driving home like a bat out of hell because I was bleeding from a gaping wound in my side. His gentle touches, tenderness of his kisses after sticking the bandage on…

What the hell was the point of it all? What was the point of letting him fight next to me when he wasn't intending on staying in the first place? Did he want to prove something?

And all that about only being here for the crown? Bullshit. Something else is up. And it fucking kills me knowing I'll never get an answer.

"Nothing. Skylan was nothing. It's just me."

"Emrie," Ophelia starts, but I brush her off. No more sympathy. Skylan is gone. And he's never coming back.

"Whatever. It is what it is," I declare and tie the laces on my boots before heading to the wall and reaching to pull down the fixture for the tunnel.

"If anyone asks, I have food poisoning," I say over my shoulder, but Ophelia steps in my way.

"Hold on a second. What exactly are you planning to do? You can't just go shooting up the place, Emryne. You're the Queen of Alorewyn, you can't afford to get hurt right now."

I would've thought of that if… no. Whatever the hell got into him, made him leave. So be it.

"I don't know, I'll wing it," I say, finally pulling the fixture down. Not like I can do much else. This is the first time since I've strapped this armor on, I'm going in completely blind, and not knowing what's in store for me by the time I figure out where this lunatic is hiding is a hell of a risk, but it's one I'm willing to take. Anything to stop this.

That familiar musty scent filters into my room, awakening new adrenaline and excitement threefold. Knowing I'm about to end this war has never been more exhilarating.

And doing it alone? Even better.

"Wait!" Ophelia says, bending down and bunching her skirt up. "Take this," she unstraps the leather and hands me a slick, sheathed dagger. Just light enough to go unbothered and unannounced.

"Just in case," she winks, placing it in my hands.

My fingers close around the hilt. "Do I want to know why you have this?"

"Nope. Just, a word of advice, the blade is laced with a heavy paralysis oil, so be careful when you use it."

"Pretty sure you just saved my life," I smile at her, strapping it to my lower arm, perfectly disguising it under the shirt.

I give my sisters each a hug, a kiss to Addylin's forehead and, "I want to hear everything about your crime fighting when you get back!" from Asaria as I head into the dark tunnels.

Lodran will damn well regret the day he thought using my people for mules was a good idea.

I am Emryne Charlotte Gwyndolyn Gennady, Queen of Alorewyn.

Every wound I have has shaped me. With every scar, I've built my throne. If I must do questionable things so the wellbeing of my people will never be called into question, so be it.

This *will* end today.

Even with limited resources, Castor pulls through. The black Chev is already idling outside the gate by the time I fly out of the tunnels and into the driver's seat, not bothering with the seatbelt when I slam accelerator and weave through the backstreets and onto the freeway.

I sent Castor what little information Addy gave me as I traversed the darkness, and received an address not long after hitting send. Back to the port it is.

That familiar smell of salt hits my nose the second I yank the door open, memories escaping their confines about the last time I was on water. No used in crying over spilled milk, so I shove them back where they belong, and stick as closely to the shadows of the surrounding building as possible in the midday sun.

Figuring the fire escape the best option to get in undetected, I make my way up to the second floor as quiet as possible. The iron steps are stable enough to stay low and survey my surroundings before entering the building in better condition than the first.

Other than the steady lapping waves against the concrete ledges, the chirping seagulls and the buoy bells clanging with the bobbing water, the docks are mostly empty. No voices from inside the warehouse either, which I find strange.

The satellite shots Castor texted showed several people moving around the lot around the building, SUVs moving back and forth. Now, it's much too quiet for comfort, and it shoots my caution radar into bright red.

Reaching the landing, I test every window I find, most of which are shut, but finally slide one open a few windows down from the edge of the building. I shimmy the glass up, just enough to squeeze through, careful not to let my boots hit the ground too hard, and close it behind me.

The hallway before me is dimly lit. Most of the doors are closed and locked when I wrap my hand around the handles, all expect one.

I stop at the half-open door, swinging the decapitated wood into the room until I'm able to walk through and reveal a small, mostly empty office, save for the empty drawers and a few papers strewn around and an old, clunky desk near the rear wall with an overturned office chair.

I stalk closer to the desk, picking up the papers and reading through what mostly looks like old delivery records and invoices from what I'm assuming is a shipping company that went bankrupt. Nothing out of the ordinary.

Until the door shuts.

And I can't say I'm surprised when King Lodran emerges from the shadows. "Amazes me how you find your way into my buildings without making so much as a lick of noise."

Oh, I can't wait to smash that ugly face into the ground.

I abandon the pages, and eye him over my shoulder. "Part of sniper training is learning to walk really, really quietly. Something you would've known if you weren't such a pussy about learning to defend yourself and relying on others who don't know their left from their right instead."

He clicks his tongue. "Foul mouth to match your foul manners. How original." *Douche.* I roll my eyes. He crosses his hands behind his back and stalks toward me, his voice low. "You know, since you had Mr. Millman arrested, you've been an irreparable pain in my neck."

I didn't think it was possible for the creep to look worse than he did the last time I saw him, but today's ensemble definitely takes the cake. His eyes are bloodshot and bulging, skin clammy and sunken, and whatever weight he had the day he arrived with Caneic has disappeared. Man looks like a bag of bones.

"And you've been one in mine," I say, slowly spinning to keep him in clear sight. No chance in hell do I want his unpredictable ass behind me. "Isn't it supposed to be an unspoken rule of traffickers *not* to get high on your own supply?" Frankly, I'm amazed he's able keep himself upright. Watching his shoulders move, he's breathing so heavily he should've passed out hours ago.

He ignores the question, "Oh, am I? How'd you figure that, Princess?"

Queen. But I bite my tongue.

"First of all, I love the fact that you thought it would be a good idea to sell your trash in my kingdom without figuring you'd get caught sooner or later, and two, that you were stupid enough to think no one would come after you."

His head falls back in unfriendly laughter. "Well, Lilliette certainly was easy enough to get around. Quite gullible, isn't she?"

"You leave my mother's name out of your mouth, Lodran," I seethe.

"And you seem to forget who you're speaking with, Princess," he spits, wobbling closer. "I am the King of Eikenish after all. Or didn't you know that?"

"And I'm the Queen of Alorewyn," I spit back, wiping his smirk off his face. "Didn't you know *that?*"

He straightens with raised brows, rubbing at his nose. "Well then, color me impressed. What exactly Loryne sees in you will baffle me for the rest of my days," he rolls his eyes, slowly stepping around me. "Look at you. So unkempt, rough. Where have you ever a princess who masquerades as some midnight crime stopper? Ludicrous."

"Aw, was that supposed to hurt my feelings?" I saw with a mocking pout, stepping closer to him. Those bloodshot eyes bore into me, sending a ripple of disgust down my spine, along with a silent retch, breathing in his wrinkled, sweat-stained shirt. And he calls me unkempt?

I'm not sure what he's trying to accomplish with this macho act either. Man's about as intimidating as a ladybug. If the ladybug was sky high on opiates.

"Enjoy this freedom while you can. I'll be dragging you out of this building chained and gagged in a few minutes."

He bares his teeth. "Oh, I hardly think that'll be the case."

Cold hits the back of my neck, and the sound of a hammer cocking cements me in place.

Not good.

"Remember Luke? Your little partner knocked his teeth out a last year."

My reflexes may be quick, but I have no way of judging whether or not whoever's behind me is in the same mental state as Lodran, not to mention how trigger happy he could be, so this situation really isn't ideal. Moving an inch would mean my death.

"Weapons on the table, love," comes Luke's voice behind me.

"Typical," I huff as I shake my head, removing my knives, gun and brass knuckles and slamming them each down on the table. "Always letting others fight your battles for you." *Shut up, Emryne, shut up…* "No wonder every monarch as lost respect for you."

"Such a brave little princess you are," he raises his hand, running his knuckles over my cheek. I yank my head away, only for the icy metal to push harder into my head. Lodran lifts his hands, "Queen. Pardon me."

"You cannot seriously be idiotic enough to shoot me, could you?" I ask, glaring at him.

That senile chuckle returns again, and he steps right into my face. "I've made pests such as yourself disappear before, what's to stop me from doing it again?" his smile drops, and he grabs my cheeks between his fingers, "You've caused enough trouble for once, vigilante," then pushes me back until I hit a solid chest. Those were the last words I heard before the world went black.

#

I woke up… I don't know how many hours later to my name being called, but it takes serious effort to open my eyes. Fuck, my head hurts. Nothing worse than being knocked out with the butt of a gun, or whatever he used.

When I finally get my eyes open, I see the room is empty. Probably one of those closed doors I passed on my way into that office. The tiled floor is cracked and filthy, so are the windows, and it's boiling in here.

Something shifts, and when I look up, I'm staring straight at the last person I ever expected to see.

"Y… Your… M-Majesty?"

"Oh, thank Christ," King Harryson breathes out a sigh as he sits back, looking at me with a swollen and bloody eye, lips turning up in a faint smile. "You're one hell of a tough kid, you know that?"

"So I've heard," I croak, trying and failing to push up given my hands are tied behind my back. "What happened?" I ask him, tucking my shoulder under me and using my stomach muscles to finally push upright.

"To me or you?" he chuckles softly. But I hear his annoyance loud and clear.

I know perfectly well how I got here. "You, Your Majesty."

The king sighs, "Couple days ago I got an SOS from your father. Now, usually that wouldn't concern me since the bozo has the tendency to overexaggerate everything," he rolls his eyes. Years and years of friendship they had between them. And always will have. Disagreements or no.

"But what I thought was strange was that it came from his pager, something neither of us have used since we left the Scorpions. I know Ryne, and he wouldn't be communicating through pager if this was something run-of-the-mill.

"So, I caught a flight down and we met at an old safe house outside the city when he told me your sister was kidnapped. We were able to trace her phone back to this place not long after, just as she and Caneic were leaving the building. He got them back to the palace as soon as he could, but I stayed behind to confront the bastards. Ask me how surprised I was to see Lodran's drug-addicted ass and his goons jump me. Took a beating, and here I am."

Hell. What is it with us Gennadys and taking the law into our own hands? I'm definitely calling a family meeting about keeping secrets when I get home.

"Are you alright?"

"I'm fine," he sighs, settling his head back against the wall. "Shoulder's pretty messed up. I can't say my ego isn't somewhat bruised, and just a little sleepy, but otherwise fine."

Oh no. Not good. Not good at all. I scan over his body, searching for any indications of more blood loss, but other than his obviously dislocated shoulder, bruised cheek and the cuts on his left eye and bottom lip, I can't see anything. Thank God. He must have a concussion, and falling asleep now wouldn't be a great idea.

"I need you stay awake, Your Majesty, can you do that?"

"Can't say it won't be hell," he chuckles softly. "But I'll do my best, kiddo. How're you doing?"

I release a sigh, wiggling my butt to scooch closer to him. "I've been better."

"Do this all by yourself, did you?" he smirks, running his gaze down the armor.

I chuckle. "I'm surprised more people haven't figured it out. Asaria gets attacked and a masked hero springs out of nowhere?"

"You've been smart about covering your tracks," the king says, wiping the blood off his eye with a shoulder. "Though I could've sworn you weren't alone in that warehouse."

My smile drops, and I lay my head against the brick, blowing out a puff of air. Of course, Father shared the footage. "Yeah."

"Skylan back you up?" he looks over, but I keep my gaze on the floor in front of me.

"He did."

From the corner of my eye, I can see him nodding. "Have you spoken to him at all?"

"Not since he left, no," I reply quietly. He made it pretty clear he had no interest in talking to me ever again so why would I?

"I'd still love to know what the hell got into him."

"So do I, Sir."

We fall in a comfortable silence for a few moments before King Harry speaks again.

"I've never quite seen two people more suited for each other than the two of you, you know that? Myself and Gilliana included," I nod, my lips turning up in a sad smile.

"You really were amazing together," when I finally turn my head to him, I watch as his shoulders sag.

"Greatest love of my life, that woman," he says. "Breaks my heart to this day that Skylan never got to say goodbye to her before she passed."

"He didn't?" My brows draw together.

The king shakes his head. "He had his flight exams that morning. He needed to be in the air at the butt-crack of dawn."

"Sky never mentioned that," I say slowly. And we talked about his mother. Several times.

"Come now, we both know my son. Talking isn't his thing regardless of how hard you push," he says. I nod again, unable to swallow the lump in my throat as he continues. "I think part of the reason he left in the first place was because of that fear of watching someone else he loves disappear."

"You think that's why he pushes people away?"

"Partly. Gilliana tried her best to get him to speak his mind, but he's inherited his old man's stubbornness, no two ways about that, so talking has never been an option. It's easier for him to leave before he gets hurt."

That I knew well. Growing up, no injury small or large would have him admit his level of pain, whether it was falling face first into concrete and smashing his front teeth before his adult teeth came in, standing up and pretending he was a-okay despite the blood running out of his mouth, or when Frolic stomped on his foot and smashed his metatarsals did he even flinch or say a word.

But I thought we moved to a part of our relationship where we could trust each other with what's going on in our heads, not run away and refuse to talk it out.

What's the point of the relationship then? Pretty sure we passed the whole 'friends with benefits' stage ended the day he told me he loved me and I said the same. I thought I must've been losing my mind, but I wasn't lying—I did love him. I still do. And I'd be lying through my teeth if I didn't admit that.

"Sometimes I wish I could read his mind. It would make loving him so much easier if I knew what the heck was going on up there."

"He'll come to his senses eventually, you can trust that. I just hope by that time it isn't too late and you haven't moved on," the king says, bumping my shoulder. "He needs you, Emryne. Sky became an entirely new person in the year you spent together, Maverick said the same thing. He's relaxed, he's more open, however little. Add how willing he was to stay beside you and become king? Three years ago, the thought alone would've driven him into a panic attack."

"He told me. That must have been difficult."

"Scared the shit out of me more than once, believe you me. Especially when he got knocked out the last time. More so because I don't know my son like that. You know how level-headed he is with stressful situations."

Yeah. I do know. He proved that much the night he dug a needle into my skin. His father didn't need to know that though. No one did.

It's the very thing that made me fall in love with him.

"Just… just do and old king a favor and don't to give up on him too soon, alright? He may be a moron, but he'll come to his senses."

"It's going to take a while for me move on, Your Majesty," I close my eyes, blowing out a breath. If I *ever* move on. And if we ever get out of this fucking place.

I have no intention of being a sitting duck for any longer than needed, so I sit up and wiggle my wrists. "What did they tie us with?"

"Cable-ties I think," he answers. Immediately prompting a laugh from me. Idiots.

"King Harryson?"

"Hmm?"

"I need you to do me a favor."

"I don't have much mobility, but I'll try," he croaks, sitting up as well.

I scooch forward until I can turn my back to him. "Reach down to my hands and pull the ties as tight as you can."

"Are you sure?"

"Trust me." This is going to be fun.

King Harry's fingers grab the plastic and he pulls tight enough to nearly cut off circulation. The perfect position for me to lift my hands off my back and slam them back down. The ties snap and my hands are free.

"Idiots," I repeat aloud, shaking my head.

King Harry's jaw falls slack. "How did you…"

I don't answer before pulling up my sleeve and slowly remove Ophelia's dagger, her warning still fresh in my mind. I spread his wrists as far apart as the ties will allow, no need to knock him out with whatever the hell this thing is laced with, before hooking the blade under the plastic and cutting it loose.

"How's the shoulder, Your Majesty?" I ask, sheathing the dagger before helping him to his feet.

"Pretty sure this isn't what people mean when asking someone what's popping," he jokes, typical Dormer humor shining in his eyes he flicks to his shoulder. "But I'll live."

"There's a car waiting around the corner," I say, pulling on the door, only to find it locked, so I free the dagger once again and jimmy the blade in the small gap where the bar is, holding the door closed. A few tries, and the bar flicks up, I slowly open the door and lean my head out, confirming the hallway is clear before leading King Harryson to the fire escape and helping him through—already finding it open. Strange. I'm sure I closed it.

"Keys are still in the ignition. Do you think you'd be able to drive?"

"I'll figure it out. But what about you, kiddo?" His eyes shine with concern. "Loryne would never forgive me if I leave you here alone."

"Oh, I'm dragging this idiot to Dispatch if it's the last thing I do. Go," I say with a smirk, beginning to shut the window. "I'll be fine. Hurry."

But his hand closes over mine. "Emryne, about Sky—"

"It's okay, Your Majesty. I'm over it." I try my best at a smile, but it certainly isn't convincing.

He hesitates, but gives me a tight nod before he turns to head down the steps and to the car. My eyes are still on the window when I slide the glass down and get to my feet, ready to end this as I take a step down the hallway, when I finally turn. Straight into an armored chest.

"Aren't you a sight for sore eyes, darling."

Chapter 34
Skylan
Can't Wait to Tell This Story to My Grandchildren

"Are you coming to the wedding?" Maverick asks when he walks into the gym and pauses the music, already in his formal red dress jacket, medals shining on his chest.

Six months without her smile, and I'm emptier than ever. I can't tell you how my body returned to a regular sleeping schedule, but by some miracle it has, and the only reason I'm in here today is because my flight suits fit a little too snug lately. And if I'm being honest, I haven't exactly bothered to change into anything other than sweats from the minute the sun rises, maybe some gym shorts when I get back.

I've spent more time in the air than the few months after I got my qualifications. Usually, it cleared by head up after running a few drills with the other pilots, but now it doesn't do a damn thing. No matter how hard I try, what I try, nothing gets her out of my mind.

I've wished for a way to fix this. Wished there was something I could do to stop her from marrying him, but let's be honest, I'm wasting my time making a scene when I know she doesn't want me.

If this... he, is what Emryne wants, then I should be happy for her.

But I'm not. I hate that I can't be there for her ever again. I hate that I have to watch her be crowned queen, watch her smile as she waves to Alorewyn next to him, kissing him, knowing he'll be buried between her legs, inside her, bringing her closer and closer—

God, this is fucking unbearable.

"The fresh air will be good for you. Might help you gain some perspective."

Oh, I've been getting plenty of fresh air, thanks. "Perspective on what?" I frown at him.

"Life, cousin. What's next. You can't stay cooped up in your bedroom for the rest of your life. Come to the wedding."

"And see her happy with someone else?" I scoff, cutting him off and slamming by back down on the bench, grabbing hold of the straight bar. "Don't be ridiculous."

"What is she to you? You never cared about her," he says, throwing me a clean towel and taking a seat on the bench opposite mine.

I can't believe my ears. "Are you fucking kidding me? Of course, I cared about her. I've been in love with her for three years! Why would you say that?" I bellow, yanking the towel from his hands.

"Come on, man," he says gently, getting to his feet and gripping my bare shoulder. "Did you really?"

"Of course, I did. I walked away for three years, *three years*, because I was too stupid to see what was in front of me the whole time, because I was too stupid to realize that she's always been there for me when I needed her most. And now I lost her. All because I was the idiot who took her for granted. I can't watch this, Maverick. I can't watch her marry Cane."

He drops his hand. "If you could just tell me why, maybe I'd—"

"Because I love her!" I roar, slamming the towel down and shooting upright. "I watched her fight tooth and nail for a better life for less privileged citizens. I watched her grow into this… woman, not a girl, a woman, who isn't afraid of anything except losing the people she loves the most.

"I love her, because even though she was perfectly aware of the danger of going after an entire drug empire, she put her fears aside and faced them head-on. She put every single citizen in the kingdom's life ahead of her own, mine included, and made sure they were safe every goddamned night for years.

"You have *no idea* how much it destroys me watching the person I don't have the words in my vocabulary to explain how much I care about, to watch the person I love beyond all rationality, fall in love with someone else," I fall back onto the bench, biting back tears, letting silent fill the room once again. "She was supposed to choose me, Maverick," I say quietly. "She was supposed to be with me."

"Then why did you leave, Skylan?" he asks, as if it's an obvious question. "Why the hell did you walk away from her if this is how you really feel?"

"Because she's getting married! Fuck man, you should've heard what Cane said to her. How was I supposed to compete with that?" What does this moron not understand? "She's marrying him. Not me. It should be me."

"Dude, that's really nice and all but you've barely spent three seconds with the girl, how are you this in love with her?" My eyes shoot daggers his way. Is he out of his mind? What the fuck isn't he hear—"I mean, Addylin's fine, sure, but she's really not all that."

"Addylin?" I recoil, pushing to my feet. "I don't care about her, I'm talking about Emryne."

Maverick goes silent. His face drops and he goes white as a sheet, and he takes a few steps back. "Oh, shit," he shakes his head. "Wait, you don't think? Oh my God, you do."

I've never been more confused. Dammit can this guy just quit talking in riddles! "Think what, Mav? The hell are you talking about?"

His gaze cements on mine. "Sky, Addylin is the one Cane is marrying. Not Emryne."

The words leave his mouth, and the floor drops from beneath me.

No. No, that can't be right. There's no way that's right.

"What?" I ask carefully. "But I… I heard him…"

"Skylan… you opened the wedding invitation, didn't you?" Mav asks as my heartbeat becomes more frantic, anxiety flooding my veins. "Oh God, please tell me you opened the wedding invitation?" At this point I can't do anything but gape at my cousin. "It's their wedding today. Emryne's not the one getting married, her sister is."

"Maverick, so help me God," I stalk toward him as he pulls a fancy white envelope from his jacket. "If you are screwing with me right now, I'm going to kill you."

I yank the fancy paper from his hands, ripping the invite free.

And there it is, bright as day: *It is with highest honor and greatest pleasure that the kingdom of Alorewyn invites you to the wedding of His and Her Highness, Princess Addylin Rose Gennady and Prince Caneic Hadrian Magnusius Loundry III, Duke of Lanercost, at 3:30pm on July 22nd, 2022.*

Oh my God, you idiot.

You stupid, stupid moron!

That's what she tried to tell me the day I left. The day I let my anger get the better of me. Stomped away and slammed the door in her face before she could get a word in edgewise.

"You're a colossal jackass, you know that?" Maverick deadpans, crossing his arms.

"Fuck. Fuck, fuck, fuck!" My fingers weave into my hair, ready to pull every one of them out. Man, this is bad. "What the hell do I do, Mav? How am I supposed to fix this?"

"How'd you fix things the last time you screwed up?" He asks, crossing his arms.

"Singing won't help," I frown at him.

"I'm not talking about a song. I mean taking responsibility for your actions," Maverick sighs, this time sitting beside me. "Look, this might not mean a lot coming from me, but it's been a long time, and I mean forever, since I saw you relaxed and smiling, with her. And that's saying something. You did this to yourself, Skylan. You let yourself wallow and suffer when all you could've done was talk to her. Or open the invitation for that matter. Instead, you let your own goddamn stubbornness get in the way. Wake up, kid. Do you love her?"

"Yes."

"You really love her that much?"

"Of course, I do."

"Then what the hell are you still doing here? Get your ass on a jet and go get your queen. She can't rule Alorewyn by herself," he pats my back. A knock comes from the door and Ambrose, Dad's assistant, pokes his head through the archway.

"Pardon the intrusion, Your Majesty. Your Highness," he says with a bow.

"What is it, Ambrose?" I ask. Not that I'm interested in listening. I've already begun backing out the other door leading to my bedroom.

"Your father, Your Highness," he says concerned. "No one in the palace has seen him since Friday."

Three days? Not unusual. "He's probably just hanging out in his bedroom reruns of M.A.S.H. like he always does."

"Normally I'd agree but his dress suit is still in the same place it was when Marcee laid it down on his bed on Thursday. He was supposed to fly with His Majesty this afternoon, but he's nowhere to be found."

"I'll call him when I get to Alorewyn," I shout over my shoulder as I sprint out the door.

Obviously, I want to know Dad's safe, but there's something else I need to take care of first.

#

I pushed the jet beyond its limits. The Gulfstream G650 never sliced the skies at the speed it did today, but I couldn't afford to waste any more time, and I made it to Alorewyn twenty minutes later.

I change into my armor, and grab what I needed from the copilot seat before sprinting down the steps and straight past the knights welcoming me back to the kingdom, making a rapid beeline for the steps leading to the palace.

Emryne's family is gathered in the garden, laughing and clinking glasses of what I'm guessing is champagne when my eye catches Addylin's.

"Sky?" she calls confused, slowly rising beside Cane. "What are you doing—"

She doesn't get a second word out before Asaria flies from her seat and stomps to me, her loose hair and pink dress floating in the breeze while her skin glowed in that typical Gennady-warrior way in the afternoon sunlight. And something about the way she's seething had me thinking she's plan—

"Bastard," she spits, swinging her fist at my jaw with a deafening smack. Fuck, these women can hit.

I don't bother blocking either and stagger a few steps before I can recover. I deserve every punch they throw my way. "Asa, please, I can explain," I try, but she has no intention of hearing me.

"Wow," she scoffs. "You've got some real fucking nerve kid. Explain? Explain why you destroyed my sister's heart?"

"I know I messed up. I just need five minutes to explain what happened."

"Not interested," she holds up a palm. "Now get the fuck out of my kingdom before I cut your head off, send it back to Callior on a spike and declare an all-out war."

"Asaria," Kind Loryne's voice booms from behind them.

"Just, let me talk to her. Please, I'm *begging* you," I plead with her. "I love her. Please, I need to fix this."

354

"Ace?" he steps closer, casting his eyes over his children, then over me. "What are you doing here?"

"She's not here," Queen Ophelia steps forward. Not exactly what I want to hear. It makes no sense why she wouldn't be here for her sister on her wedding day.

"What?" The king and I say in unison.

"Emryne left," she says, stepping closer.

"What do you mean left? Left where?" he asks. "You said she'd be joining us not five minutes ago?"

"She found out who was supplying the Purple Sprinkle," Addylin answers.

"She did?" I breathe out. That's my girl. My strong, intelligent, gorgeous girl.

"Turns out it was my father," Cane says. Usually, that would be more shocking news but right now I didn't care. "That's why we had the wedding here. Parliament will have a ball with this, but as soon as we get home, we'll be crowned as King and Queen of Eikenish," he beams at Emryne's sister, his wife, taking her hand.

They're leaving? So… that means… "Emryne is… queen?"

"Purple what? Your father?" The king recoils, eyes darting between Cane and mine. "What on earth is going on here? Why wasn't I informed of this?" he asks, none of his questions are answered though.

"She is," Asaria crosses her arms.

My heart squeezes. Of course, they named her queen. Who in their right mind wouldn't? The Gennady sisters are a solid bunch, but Emryne is the only one of them with the backbone to commit.

I have to fix this. I have to fix this now. "Do you know where she went?"

"To end this," is all Cane says.

"Alone?"

With all those guns? Emryne was good, but alone in a warehouse full of slimy goons? She's outnumbered by threefold.

"She armored up and left. We don't know where she went through," Ophelia adds.

"Not a problem," I say, yanking my phone out of my pocket. "I know exactly who can."

"My daughter is heading to her death and your texting!" he bellows, stomping forward and around me. "She needs help! She can't go up against those maniacs—"

"With due respect, Your Majesty," I say after sending the message. "If you think your daughter needs protection you don't know her at all. Emryne doesn't need a savior. She needs backup."

All I can hope is that she'll accept it.

Chapter 35
Skylan
The Final Plea

"I better be dreaming and you better not be here," oh, she's angry. Of course, she is, why wouldn't she be?

My hands are on her in an instant. "Are you okay? Are you hurt?" I ask, taking her hands in mine, scanning her body for any injuries. I'd never forgive myself if she was hurt and I couldn't help. But she yanks them right back.

"How did you even get in here?" she grabs my arm, dragging me into an empty room and shutting the door behind us.

"Fire escape," I nod to the door.

"And how did you find out where I was?"

"Castor." Who apparently never got the memo of our break-up. At least he sent the location anyway. I take her hands again. "Please tell me you're okay."

"I'm fine. No thanks to you," she scoffs.

"That's good," I nod, relief settling my raging heartbeat. "That's good to hear."

She crosses her arms over her chest. "You didn't answer my question."

"I'm an asshole," I step forward. "A stupid, inconsiderate, judgmental asshole."

She pauses, then raises an eyebrow. "Are you expecting me to disagree or?"

"I just—"

"What are you doing here, Skylan?"

I risk taking another step. She's fuming, but I need her to hear me. "I'm here for you."

"Does it look like I need to be saved? Have I always been a helpless *little girl* to you?"

My eyes shut as shame clouds my vision. Her words cut deep. The one time we had a fight in middle school and I said the same thing, she didn't speak to me for weeks. It's a miracle she's speaking to me now. If you can count this as conversation. "No, of course, not."

"Then what? What is it?"

"I love you," I say quietly.

Her scowl falls, however little, and she takes a step back. "He loves me," she mumbles, rolling her eyes.

"I'm here for you, Emryne. I've always been here for you."

"No thanks. I'm fine. You can leave now," she tries barging past me, but I step in her way, slamming my palm on the door.

"I'm not going anywhere."

"Jesus Christ, Skylan! Make up your fucking mind!" she says through gritted teeth. "I swear, you're worse than a woman. I can't keep up with you!"

"I know. I messed up, I know. I'm sorry."

"And I'm telling you I don't care. Go home."

"And leave you here alone? I don't think so."

"You've done enough. And by enough I obviously mean nothing at all. I started this alone, and I'll end it that way too. I'll handle this, now get out of here."

"I'm not going anywhere," I repeat, gentle but firm. Regardless of the risk, I won't ever leave her, and deep down, she knows that. I know she does.

"I don't want you here," she says quietly, despite the resistance in her voice. I know she's lying; any normal person would see that. Emryne isn't normal, but she's in pain.

"I'm sorry, Emryne," this time, I don't bother keeping the distance between us when I step closer, cupping her cheeks. "You have no idea how badly I wish I could change how I acted that day. Or these last few months. I've been in agony," I say, breath catching in my throat.

Her eyebrows shoot to the tattered roof and she rips herself free. "You've been in agony?"

"Okay. Okay, I know," I hold up my hands in defense. Not that it'll do much to stop her from kicking my ass if she wanted to. "This is messed up. And you probably want to hurt me right now."

"Hurt doesn't even begin to cover what I want to do to you pal, trust me." She declares, freeing a nasty-looking dagger from her right arm and tightly gripping the hilt in her hand.

No idea where that came from, or where she's planning to stick it, so I take a few steps back, giving her space. "I know. I know. I'm sorry."

"Stop. Stop saying that! You say you were in agony, how the fuck do you think I felt, huh? What do you think I went through when you did the same thing you did when I graduated?"

"Emryne, I—"

"You left, Skylan," she deadpans. "Again. You left without so much as an explanation."

"If you just let me—"

"And now all of a sudden, you're here saying 'I'm sorry'?"

"Yes, I—"

"How about this? How about not doing something to be 'I'm sorry' for? For the love of God Skylan, for once in your life just be honest with me and tell me what you want!"

"I'm trying to but you keep interrupting me, woman!" Her gaze widens, but she goes quiet, crossing her arms and waits for me to speak. I don't. Dammit, why'd she have to look so fucking incredible in that armor?

"Well?" her brows raise expectantly.

"I was an idiot—"

"Was?"

"For fuck's sake Emryne, quit interrupting me!"

She huffs, but shuts her mouth, tucking the knife away.

"I *am* an idiot. I know that now. I run away at the first feeling of emotions I can't explain to myself, let alone to you. You have to know how much you mean to me."

She rolls her eyes. "I know—"

My fingers close on her lips, clamping her mouth shut. I can't see getting through conversation any other way. "No. You don't know because I've never had the courage to tell you how much I care about you."

Her eyes stay fixed on mine. I watch her anger subside, and her breathing even. Slowly, I let go of her mouth and take a step back. Ready to tell her everything I should've said the day I left.

"What happened?" she asks when she's calm, leaning her back against the wall.

"The day I left I went looking for you after going to my room. And when I found you in your father's office, I heard voices coming from inside. The door wasn't closed so I could hear most of what you were talking about. I saw you standing next to Cane, smiling, with tears in your eyes. You looked so happy," I say, swallowing the bitterness. "But then I heard him telling your father how much you meant to him."

Slowly, her brows furrow. "Oh my God, Skylan."

"I heard Cane talking about how much he loved you, how happy he'll make you. How you'd never go to sleep hungry, or angry or lonely, and that he'd be honored to be your husband, and…"

"You thought he was proposing to me," she finishes my sentence, shaking her head as her eyelids fall closed.

I laugh, despite the lack of humor. "Stupid right?"

"Why didn't you say anything?" she cups my cheeks.

I take my time answering. The only thing I can tell her is the truth.

"Because I didn't want to believe it. I didn't want to believe you were giving in to protocol. And I was so, so jealous. I didn't want to face the fact that my own selfishness and stupidity finally caught up with me, and I lost you forever. It shattered my heart in more ways than I could ever have words express." I take her hands in mine and pull her into my chest, leaning my forehead to hers.

"I love you, Emryne," I choke out. "I love you so much it hurts."

Her blue irises fill with tears, and her lips turn up. "That much, Your Highness?"

"With every fiber of my being. Every breath I take. I can't stand the idea of anyone else having the extraordinary honor of loving as much as I do. You make me laugh; you challenge me. You make my life better, my mornings brighter, my evenings less lonely. And you suck my dick like a goddess," she laughs, and the glorious sound warms my heart. Man, I've missed hearing that.

"You are everything I've ever wanted, and more. And if you're ready," I unzip the pocket on the right thigh, pulling out the black velvet box out and get down on one knee.

"Emryne Charlotte Gwendolyn Gennady, marry me. You are my world. You are my home. I know I might not always get it right, but I promise I will love you until the end of my days. Until the sun stops shining and the world stops turning. And even after that. I promise I will love you unconditionally, no matter how much we disagree, or how much you piss me off that day, I will love you, because you are everything to me. Marry me, Emryne. Be my queen."

Her tears are running freely now as she bends down and caresses my cheek. "All I've ever wanted was to hear you say you love me. That you can't stand to think about living a day without me. Because that's how I feel. Skylan Henry Alexandrius Dormer, I've loved you from the moment I was old enough to understand what love is. And even when I didn't, I still had those little flutters in my heart, I'd smile wider when you were around, and I wanted you to feel the same way I did."

My breath catches in my throat. "I did. Trust me, I did. I was just too afraid say it because…"

She nods, finishing my thought, "Because you were scared if you said it out loud, I'd go away. Just like your mother did. I know. And I saw it. Every day, I saw how hard you tried, how much you cared. I knew you were going to say it eventually, but you know me. I have the patience of a kindergartner," she says, and I laugh with her. Her fingers close around my shoulders. "You are the love of my life. And I can't think of a better king to serve Alorewyn."

My heartrate shoots sky high. This is happening. This is really happening. "Does that… are you…?"

"I'm not done yet," she says, wiping her tears. I'm sure she has more to get off her chest, so I nod, let her continue.

Her eyes fill with fresh tears, and she shakes her head. "I appreciate everything you said, Skylan. But I just… don't know if I can."

No… No, no, no… Please no. "I'm sorry, Emryne, I'm so, so sorry."

"I know you are," she nods, cupping my cheek. "I just don't know if sorry is enough."

"So, are you… s-saying no?" I feel the color draining from my face, regret claiming what little hope I had left in my body.

"I should. After all this, I have no idea how I'm supposed to trust you again."

I nod solemnly, lowering the ring. My mother's ring. The one I couldn't wait to give her six months ago. "I get it," I say, devastation gripping my heart. "I uh… I guess I really fucked up this time, huh?"

Idiot. I did this. I destroyed what we had. Destroyed the single greatest thing that's ever happened to me. And I deserved it. I'll hate myself for the rest of my life knowing I caused this.

Knowing I pushed her away.

Fuck.

I'm such a fucking idiot!

"But no," her soft voice says, surprising the hell out of me. My eyes shoot to hers. I had to make sure I heard her right. "I'm not saying no." And I did. It brings hope back in my heart. "I'm saying yes."

"You… are?" I ask slowly.

"I want you, Skylan. I know who you are, and I know that I love you. I know that I'll never love another man the way I love you. I've tried everything I could to forget you, but you find your way back into my life regardless of what happens. And that can't be a coincidence.

"So, I'll take you. Just the way you are," she says, cupping my cheek with a smile. "I'll take your ring, and I'll take your name," her assured words had me beaming in no time, and choking back tears. "But I won't take your bullshit," she says, leaning down with a cocky smile as her hand slides around my neck. "Ever again. Understand?"

My eyes close and I let the welcome relieve flooding my body before opening them again, and finding her beautiful blues with a massive smile on my lips. "I do."

Her eyebrow raises, and she flashes a smirk, "Not the answer I'm looking for, Your Highness."

"Yes, my queen," I swallow, my body filling with a rush of lust. Damn, the things she does to me with a simple smirk.

"And the only sex tape you're ever allowed to record will be of us, you get me?"

"Yes, my queen."

"Good boy," she says, and I chuckle, taking her hand and sliding the Asscher-cut diamond on her finger, placing a delicate kiss on her knuckles.

Until that day, I had no idea I had a submissive bone in my body, but fuck it felt good. And I wanted it.

I wanted her.

She has free rein to dominate my body any day she wants, any damn way she wants, as long as she falls over the edge with me. Hell, my pulse races just thinking about the endless possibilities. Endless adventures we get to have, in and out of the bedroom.

No man will ever take her from me. I'm hers, forever.

And she's finally mine.

"Marry me, Emryne," I ask again, getting to my feet, and the only reason I do is so I can hear her say it again. I'd do it a thousand times just to prove this isn't a dream.

"Yes," she chuckles softly, climbing into my arms and hooking her legs around my waist. "Yes, I'll marry you. My answer will always be yes." And our lips crash together. My arms wrap around her, holding her tight. Her lips part, her tongue tangling with mine, setting every one of my nerve endings on fire.

"I love you," I whisper against her lips. "I love you so much."

"I love you more, you pain in my ass."

"Sexy ass," I moan into her mouth as my hands cup her butt and give her a firm squeeze. "Sexiest ass in the whole damn kingdom."

She breaks our kiss, and beams at me. "Our kingdom."

"Now, tomorrow, and forever," I say proudly, and press my lips to hers once again.

Taking on Alorewyn will be one hell of a challenge, but with Emryne beside me, I'm more than ready to take it on.

"Well, isn't this a wonderful sight?" The unwelcome voice is like razors in my ears. "Alorewyn will have a new king after all."

King Lodran scrawny form slants against the frame, barely able to keep upright. I can't begin to imagine how good she must feel knowing this scumbag is done for, months of hard work finally paying off.

He will be locked away if it's the last damn thing I do.

"Lodran!" I exclaim cheerfully, holding Emryne steady. "Still an ugly piece of shit, I see."

"You filthy little brats," his sways from the doorframe and wobbles closer. "If this were Eikenish, I'd have your tongues for slander!"

"Oh, you mean same way you had Caneic's leg for fighting for equal rights for your people?"

"What?" Emryne shouts above me.

"Caneic is no son of mine," he glares at her, those baron eyes lighting my own fury. "The boy's more pathetic than the two of you combined."

"Keep running that mouth of yours, Lodran," Emryne bites. "You won't be saying anything at all after today."

Lodran leaves the doorway, "If anything, you should be thanking me for contributing to your economy…"

I'd listen to whatever bullshit justification he spews, but I've already zoned out. So has Emryne it seems. "Guns of knives?" she mouths through gritted teeth.

"Knives," I mouth back, keeping my eyes on his mumbling form.

"… and I would've gotten away with it—"

"If it wasn't for us meddling kids?" Emryne and I finish his sentence in unison. "God, could you be anymore cliché?"

"Get them!" He demands, backing from the room.

My hands drop from her butt, and her feet finds the floor, the knives I had strapped to my thighs in her hands as she shoots upright.

Bodies of all shapes barrel into the room at once, and all equally as frenzied. Two blonds, one with ugly scabs on his bald head and jaw, and another with thick dreadlocks Emryne knocks out first, conveniently with the first blond to advance at her.

"Any chance of explaining what happened now?" I ask above the angry grunts, narrowly missing a fist flying into the face.

"Came here, snuck in, got knocked out, woke up next to your father. The end."

"Is he alright?" I ask, still gripping his jaw in my hand as his arms flail at his sides. If this asshole laid so much as one finger him…

"His shoulder was dislocated when they locked me in here," another hook, and she shoves him face first into the wall, says as his unconscious body slumps down shodden paint. "But I got him out. He's safe."

"How the hell did he even end up here?" I yell at her over the commotion.

"Can we talk about this later?"

Scab-face grabs for her, but she catches his hand and swings him into another one, sending him over the desk, before she spins and holds him in a headlock, yanking him before me to finish him off.

Three down… and one still lingers in the doorway. Watching us closely. Not bothering a blink at his unconscious compatriots at his feet.

That sullen expression, dirty, shady blond hair… I'd recognize him anywhere.

"I've got this," I assure her, still hesitating as Lionel, or whatever the hell his name is, sneers at me, and I send her a wink of encouragement. "Go get 'em, darling."

Emryne wastes no time. She slips on her heal, and heads down the hall to wherever Lodran has run off to.

Leaving me with Lucian.

"You do know neither of you will be walking out of here alive, right?" He glares, prowling closer and closer until he stops just short of my right.

"And here I thought all psychics were frauds," I roll my eyes, and barrel toward him, slamming him into the head-first into wall before he could react. He chokes out a breath as I fist the material of his shirt and slam him a second time.

What luck that the idiot must be high on Sprinkle.

I almost feel bad for the sad sap. Almost.

Though he proves to me why I shouldn't when he spins on his heels, elbow shooting toward me.

I lean away from him just too late, and he catches my jaw. Hard enough that my bottom lip catches between my teeth, and the skin splits. I'm prepared this time, and when he lifts his fist to deliver another blow, the tip of my boot hits his stomach, and he juts forward, right as I drag an uppercut through his nose.

Luke stammers back, completely losing his footing as the disorientation wracks his senses. He takes a single step backward before his foot slips on a stack of papers, and his back hits the ground.

Blood is already trickling down the cut when I lean down in his face. "That the best you got, Leonard?"

"It's Liam!" he grunts, clawing at my face.

"No one cares, sweetheart," the heel of my boot flies through his jaw, and he slumps against the wall.

I leave sleeping beauty to his dreams, and spin on my heels to find Emryne, barreling down the hallway and down the stairs. Most of Lodran's lackeys are already rolling around on the floor in agony.

When I turn back to the chaos ahead, all I can do is stare as Emryne catches up to Lodran. She has him by the collar, dragging him my way, when he gets his feet under him, somehow under hers, and the two sprawling on the ground.

She has him straddled under her, fists barreling into his face in steady cracks, but he once again frees himself with an upward shove of his hips, forcing her forward fast enough for him to push Emryne off and scrambling to his feet and away from her. Face bloody and bruised and a mess of heavy pants.

Lodran's heavy, labored pants break from his throat as he heaves himself back up the stairwell, the drugs obviously impairing his ability to function.

Where to, I can't say I know. But Emryne is on his ass regardless. And Emryne, mighty, fierce, and fucking stunning Emryne, doesn't bother with the stairs.

No, she leaps for the bench under the iron walkway, jumps and grabs onto the jutting piping just below. She tucks her legs under her, and with a mighty swing, thank God the structure is strong enough to hold her weight, she vaults herself up and over the railing, straight into Lodran's path.

He has no time to gauge a reaction before she has him by his collar once again, and heaves him over, sending him crashing him a mess of empty crates below him, the moldy wood splintering in every direction at the hefty impact, knocking the breath clean out of the king's body.

Pride blossoms in my chest as my princess, once again ignoring the stairs, leaps over the railing and her boots slam onto the floor. Emryne straightens, sweat and dried blood sticking to her forehead as she settles her gaze on Lodran's moaning form, and I join her stalking toward the slimy cockroach at our feet.

"Allow me to guess," Lodran groans, blood gushing down from his nose. "This would be the part of the film where you ask if I have any last words?"

Emryne simply shrugs her shoulder. "I would, but you look like you're about to pass out. Just remember, by the time you wake up, you'll be behind bars. Exactly like I said you would."

"I'm not going to prison," he says, rolling to his left and failing to sit upright.

"Didn't know Purple Sprinkle caused delusions. Quite the product you made there, Lodran," I say, crossing my arms.

He grunts, and flings a broken piece of wood at my feet. I kick it away easily enough, and press the sole of my boot down on his arm, "King! Get off of me! I am the King of Eikenish! And I will have your heads for this!"

"Not before Alorewyn has your soul for all the trouble you caused," I defend, pressing his wrist harder.

"You hardly have jurisdiction here, Your Highness," he grumbles, yanking at this arm.

"As my fiancé, I can assure you he in fact does," Emryne declares, kneeling low and grabs him at his collar. Man, I love hearing her say that. "The only thing I'd like to know, is why? Why, of all the kingdoms you could've targeted in all the damn world, you chose the one you know perfectly well you couldn't afford to gain as an enemy? Where's the logic in that?"

"I already have product on every other continent. Emarica was the final frontier," he grits out, a dark, humorless chuckle escaping his cracked lips. "Your people are gullible. Easily convinced. It's already happened," his lip curls in a hideous, bloody smirk. "You'll never stop this, Princess."

Emryne hears none of it. "Eat shit," she deadpans, and knocks him unconscious with that signature right hook.

King Lodran's eyes roll back in his head, and his unconscious figure slumps to the ground, and we lock his body in the trunk of a nearby SUV.

"Boring conversation anyway," I say, relief at once flooding my body after the door slams shut. Emryne's eyes find mine, and our smiles return, both of us folding over with laughter. She steps closer and wraps her arms around my shoulders, pulling me into a hug.

"Thank you," she says through her chuckles, sliding her hands down my arms and pulling away to cup my cheeks. "Thank you for everything."

"I love you so much," I wrap her in my arms, leaning my forehead to hers. Over. This is finally over. And fuck, it feels good.

"I love you too," her soft lips press to mine. "Fiancé," she says, then pulls me into another kiss, sucking the breath from my lungs like only she can. Fiancée. My new favorite word.

"Emryne!" A panicked voice calls from outside. "Emryne! Skylan!"

She sprints over to the loading bay doors and pulls up the lever to open them. The iron screeches as the engines battles to pull the rusted chains up, and the late-afternoon sun pours onto our feet.

"Oh, thank God! I was worried sick about you!" King Ryne storms into the warehouse and closes both of us in a tight hug. "What on earth were you the two of you thinking coming here alone?"

Prime Minister Fredrich runs up behind him. "Not to worry, help is… uh… Help is… here," he frowns, eyeing the moaning men on the floor with a raised brow. "Your Majesty," he turns to us and bows. "Your Highness. Are you alright?"

"We're fine, Prime Minister," Emryne says, taking my hand and locking her fingers in mine. "Nothing we couldn't handle."

"Well," a smile spreads over the big man's lips, and he shakes his head. "No wonder we couldn't find you. You've been under our noses this entire time."

"I had some help," she smirks, turning her gaze toward me.

"Alorewyn owes you a great deal, Ace," King Ryne says, gripping my shoulder. "And I owe you my life for keeping my daughter safe."

My gaze locks with hers, and I pull her into my side. Her beautiful smile turns her lips upward and her hand crosses my chest, putting her engagement ring on display. "We take care of each other, Your Majesty."

Her father's eyes travel to her hand, to the massive stone shimmering in the sunlight, and his lips spread in a wide toothy grin. "Well, well. Quite the action-packed day for the two of you."

"I realize I should've asked you permission first, but a few things—"

He holds up his palm, "Ace, you had my permission the day you stepped up to be by her side," then extends hand for me to shake. I close my hand around his, and he steps closer, "Just remember, the only other things of hers you're ever allowed to break is bad habits. Break her heart again, and you will never live to see the light of another day. Understand?"

"Yes, Sir," I swallow, squeezing her tighter as she chuckles, standing on her tiptoes and pressing a kiss to my cheek. Glad she thinks this so funny. I'm pretty sure I just broke the record for receiving the most death threats in a single day. Doesn't make me love them any less.

The king winks, then turns back to the Prime Minister. "Let's make sure to keep the media at bay for now. At least until I can get my children out of here." Looking over his shoulder, for the King of Eikenish I'm guessing, the Prime Minister asks, "Should we put out an APB for Lodran's arrest?"

"Oh, don't bother. He's in the trunk," Emryne deadpans, pointing over her shoulder. "If what Lodran is saying is in fact true," Emryne says, "and he did get shipments distributed, we need to get every king and queen on a conference call immediately. If they aren't already aware. I want us to get ahead of this, Prime Minister."

He pulls out his iPad and types at the screen. "Yes, Your Majesty."

"We'll deal with it," I say, weaving my arms around her waist. "Right now, we have a wedding to plan."

Chapter 36
Emryne
The King and Queen of Alorewyn

There are a lot of things you wish for before big moments.

I wish had more control over my life. I wish I had more time to do what I wanted, see what I wanted.

I wish I asked for help sooner. I don't want to do any of this alone. And I never realized the value in that until Skylan and I took Lodran down. It's not because you're incapable, or cowardly, but because you respect yourself enough to know when you're at maximum capacity and in danger of completely burning yourself out.

It's impossible for a single person to do it all. To rule a kingdom, protect your citizens, raise a family. None of which I ever could've done by myself. I get that now.

I used to think I never wanted a king, that I didn't need someone serving next to me or to fall in love, and people who did were idiots, but I get it now. Turns out, what I needed was to change my point of view. What I needed was to realize that I wasn't signing myself up for a death sentence.

Between all the people who've come in and out of my life, I thought it would be impossible to find someone real. Someone who got what was happening, who'll be there to tell you that you weren't crazy, that you weren't being stupid. Someone to tell you, I'm proud of you.

I'm proud of who you are, who you've become, and more than anything, I'm proud to stand here as the person you'll spend the rest of your life with. My boyfriend—I'm sorry, fiancé—helped me see that.

Surprise, surprise. Little Miss Guided made it out alive.

And if I could go back and do it all over again, I wouldn't change a thing.

The first thing Skylan and I did after Lodran—who myself, my father, Skylan, and Parliament have ruled would never walk among decent people again. He was found guilty of selling and distributing illegal substances, intent to sell and distribute illegal substances, assault on a minor, and attempted murder, all of which earned him fifty-six-years to life with no chance of parole, early or otherwise, not to mention being stripped of his title and banished from Adlengn, which meant Addylin was now officially queen next to Caneic—was arrested was check on his father.

He wasn't particularly happy about being confined to a hospital bed for as long as he had, but I know he couldn't be happier sitting in the chapel today, waiting for his son to say his vows. Just as excited as mine is, seeing his child finally become queen.

I couldn't sit still in that vanity chair for a second. I was filled with too much excitement. My sisters basically had to hold me down to keep me from bouncing out of my seat while Tory and Asa were doing my make-up and Addylin was helping Desirée braid and pin my hair up while Ophelia and Monique finished steaming my dress. As much as I love the palace seamstresses, I wouldn't trust anyone but my sister to design the gown.

Ophelia was on the phone not a split second after we told them we were getting married, reaching out to her contacts, and ordering as much pearl-white silk as was available, price be damned, and had it shipped to Alorewyn. And she finished the dress in record time.

I wanted something simple and classic with a straight neckline, after which she looked at me asked if I'd lost my mind, then insisted a sweetheart would be much more flattering. Not that it mattered to me, I just wanted my sisters and my best friends, and Skylan.

I talked them through the Dark Warrior journey, and their jaws fell on the floor more often than not. Asaria hasn't exactly forgiven Sky for what he did, I'm pretty sure she never will, but she's accepted the situation for what it is when I explained what happened. All to which my very pregnant sister couldn't believe her ears.

We all sat beside Ophelia as Addylin helped her sew the precious jewels around the neckline, bringing the gown to life. And seeing her masterpiece today? I don't think I've ever been more ready to walk down that isle.

"Come on!" my hand finds Ophelia's, almost running Asa, Beth and Addy over as I sprint into the hallway.

"Slow down, speedy!" Asaria giggles, handing me my bouquet. "We're barely running half an hour late."

"I can't! I want to get married!" I beam, but stop at the stairwell to wait for them to catch up.

"I think she's been replaced by an alien," Beth yells with a laugh.

"Seriously, Emrie, slow down," Addylin calls, rubbing her swollen belly as she waddles behind us. "I can't move that fast."

"Sorry," I say, reaching for her hand. "I'm just… beyond excited."

"Yes, I know. But I do need to keep this baby in here for at least three more months before meeting them."

Asa catches up and crosses her arms. "I still can't believe you're keeping the gender a secret."

"Cane and I agreed we want it to be a surprise," she says, rubbing her belly. "I like the mystery."

"Oh, I want it to be a boy!" Ophelia claps her hands as we continue down the stairs and toward the chapel. "This aunty will be spoiling him rotten."

"This aunty better watch it," Addylin warns playfully. "I'd still like him to be a gentleman, if it is a him."

Cameron's waiting at the chapel doors when arrive. His face lights up when he catches my eyes, and I reach for his hands. "You look like a goddess, Emerhino," he says, pulling me into a hug.

It's Alorewynian tradition for the king to marry his children, and it falls on the eldest son to walk his sisters down the aisle, I'm just happy he could be here for once. And a married man. Turns out having a rival in the office wasn't nearly as fun as having him in the bedroom apparently.

Or it was. I really didn't need details.

"She looks like a queen," my mother says quietly from behind us. I leave my brother's arms, and turn to face her.

Other than a few friendly encounters, Mother's been keeping her distance the past few months, and in that time, I had no idea what to say to her.

Hell, I have no idea what to say to her now.

"Emryne?" she takes a step forward, keeping her hands curled in anxious fists at her side.

"Yes?"

"Do you think we could… talk, for a moment?" I never known her as anything other than hotheaded, so dealing with this gentle woman is extremely strange. Most of our chats happened this way, calm and quiet, and it freaks me out. I've never seen her this distressed either. And that freaks me out even more.

All I want to is get married… but, sure. So, I nod, and we walk away from the doors and into a small hallway for more privacy.

"Is everything okay?" If she's vetoing this, I'm going to kill her.

"Yes, yes fine. Everything's fine," she shakes her head, taking my hands and squeezing them. "I just wanted to say… I just…" she swallows, choking back tears. "I'm so…"

Oh great, here come mine. "Mother, it's okay, you don't have to—"

"No, no I do. You have to know how proud I am of you and the incredible woman you've become. I know I've been hard on you, and I know I haven't been the easiest or most understanding mother, but you have to know that I was only doing what I thought was best for you and your sister.

"I am so, so honored to give you my crown, my sweetheart. And I know with every fiber of my being that you and Skylan will do remarkable things together."

I'm mad at my mother.

I'm mad at her for so many things. For the way she's treated me, treated my father, Addylin. It pisses me off to no extent how much work she's created for me and Sky.

Still doesn't change the fact that I can't change *her*. I can't change who she is, or what she's done, and justifying it would be as useless as trying to teach a dog how to moo.

But the only way to begin healing, is with forgiveness. Not immediately, both of us have too much to work through, but for the sake of today, and my own mental health, I'll set aside our differences. I don't want to focus on anything other than happiness for the next few months.

"Will you walk down with us?" I smile at her, my heart squeezing in my chest as I watch her face light up.

"Really?" she asks, tears streaming down her cheeks. I hold out my hand, linking our fingers and I turn back to my family. Addylin clips my veil on my head, and smooths out the creases before Cameron knocks, letting them know we're ready.

And the doors swing open.

The palace chapel wasn't very big, but has enough seating for family, friends, our leading members of Parliament to attend.

The afternoon sunlight illuminates the room in hues of pink and yellow, warming the atmosphere inside, and every inch of it is covered with white daisies and bright yellow daffodils. I wasn't sure which flowers to go with given the little time we had to prepare, but I'm overjoyed for trusting with my fiancé with picking the arrangements.

Skylan only turns when Father nods, and his breath is knocked out of him. His smile lights up my world, setting my own tears free as we walk down the aisle and toward the love of my life, looking as dashing as ever in Callior's bright red dress jacket, and the rows of his medals adorning his chest.

Mother and Cam sit down in the front pew, Tory and Beth next to them, and Asa takes my bouquet, helping me up the steps. My hands find Sky's, and I lean in close. "Nervous?" I ask with a whisper.

"Not at all," he replies assuredly, giving my hands a squeeze. "You look so beautiful, darling," he chokes on his tears with a smile.

Father straightens and puffs out his chest like he's been waiting for this opportunity his entire life, and his hands close on our shoulders, excited to begin.

"Dearly besotted—"

"It's beloved, you moron," King Harryson shouts next to Maverick and his girlfriend, Sapphire.

"Don't tell me how to live my life."

The guests laugh, shaking off the last of our nerves. Won't be a Gennady gathering without our parents' humor.

He winks at me and clears his throat. "We are gathered here today to join together two of my favorite people in all of this world. I don't know how to begin expressing my pride in the two of you. Of who you are, how far you've come, how you've grown, and the things you've accomplished together in the past year alone. I am so thrilled to see whatever else life has in store for you. Because I know, beyond a shadow of a doubt, you will conquer whatever comes your way, I—we, raised two incredible, strong-willed children who won't shy away from challenge, or adversity, and standing here today, I couldn't be prouder," he gives us a squeeze, then drops his hands, and takes a step backward. "I believe you've prepared your own vows?"

I insisted on it the second I found what I was looking for a few days ago.

And I made sure I handed it to Asa before we left my room.

Father pats his back. "Ace, you okay to go first?"

Sky nods, reaching for a piece of paper in his back pocket and he unfolds it before he takes my hand and pulls me closer, cementing his loving gaze on mine.

"I know your body like the back of my hand. I know every scar and the story behind it, mostly because I gave them to you," he winks, and I nod with a laugh. "I know your mind, because it works twice as fast as mine, rightfully so, and without it, I wouldn't have been as in love with you as I am today. Or the first time we kissed. Or when you told me you loved me. Every part of you never ceases to amaze me.

"I know your heart with all of mine because you wear it on your sleeve, and you don't know how to love other than with your entire soul. I vow to you today, I that will never love you any different. Not for a second. I vow to be by your side, to be your shoulder to cry on, your pillow to sleep on, and your support in whatever way you need. As you husband, as your king. And most of all, as your best friend."

Fresh tears trickle down my cheeks as his vows echo in my mind. Vows I will carry with me for eternity.

Because that's how we started. As best friends.

Best friends who were never supposed to kiss, let alone fall in bed together. But we wouldn't be here today if we didn't.

"Emryne?" Father turns to me. Guess it's my turn. I smile and turn to Asa, taking my vows from her.

My hand is still in Sky's, and I give him a gentle squeeze. "Remember that poem I told you about? The one your mother wrote I had no idea what it means? Took me a while to realize what she was trying to say, but today, I think I do," I unfold the page, and read his mother's words. The most beautiful words written, and the greatest gift she could ever have given us:

Magnificent Thine
Of eyes the bluest blue
Magnificent Mine
Of heart the gilded truth
Magnificent Son
Take note the ardent whispers

"Gilliana gave that to you?" King Harryson from the pews, voice thick.

"She did," I smile, but my eyes never leave Sky's.

"She knew," Sky says, blowing out a breath, fresh tears streaming down his cheeks as he leans his forehead to mine. "She knew we were going to be together."

"Your mother was a smart woman," I squeeze his hand. "She taught me the value of observation. Of watching your surroundings and appreciating what's in front of you, especially the people, and I am so thankful that she did. I'm thankful that she brought you into this world, and to me, and for letting me love you with everything I am, and everything I have.

"I vow to you today to be your partner in justice, in life, and, if need be, in crime." I wink, and he chuckles, giving my hand a squeeze. "I vow to stay at your side faithfully, and honestly, as we embark on the biggest adventure our lives. I vow to keep your heart safe, your days busy, and your nights entertained. And I vow that you will never spend a day not knowing how much I love you."

I wipe away the few tears running down my cheeks, and hand my husband his mother's poem, my vows, and everyone of their beautiful memories they've shared between us. I only wish she was here to witness this. But in my heart, I know she is.

He kisses my knuckles before gently tucking it inside his jacket, and my father clear's his throat.

"Well, beats anything any of us said on our wedding days," Father sniffles, earning a few giggles from the room after before clearing his throat. "By the power vested in me, by the kingdom of Alorewyn, it is my privilege to announce you husband and wife," his fingers close in Skylan's shoulder and a new wave of excitement floods my body as he says his final words. "You may kiss the bride."

The room erupts in applause as I leap into my husband's arms and our lips crash together in a soul-binding kiss. With the promise of more to come. Of love. Of light. Of eternity.

"Today. Tomorrow."

"And forever."

#

Coronation day is one of the singular events where live media coverage is permitted within palace walls. Every news channel imaginable is lining the walls of the throne room, an ocean of chaos echoing against the chamber door Skylan and I await Prime Minister Fredrich's call between the rows of portraits of queens and kings passed. And soon enough, our own legacy will be added to these walls.

Sky and his family had a farewell evening for his Callior dress uniform before his official coronation white, red, and navy dress jackets, and the red, white, and blue sashes and white aiguillettes replaced them. And today, he's wearing them along with his medals, and a few new ones, proudly.

Since Sky's officially in our kingdom's uniform, I went with a navy gown of the same shade to complement the colors. Though I could've done without the heavy sequins and the lace cape around my shoulders dragging behind me, Sky assured me it was phenomenal. And I wasn't about to argue with my husband after he promptly shooed Claire and Justine from the sewing room so he could climb under the dress and eat out my soul in broad daylight.

We woke up the same way we have since our wedding night. Naked, sated, and wrapped in each other's arms, but now, it's not difficult to tell my husband's anxiety through his pacing. Sky's almost walked a trench in the sandstone tiles below us, and I won't say I'm not nervous either.

"Emryne," he stops, spinning toward me. I press the lock button on my phone, making sure the plans are set for after our coronation, and walk to him. There's no better day for Alorewyn to learn the truth.

"Are you okay?" I ask, taking his hands in mine.

"I just... I..."

"Are you... having second thoughts?"

His eyes snap to mine. "No. Not at all."

"Because it's okay if you are—"

"I'm not. I promise," he assures me. "I'm just... nervous."

My heart squeezes in my chest. I would never be able to forgive myself if he had a panic attack when I could've done something to help, so I hook my finger under his chin and lift his eyes to mine, a soft smile on my lips. "So am I."

"You are?" he asks surprised.

"Of course, I am. We're about to take the biggest step in your lives, Sky. Something's wrong if we aren't nervous."

He nods, laughing as he shakes his head, "I'm sorry. This is stupid."

"No, it's not," I reassure him, wrapping my arms around his shoulders. "Breathe. There is no one I'd rather be here with then you. You are the love of my life, and you are going to be an incredible king, Skylan," I say, standing on my tiptoes and kiss him tenderly. "You already are an incredible husband."

He chuckles again, letting his shoulders relax. "Just… please keep being my gorgeous wife and don't let me fall on my face?"

"Never." My fingers curl around the back of his neck and I pull him down for another kiss, whispering I love him before we hear the Prime Minister call us to the throne room.

I keep a close eye on Skylan as the bombardment of flashes snap in our eyes. The minister introduces us to the adoring crowd, the masses at home watching our coronation, and leads Skylan left, next to my father, and me right, next to my mother.

He leads Skylan to kneel, and Father steps beside him as Minister Fredrich reads forth the oath both of us will be making.

Every bit of confident Sky has returned. He repeats the oath word for word without hesitation, and the king's crown is placed on his head.

Mother grips my shoulder, smiling warmly after the Prime Minister calls me to kneel. She takes my hand, helping to my knees next to Sky, and my heart jumps to my throat. This is it. This is the moment I've been waiting for my entire life.

I open my hands. He places the jeweled scepter and the golden cruciger globus in my palms, and smile as he chokes on his words as he instructs to repeat the oath.

"I, Emryne Charlotte Gwyndolyn Dormer, do solemnly swear to protect, defend, and govern the great kingdom of Alorewyn.

"To act just, and fair in executing the constitutional laws as set forth by the authority of Parliament, past and present.

"To withhold prejudiced judgement, punishment, or prosecution on any citizen, civilian or otherwise, not proven guilty by a federal court of law, or face prosecution of my own misconduct.

"Until such time where my progeny prevails me. So, help me God."

He places my mother's crown on my head, and takes the globe and scepter from my hands. Sky's at my side, helping my back to my feet. The crowd bursts into a new fit of chaos and applause, and the knights step between them, forming a path for us to exit the room and make our way to our citizens, all gathered outside the palace once again, crying out our national anthem at the top of their lungs alongside the choir and orchestra seated on the palace steps. Earsplitting cheers erupt after they go from belting the anthem to chanting our names at the top of their lungs.

"Ready?" Sky says next to my ear as we stop at the balcony. I nod, and he reaches into his pocket pulling out his phone.

"You're up, Cas," he says into the speaker, and wave upon wave of notification sounds chime in a never-ending chorus.

Breaking News: Dark Warrior Duo Finally Unmasked!

Addylin

My sister is a superhero. Super queen, I should probably say. I never thought I'd be alive to see this day, let alone be a queen myself. I definitely never planned for the tiny life growing inside me.

My family is gathered at the base of the mahogany staircase in the grand foyer, laughing and chatting while I waddle closer from the bathroom after yet another glorious round of morning sickness.

"How are you feeling?" Cane asks, taking my hand.

"Better now," I say, sinking down into the plush side chair just off the banister. "Geez, but do you think you could tell your child to get their foot the heck out of my spleen?"

He chuckles as he kneels beside me, "Listen to your mother, poppet. I know she's your home, but she's mine as well," he whispers, rubbing my swollen belly. "And I'd like her in one piece."

"Everyone picture, now!" Cameron calls, dragging his husband behind him.

"Oh, come on, Cam," Asaria protests. "Do we have to do? I'm starving."

"Shut up and smile, you can stuff your face afterward." Cam steps up, my siblings behind him, and he lifts his phone with his front-facing camera open. "To our glorious new king and queen!"

"If he ever breaks my sister's heart again, I'll rip his legs off and beat him to death with them."

Asaria says, flashing a teeth-baring grin while Cameron snaps the pictures.

"You hear that, you moron?" she flicks her head around, calling out to him. "Death! I don't care if your king or not!"

But my sister and her husband… seems to have disappeared…

"Uhm, where are they?"

Epilogue
Emryne

Heaven. Ecstasy.

Finally.

What are we doing? Making up for lost time, of course.

Six months without his tongue on mine, without his body on mine, and I'm starving.

Our crowns barely made it to the table safely after we burst through our bedroom door and slam it shut, tearing into each other like rabid animals on heat.

Well, I am on heat, and I fucking want my husband.

My king.

"That feel good, Your Majesty?" I tease, down on my knees in front of him, flicking my tongue over Sky's wet tip and savoring the taste of him.

"Fuck," Sky chokes out, twisting my loose hair in his fist. "Keep going, my queen," he grits out.

A deep chuckle leaves my lips and I moan into him, working his hard shaft in my mouth in slow, deliberate movements.

I feel his body stiffen, and he grips my hair tighter. "I… I need… I'm going to come," he rasps. "Please, my queen, I want to come."

"Only place you're coming is inside me," I declare, sucking him harder.

He releases a heavy grunt, and wraps his hands around my wrists, pulling me up and lifting me into his arms so I wrap my legs around him.

Sky slams us against the wall next to the dresser, and crashes his mouth onto mine, his steady grip keeping me secure around his hips.

"Show me the way home, darling," he smirks, rasping, and pushes this thick length all the way into me.

I grip his shoulders, arching my back so my piercing rubs against him. Sky finds his rhythm, our bodies grinding together in what has officially become my new favorite position.

"Oh, God. Skylan," I whimper, squeezing his shoulders.

"Tell me your mine, Emryne," his heavy breaths demand, lighting my heart with a new wave of unquenchable thirst for him. "Tell me whose pussy this is."

"Yours! I'm yours, Skylan, I'm yours." Just as much as he is mine.

"Fuck yes you are, darling. All. Fucking. Mine," he moans with every thrust, until his head falls back, and I feel him stiffen inside me, just as my own sweet orgasm is begging for release.

"I'm going…" I weave a hand in his hair, gripping his shoulder tight. "I'm gonna come!"

"Come for me, my queen. I want to feel you," he moans, grabbing my thighs and giving one final thrust, and we both come apart, our moans shatter the air, ripping free from our bodies.

His hazelnut eyes settle on mine as we come down from the high, and a lazy grin curves his lips upward as he leans his forehead against mine, still puffing out air.

"Round two?"

"Bed or table?"

"Balcony," I reply breathless.

"What if someone sees?"

My lips turn up in a devious grin, and whisper, "Let them."

Sky chuckles, leaning down and pressing his lips against mine. "That's my girl."

And we fucked—ahem, lived—happily ever after.

THE END

Playlist

Trouble—P!nk
Hollaback Girl—Gwen Stefani
You've Lost That Loving Feeling—The Righteous Brothers
Somewhere Only We Know—Vitamin String Orchestra
Maybe I'm Amazed—Jeremy Jordan & Keke Palmer
Watch Out (Max Lean & Avari Remix)—The Disco Boys
In My Head—EVA SEVEN
War—grandson
Easy On Me—Vitamin String Orchestra
Poison (Zdot Remix) (feat. Krept & Konan)—Rita Ora
Lovebug—Jonas Brothers
Your Song—Kate Walsh
Daisy—Ashnikko
9 to 5—Dolly Parton
Castle—Halsey
Paradise—Epic Orchestra
Photograph—Ed Sheeran
Cold Water (feat. Justin Bieber & MØ)—Major Lazer
Wildest Moments—Jessie Ware
How To Lose A Friend—Wafia
When I Was Your Man—Bruno Mars
Believe—Cher
Fall for You—Secondhand Serenade
Give It All—Rise Against
You Are The Reason—Calum Scott
Star Spangled Banner—First Baptist Choir & Orchestra Dallas
Stop This Flame—Celeste

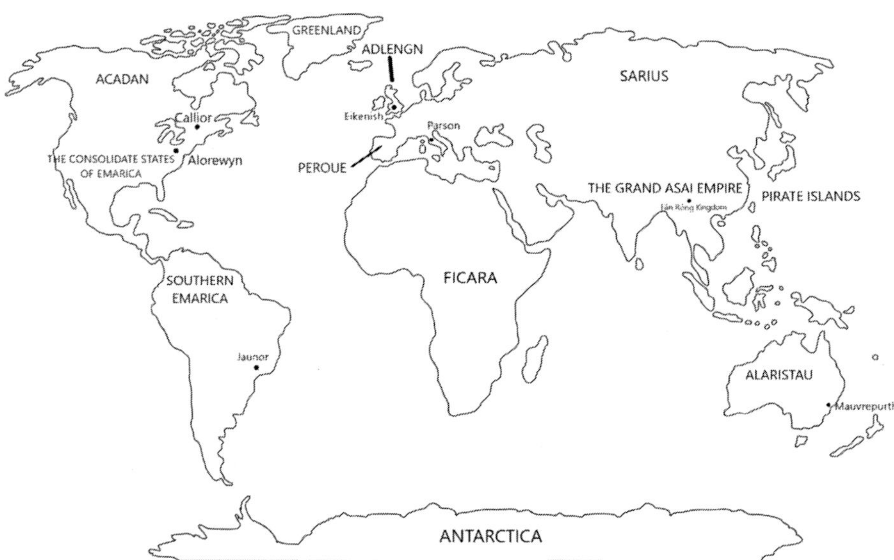

GREENLAND
ADLENGN
ACADAN
SARIUS
Callior
Eikenish
THE CONSOLIDATE STATES
OF EMARICA
Alorewyn
Parson
PEROUE
THE GRAND ASAI EMPIRE
PIRATE ISLANDS
Lán Róng Kingdom
SOUTHERN
EMARICA
FICARA
Jaunor
ALARISTAU
Mauvrepurth
ANTARCTICA